TEMPT THE DEVIL

JILL BRADEN

WAYZGOOSE PRESS

TEMPT THE DEVIL

Copyright © 2014 by Jill Braden

Published in the United States by Wayzgoose Press.
Edited by Dorothy E. Zemach.
Maps by Will Mitchell.
Cover design by DJ Rogers.

ISBN 10: 1938757149
ISBN 13: 978-1-938757-14-3

This is a work of fiction. Names, characters, places, brands, media, and incidents are either the product of the author's imagination or are used fictitiously.

TABLE OF CONTENTS

MAP OF LEVAPUR

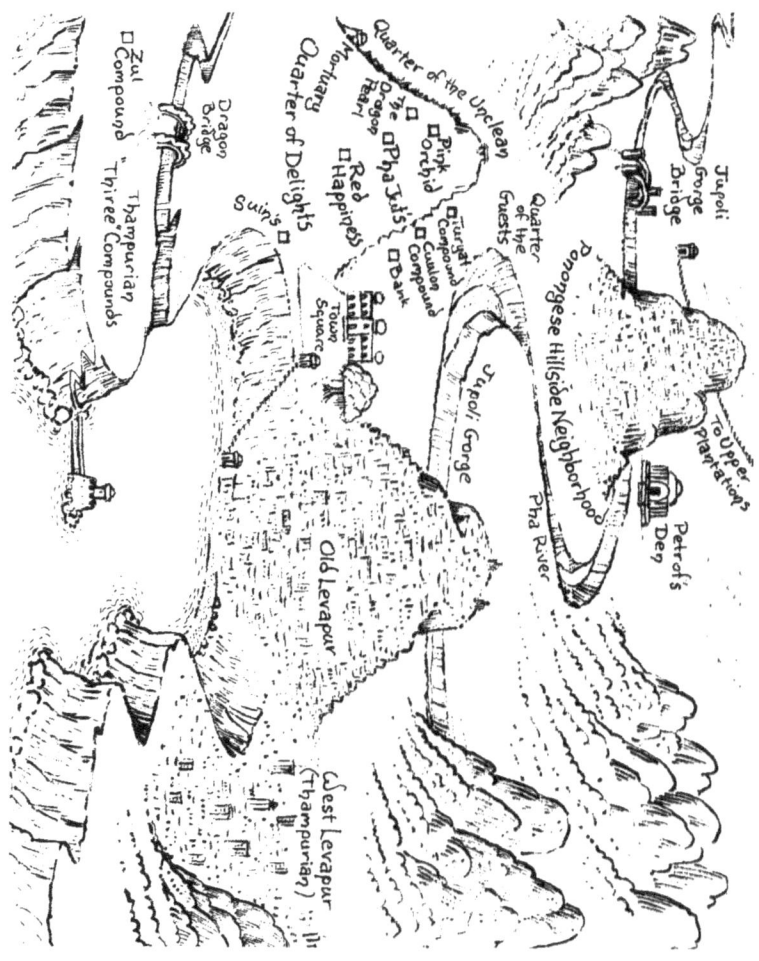

CHAPTER I: A NEW ARRIVAL

*S*he was vapor: insidious, addicting, forbidden.

She was QuiTai, the Devil's right hand – and often his left one too. Former actress, former prostitute, former mistress to kings and prime ministers, she was a dangerous mixture of ruthlessness, charm, intelligence, and cunning. And she was in Kyam's dreams again.

This time, she wasn't a lover or his partner in adventure. Instead, she showed him the slums of Old Levapur, and forced him to look at the bodies of executed prisoners hanging from the fortress walls. Nothing he said would stop her from revealing horrors.

He woke relieved to find himself alone, yet he reached across the sheets to make sure she wasn't beside him. It was his ritual after dreaming of her.

Birds chirped happily in the snakeflower tree outside his window. He pulled the pillow over his head, but there was no way he could fall back asleep.

He sat on the edge of the bed a long while. From the angle of the sunlight coming in through the typhoon shutters, it was already late morning. He had to be at the wharf when the *Golden Barracuda* arrived, and according to the farwriter message he'd received last night, they expected to be dropping anchor about now.

Still, he didn't rise. Sighs lifted his shoulders. Time slipped past and he let it go.

He ran his hand over his face. He could rub away sleep, but he couldn't erase his sense of dread. It clung to him every day that he was stuck on this infernal island. The worst of it hit him in the morning as he walked across the town square to his office. The sight of the gold sea dragons wrapped around the red columns of the government building was like piling stones on his already sinking heart.

It was QuiTai's fault. She'd condemned him to this when she'd made him look like the hero of the rice riot, and Thampur's grateful king had named him governor of the colony. Grandfather had made sure of that.

He had to escape from this damned island. Last night, he'd seen a glimmer of hope; this morning, he couldn't decide if he dared think of freedom. He would make up his mind later. For now, he would go through the motions as he did every day. He would get up and shave. He'd get dressed. Any moment now.

Eventually.

Kyam pushed aside the mosquito net and rose from his bed. The household staff he'd brought to Levapur had already deserted him for better positions, so he didn't have a valet to pick a sherwani jacket that conveyed the right message for today. What did one wear to greet one's wife when she appeared uninvited on one's doorstep? In their eight years of marriage, Kyam and Nashruu had never spent a full day in each other's company. Now they were to live under the same roof. They'd be trapped together in hell. No jacket, no matter how perfect, was going to make that any easier to endure.

The Zul family compound had been the first one erected in Levapur after Thampur claimed the island archipelago as a colony. It was on flat land – a rarity on the mountainous island – near the sea bluffs. It was also a rather long, hot, walk from the town square, much further than the less exclusive neighborhoods. By the time Kyam reached the Dragon Bridge, which connected his neighborhood to the outskirts of the Quarter of Delights, his collar was already damp with sweat.

The jungle had reclaimed the ravine under the bridge like an invading army digging under fortress walls. It climbed the steep dirt walls and spilled out into a small stand of trees. Somewhere in the undergrowth were the remains of a drainage system and stone walls from the pre-colonial days, when the native Ponongese had farmed this land. He averted his eyes when he passed the ruins, but that didn't stop him from knowing they were there.

A flash of bright yellow through the trees reminded him of Ponongese eyes. The first year he'd lived in Levapur, he'd spent far too much time wondering if it were the Ponongese's oval pupils or the narrow yellow irises that made their eyes seem so alien. Since meeting QuiTai, he'd decided it wasn't her eyes but what lurked behind them that chilled the heart.

He stopped abruptly and darted into the trees as he realized what the yellow was.

QuiTai was heading downhill to her brothel, the Red Happiness. She wore the latest Continental fashion – a form-fitting jacket with military flourishes over a long, narrow skirt that hugged her legs to below her knees.

Longing for her pained him. He hated himself for wanting to hear her voice, for wanting to speak to her. She was vapor, and he was an addict. He had to get as far away from her as he could, far from this island, where he wouldn't be tempted by his desires anymore.

With some difficulty, QuiTai climbed the first step to the

wide, white veranda that wrapped around the pink building. Her skirt was too narrow. He heard the seam rip as she forced the step. Frowning, she twisted around to look at the back of the skirt. A flicker of annoyance passed across her face. As she turned back to the brothel, something on her sleeve caught her eyes. She lifted her arm to peer at it. Her frown deepened.

Kyam hadn't noticed the two men in the white wicker chairs until the former colonial governor, Turyat, rose and staggered to QuiTai. The other one appeared to still be asleep, but from that distance, with the veranda railing and the side of the chair blocking his view, Kyam couldn't be sure.

Since Kyam had been named as Turyat's replacement, the avuncular man had turned from a causal user of black lotus into a vapor ghoul. His belly no longer filled his jacket. Pale skin made his addict's red lips seem brighter.

QuiTai unlocked the typhoon shutters as Turyat advanced on her. Her shoulders tensed. Turyat smoothed a lank strand of hair across his balding head. He had the look of a kicked dog. As QuiTai opened the shutter, she shook her head in one, firm motion. Turyat shouted. He gripped the shutter so she couldn't close it.

Kyam held back. If he swooped in to save her from Turyat, she might be grateful, but more likely, she'd give him *that* look, the one that always made him feel like an idiot. She could take care of herself. He needed to talk to her, but this wasn't the place or time. She looked busy. Besides, meeting with her inside the Red Happiness would give her the advantage. It was better to bring her to his office.

Who was he kidding? She held all the tiles. Always. He would be at her mercy no matter where they talked.

The *Golden Barracuda*, pride of the Zul clan's merchant fleet, had already set anchor before Kyam arrived. The painted eye on the hull watched disapprovingly as he stepped out of the funicular car. Maybe he should have worn the blue jacket.

The briny scent of the harbor taunted him. As he crossed the white sand beach, waves surged toward his boots and then merrily slipped away. They could return to the sea. He was marooned here.

The wharf sat on a narrow band of beach under fern-dotted red dirt cliffs. A miniature marketplace did a lively business on the weathered wooden walkway in front of the warehouses. Cargo men shouted at vendors to get out of their way.

Kyam shoved his hands into his pockets and lowered his chin as he walked past a sailor haggling over a caged gray monkey. He could have told the man that Captain Zul wouldn't let him bring it on board, but he didn't want to explain how he knew. He glanced up at the hull towering over him. His cousin, Hadre Zul, captain of the *Golden Barracuda*, was probably still on board. They'd once been the best of friends; then QuiTai came between them, but not in the usual way. Hadre had sided with her and Grandfather in the conspiracy to make him Governor. That stung deeper than anything QuiTai had done. After all, only a fool trusted her. Then again, when you were a Zul, only a fool trusted family.

Yet, he understood why Hadre had lent QuiTai his support. One day he'd forgive his cousin and extend a hand. His hands shoved deeper into his pockets. Today was not that day.

As the gangplank lowered, unexpected worry gripped Kyam. What if he didn't recognize his wife Nashruu and her son Khyram? The wharf was crowded. Everyone would witness his mistake, and the gossip might fly as far as Thampur.

He'd lain awake many nights dreading this moment since receiving Grandfather's message that Nashruu would be joining him in Levapur. He had no idea how to be a husband or father. He couldn't even pretend well. What if they hated each other? He'd seen too many family compounds at war within their walls. What if she blamed him for taking her away from her posh life in Surrayya and bringing her here, to exile and imprisonment? What did she expect from him? He felt as if he owed her apologies, some for other things he couldn't even think of yet.

Despite his worry, he knew Nashruu immediately when he saw her on the deck. She was nice. He remembered that now. You could tell by looking at her that it wasn't in her nature to be cruel. His smile grew.

Her boy, Khyram, hung over the junk's railing. She pulled him down gently. The boy had grown so much in the past three years. No longer a toddler, his face had thinned. His boney wrists showed as he pointed at everything interesting on the wharf. Questions spilled from his mouth, but he didn't seem to expect answers from his mother or the cluster of servants huddled on the deck as if afraid to set foot on the island.

Nashruu lost her grip on Khyram as he darted down the gangplank to gape at a man's articulated leg. Before she could catch up, he'd moved on to poke at a basket of spiky huwewe fruits. She called after him, but the noise of the crowd swallowed her voice.

A cargo net swung over the wharf directly over Khyram's head. Kyam lurched toward him but the crowd held him back. He shoved people aside.

"Khyram! Careful!" Nashruu yelled.

Khyram looked up, and then bolted out from under the net. Still running, he looked back over his shoulder at his near miss. Kyam and Nashruu shouted warnings as the boy raced toward the edge of the wharf.

Khyram came to a sudden halt as someone gripped his arm. Startled, he stared up at the person who'd saved him from plunging into the shark-infested harbor.

Kyam's temper boiled. Why was QuiTai here?

Khyram shrank back from her.

She wouldn't hurt a child, would she? Had she come here to meet his wife? Did she plan to make a scene?

The corner of QuiTai's mouth curved into a smile as she looked down at the boy. She said something to Khyram that made him stop squirming. He glanced at the water, then tugged on the hem of his jacket and spoke to her.

Despite her narrow skirt, Nashruu edged around the cargo net and through the men unloading it before Kyam thought to move. She hurried over to QuiTai and Khyram.

His heart froze. They were talking. His wife and his… he could hardly call QuiTai a former lover. She was his obsession. His enemy and passion. His ticket off this island.

Fate had a nasty sense of humor, and he was the butt of her joke.

"Excuse me." Kyam scrambled around a black lotus seller talking to the ship's doctor.

QuiTai let go of Khyram. She bowed to Nashruu with her palms pressed together. Whatever Nashruu said seemed to strike her as funny, but her expression was polite enough.

Three sailors strolled down the center of wharf as slowly as they could, boasting about their plans for the Quarter of Delights. No one could get around them. Kyam shoved them out of his way and hurried to Nashruu's side to protect her.

QuiTai craned around as if she'd lost sight of someone. The hairs at the nape of Kyam's neck rose when her gaze fixed on a shadowy warehouse doorway. He didn't see anyone, but there was a subtle shift in her face. She turned back to appraise Nashruu, as if suddenly finding her interesting. Her gaze dropped to Khyram. Kyam's heart caught in his throat. He knew that expression. It was the most frightening look he'd ever seen, and he knew it all too well. QuiTai was thinking.

Her gaze flicked up to him. Now her face was a mask. Did she know? She couldn't know. There was no way she could know from a glance.

QuiTai said something to Nashruu, inclined her head, and stepped away. He would have followed her and demanded to know what she was thinking, but the crowd closed behind her and he lost sight of her.

Nashruu turned and seemed surprised to see him. "There you are."

Kyam offered his arm as his spirits sank. This was real. She was here, anchoring him to the island more firmly than before.

He had to talk to QuiTai. Today. It was probably too late already. He'd waited too long. Again.

On her mother's side, Nashruu Zul was third cousin twice removed from her husband, Kyam. They were also first cousins on her father's side, at least on the family's official scrolls. Her true sire had been recruited for breeding, without his knowledge or consent, from the crew of a Zul junk. The donor had not been chosen by her mother. Rather, her grandfather, Theram Zul, had selected him because he possessed three prized qualities: intelligence, excellent health, and no Zul blood.

From her unknown father, she'd inherited her enviable nose, gracious nature, and hair that could not look bad under any circumstance. Her height and elegant hands came from her mother. Grandfather Zul took credit for honing her native intelligence through his unconventional tutoring, but stopped short of claiming he'd taught her how to think. Her sense of humor was entirely her own.

Nashruu hadn't expected a warm welcome when she stepped off the *Golden Barracuda*, but Kyam barely seemed to notice her. He'd behaved atrociously to that native woman, barking at her like that when all she'd done was save Khyram's best suit from a dunking. As they walked to the funny little shack on the beach to buy tickets on the funicular, he glanced behind them several times, presumably to glare at that woman.

"What did she say to you?" Kyam snapped.

For a moment, she thought about pretending she didn't know whom he meant, but until she knew him better, she didn't dare provoke the Zul temper. "She said, 'Welcome to Levapur, Ma'am Zul.' Her Thampurian was quite good. I told her we had no need of staff right now, but to keep in touch. Oh, I suppose I should have asked for her name."

Kyam pinched his nose and coughed as if he'd swallowed one of the tiny gnats hovering about. "What did she say to you, Khyram?"

She fretted that her son might let the strange land distract him, but he seemed as wary of Kyam as she was. He answered as if he were addressing Grandfather.

"I said her eyes were strange, Sir. She said she was Ponongese and that I would see a great many people with eyes like hers. Then she warned me to be more careful on the wharf." Khyram's thin chest puffed out. "I reminded her that I'm a sea dragon, and I'm not afraid of falling into the water. She pointed to a shark and said my parents would probably want to know about them."

Nashruu was glad to see Kyam relax.

"Is that all?" he said.

"Then Mother came over."

More tension ebbed from his shoulders. "Very well. Uh, how was the weather on your trip?" His gaze already rose over her head.

"It rained fish and the main sail caught fire," she said. He'd asked already. She saw no reason to answer truthfully if he wouldn't listen.

"Splendid."

Her forlorn servants were gathered in the sparse shade of a palm tree. Piles of luggage surrounded them. Khyram dug the toe of his boot into the sugary sand. She despaired that everything would be left to her, but Kyam finally stopped peering off into the distance and focused. He spoke to native men lounging about by the station and arranged for them to carry the luggage to the compound. She was now quite pleased with him.

"As soon as we've settled in, I'd like for you to arrange an introduction to Lady QuiTai," she said.

Kyam seemed to have swallowed yet another fly. "Lady QuiTai?"

"Grandfather wants me to have tea with her."

"Tea?" He didn't seem to know if he wanted to laugh or cringe.

"I've heard so much about her. I assume she already knows I'm coming. She seems to have excellent sources of information."

Kyam lost the battle with his control and laughed out loud, though not unkindly. "She most assuredly knows you're here. She's the woman who stopped Khyram from taking an unexpected swim."

"Oh, the green sarong! I should have known." Nashruu stood on her tiptoes and peered back at the wharf. She felt stupid for not realizing to whom she'd been talking. Somehow she'd expected the infamous QuiTai to be more intimidating. Haughty. And much taller. Instead, QuiTai had been polite, even though she'd clearly known who Nashruu was.

Her cheeks burned under her palms as she tried to hide her shame. She'd actually told QuiTai she might hire her as a servant. Grandfather would be furious. Had QuiTai been insulted? She'd seemed amused, but not angry.

"Do you see her?" she asked Kyam.

His eyes swept over the crowd. He tensed. The change on his face frightened her. He looked too much like Grandfather.

She couldn't tell where he was looking. She looked over the sailors and dock workers but couldn't see anything that would anger him. Mityam Muul, a fellow passenger from the *Golden Barracuda*, shuffled down the gangplank, but an elderly legal scholar wasn't anything to get upset about. Besides, she doubted Kyam knew the man. Her gaze continued over the crowd.

She sucked in her breath.

Captain Voorus was standing behind a stack of crates at the entrance of a warehouse. She hadn't expected to see him yet. Why hadn't she seen him on the wharf?

He bent down as if listening intently to someone.

The crowd parted enough to show her a flash of virulent green. Jealousy surged over her as Lady QuiTai placed a finger against Voorus' lips. It was such an intimate gesture. He bent closer to her face. Were they kissing?

Kyam's jaw clenched as he, too, watched the couple.

QuiTai caressed Voorus' cheek. He captured her hand in his and pressed it to his heart. Nashruu gasped at the anguish on his face. He tipped back his head and laughed, but she knew it could only be bittersweet.

She would have given anything to hear what they said. She wasn't prepared for this. Her corset strangled her as she fought for her breath.

Khyram tugged on her hand. "Mama, what's wrong?"

She forced a smile onto her face. Her hands shook as she opened her little coin purse and drew out a perfumed lace square. "It's the heat, darling." She waved the lace before her nose.

Voorus and QuiTai peered around the crates before emerging from behind them. As they walked down the wharf, they made no effort to hide that they were having a conversation, so why had they ducked behind the crates?

They stopped in front of Mityam Muul. For a moment, she thought they'd parted so the elderly man could hobble by, but from her gestures, QuiTai was introducing the men to each other. Then she gently took his arm, and Voorus picked up Mityam's valise. They headed toward the funicular.

"What the hell is she doing with a man like that?" Kyam growled.

Nashruu wasn't sure if he meant Voorus or Mityam. She wondered about both. Mister Muul had said nothing on the trip over about working for the most notorious woman on the island. Their spies had never mentioned that Voorus had taken a lover, much less QuiTai. They'd been too busy trying to catch Kyam in her bed.

Grandfather would want to know about all of this.

CHAPTER 2: THE GOVERNOR'S FAVOR

Kyam crushed the invitation he'd been writing into a ball and tossed it in the wastebasket under his desk. He reached for another thick card embellished with the colonial government's chop in gold leaf – another waste of money they didn't have. He dipped his brush into the ink tray and tried again to find the words that would bring QuiTai to him. Something that wouldn't arouse her suspicions. Something polite.

He splashed a thick, angry line across his latest attempt. Polite wasn't coming easily for him.

He dropped the card into the trash with the others. The brush clattered against the crystal ink tray as he set it down. He put his feet up on his desk and leaned back to stare up at the delicate gold filigree in the center of the ceiling, something he did for hours most days. He hadn't changed anything in the office since he'd become governor. The fussy, overstuffed furniture reminded him of his mother's salon, but he couldn't be bothered to replace it. After all, he didn't intend to stay.

Last night, he'd received a communication from his old masters in Intelligence. They wanted him to recruit QuiTai to work for Thampur. A simple matter, they seemed to think. They had no idea what they were asking.

Unless he counted shouting at her earlier today, he hadn't spoken to her since the rice riot. Levapur was a small town, so it wasn't as if he could avoid her entirely, but he could nod curtly and move on. She didn't seem to care that she was being shunned, though, which made it pointless.

He tapped his bottom lip.

How was he supposed to convince her to become an agent for Thampur? She hated the Thampurians. She'd never forgiven them for stealing her people's land or for the injustices heaped upon the Ponongese by the colonial government. She only had one loyalty, and that was to the Devil.

Leaning forward again, he picked up the brush. It hovered over the card.

Convincing her to work for Thampur would be simple compared to writing this invitation. The first meeting with her would not go well. She'd smile coldly at him. She'd give him that look. He might as well get the humiliation over with, but how? Nearly a year of silence made it awkward.

Except for the dwindling stack of invitations and the inkwell, Kyam's wide desk was clear. He'd stashed his reports in the cabinets behind his desk, but if she came now, it would look as if he didn't do anything all day. She didn't need to know that he was idle.

He spun around and opened the drawer under the map of the Thampurian Empire. Surely something would be safe enough to leave out. He put the dullest report he could find on his desk.

He spread the papers around artfully.

I'm using props, he thought with disgust. QuiTai would mock him for that, because she could always tell. He shoved the papers away.

What if she refused to answer his invitation? He had to

talk to her. She was his only hope.

He buried his face in his hands.

He'd known better than to get involved with her, but he'd done it anyway. He'd thought he could walk away. Instead, somehow, she'd crept under his skin. No, not under his skin. Her hold on him went much deeper than that.

His superiors shouldn't have asked him to do this. They'd said her services were essential. He'd told them it would be useless to try to recruit her and that he wouldn't attempt it. He had folded his arms across his chest. He'd been adamant. But they'd known his price: he could return home if he delivered her to them.

They didn't seem to understand that they had to offer her something in return for her services too. Did those fools think she'd be so flattered by their interest that she'd say yes? If they thought he knew her price, they were wrong.

This meeting was going to be brutal. She'd draw his soul's blood and leave wounds that might never heal.

A restless murmur rose from the marketplace below Kyam's office. Something had the shoppers upset. Things would calm down in a few hours, on the surface, but the tension never fully went away.

If only his people would understand that the rice riot had irrevocably changed Levapur. They couldn't keep pretending that they could carry on as they had before. He'd have to start drumming that message into his fellow Thampurians soon – but right now, he had to figure out how to phrase his invitation to the woman who had sent that seismic shift rippling through the town.

Lady QuiTai, I know this invitation will come as a surprise...

Except nothing surprised her, ever.

His office door flew open. The brush blotted the last word as he fumbled it.

QuiTai herself stood on the threshold. She never simply walked into a room; she made an entrance.

It was as if he'd spoken of the devil and summoned her. Did she have a spy in his office? Indignation followed swiftly on the heels of shock. How dare she barge in unannounced?

Like the halo of light around a jellylantern, an aura of power surrounded her. Others reacted to the space her personality devoured, but he knew from experience to keep his eyes on its nucleus.

Earlier this morning, she'd been dressed for business in the newest Ingosolian fashion. What did it mean that she was now wearing a lumpy sarong? Wasn't *this* business? Was she insulting him?

What was she doing here? It was eerie how she seemed to anticipate the future. Had she known he'd planned to send for her today?

Her lips parted slightly. A frisson of anticipation invigorated him. Any moment now, the verbal battle would begin. He had the sensation of rousing from a long sleep, of shaking off a lethargy. Her presence was electric. He'd forgotten the rush he got from sparring with her.

Soldiers appeared in the doorway behind QuiTai, jostling for position. No Ponongese was allowed to walk through the government building unescorted.

"Only five guards? It seems the militia vastly underestimated you," he said.

He'd practiced that tone in so many daydreams. Light, pleasant, slightly teasing. It was supposed to show there were no hard feelings. It was supposed to make her pause.

She hardly seemed to have heard him. Then, as if someone had thrown a switch, she indulged him with a tight smile.

"It's time we had a little chat, Governor Zul."

Her mouth had no business caressing his name like that. The silky insinuation in her voice traveled across his skin and down– Kyam cleared his throat and scowled at her.

She walked toward his desk but did not sit. She turned to the soldiers flanking her. "Thank you, gentlemen. You may go," she said coolly, as if they were hers to command.

"You're dismissed," he told them. "Please, Lady QuiTai, have a seat," Kyam said more courteously, indicating a chair.

Her eyes slid sideways and remained there until the door closed behind the soldiers.

He hoped she'd say something cruel to him, so he would feel better about the confrontation they were about to have. It didn't matter what, as long as it made it okay for him to rage back and then demand a favor from her.

He didn't feel angry at this moment, though. He didn't feel worried about her anger either – because she was here, with him, and the old feeling of adventure was back – and something more. That was part of her charm. Calamities always followed in her wake, but she was impossible to resist.

Her hands lay folded in her lap, but at any moment she might flick her long black braid over her shoulder or smooth her sarong. She might smile mockingly at him. He drew a deep breath, hoping to catch the spiced scent she wore at the hollow of her throat, but she was too far away.

"To what do I owe the pleasure of this visit?" He sat down and nudged the wastebasket under his desk with the toe of his boot. He hated the way he sounded. He'd become an Intelligence officer to escape the starched formality of his mother's salons, but here he was, talking as if he were back in Thampur, wearing a velvet sherwani jacket and holding a silver-tipped walking cane.

"We need to talk about the ludicrous new law forbidding my people to assemble," she said.

He clasped his hand together on his desk. "I regret that we cannot."

"It was a serious mistake when your Grandfather first enacted it, and an even worse idea to bring it back. Normally I'd blame Chief Justice Cuulon, but he seems to have your support."

"It doesn't matter what I say. Cuulon controls the laws." It was true. There was nothing he could do.

"Arresting my people for gathering, even in the marketplace, and especially on festival days, is an error you're going to regret. It's the first step down a very dark path."

It dawned on Kyam that, after all, she had no idea he'd been about to invite her to come see him. What a relief. She wasn't clairvoyant. She wasn't spying on him. This visit was a coincidence.

"I cannot discuss it with you." It made him strangely happy to deny her.

"I thought you wouldn't. Coward."

The insult didn't dampen his relief. "I'm quite busy," he said dismissively, covering his reaction.

She rolled her eyes.

"Unless you have something else to say to me, Lady QuiTai, it's time to leave."

He was bluffing, of course. They had barely started, and she'd already given him leverage to use against her. She wanted the law repealed; he wanted her soul for Thampur. Could it possibly be this easy? He felt almost giddy.

"I had somewhere else to be today. Unfortunately, circumstances forced me to delay my plans. As you can imagine, I don't care to be inconvenienced like this. We've lost enough time to your nonsense already. It's time for you to stop sulking," she said.

His jaw dropped. He'd forgotten how blunt she could be, and how rude. "I have not been sulking!"

She made an offhand little noise of disagreement that set his teeth on edge.

He disciplined himself to a reasonable tone. "I'll admit I was angry about the rice riot and being forced to take this office. I'm not as quick as you, but I finally pieced it together. Grandfather had you neatly trapped. You didn't have many options. I understand why you chose to betray me."

She clasped her hands together and batted her eyelashes theatrically like a pantomime princess admiring her hero. "So all is forgiven. You have no idea how much better I'll sleep tonight." Her hands dropped as her face settled into a darker expression. "Like the dead."

This reminded him of the old days – back before they'd

worked together, when they'd been bitter enemies. He didn't like it. What he longed for was that magical sliver of time when they'd been allies in their search for the Ravidian bioweapons farm. Their lives had been in peril, but working together had been thrilling.

It felt as if his chance to bargain with her was slipping away. He needed to remind her that she'd come to ask him for a favor.

"I don't see that the law harms your people. It's only applied when crowds are deemed to have a potential for violence."

The waters were chummed. All he had to do was wait. Any moment now, she'd jump to her feet and lecture him on all the ways he was wrong. Any second now, she'd lose her temper. She'd rail against injustice and the militia and... She wasn't moving. If she wasn't going to demand he change the law, how could he negotiate with her?

"You don't wish to discuss the assembly law. You won't admit you've been sulking since the rice riot. I see no further need to talk," she said.

No! This wasn't supposed to happen. She never gave up that easily. This was one of her games. It had to be. Despair washed over him. What was she up to? How had she slipped through his fingers?

"Is there anything else I can do for you, Lady QuiTai?" He hoped he didn't sound desperate.

She mulled over something. His spirits cautiously edged up, wavered, and then tried to rise still further as he watched her for the slightest hint of what she was thinking. He leaned closer.

Her shoulders lifted in a slight shrug. "I almost hesitate to mention it."

Sure she did.

The words seemed to prick her lips as she spoke them. "There is a small matter of murder."

What murder? He didn't know about any recent murders. His mind raced but got nowhere. Family lore held that his great-grandfather had once escaped a sinking boat with only a sock and a candlestick in his hands; Kyam felt as if he didn't even have a sock.

He didn't recall hearing about any murders of note recently, but official reports took weeks to reach his desk, and since he'd become governor even gossip seemed to bypass him. It was entirely possible she knew about something he didn't. It was also entirely possible she was the murderer.

If he gave a flippant response, maybe she wouldn't see that he didn't know what she was talking about. "Small? Since when is murder a small matter?"

Contempt sparked in her odd eyes. "The way your militia is handling the investigation, one might think they've decided murder doesn't matter. I'm glad to know that you still take it seriously."

"What investigation?" he asked. He didn't know of any investigations. If he had, he might have helped. It would have given him something useful to do.

"What investigation, indeed, Governor."

There was still a chance he could bluff his way through this. "Well, you know…" He tried to think faster than he talked, but he needed more time. "The militia are soldiers, not police. Their job is to defend Levapur from foreign invaders. They aren't trained in the art of detection."

"Exactly. So why don't you put your police force on the case instead? Oh, that's right. You still haven't created one."

He jabbed a finger toward her, but stopped himself before he raised his voice. The important thing to remember was that he needed a favor from her. Pride be damned. He wanted his freedom. He settled back in his chair, lowered his hand, and tried to look like a hapless civil servant. "I've been busy."

Now she'd ask what he'd been busy with and make sharp comments about how little he'd accomplished.

Except that she didn't.

"Two bodies found mutilated in alleyways in the past week. Both alleged smugglers. Does that sound familiar?" she asked.

Now he remembered Voorus telling him about the grisly findings. "Oh. Those. I didn't suspect you… much. I'm sure the Devil–"

"You shouldn't blame me at all. They were my people." Her anger cracked, and pain shone through it so acutely that his breath caught.

The criminal network in Levapur existed outside the Thampurian sphere. Kyam had no idea what happened in the alleyways of the Quarter of Delights. She shouldn't expect him to know.

She composed herself. "Are you going to see to it that these murders are properly investigated?"

Here was another potential bargaining tile. He could offer to investigate the deaths in exchange for her help. It seemed to be something that mattered to her. Maybe this was her real reason for coming today.

He decided to be frank. "I have limited powers here. I'm up against every government clerk in this building. They make glaciers look fast. They demand obscure forms that can never be found. They get offended if I ask them to do anything, but I can't fire them. Besides, I can't create a police force out of thin air. We don't have the money. Turyat drained the treasury. I don't even have enough to remit taxes to Thampur."

There it was at last, the wicked little smile that haunted his dreams. She was laughing at him, but he thought it was with some fondness. What a relief that she didn't seem to hate him.

"Does the Colonial Government need a loan?" she asked.

He laughed.

"You won't like my terms, but if you're desperate enough, let me know."

He was desperate, but not for coins. He kept his tone light. She liked banter. He'd give it to her. "What are your terms?"

She gave him an appraising look. "Repealing the assembly act is out of the question?"

"Yes." Not really, but negotiations always began this way.

"What would it take to convince the colonial government to go through the pretense of giving a damn and investigate the murder of my lieutenants?" She rose and walked across his office to open the typhoon shutters. Indicating the marketplace below with a sweeping motion of her arm, she said, "Show them that you're the governor of everyone on this island, not only the Thampurians. Show them that justice is for everyone."

"I can't–"

"Don't be such a coward. Anger your own people. Make enemies. Prompt them to write outraged letters to the papers back in Thampur and denounce you to the King. After all, when the war comes, you don't want my people to side with the Ravidians against Thampur."

Kyam jumped to his feet. His hands clenched into fists. He pressed them against the desk and leaned on them. "You wouldn't dare. The Ravidians would enslave you."

"The Ravidians swear that putting the Rhi in chains was Turyat and Cuulon's idea, not theirs. And after the Ravidians were gone, the Thampurians tried to keep my people in slavery, so don't preach to me about Thampur's moral superiority."

He took deep breaths and slowly sank back into his chair. Too much was at stake. He couldn't afford to lose control. He swore she made him angry on purpose.

After several false starts, he was able to speak calmly. "How do you know what the Ravidians said?"

She sauntered back to her chair and sat down. "I asked them."

"The Ravidians?" She was not to be believed. He couldn't even begin to make sense of her thinking. The Ravidians were pure evil. You didn't talk to Ravidians, you killed them.

"When you want to know a person's version of the story, you ask them, not their mortal enemies. A most enlightening conversation." She looked pleased with herself.

He wasn't sure he could speak without sputtering. "You're committing treason by even thinking of talking to them."

She shook her head. "As I told you long ago, they're your enemies, not mine."

"But you're a Thampurian citizen."

"I'm a Thampurian subject, not a citizen."

Knowing he'd regret it, he waved a hand dismissively. "Same thing."

"You can gather with friends in the marketplace without the militia beating you. I can't."

"You have friends?"

Her eyes narrowed, but she let it pass. "Tomorrow, Thampurians will celebrate a very minor festival with feasts and balls. My people have been warned that if we gather at our ancestors' altars for the Day of the Spirits, our most holy day, we might be arrested. I could go on, but I can see that you've already stopped listening. You think that you're a good man, and none of this is your doing – but it is, because you won't stop it."

He hated how uncomfortable she made him.

She growled in frustration. "Your face shrinks against your skull as you try to hide from the truth. Your eyes can roll back in your head so that you no longer have to see. You can hold your breath so you don't have to smell your corrupted soul. But your ears can't stop you from hearing this: I am not a Thampurian citizen. I'm a native of an occupied land. To call me a citizen is to insult my intelligence."

"Spare me your political lectures." His temper was almost beyond his control.

"Are you going to seek justice for my murdered lieutenants?"

He struggled to calm down. She was right, he shouldn't let murders go unsolved, no matter who the victims were. But at present he was tired of being the hero and getting nothing for it.

Abruptly, he recalled the events of the morning, and his anger dissolved into meanness. "Why don't you talk your Captain Voorus into investigating the murders?" he asked.

So that's what she looked like when taken by surprise. She blinked rapidly and seemed confused. "Captain Voorus?"

"The two of you were behind the crates at the warehouse. You reached up to touch his lips. He bent down–" He swallowed the lump in his throat. The jealousy was as raw as it had been this morning.

She laughed derisively. It was like a knife twisting in his gut. "He's not smart enough for me."

That had been his first reaction when he'd seen them together. He'd almost convinced himself he'd misunderstood what he'd seen, but then she ruined it by adding, "Not that I'm looking for conversation in bed, as you may remember." Her gaze dropped to his waist as she smirked.

It wasn't fair that her cruelest smile could make him clear his throat and cross his legs. He remembered, all right. Every delicious moment.

He glanced at the folder on his desk and thought about dragging it into his lap. He was supposed to have better control over his body at this age.

If she'd been Li instead of Ponongese, she would have purred. She certainly looked content. "Captain Voorus has such a strong body. A lot like yours. Almost exactly like yours. Not surprising, since you have the same father."

Was she guessing? Even he hadn't known Voorus was his half-brother until recently.

She didn't seem so amused now. If he felt mean, she must have felt vicious. It showed in her eyes. "That's only one of the Zul clan's dirty little secrets I stopped him from spilling at the wharf, where spies might overhear. Would you like to know the others?"

He remembered the long look she'd given his wife, Nashruu, and her son. The gears had been spinning in QuiTai's mind, he'd seen it. How much did she know? Was she bluffing?

She flicked her hand and looked around his office. "This bores me. Are you going to investigate the murders, Governor Zul?"

One of the Devil's sidelines was blackmail. Was she hinting that she'd spill the Zul clan's secrets unless he investigated the deaths of her lieutenants? There was only one way to find out.

The game excited him more than it should have. "No, I won't."

"Very well, then. I suppose I'll have to take matters into my own hands. I gave you a chance, Governor. Remember that."

Kyam rested his forehead against his hand. This was not the conversation he had wanted to have with her. She didn't use threats unless she had to, but what exactly had she warned him about? As usual, when she was around, his head was swimming. "What do you have planned?"

"Something impossible." She sounded annoyed. He knew for certain she was when she bowed her head and ran her palms over her sarong, smoothing the bulky fabric as if the task required her complete attention. She lifted her head. "Governor Zul, I very much regret to inform you that you must arrest me and take me to the fortress."

He peered at her through his fingers as he tried to decide if she were joking. "For what? What have you done?"

"Me? Nothing." She looked so innocent. He didn't believe it for a second. "This time," she conceded.

"I'm sure it makes perfect sense to you, but why do you want me to arrest you?"

"You don't want to know."

"No, I'm fairly sure that I want to hear a reason."

"No, you don't, Kyam. You never do."

He was about to argue with her, but he realized there were so many crimes she was suspected of, including several disappearances he believed she'd arranged, yet he'd never investigated because he couldn't bear to put her at Cuulon's mercy. He justified everything she did as necessary. She was right – he didn't want to know.

Kyam spread his hands. "Let's say you're right, and it's none of my business why you want to be taken to the fortress. Why would I arrest you? I need a reason."

"I'm Ponongese. That's good enough for the militia."

He would not take that bait. He wanted to reach an agreement with her, not fight.

"Assuming that's true – not that I agree with you – I hope you realize that once you're in the fortress, I can't protect you. You escaped once. You can't possibly hope to leap from the ramparts a second time. And as you are well aware, you're the only Ponongese who has ever left the fortress alive. Why would you risk it again? The odds are not in your favor."

Her eyebrow rose at his pleading tone.

He couldn't decide what to do. The neat plans of the morning had gone to hell already. All he knew was that he couldn't let her die, at least not until he'd used her to escape Ponong.

He walked around his desk. "If I do as you ask, I want something from you in return."

"A deal?" Her mouth curved into a smile as she sat back. "What do you want?"

"Agree to work for Thampur."

Her face became a mask. He knew her better than almost anyone, and even he couldn't tell if she were outraged or amused... or even surprised.

"If it's not too crass to ask, what do you get for delivering me to your old masters?"

There was no hate or malice in her eyes. He decided to be honest. "I get to leave this island."

"Ah." Whatever she was thinking, it took all her concentration. She tugged on her bottom lip as she scowled at the floor. The wrinkles across her forehead eased as her eyebrows suddenly shot up. "May I make a counter offer?"

"You can try, but I don't think I'll change my mind. You know I've been trying to escape from Levapur since the moment I arrived."

"I can give you what you've been searching for since the rice riot. The Devil's name."

She knew him too well. That was the only temptation she could dangle before him that was almost as enticing as his freedom. He'd always thought if he could capture the Devil, she'd be free.

"I always wondered why you protect his identity when as far as I can see, he's never done anything for you. I know you're going to hate me for this, but between Jezereet and the Devil, you've had terrible taste in lovers."

"Don't you dare speak ill of Jezereet, Kyam. Ever."

He'd never seen such blazing anger in her eyes, but he wouldn't back down or apologize. "They treated you so badly, and you excused it away."

"Is asking me to bow down to Thampur for your sake any better?"

He wasn't betraying her, he was giving her a choice. That wasn't the same at all. Jezereet and the Devil used her. "You always say such heartless things."

"It only stings because you know it's true. Don't think for a minute you're such a paragon of virtue. Jezereet's corpse was still warm when you insisted I help you find the Ravidian's bioweapons farm. Even now, you dare tell me not to mourn her death."

From the moment they'd first met, they'd been able to find each other's weak spots.

"I'm not saying you shouldn't mourn her. I'm saying that she didn't…"

"What?"

"Nothing." He shouldn't have brought it up. They would always have different ideas about Jezereet.

She mastered her anger. "If I survive the fortress, you have my solemn word that I will give you the name of the Devil. No tricks. No games. No sleight of hand."

"You're assuming I care about him."

QuiTai prepared to leave. "You don't have to choose now. Arrest me, take me to the fortress. We'll work out the details later."

She acted as if they had a deal, but he didn't understand any of it. "You want to leave the fortress at some point, don't you?"

"Of course. You can come get me before the sun sets. I expect that will be enough time."

She was the most maddening person ever to walk on the face of the planet. "Time for what? What exactly am I agreeing to?"

She patted his cheek. "In exchange for getting me in and out of the fortress, I will give you the name of the Devil– Calm down and listen to my full offer before you go off on one of your rants."

It was nearly impossible, but he held his tongue.

"Thank you. As I said, I will give you the name of the Devil, *or* I will agree to work for Thampurian intelligence for the term of one year. Is that an acceptable deal?"

There had to be a catch. Was it going to be this easy? Hope was a cruel mistress, and he knew better than to trust it. But this might be his only chance, and she always kept her word.

He took her hand and pressed it to his lips. She gave him a fleeting smile. Then her fingertips were trailing across his palm as she withdrew her hand from his.

"I know you're manipulating me. I only wish I knew what's really going on," he said.

"You'll figure it out, eventually. You always do." She paused at the door. "I'm ready if you are. Shall we go to the fortress?"

"Right now? Don't you have to get your affairs in order?" He didn't know why he wanted to talk her out of her plan – whatever it was. This was good for him. He'd get to leave Ponong. Why did he want to stop her?

"You know me, Kyam. I came prepared." She gestured for him to come along. "It's nearly midday already. I can't afford to waste a moment from now on."

CHAPTER 3 : THE MARKETPLACE

"*P*ui, Mister?"

Ponongese boys surrounded Kyam and QuiTai as the government building's brass doors clanged shut behind them. Hands pushed too close to Kyam's face.

"Pui?"

"I'll carry anything for pui, Mister, no matter how heavy."

"Pui, please, Mister."

Their hands quickly dropped as he shook his head. They scattered, returning to sit on the steps. He stepped carefully over their pitifully thin legs. Most boys that age didn't wear blouses like their fathers. Their spines showed each bone, while their distended bellies bowed over their threadbare sarongs.

They used to carry packages for Thampurians, but few were hired anymore. No Thampurian would ever admit it, but they didn't want the boys to know where they lived.

"You have to be so careful nowadays," everyone said. At dinner parties, the guests nodded sagely. If one of the ladies confided that she'd felt uncomfortable around a servant, compassionate friends said, "But what can we do? Are we to cook our own meals, too? Our lower castes here are spoiled. We never should have allowed them to leave service." And the women whose parents had come freely to Levapur as servants but now owned shops stared at the tightly clutched hands in their laps as anger and shame in equal parts glowed on their cheeks.

In their dark-paneled bars, men swished their walking sticks about furiously and swore to "show them a thing or two." And what *they* had to be shown, of course, was their place. They had to be kept there by force. What was needed now were harsher measures, so Thampurians might sleep at night when the sounds of the jungle made them pull the covers up to their chins.

A year ago, Kyam wouldn't have thought twice about the teen boys loitering at the fringes of the marketplace. He might have even nodded to a few of the lads he knew by name. But ever since his grandfather had pushed the Ponongese dangerously close to the point of rebellion, he worried when the boys laughed, and moved his hand to his baton when they fell silent.

QuiTai surveyed the marketplace from the top step as if awaiting her audience's attention. She stretched the fingers of both hands into painful poses like a temple dancer with golden fingertips. He went down the steps, and then realized she still hadn't moved. He extended an impatient hand to her. She was the one who'd said she was in a hurry. She finally deigned to take it.

He would have gone around the edge of the marketplace to the funicular station, but she plunged ahead of him into the midst of the most chaotic section. He ducked beneath red and orange festival flags slung between leaning poles and swatted banners out of his way to keep her in sight. The aisle meandered like an ill-planned labyrinth. Noisemakers blared too close to his ears.

Sellers didn't call out to QuiTai as she glided past their stalls. What use would a Ponongese have for costume fangs, a wig of wooly hair, or lenses to give her eyes a reptilian shape?

But they held out to him cheap sarongs in colors too somber for any real Ponongese. When he'd been an itinerant artist, he'd shoved the costumes away; but now that he was governor, he had to be more polite about it and not rant about how much he hated this ridiculous festival.

Back in Thampur, the last long voyages of the season were beginning ahead of the monsoon season and the typhoons that made crossing the Te'Am Ocean to the southern continent so dangerous. If they remembered the minor festival at all, people celebrated by slipping an extra coin to the priests or placing a sweet bun sacrifice on the gold platters at the temples. In Levapur, Thampurians celebrated with fancy dress balls and great feasts of Thampurian dishes, as if it were the King's birthday rather than a footnote on the maritime calendar.

He swerved around a lower caste Thampurian woman and her twin boys. Under the awning of a yellow and beige striped tent, a basket of fruit appeared inches from his nose.

"Ambrosia fruit! All the way from Thampur! Ours come on the fastest ships, only nine days from port!"

He used to climb the tree in Grandfather's garden and gorge on the honey-perfumed pink fruits. The best part was the thick nectar that gushed out with each bite.

The seller's grin widened as he saw Kyam's expression. He pushed the basket closer to Kyam's face. "How many, Governor? For you, a special price."

The ambrosia fruit in the basket looked sun-wilted, but he hadn't eaten one in years.

Ahead of him, QuiTai moved through the crowd with measured steps, as if she were keeping count of each one. He told himself he could keep sight of her long enough to buy one.

"One, please."

"Discount if you buy more."

"One," he said firmly, as he plucked the least bruised one from the basket and handed over a coin.

As he rushed after QuiTai, he cupped his hand under his lips to catch the juices and bit into the flesh. But there was no juice, and it wasn't the taste of home he expected. He spit the dry, woody mouthful into his hand and dropped it into the dust.

They were almost past the stalls when a Ponongese woman bumped into Kyam hard enough to spin him. She yelled at him, even though he was sure it had been her fault. He knew he recognized her, but couldn't immediately put a name to her face. Since he'd moved from his old apartment to the family compound, his relationships with the Ponongese had grown formal and distant. Kyam the painter, they knew. Kyam the governor was just another Thampurian.

Kyam caught up to QuiTai. He almost grabbed her elbow but thought better of it. He didn't want anyone to think he was dragging her somewhere against her will. The last thing he needed now was a riot.

This was all too easy. That was the most unsettling part. She'd agreed too quickly, as if she'd already known what deal she was prepared to offer. He didn't trust it. Fate was going to cheat him out of this somehow, and if Fate's name was pronounced QuiTai, he'd never forgive her.

RhiHanya bumped into Governor Zul in a narrow aisle in the marketplace and then scolded him loudly, so everyone would look. That was all she'd been told to do, so she sailed away on a cloud of theatrical indignation as he tried to apologize.

She hurried back to the banyan tree at the edge of the town square. Clusters of Ponongese squatted in the shade of the enormous tree. She stopped short as a little girl ran in front of her.

LiHoun raised his hand to get her attention. RhiHanya picked her way over the women weaving baskets. She made sure her bright orange sarong was secure before she squatted. The gap in her front teeth showed as she grinned at him.

"Have you eaten, brother?"

"Yes, sister. And you?"

She switched to LiHoun's native language. "We both eat

well, thanks to Little Sister. May she have a plump chicken for her rice bowl, and praise the gods, maybe we'll continue to share."

He coughed until he gasped in shoulder-wrenching whoops. He turned his head and spat bloody phlegm into the dirt. "It went smoothly?"

"You don't hear him yelling, do you? She has quick hands. Even I didn't see what she did, and I was looking."

LiHoun fished a small spiked huwewe fruit from his pocket and held it out to a gray monkey. It paced at a skittish distance, sat for a moment, and paced again. Then it darted forward and grabbed the huwewe from him. As it scampered up the banyan tree, a gang of bigger monkeys tried to take it from him. LiHoun laughed as a bold monkey ran up his back and stuck a hand into his pocket. Finding it empty, the monkey dashed up the tree and scolded him from a safe branch high overhead.

LiHoun coughed until his face turned ashen. He turned to RhiHanya. "She was a magician's assistant when she lived on the continent." He liked knowing more about QuiTai than anyone else. He hoped she wouldn't decide he knew too much.

"No one gets hands that fast by folding herself into a compartment at the bottom of a cabinet."

"She only talks about the tricks she doesn't mind you knowing about."

RhiHanya watched Kyam and QuiTai emerge from the market. "I hope our Wolf Slayer knows a trick where she can survive being hanged, uncle."

"She will find a way." He folded his arms across his knees and rested his chin on them.

"So you think she has something up her sleeves?"

"I know better than to try to figure her out. You'll drive yourself as mad as nesting gregru if you spend time worrying about her."

"Of course I'm worried. She's going to the fortress, isn't she? That means the sea dragon wouldn't investigate the murders of SungHi and ChiHui."

"I told her he wouldn't."

"Why doesn't she tell him we already–" Her mouth snapped shut as he jutted a thumb toward the circle of mothers several feet away. Her sigh was long on suffering.

LiHoun chuckled. "Mad as a gregru." He formed his hands into beaks and mimicked a pecking fight between the strutting male birds. "Worry about what happens to us if she fails. She is the Wolf Slayer. We are lowly jungle fowl – snacks for those who hunger for power."

Peels of lavender paint clung to the weeds at the base of the funicular station's ticket shack. Dust coated the single window. A double line of yellow ants flowed across the exposed wood and disappeared into a wide joint.

The back door squeaked open. A Thampurian in a creased uniform stepped out of the ticket shack and kicked a crate toward the door to stop it from swinging closed. He listed as he carried a tin of juam nut oil to a disintegrating shade hut on the other side of the track terminus.

Grabbing a grimy cloth from a nail on a post, he gingerly unscrewed the funicular engine's fuel tank. He pulled back his fingers between twists to blow on them. The oil tin's sides collapsed inward until the flow slowed. Air rushed in, popping the sides out again. Amber oil gushed out, then trickled, and finally fell in drops. The operator screwed down the tank cap and wiped his hands on the cloth. He started the engine again, and it belched black smoke. After watching it for a bit, he nodded and returned to the shack.

QuiTai went to the end of the ticket line. As Kyam waited behind her, he noticed her sarong was bulkier than usual. How many times a day did she change clothes, anyway? She was usually so meticulous about her clothes, but her choice this time he found unflattering.

"Seeing as the colonial government is so poor right now, I'll buy my own funicular ticket. Shall I also buy one for you?" she asked.

He wished she wouldn't say that where anyone could hear. "Thank you, but I can—"

She turned to the window. "One, please. I'm feeling hopeful. Make it a round trip."

The quip was vintage QuiTai, but her heart didn't seem to be in it. Maybe she was thinking ahead to the fortress. He was tempted to give her shoulder a friendly squeeze of support, but then reminded himself that she was his article of transport out of this place. This was business. She always made that clear in the past, so he wouldn't make the mistake of thinking it was something more this time. It was her choice to face her biggest fear. It was her fault he had to be beside her when she did it.

Kyam told himself he could admire her and still lock her away. But damn it, why? Why was she doing this? And how was he going to rescue her? She trusted him to do it, maybe because she knew what he'd lose if he didn't.

Chapter 4: Nashruu Begins

After Kyam brought Nashruu and her servants to the family compound, he muttered an excuse and left her to deal with the household, furniture, luggage, and a million other matters that she of course could manage but wished hadn't been so abruptly dumped into her manicured hands. Two years living in exile had roughened his edges, she decided. The alternative was that he was simply that rude, or that he hated her. She preferred her first explanation.

She was cross, a mood she had no patience for. Kyam had been out of sorts too, although neither of them would admit to it. If they had, they would have blamed the searing heat of the day, or perhaps – she slapped a gnat that seemed determined to share the shade of her parasol – the abundant insect life with a taste for flesh. Because they were Thampurians, they would never confess that their bad moods had begun when they'd turned to look back at the wharf from the lower funicular station and had seen QuiTai and Voorus huddled together behind a stack of crates at a warehouse door.

Nashruu and Kyam had turned sharply away from the scene when the couple went to greet Mityam Muul. Thankfully, Mityam shuffled so slowly that the funicular left that station before they came up from the wharf, and Nashruu was spared the indignity of sharing a car with them.

On the funicular ride up to the town square, conversation between Kyam and her had gone from strained to unbearable. They seethed in their private hells of jealousy and humiliation. No wonder Kyam took the first opportunity to go pout in privacy. Unfortunately, that left her to handle greeting his servants and moving her staff into the house alone.

The interior of the compound consisted of only two buildings. Back home, wealthy families often had four or more, as each generation added to the clustered houses inside the walls. Squatting women stared at her from inside the smaller of the two buildings. The bright yellow band around their oval pupils glowed in the deep shadows. They held woven fans that they passed over a ring of stones on the ground, probably fanning the coals of a cooking pit. In Thampur, the kitchens were in the main house, but she'd heard it was so hot in Ponong that only the poor cooked in the same building where they slept. She wondered if that was true during winter, too.

The main house looked almost like a typical Thampurian mansion, except for the odd ways in which it didn't. Every room on the ground floor opened onto the courtyard through glass doors, which she could see through. If there were curtains, they were pulled aside. At least upstairs, the glass in the typhoon shutters was frosted at the bottom, so anyone looking up from the courtyard wouldn't see much below the ceiling murals, but they still opened onto a shared veranda. Having servants meant never having true privacy, but this was so *exposed*. She felt as if she would be living in a shop window along the Lirhumet Canal in Surrayya.

Although the wide canopy of a single tree shaded most of the main courtyard, the sun was too brutal to endure for long. Since Kyam hadn't bothered to introduce his staff, and they didn't seem inclined to come out to greet her, she'd have to invite herself in and take over.

It struck her that during the years she'd been married to Kyam, they'd spoken, to the best of her memory, six hundred and thirty-nine words to each other. Well over a hundred of those had been exchanged this morning. She wondered when he'd become so chatty. He'd used only four to propose marriage; she'd used one to answer, and those had been a mere formality for both of them. On their fifth anniversary, he'd accidently walked into her parlor and sputtered as he'd grasped frantically behind his back for the doorknob, "Oh, wrong room. You're looking well. Splendid. Is that a new frock? Color suits you. Is that the boy? Wonderful. Must run. Love to auntie."

When he returned later today, she would definitely have a few more words to say to him. For the first time in their marriage they would live together, and that meant someone had to change his ways.

Stepping into the foyer of the compound's main house was a bit like crossing the Sea of Erykoli back into Grandfather's mansion. The dark wood floor and paneled walls cast a welcome hush. It wasn't that Levapur was loud; it was the bright turquoise and yellow buildings, the squawking birds, and the intense scent of jungle that made it seem as if the island were constantly shouting for her attention. This dark, monochromatic place was like a cool rag on her forehead and cucumber slices for her eyes.

Then the servants shuffled in behind her, and although they apologized, they banged the luggage about and brushed against her, destroying her moment of peace. While the foyer was quite large, twenty people, a small boy, and their collected possessions filled it quickly. She quashed the desire to rush outside and fill her lungs with air. Nerves, Grandfather often said, were an indulgence for women with little else to occupy their time, and she had plenty to do.

First order of business: settle the household.

Before her was a broad staircase behind which she glimpsed a door. If this were grandfather's mansion, that would be his office. From what she'd seen through the glass doors, there was a formal dining room to her left and a parlor to the right. She hadn't looked into the outermost rooms of each wing but assumed they were the sorts of spaces one often found in palatial homes, such as a music room, a library, and one of those long, wide rooms that wasn't big enough or small enough to be of any real use so you hung artworks you didn't much care for on the walls and only opened the doors for those horrible parties where you couldn't hear what anyone said and people kept stepping on the hem of your dress.

She realized she wasn't going to miss Surrayya much. It was too bad that as the governor's wife she'd be expected to play hostess to the exiles of Levapur. On the voyage over, Cousin Hadre had quipped that for a group of people with dark secrets, the Thampurian citizens living in exile in Levapur were inexplicably dull. It was too bad they didn't have the nerve to celebrate their wicked reputations. What was the worst that could happen? Someone back in Thampur would get angry? Who cared? This place was freedom from all that.

Khyram escaped from his tutor and threw open the dining room door. "Food!" He rushed inside before anyone thought to grab him. Nashruu knew she should scold her son, but she was hungry and her servants probably were too, so she followed him into the dining hall as if it had been her plan all along.

It was bad enough that Kyam's servants hadn't bothered to greet her; did they have to be bad at their jobs, too? It was a nice thought to set out a meal for her, but someone had simply dumped the fruits into silver bowls rather than arrange them with any eye for art. There were no cloths under the bowls to protect the long, polished table. She lifted the heavy lid of an elaborate chaffing dish. The scent of the curry rose in a puff of fragrant steam.

Her maid, Simran, darted forward to take the lid from her. "Please sit, Ma'am."

Nashruu sank into the seat at the head of the table. The master had bolted for safety rather than grace them with his presence, so she felt entitled to the most comfortable seat.

Simran couldn't figure out where to put the lid. She devoted her life to making sure everything stayed in its correct place, and this was a small nightmare in the making for her.

"Set it down in a corner for now," Nashruu told her.

"Where?" Simran wailed.

"On the floor."

Simran shuddered, but set it down.

"We'll have to see about training the household staff, won't we? Assuming they even exist," Nashruu said.

Her servants laughed. She always wondered if they ever meant it, or if humoring her was like cleaning mud off boots – simply another duty.

"Sit, sit. Someone hand around those plates." Nashruu extended a graceful hand.

Her servants seemed scandalized, but her son and his tutor plopped into chairs and ladled hefty servings of curry onto their plates. With some urging, the rest of the staff shuffled forward, but they still waited for someone else to make the bold move.

"Either sit down or I will revoke your articles of transport allowing you to return home."

The senior staff reluctantly took the seats past her son and tutor. The rest followed the intricate rules of hierarchy to decide if her maid or a footman should sit in a particular place. They perched on the edge of their chairs as if they would run away the moment they were allowed to. Most seemed perplexed by the array of spoons and forks before them.

She suspected they would have eaten much more heartily if she hadn't been there. Their discomfort was her fault. She'd expected them to have more of a sense of adventure, but perhaps that sort of thing was something only the rich, and socially secure, could risk.

After she had her fill of curry and rice, she rose, but gestured for them to remain sitting. "I'm going upstairs to find my rooms – and hopefully the household staff."

Definitely fake laughter, she decided, as the staff once again tittered on cue.

"Please feel free to continue your meal. We've all had a long trip, and this heat is not to be believed. Take the rest of the afternoon to settle. Tomorrow morning we begin our regular schedule. That means lessons."

She gave Khyram a meaningful glance. He groaned and slid down in his chair until she could only see the top of his head. He'd been allowed to skip formal lessons on board the *Golden Barracuda* and spend time on deck, as every Zul male should. Now it was time to return to his books.

"Master Zul! Sit up at once." The tutor, it seemed, was ready to reclaim control over his pupil. That was one worry off her list.

On her way out of the dining room, Nashruu took the farwriter case from her protesting footman. The doors shut, and she took a deep breath. It was exhausting to be in charge of that many people. She'd managed much of the staff in Grandfather's house, but they had little need of her direction. On board the ship, few of her servants had been able to perform their regular duties, which made them far more dependent on her for guidance than she'd anticipated. This was the first moment she'd had to herself in over two weeks. What a shame she had no time to enjoy it.

She paused on the stairs as she saw movement high in shadowy peak of the ceiling. A lock of hair that had escaped her perfect curls rose as if lifted by invisible fingers. She knew it was a waft of air from the overhead fans, but enjoyed a brief fantasy that the house was deserted and haunted. She smiled as she walked the rest of the flight of stairs. How could any place this sunny and cheerful be haunted?

At the top landing, the hallway branched right and left. One direction presumably led to her rooms, the other to Kyam's. There was nothing to do but open doors and hope it was obvious where she was meant to live.

The heavy farwriter case banged against her leg with each step down the lushly carpeted hallway, as if it were grandfather tapping her with his cane to hurry up. She pictured him pacing angrily between the rows of hundreds of farwriters in his ballroom as he awaited her message. He probably already knew the *Golden Barracuda* had arrived in port.

The short hallway to the left led to double doors with a high, peaked arch. The moment she opened them she knew the rooms were Kyam's. Every door to the veranda was wide open, but the room still smelled of oil paint and thinner.

Someone had told her he painted flowers. She'd pictured tasteful bouquets. These flowers however were bold and bright, and vaguely obscene, although she couldn't say why they made her feel that way. One looked like a bratty child sticking its tongue out at her.

Curious, Nashruu flipped through a sketchbook on the corner of a paint-spattered table. She liked the charcoal drawings on those pages much more than his paintings. Some were sketches of women balancing large, flat baskets on their heads. Others were groups of Ponongese squatting under a tree like that gigantic one on the edge of the town square. He'd drawn several of an ancient cat-man smoking a kur.

Nashruu drew in a breath as she flipped the next page. At some point, he'd sketched QuiTai. The sharpness of her features was exaggerated to make her look cruel. Page after page, her glare challenged anyone who dared gaze at her. Nashruu flipped back toward the front of the book and stopped when another picture caught her eye. Kyam had drawn QuiTai again, but this time she sat on steps with her arms wrapped around her knees, looking as if she were about to laugh. She appeared younger, more carefree than she had on the wharf. The sketch was lovingly rendered. Intimate.

At some point, QuiTai and Kyam had shared this moment; he'd wanted to capture it. It meant something to him.

It felt as if she'd peered into something too personal. Grandfather would want to know about this. He'd badger her for details. Maybe when she was a seasoned agent, such things would come easily to her, but for now, she saw a line she would not cross.

She closed the sketchpad and hurried out of the room.

Nashruu found her suite across the landing from Kyam's room. Filtered light cast the sitting room before her in a soothing glow. A little yellow and white striped settee and two delicate chairs were arranged before an ornamental fireplace. Unlike the dark carpet covering Kyam's floor, the one in her room was cream with pastel yellow and pink flowers. No one could have matched her taste so exactly without going to great effort.

She would write Kyam a nice little note of thanks. And she might even say it to him over dinner. The idea delighted her. They'd have something to talk about.

She set up her farwriter on a petite dressing table in her bedroom. Even though she knew she was alone, she cast a glance over her shoulder and at the veranda before pressing her fingertips against the biolock. She pried her frequency book out of the tight, hidden compartment in the copper-bound leather case. She'd randomly selected frequencies from the master list and diligently recorded them in two books – one for her, the other to sit beside the farwriter assigned to her in Grandfather's ballroom.

She hugged the book to her chest and tapped her toes in a quick little dance of joy. Then she opened it to page one and hummed a jaunty tune as she set the frequency on her farwriter to the numbers on line one of page one.

Now singing, she wound her field battery. It took about a hundred churns of the handle above the copper wire coil to charge the battery, but rather than count the spins, she wondered who consulted the books and adjusted the frequencies on all Grandfather's farwriters now. Surely not he himself. But whom could he trust? Not his servants. Perhaps her mother-in-law was Grandfather's new assistant. The thought of Liragme Zul rising before noon made her laugh. Only Grandfather would dare make the Grande Dame of Surrayyan society do such a thing.

The moment she secured the battery to her machine, the incoming bell rang, and paper coiled out almost faster than she could read. The gist was that Grandfather wanted her to report immediately, and where was she, damn it? The message repeated. Only Grandfather's scolding varied.

Feeling bold, she spoke to the machine. "I've just arrived. The voyage was pleasant enough, thank you very much. Cousin Hadre sends his... not love, but his greetings." She'd never type a message like that, but it felt good to say to out loud. Now that she was almost free, she wanted to try all those things she'd never dared do before – like talking back to Grandfather.

She let the paper scroll to the floor as she prepared to send her reply. She scooted her chair over a bit, then a bit more. She cleared her throat. Her fingers curved over the keys as if she were about to play a concerto for a salon filled with the cream of Thampurian society.

Have arrived at the family compound. NaZ

I have been kept waiting. TtZ

The machine couldn't sense emotion, so it wasn't possible for it to pour out messages faster when Grandfather's face grew red and he jabbed his fingers at the keyboard, but it felt as if it did. She tore off the long ribbon of paper and searched around the room for somewhere to burn it. There was no fireplace in her room and nothing with a flame. She placed it beside the machine as she reached for the incoming message.

She read the paper with increasing panic. No wonder Grandfather was so wild to reach her.

Why did Kyam arrest Lady QuiTai? TtZ

Go to the fortress and make sure those fools don't hang her. Talk to Colonel Hurust, head of the colonial militia. Use your discretion, but evoke our royal cousin if you must. TtZ

Nashruu wasn't sure how he expected her to convince Colonel Hurust without evoking the power of the King, in fact.

"Excuse me, Colonel, but my husband the governor arrested Lady QuiTai an hour ago. And even though you don't know me or understand why I think I should be able to override my husband's decisions, why don't you let her go?" Yes, she imagined that would be an effective tactic.

Why would Kyam deliberately deliver Lady QuiTai to the one place we can't protect her? TtZ

She'd never suspected the old man of musing in his communications, although she'd often seen his fingers hover over a keyboard before as if he were deep in thought.

"Maybe, Grandfather, he did it because he hates you."

She had to stop saying such things out loud. Her servants would report it to him. But it felt so good to blurt out the bitter words she'd been forced to swallow for so long.

Enough of that. Time to work.

Why had Kyam arrested QuiTai? According to their information, the two had been close at one time. Kyam's sketch of QuiTai confirmed it. Grandfather suspected Kyam and QuiTai were carrying on an affair, but his agents swore that if they were, they were so discreet that it was impossible to catch them together. Or perhaps they hadn't been caught together because Lady QuiTai's lover was Captain Voorus, not Kyam.

Nashruu shook her head so hard the fall of curls down her shoulder bounced. Voorus would never touch a Ponongese woman. In the Zul clan, Grandfather urged respect for the Ponongese; but Voorus, like most Thampurians, had openly made derogatory comments about the colony's natives years ago. Grandfather's agents said his stance hadn't changed much in the years he'd been exiled to the island. But their reports also said he had never taken a lover, and she'd seen how closely he stood to that woman.

Now is not the time for petty jealousies, she scolded herself.

She realized Grandfather must be waiting for a reply. Her graceful fingers struck the keys in quick succession.

I will see what I can do. NaZ

Why are you still sitting there? Go! And you better do more than try! Keep me informed. TtZ

Nashruu emptied her purse onto the bed and shoved the farwriter paper into it. On the way out, she'd stop by the kitchen and put the papers in the cooking fire. Hands on her hips, she took a deep breath. This was it. This was what she'd been trained to do for years.

She was going to have an adventure.

Chapter 5: To the Fortress

Kyam looked for an empty car when he and QuiTai boarded the funicular, but there wasn't one. They handed their tickets back to the operator, even though he'd been the one to sell the tickets to them. Only in Levapur, Kyam thought.

The operator slammed the door shut and locked it.

QuiTai faced the window with her hands clasped loosely at her waist. With the first jolt as the funicular began its long trip down to the harbor, she laced her fingers into the grill under the window. No matter what she did, her pose was graceful.

His arms felt awkward when he held onto the grill. Flashes of pity for her made him feel as if he was doing something terribly wrong. But she'd agreed to the deal. She'd proposed it!

Why did he feel so guilty?

Would she keep her word? The only promise he'd known her to break was when he'd asked for her help escaping the island before the rice riot. Okay, it wasn't a promise, exactly. She'd offered to find him berth on a smuggler's boat. He'd taken too long to say yes. Whose fault was that?

Hers.

He winced. She was right. He was sulking. Angry with her for being right, he stared at the dusty spider web in the corner of the window the rest of the trip.

At the harbor, the other passengers rushed the door as soon as the lower station operator unlocked it. Kyam and QuiTai followed them at a slower pace.

As they passed the Harbor Master's office, Kyam whistled sharply to get the attention of two soldiers slumped in the shade and motioned for them to follow him.

"They'll row us out to the fortress." He didn't know why he was telling her what she already knew. His nerves were showing.

QuiTai sauntered across the small beach at the bottom of the cliff. He helped her over a tangle of kelp in the sand. Small crabs scuttled over the slick leaves and avoided the sandy jellyfish nearby.

"Did you ever finish that portrait of me?" she asked.

He'd been thinking of that afternoon too. "No."

"Hmm. The Devil paid you handsomely for it, in advance."

He was sure she was teasing him, maybe to help calm his nerves. "Tell him I'll gladly return the coins."

"You can tell him yourself if you decide you want his name."

"You're crazy if you think I'd give up articles of transport, even for the name of the Devil."

"Thank goodness you're being sensible, for once," she said.

He cast a dubious glance at her.

"Let me explain. You can't have your articles of transport if you don't get me out of the fortress. So I hope you want them so badly your skin itches for them. And I want you to know that the only way you'll ever relieve that itch is to hold up your end of our bargain."

They reached the militia's private dock, jutting from the beach near where the fishermen hung their nets to dry. The drying poles were mostly empty this time of day, and it would be several hours before they returned to the small docks in the shallowest part of the harbor.

QuiTai tapped her sandals against the dock to knock the white sand from them. The breeze sent a lock of her hair fluttering against her cheek. Her fingers curled around it and slowly pulled it behind her ear.

If he had been facing his last hours, he would have looked to the sea. She turned her back to it. Her gaze climbed past Levapur to the high, mist-shrouded mountains. She seemed to drink in the rich green. Then she closed her eyes and turned her face to the sun.

"The soldiers are here," he said quietly. He hated to disturb her meditation.

"It will be all right. I will survive."

At least that's what he thought she said, but then the soldiers stomped across the creaking dock and complained to him about rowing across the harbor while the sun was high. While they argued, she climbed into the boat, folded her hands in her lap, and waited.

As the boat made its way across the harbor to the fortress, she turned from her beloved island to face the stone walls. Distress etched deep lines around her eyes as she gazed at the bodies hanging from the ramparts. By sunset, unless he got her out, she might be one of them.

He liked this deal less with each moment that passed. It looked too easy because it was. He didn't have to charge her with anything to arrest her, and the militia didn't need an excuse to hang her once she was in their clutches. Thankfully, they tended to wait until sunset to execute prisoners, but that wasn't guaranteed.

The rowboat collided with the short dock outside the fortress gate. He climbed out first and extended a hand to her. She seemed calm, but her hand trembled in his.

Despite the months of silence between them, he felt as if he should comfort her. Again it seemed to be his fault she ended up here. He stood beside her as the towering gate of the fortress swung open and revealed the dark maw of the tunnel behind.

"You could have asked me for almost anything else, and I

would have done everything in my power to give it to you," he whispered. His heart pleaded with him to ask, *So why did you ask for this?*, but he refused to listen to it.

She pushed his hand away and stepped forward. "I know."

"You want to be here?"

"Want isn't the right word. It's my duty."

The interior doors shut behind Kyam and QuiTai. She put her hands to her ears as the clanging echoed down the arched tunnel. She'd done the same thing a year ago when Voorus had brought them here. He should have asked her what had happened between her and Voorus. When had they become friends? What had he missed during the past months?

Flecks of mica in the stone reflected the green glow of jellylanterns along the tunnel. He squinted at the bright sunlight at the end of the tunnel, where lush grass and the brilliant blue sky made the prison section look almost cheerful. The sun overpowered the white light jellylantern inside the barred admittance window carved into the wall.

A bored soldier lifted his pen over his form as they stepped closer to it. "Name?"

"Lady QuiTai," Kyam said.

The pen didn't move, but the soldier's eyes rose. He slowly smiled. "We've been waiting for you for a long time, snake."

She turned to Kyam. "I do hope you'll escort me to my cell. One would hate for there to be an accident."

He knew what she meant, but he said, "An accident?" because he knew instinctively that was his line. Moments like this were when he missed working with her the most.

Tiny smile lines formed around her eyes. She tilted her head and gave the soldier a coy side glance. "The proper term should be an on-purpose, because there wouldn't be anything accidental about it at all."

"I assure you, nothing will happen to you here. Correct?" He glared at the soldier but received no assurances.

QuiTai's hands clasped at her chest. This time she looked like a hapless ingénue pleading with the villain. Her transformation caught him off guard. She so rarely acted for his benefit.

Unless she always did.

He didn't know.

She turned wide eyes on him that brimmed with tears. "You have my word that I have no intention of attempting to escape, and my fangs will remain firmly against the roof of my mouth."

The soldier grunted as if he found that funny. Kyam didn't. She was in real danger here. No matter what insurance she thought she had, it wasn't enough.

He grabbed her arm. "I'll take charge of my prisoner. I may have questions later, and I want her alive to answer them."

"Do what you want, Governor. It won't change her fate," the soldier said.

He pulled her back even though he knew the soldier couldn't reach through the bars. Fear set an icy finger on his soul and made its mark. "This is a mistake. You're coming with me," he whispered.

He grabbed her forearm to pull her out of the fortress. Her sleeve pulled up and he saw another cuff at her wrist, as if she were wearing another blouse under this one. That explained her rumpled appearance. Had she thought to keep herself warm in her cell?

She leaned into his hold and twisted her wrist out of his grip, pulling away in a smooth motion. The double layer of cloth made her impossible to hold. "We have a deal, Governor. You're not getting out of it so easily."

The soldier from the admitting window came out of his office and hailed another soldier out on the parade grounds. Both men raised their hands to the biolocks that activated the gate.

The gate opened. She walked to the middle of the grassy parade ground and stopped. Was she remembering how the werewolves shifted and then slipped through the bars of their cells? He still had nightmares about that insane leap she'd made into the harbor, barely missing the rocks below. Was she plotting yet another fantastic escape? She wouldn't need to if she would come away with him right now.

A soldier led them toward one of the cells built into the fortress wall under the ramparts. They were open to the elements, but she'd be able to see the sky and the mountains of her beloved island over the fortress walls.

"You are going to die here," he whispered to her.

She continued her inspection of the fortress. "Then you will never go home."

"Why are you doing this? Why?" But he knew it was futile to demand answers from her.

"This cell is charming, but I fancy a bit of privacy. Do you have something in a dungeon, perhaps?" QuiTai asked the soldier. A fake smile appeared on her face a few seconds late.

What was she up to?

He smiled weakly at the soldier as he pulled her across the grass. The soldiers were going to wonder why they kept doing this.

As soon as they were far enough away, he scowled down at her. "It's going to be harder for you to escape if you're in a dungeon."

"I have no intention of escaping, in the conventional sense. You will return an hour before sunset and take me out of here. It's not dramatic, but it'll get the job done." She had the nerve to wink at him.

"Do you want her in the dungeon or here in the cell, Governor?" the soldier asked.

Against his better judgment, Kyam said, "The dungeon." He gave her a hard look, which she ignored.

"This way, then." The soldier led them to a thick wooden door under the south rampart stairs.

Right inside the door, a roughly hewn table and a few chairs sat tucked into a small alcove. A guard seated at the table turned a bone tile end to end.

Kyam put his hand over his nose as the stink of the marsh at low tide choked him.

The soldier threw a salute and thrust out his chest. "I have a prisoner for you."

The guard at the table smacked his lips and turned the tile a few more times before slowly coming to his feet. "Sure. Follow me."

He grabbed a white light jellylantern from the wall and a large iron key ring before leading them down narrow, twisting stairs. The smell of damp stone and stagnant mud grew worse as they descended into the dungeon.

The green light jellylanterns in the wall sconces needed replacing. Kyam could barely see beyond the first cell. They were a bit smaller than the outside cells. The walls looked solid enough, even though they were damp in a few spots. Iron bars separated the cells. At the far end of the space there was a door, but he didn't think it was a cell. Unless she knew of a hidden passage, there was no way QuiTai could manage a disappearing trick from this place.

QuiTai jutted her chin at the dim row of cells. "No other prisoners? Good."

Kyam looked in that direction, as did the soldier. Keys jangled, but underneath the noise, he thought something skidded across the stone floor and came to rest in a shadow.

"Don't touch my keys!" The sleepy guard slapped QuiTai's hand.

"Sorry. I'd hoped that the Governor himself would hold onto the cell's key." She stepped into the cell, gripped the bars, and pulled the door shut. The clanging echoed through the dungeon.

"Wait. We have to search her," the guard said. The man sounded so sleepy he could doze off any second now.

QuiTai had thought this through. She had some kind of plan. At least, he hoped she did. He had to help her. He shot a glance to the gods above. Only QuiTai could get someone to talk himself into helping her and betraying his own.

"Ah, she's already in the cell. Why bother dragging her out? She might not go in so easily next time," he said. "Besides, she isn't charged with anything. I'm just holding her here for questioning later today. I'll come back later today and question her." He stopped talking, but it was too late to stop looking stupid.

The soldier and the guard seemed uneasy with that, but they didn't want to go to any more trouble than they had to. "Okay, but if anyone asks, you told us not to."

"Give me the key to her cell." Kyam put his hand out. He had no idea what this was about, but he took his cues from her, and if she thought he should hold the key, then he would.

"We can't give you the key."

He grinned at the guard. "Yes, you can."

"No, Governor. Afraid I can't."

"I command you."

The guard shook his head slowly. "No."

Kyam stuck his hand into his pocket and withdrew a handful of coins. The soldier's fingernails rasped against his palm as he scooped the coins. The key dropped into his hand.

QuiTai patted her hip. He dropped the key into his hip pocket as instructed. Her lips pulled into a tight smile. The guards rattled the door to her cell to make sure it locked.

Whatever she had up her sleeve, it was up to her from now on.

"Give me half of that," said the other guard, trying to take some of the bribe from his friend.

He wouldn't be frightened for her. He wouldn't think about torture. She was brilliant, and cunning, and ruthless. Gah! But none of that mattered much if a few soldiers decided to go into that cell and hold her down. A wave of nausea hit his stomach.

As if she read his mind, she whispered," I will see to it that you're stuck in Levapur until your dying day if you dare interfere with my plans. Go away. Go now."

Chief Justice Cuulon darted panicked glances over his shoulder as he rushed into the government building. The

Ponongese wouldn't be able to break down the massive brass doors and drag him into the town square if they decided to riot over QuiTai's arrest. He'd seen what those snakes had done to the werewolves several years ago. Savages, all of them.

He forced himself to slow down as he stepped into the center atrium. His heart pounded as he paused to admire a purple lily in the ornamental pond. Seven, eight, nine, he counted the seconds. When he reached thirteen, he headed for the staircase.

Cuulon didn't acknowledge the deep bows of junior clerks on the first landing of the staircase, or those of senior staff as they pressed against the railing to clear his path. He held his head high through the long climb to his office on the third floor. No one must guess how the snakes made him tremble.

Somehow, QuiTai always managed to make things difficult. How did she happen to have one of Thampur's finest legal minds in her employ now? She had supernatural powers. That was the only explanation.

He took a calming breath and opened the door of the justice department.

Legal clerks sat at small desks arranged in neat rows in the front chamber. Dressed in nearly identical sherwani jackets, they reminded him of schoolboys. None of them lifted their eyes from their work as he strode past the desks. The only sound in the room was the soft lop-lop-lop of the ceiling fans and the banging of message cylinders in the pneumatic tubes along the wall.

His secretary tried to hand him a stack of papers, but he waved them away.

He shut his office door a bit too forcefully and sank onto a settee. His hand rested at his temple to shield his eyes from the blinding sunlight streaming through the glass typhoon shutters.

If only Petrof had killed QuiTai before the rice riot, or even back during the Full Moon Massacre, he lamented. It was just his luck that QuiTai had been the one to escape the assassination of her family. The dangerous ones always found a way to survive.

His hand slipped down to support his chin.

That old bastard Theram Zul might have made it clear QuiTai was under his clan's protection, but the Ravidians had found a way around that. They'd tortured Petrof until he'd agreed to kill her. But after a few senselessly theatrical attempts on her life, Petrof had suddenly stopped trying. What was he waiting for?

Maybe Petrof was being cautious. He was the only werewolf known to have escaped the mass hanging at the fortress. Petrof didn't need to come out of hiding to kill QuiTai, though. He could still attack from the shadows – if he were still alive. Was he? He had good reason to stay in hiding if he was. Theram Zul and the Ravidians probably both wanted his hide nailed to their walls. QuiTai too. She was a vicious little thing, and she wouldn't be content to kill a man quickly. Oh no. She'd do it slowly and enjoy every second of it.

That woman!

He leaned back and crossed his legs. His arms spread across the back of the settee as he surveyed his grand office. With a sniff, he tried to convince himself that he'd never been infatuated with her. His fingers drummed against the dark wood frame of the furniture. Never, he thought.

Maybe he should hire someone to kill her; but now that the werewolves were dead, he wasn't sure who handled contract killings in Levapur. Every discreet message left at the usual places had gone unanswered.

Maybe the Devil had killed Petrof.

No. It couldn't be. The Devil was smart and ruthless, not a fool for love. The Devil wouldn't kill Petrof to protect QuiTai. Petrof was too important to the Devil's business. But where had Petrof disappeared to? He'd never been easy to find, especially after the militia went a bit too far with that ant torture. But he'd still slipped into town occasionally after that. Now he was as elusive as a maishun spirit.

Who knew where to find Petrof? Probably only the Devil. And who knew how to get an audience with the Devil?

Probably only QuiTai.

Frustrated with his circular thoughts, he slapped his hand against the upholstery. There were too many unknowns. It used to be that he knew every major criminal in Levapur and what they might do, but that had changed as soon as the Devil muscled in and took over. Now everything was a secret, and the Devil was the biggest secret of them all.

It was too late anyway. Too late to kill her.

At least she had been taken to the fortress. He was surprised that Kyam Zul had acted so quickly. She was defenseless now; even the Devil couldn't save her there. He looked forward to hearing her beg. That would be the sweetest thing. As she had once humiliated him and made him plead, he would now make her grovel. The natural order would be restored.

But none of that would bring back Turyat.

That bitch! Why would she kill a man who was already a ghoul?

He bowed his head. Tears fell.

CHAPTER 6: MOTIVES

Kyam returned to his office in a restless state. There was no taking back the morning, was there? Qui-Tai had him in a strange bind. He couldn't save her too soon, but if he were too late, he was screwed that way too. Every deal with her was a trap. He knew that. He should have asked her why she wanted things done this way. It made no sense.

A deep sigh lifted his shoulders. He poured a drink but left the glass untouched as he tried to remember his exact conversation with her. The Ponongese could listen to a saga once then repeat it flawlessly. He wished he could do that, because he knew she'd told him things she thought he needed to know. But being typical QuiTai, she'd refused to say 'remember this,' or 'this part is the most important.' She trusted him to be smart. Sometimes he wished she would treat him like an idiot instead.

Kyam's office door rattled. Voices rose outside as something slammed against it. No one had talked to him in months, and now twice in one day he had urgent visitors. He had no idea what would happen next.

The door flung open and Voorus stumbled in, followed by Kyam's outraged secretary – a young man with far too much nose and not enough chin. While his secretary alternately apologized to him and scolded Voorus, an elderly Thampurian gentleman shuffled through the doorway and into the room.

The man carefully made the transition from the wood floor to the thick carpet. He grasped his cane with cruelly contorted hands. While every step seemed difficult, the man never faltered. Kyam thought he recognized him, but no name came to mind.

Kyam raised a placating hand to his secretary, "It's all right."

Offended, his secretary sniffed deeply though his prominent nose and turned on his heel. The office doors banged shut behind him.

Voorus seemed extremely nervous. The captain wouldn't look him directly in the eye. Instead of sitting, he rushed to the old man's side, but couldn't seem to decide if he should help the fellow or simply hover. What he should have done was make introductions, but after a long, painfully awkward moment, Kyam decided he'd have to take care of it.

"Sir, you look familiar, but forgive me, I cannot recall your name," Kyam said.

The man made a small bow. "Mityam Muul. You need not introduce yourself. I recognize a Zul when I see one."

Kyam wasn't sure if that was meant as an insult.

It took a moment, but it dawned on him where he'd met Mityam before. Mityam Muul might have been a scion of the least powerful among Thampur's thirteen families, but a man of his reputation barely needed of a family name. Mityam had never served on the nation's high court, but he was a mentor to every man who did. Diplomats and government officials turned to him for advice, and he was often referred to as the nation's 'sage uncle.' Kyam thought he'd retired a few years ago. What was Captain Voorus doing in the company of such a man? The best way to find out was to ask, but he'd have to ease into it.

"Gentlemen, please have a seat," he said.

Kyam remained standing until Mityam painfully lowered himself into a chair. After Kyam took his seat behind his desk, Voorus also sat, but almost immediately jumped to his feet again and paced.

"Is something troubling you, Captain?" Kyam asked.

"Well, yes. Former Governor Turyat's murder."

He didn't like this. "I hadn't heard."

Clearly confused, Voorus looked to Mityam for help. "But then why did you arrest Lady QuiTai?"

"She asked me to." He was never going to be able to explain it to them. QuiTai always made things sound so logical, until you tried to explain them to someone else. Only then did you realize you were spouting gibberish.

Voorus looked at him as if he'd done something unspeakable. "You know they mean to hang her for it."

That sinking feeling only worsened. "For what?"

Voorus had been sitting on the edge of his chair for a moment but sprang to his feet again. "For murdering Turyat!" He jabbed Kyam's desk with his finger. "Right in this room, after the rice riot, she swore she would not kill Turyat or Cuulon. She swore she wouldn't have them killed. You heard her. But that won't stop the militia from hanging her for it."

Astounded, Kyam leaned back in his chair. Voorus acted like a passionate lover. Had QuiTai lied to him about her relationship with Voorus? Had she ever made it clear what was between them? He couldn't remember now. How very like her to avoid a lie by changing the subject.

Voorus still glared at him.

"Okay. I'm lost. I'll admit it. Why would anyone think QuiTai murdered Turyat? We all know she hates him, but as you said, she gave her word she wouldn't kill him," Kyam said.

"Because Turyat's body was found in the Red Happiness. On the floor. In a pool of blood."

"Oh, hell!" Kyam clutched his head. "I should have known."

He had to rescue her. He had to get her out of the fortress

right now. She couldn't know how much danger she was in.

"And now Cuulon is calling for her neck, and you delivered her to the fortress."

"Do you think I don't know that?"

They glared at each other until Voorus blushed and glanced away.

What was he going to do?

Not panic. That was the first thing. The next thing he would do was think. They generally didn't execute prisoners until sundown, so he had a few hours to come up with a plan.

He would hear what Voorus and Mityam had to say, show them out, and then come up with a brilliant plan to rescue QuiTai. He took a deep breath. That sounded about right.

Kyam pointed to Mityam then Voorus. "What's the story here?"

Voorus waved a dismissive hand at Mityam. "It's a long one, and we don't have time to waste."

"The finest legal mind in Thampur magically appears the same day Lady QuiTai is arrested. I want to know why." How long had she been planning this?

Voorus sighed dramatically. "I told you I wanted to study the law. She hired him to tutor me."

"*She* hired him?" What had been going on in the past nine months?

"You know they'll torture her down there. The Colonel in charge, Hurust, is one of these moral absolutists. He won't even set foot in Levapur because it's polluted with Ponongese. And don't even get him started on the degradations of the Quarter of Delights. How could you deliver her into the hands of a man like that?" Voorus asked.

"I warned the militia not to touch her."

Voorus scoffed. "She did everything she could for you before the rice riots! Everything. And you're going to let her die because poor Kyam got a cushy political post with a huge salary and he didn't want it? Be a man, Zul."

Only a man in love would come to her defense like that. He could see why Voorus worshipped her, and if she'd hired

Mityam Muul to tutor him, the feelings must have been mutual. But didn't the Devil mind that his concubine had another lover? Maybe not. After all, she'd been married to Jezereet while she'd served the Devil.

He rested his elbows on his desk and leaned forward. "May I remind you that she *caused* the rice riots?"

Mityam seemed puzzled, but rather than interrupt, he rested his forehead on the silver knob of his cane. His intense focus was frighteningly similar to QuiTai's manner when she caught the faint scent of the truth hiding behind other words.

Incensed, Voorus gestured emphatically down to the marketplace. "Greedy Thampurians caused that riot. There was plenty of rice. There was always plenty of rice. All people had to do was pay the full price with the taxes, only buy what they needed instead of trying to hoard it, and none of that would have happened."

"Spoken like a man smoking her vapor."

"I—" Voorus stood straight and yanked on the hem of his jacket. His forehead wrinkled then smoothed as a wry smile spread across his face. "You think we're lovers. You actually think Lady QuiTai and I are..." He cast a glance at Mityam. "Together. Is that why you're letting Cuulon murder her?"

"Execute," Kyam quietly corrected.

Voorus raised his hands to the ceiling then let them drop with a loud slap against his thighs. "You used to hate the colonial government. Now you're nothing but their hand puppet." He made a rude gesture that left no doubt as to where he felt the government's fist had been rammed.

Kyam tried hard to keep his temper in check.

Voorus paced across the rug again. "She barely tolerates me. Still. And believe me, we have no interest in each other that way. None."

"You two seemed to have a moment at the harbor. I saw you behind the crates." Between Voorus and QuiTai, he might get the truth about what they had been up to.

Voorus' mouth opened and closed a few times. He pointed at Kyam. "That's right! You were there! You know she has an alibi for the time of Turyat's murder because you saw her! You know she can't possibly be guilty, but you won't lift a finger to save her. Is being governor so terrible that your revenge has to be her life?"

It wasn't like that. Did Voorus think so little of him? "I can't comment on a case."

"It's a case? Wait, are you going to investigate the murder?" Voorus' temper turned instantly to relief. "Thank goodness. For a moment there, I actually thought you were going to let Cuulon murder her."

"Execute." Kyam wasn't sure why he bothered.

He leaned back. If he found Turyat's real murderer, they couldn't hang QuiTai for it. The more he thought about it, the more he liked the idea. Except for one small problem: QuiTai was the one who solved mysteries with a mere glance at the scene, not him. It took him days to catch up to her – and he didn't have days.

"If Cuulon hangs her for a murder she didn't commit, then it's murder, Zul, and you know it. No amount of political double-speak will change that fact. Hide behind the state, and I'll call you a coward." Voorus flopped down in the chair next to Mityam. "Not you, of course. 'You' meaning anyone who would do that."

"She's safe enough, for now. I have the only key to her cell."

Voorus laughed. "Do you think we're stupid enough to have only one key to any cell down at the fortress?"

A bad feeling washed over Kyam. He felt stupid. "The militia assured me–"

"They lied. And you better be careful, because everyone in the marketplace saw you take her to the fortress. If she dies, you'll be blamed. The Ponongese are already angry about the assembly law. Kill their favorite outlaw, and who knows what they'll do?"

Kyam cursed. Was that her game?

"I've warned you before what could happen if the Ponongese decide they're tired of us," Voorus said. "There's ten of them to every one of us, and that's just in Levapur. Do you have any idea how many Ponongese live across the Jupoli Gorge Bridge? I don't. None of us do. But I have a feeling we will if QuiTai is executed this evening. They still haven't forgiven us for what your grandfather did to them before the rice riots."

"No need to lecture me about that," Kyam snapped. He didn't want Mityam Muul to hear that juicy piece of gossip. As far as he understood it, no one back in Thampur, and no one in Levapur, knew that his grandfather had manufactured the crisis that eventually made Kyam governor.

Voorus shook his head. "Thampurians think you gave us rice to end the riots. What our people should be told is that *she* gave you all that rice, for free."

"The Devil gave me the rice," Kyam said.

"Why would the Devil help you? That rice was hers."

Kyam gave Voorus a sharp look. Ideas kept flitting into his mind. The problem was that they flitted out just as quickly. There was a tantalizing glimpse of something big beyond his perception. He wished everyone would leave him in peace so he could try to coax it into view.

"Meanwhile, the Ponongese now think she's the only one standing between them and a police state," Voorus said. "Guess which leader has the most popular support? You or her? Here's a clue. We Thampurians have rice now. A full belly forgets hunger."

Mityam snorted. "Police state? If the Chief Justice can execute someone without a trial, this already is one. Poor deluded fools, thinking only the guilty are arrested."

When had Voorus gotten so insightful? Kyam suspected his bastard half-brother had spent a lot of time in the past months learning at QuiTai's feet. What else had they done other than talk politics?

"What do you expect me to do?" Kyam asked.

"What you're already doing. Find the real murderer and free Lady QuiTai." Voorus checked his watch. "Tick, tick, Governor. We'll leave so you can start your investigation. Call on me if you need any help." He rose and offered to help Mityam from his chair.

"Was the militia at the scene already? Do we know exactly when Turyat died? After all, there was at least half an hour between when I last saw QuiTai at the wharf and when she came here."

"She was in my company the entire time, from the ride on the funicular down to the harbor to the moment I escorted her into this building for her meeting with you. I would swear to it in court if there were such a thing as a trial in Levapur."

"No trial?" Mityam bellowed. "I don't care if this is Levapur. It's a royal colony, and the law of the land must be followed. Everyone is entitled to a fair trial."

"Yes, well, welcome to Levapur, Mister Muul." Kyam's dark humor showed in a sour smile. 'Welcome to Levapur, Mister Zul,' had been QuiTai's' first words to him, before she'd stepped over him in the middle of the street where he'd lain, bleeding, from the assault she'd arranged.

"Thampurians only pay fines. Ponongese are hanged. There hasn't been a trial in Levapur in… since I was sent here," Voorus said.

"This is wrong, sir, wrong!" Mityam banged his walking stick against the floor to emphasize each word. "I will make reports. I shall write letters!"

"Maybe it won't come to that. The Governor is going to find Turyat's real killer and free Lady QuiTai. Isn't he?" Voorus stared hopefully at Kyam. "He found the– Oops! Can't talk about that, but he solved the Harbor Master's murder almost a year ago. He was an agent with His Majesty's Intelligence. He can figure it out. Can't you, Kyam?"

"I'm not sure how to solve a murder. If the militia destroyed the crime scene, I'm not sure I can read what's left," Kyam blurted out. It felt good to admit that. The Thampurian way was to hide all weakness, but he was out of his depth. Maybe Thampur's finest legal mind could offer some valuable insight.

Mityam's hand trembled on the head of his cane. "Or you could ask QuiTai. She's a clever girl. From what I hear, it was her brothel where the body was found. Surely she would have some idea."

Kyam gulped as Mityam's piercing gaze shone from behind his heavy, wrinkled eyelids. For a moment, it felt as if his grandfather were in the room. He wouldn't shiver, but it was hard not to.

A suspect thought infiltrated his brain. What if QuiTai knew about Turyat's murder and set up her arrest to divert attention? That was convoluted even for her. It didn't make sense. But her wanting to be taken to the fortress didn't make any sense either. The further he stepped back from this, the worse the big picture looked.

"Would you believe the prime suspect if they pinned the murder on someone else?" he asked.

"Who said she was the prime suspect? She has a solid alibi. It's circumstantial that her place of business was the scene of the crime," Mityam said.

"If anyone could murder someone while she was somewhere else, especially with a perfect, unshakable alibi, it would be QuiTai."

Kyam grabbed a bottle of aged whiskey from the bar in his office and hooked two glasses with his fingers. He could never get past Chief Justice Cuulon's secretary, so he went out on the veranda and let himself into the chief justice's office through the typhoon shutters.

Cuulon sat on a divan, elbows on his knees, his gaze fixed on something that wasn't in this world. "Go to hell, Zul." He sounded exhausted.

Kyam set the glasses on Cuulon's desk and filled them with whiskey. He put Cuulon's drink on a low table by the settee. It was rude enough that he'd come in uninvited; taking a seat would have been beyond the pale. He leaned against a bookcase. He started to say something, but then realized he should have thought this through before he left his office.

When offering sympathies for any misfortune, but

especially death, the less said the better, his mother had told him many times. If you're truly sorry for their loss, visit them the week after the funeral, and at least once a month after that. That's real manners. If you aren't sorry, keep your visit short and don't be a hypocrite. Unless, of course, they matter socially. Then you had better make a good show of it.

"I came to offer my condolences." That was honest.

It made him uncomfortable to see that the man he hated had real feelings.

Cuulon's gaze finally made the long climb up to meet Kyam's. "He'd be alive now if it weren't for you."

Why did he even try to be nice? He always regretted it. "I didn't kill Turyat."

"No, you idiot! He wouldn't have become an addict if you hadn't ruined his life." Cuulon looked as if he might say more, but changed his mind and gulped the drink Kyam had poured for him.

Kyam winced. That whiskey was almost as ancient as Grandfather. "I'd appreciate hearing any theories you might have as to why Turyat was murdered."

Cuulon's ears turned pink. He tipped the glass to his lips again and licked the drops away. "Who needs theories? The Devil's whore killed him."

"Do you have proof?"

"I don't need proof. If I say she's guilty, then she's guilty."

Kyam pointed to the law books lining the shelves. "Is that what those say?"

Cuulon's wagging finger reminded Kyam of his least favorite uncle. "You've been talking to that old fool Captain Voorus dragged up from the harbor."

"Mityam Muul happens to be the finest legal mind of our age. I suspect he knows a thing or two about the law."

"But you don't, so leave the legal questions to me." Cuulon gave Kyam a nasty look. "Unless Theram Zul wants you to be the chief justice too. Tell me, are any Zuls allowed to think for themselves, or are you all puppets for him?" Cuulon raised his hands and jerked them in a pantomime of a marionette.

It was true, they were puppets. His cousin Hadre fought it as much as he could, but even he eventually did what Grandfather wanted too.

"Do you believe beyond all doubt that she killed Turyat, or do you want to execute her for another reason? Come on. You can tell me. Your answer won't leave this room. I'm just curious."

Cuulon rolled his empty glass between his palms. "I have no idea if she's guilty of his death, but she still deserves to die."

Why was this man so determined to see QuiTai dead?

Kyam went to Cuulon's bar. He carried a decanter of honeyed whiskey to Cuulon. Cuulon nodded and lifted his glass. Kyam poured a generous serving and returned the crystal decanter to the bar.

"Be that as it may, executing Lady QuiTai won't fix your problem," Kyam said.

"What problem?" Cuulon asked.

"Your friend is dead."

"Damn it, Zul! I know that!"

"His real murderer will still be out there after you hang Lady QuiTai, and he will never pay for killing your friend. That, as I see it, is a problem – the kind of problem that will make food taste like dust in your mouth and whiskey like marsh water, the kind of problem that eats at your soul."

Cuulon covered his face. Sobs shook his shoulders. When he took his hand away, his face writhed with anger.

Unexpected pangs of guilt and sympathy pricked Kyam's conscious. When your enemy was vulnerable, did you take advantage, or do the compassionate thing and give them space to grieve?

Of course you took advantage.

Kyam was surprised how disgusted he was with himself. He'd been much harsher with QuiTai after Jezereet died than he was with Cuulon now. Turyat had only been Cuulon's friend; Jezereet had been QuiTai's spouse. At the time, he hadn't felt guilty about how he'd treated QuiTai because he'd felt it was necessary. But afterward? Afterward, guilt had crept into his bed in the middle of the night and propped open his eyes. It made it impossible to look in the mirror some mornings. He didn't look forward to losing sleep over Cuulon too.

"A witness saw you on the veranda of the Red Happiness early this morning, with Turyat. He was alive then. Why were you there?" Kyam asked.

"Those snakes will say anything against their betters."

"The witness is Thampurian." There was no reason to admit he was the witness. It would sound as if he'd been lurking outside the Red Happiness when nothing could be further from the truth.

Cuulon shook his head. "There weren't any Thampur—" He slowly smiled and steepled his fingers together. "All right. I was there. Am I to take it that you're investigating Governor Turyat's death? Are you playing policeman?"

That was a punch to the gut Kyam should have seen coming. Police in Thampur were recruited from the lower castes on the theory that brutes knew how other brutes thought. Calling Kyam a policeman was a deliberate insult. But Cuulon had been in charge of a police force back in Thampur, so the meaning might equally be 'Now you're no better than I am.' Cuulon was no salon wit, but even he could turn an insult into a stiletto through the ribs from time to time. Kyam wouldn't rise to the bait, though, no matter how much he wanted to beat Cuulon's head with his shoe, because his freedom depended now upon solving Turyat's murder.

With exaggerated patience, Kyam said. "I want to make sure the right person is hanged for it. Isn't that what you want too? As chief justice, I'm sure the concept of fairness interests you."

Sly wariness settled around Cuulon's eyes. "Maybe you had Turyat killed. Maybe stealing his office wasn't enough. Your Grandfather was like that when he ruled here. Absolutely ruthless. Once he had your scent, he'd hunt you down to ground even if you weren't a threat any more, like one of those werewolf barbarians."

Kyam forced his anger into the coldest portion of his heart.

He set down his drink carefully, so the glass made only a muted *thunk* against the wood. QuiTai had taught him how effective quiet could be when it was used in anger. He kept his voice calm, low, and chilly. "Ah, now you see, that was a mistake. First you call me dirt for wanting to find the real murderer of your friend. Now you try to insult my clan by bringing up the werewolves. Are you sure you want to remind me of your involvement with the werewolves?"

Panic flashed across Cuulon's face.

"We know you paid Petrof to kill Lady QuiTai and her family," Kyam said.

Cuulon gave him a haughty look. "When you eradicate vermin, you set dogs to it."

"So you're finishing the job by executing the last Qui?" Kyam leaned down close to the older man's face. "She knows you're the one who paid Petrof to devour her daughter. Do you think she'd let a little thing like death come between her and revenge? She won't come back as a shy little maishun spirit, either. Instead, she'll probably hunt you down like an anmau. I hear they eat your liver every night. It grows back during the day. Sounds painful."

Cuulon trembled. "You don't understand anything. We didn't have a choice." His voice sounded as if it had been dragged over a gravel road.

Something about the past had left a bitter taste in Cuulon's mouth, but Kyam didn't believe it was the unjustified murders of the Qui clan.

Cuulon rose with a heavy sigh and went to his desk.

"The witness said Turyat quarreled with her. Do you know anything about that?" Kyam asked.

"Let me tell you a little something about that bitch you're trying so hard to save. You know she controls the black lotus trade in Levapur now?"

Kyam nodded. "Since the werewolves were executed."

"She let Turyat binge on vapor for a month. Then she cut him off for a week. Nearly drove him mad. Then she let him have as much as he wanted for three weeks, then cut him off again." Cuulon's face reddened alarmingly. "She toyed with him, and she enjoyed every second of it." Spittle foamed in the corners of his lips.

Kyam didn't doubt it was true. That sounded like something QuiTai would do. Technically, it was within the bounds of her promise, but it was also far crueler than killing Turyat.

"I couldn't buy black lotus anywhere on this island because I might have given it to him. She cut off Lizzriat at the Dragon Pearl for a month for allowing Turyat a single pity pipe. After that, no one would dare challenge her decree. The itching got so bad yesterday he flayed his own skin. I had to cover his forearms in balm and wrap them in gauze. You know how easily scratches get infected on this cursed island."

Kyam nodded.

"Last night, he went to grovel to that bitch for a pipe."

Kyam could imagine QuiTai enjoying Turyat's debasement. That curve of her mouth. The sinister sideways glance of her eyes. Her standing rigid and regal while she watched her enemy suffer at her feet.

"Madam Inattra said he couldn't allow Turyat a pipe without QuiTai's permission, and that she wasn't expected back for a while. The hint was that we should go away, but Inattra knows how to walk that fine line between his customers and his employer, so he didn't have us thrown out. While we drank out on the veranda, one of the whores whispered that she'd bring us a pipe, but Madam Inattra saw her and started to head our way, so she had to slither away. You know how dreamers are — Turyat thought if he waited long enough, the snake would come back with some. There was no way to convince him it was a lost cause. At some point I fell asleep. When I woke the next morning, Turyat was gone."

"Did you look for him inside the Red Happiness?" Kyam asked.

"It wasn't open yet."

"What time did you wake?"

"When did your witness say I woke?"

Kyam spread his hands.

Sighing, Cuulon picked up a file from his desktop and opened it. He peered at the papers, but Kyam doubted he read a word. Without looking up, he asked, "Am I a suspect?"

"You're a witness."

"You are investigating his death. Admit it." Cuulon leaned back in his seat and folded his hands in his lap with the air of a man who'd laid winning tiles on the table.

Everything Cuulon said made sense. Kyam prayed to the Goddess of Mercy that he never ran afoul of QuiTai.

"Why would Lady QuiTai kill Turyat when she could torture him instead? Wouldn't that ruin all her fun?" Kyam asked.

"Does it matter? She's guilty of many things. Why worry if we execute her for the wrong reason? Come on, Zul, you know I'm right."

"We have a town full of Ponongese who would care very much if we hung her without just cause. I don't like the mood in this town, Cuulon."

"That's why we agreed the assembly rule was needed. If the snakes start gathering to cause problems, we'll hang them by the dozens until they get the message."

Kyam felt sick. That wasn't what he'd envisioned when he'd agreed to that rule, not that his opinion mattered. Cuulon was the one who made up the laws in Levapur.

"We still have to tread carefully here. Don't do anything without talking to me first. Don't torture her, and definitely don't hang her until I've had a chance to build a case against her."

"Against her? For a moment here, I thought you were trying to exonerate her."

"Just playing devil's advocate."

CHAPTER 7: KYAM INVESTIGATES

Kyam shielded his face as he ducked into the small Thampurian neighborhood on the southern slope of the Quarter of Delights that was known as the Quarter of the Unclean. He made sure no one important was nearby, and then hurried down the narrow street lined with butcher shops, tanneries, mortuaries, and tenements. Ocean breezes hadn't purged the air here as they did the rest of the town, and the sharp stink made his eyes sting. No wonder the rest of the Thampurians made this caste live off by themselves. His hand moved from the side of his face to his nose.

He stopped at a white building with sky blue shutters and checked the name on the simple plaque by the door. No one came when he knocked, so he stepped inside. Although it was midday, the dim light from the shrouded jellylanterns made it seem like twilight. The transition made him feel as if he'd suddenly lost time he could never make up.

The room smelled strongly of wood oil, a welcome change from the tannery down the road. Stairs before him led into stifling darkness. On both sides of the foyer, he caught glimpses of richly appointed parlors through sliding screens.

Muffled footsteps shuffling over polished wood enforced a sense of silence weighing down the air inside. He turned toward the sound and waited with growing impatience.

A thin, elderly Thampurian dressed in white bowed deeply before stepping into the foyer. His expression conveyed condolences. If this man had been in any other profession, Kyam would have returned the bow, or offered his hand, but it simply wasn't done.

"I understand you serve as the coroner for the government," Kyam said.

The man bowed again. "I have been honored with that trust." His grating accent proved he'd been born in Surrayya, but in a neighborhood above the canals. He'd moved as far as he could from Thampur, but he'd never escape his caste.

Kyam's mouth was dry. Too late, he realized how odd his questions were going to sound, even to a man who prepared bodies for cremation. Once it was known he'd come here to look at the body, the stain on his family name would be nearly impossible to remove. Even this man would think less of him. It had to be done though. With the scene of the crime hopelessly contaminated by those idiot soldiers, the body was the best evidence he had.

"I understand Governor Turyat's body was brought here," Kyam said.

"Yes."

Even though they were alone, Kyam didn't trust the foyer. Anyone could be in the shadows of the upstairs landing. "Is there somewhere private we can talk?"

The man gestured to one of the parlors.

Kyam walked in and sat on a dark red settee. His spine ached from the stiff posture. His hands rested on his thighs inches from his knees, as was proper. The man did not sit, and this too was right.

He pulled on his collar. "If I may ask, in your professional opinion, how did Governor Turyat die?"

QuiTai had once observed that respect was in such short supply in Thampurian culture that the smallest drop of it spent further than coin. From the change that came over the man, that was true. Of course it was; QuiTai understood people better than anyone he'd ever met. A member of the thirteen families asking for such a man's opinion was unheard-of flattery.

"As a professional." The mortician smiled into his fist then coughed to hide it. "I do not wish to bring up unpleasant topics."

"And I do not wish to make you uncomfortable."

"You honor me, Governor Zul."

Kyam realized he was in for a very long conversation. While QuiTai's directness often struck him as rude, he missed it at times like these. As he went through the motions and said the proper words, his patience thinned. They slowly circled on the topic of Turyat's manner of death, but ricocheted off into safer topics each time they got close. QuiTai would have made it a tantalizing dance of wits. This man didn't.

The man glanced a third time at Kyam's leg. It bounced as he tapped his foot. Kyam willed it to stop.

"If I might see the body," Kyam said.

"See?"

Kyam was certain he'd spoken Thampurian, so the lack of understanding wasn't his fault. "Yes. See. Before you cremate him."

Flustered, the man shot a glance at the parlor door. "It is my professional opinion that the governor died from blood loss. His right temple was wounded, and that might have killed him, but from the amount of blood surrounding the body, I estimate that he was alive for a few minutes after sustaining the wound, although he was probably unconscious. Praise be the Goddess of Mercy that he did not suffer."

"Praise be." Kyam echoed the words without thought or feeling. "Were there any puncture marks on the body?"

The man seemed surprised. "I didn't look for them."

"Why not? Surely you heard a Ponongese was accused of the murder."

"If a snake bit him, she didn't share enough of her venom

to kill him. I assumed she had been caught delivering the blow to his head."

Kyam didn't know why he felt like defending QuiTai. "Truthfully, she wasn't even in the building at the time of the murder."

"Ah. That makes it much more difficult to kill a man."

Was that a slight twinkle in the mortician's eye?

"Do you see many deaths by Ponongese venom?"

The man shrugged. "A few cases since I moved here forty-six years ago. Much more common before Governor Turyat took the office. Since then, only one that I can remember."

"How did you know Turyat didn't die from venom if you rarely see cases?"

This time, the man chuckled. "When I came to Levapur, it wasn't like this." He gestured around the room as if it encompassed the whole town. "There were very few Thampurians. We lived with them, the snakes. It was primitive." He wrinkled his nose. "I learned to tell a boar brought down by a Ponongese hunter from one our men killed."

"Is it safe to eat that meat?"

"We survived. So do they. They aren't immune to their own venom, did you know? We cooked the meat well, of course, and the Ponongese swear you must cook it with a root and spice preparation that nullifies the venom. I don't know if that's true, but who would be the first man to risk eating meat not cooked that way? We got used to it, but I never liked it."

Kyam had never heard any of that. Meat in the marketplace all came from Thampurian butchers because the Ponongese were only allowed to sell fish, but he'd never known why. He'd assumed it was simply to protect Thampurian butchers from competition with the Ponongese.

"How could you tell if the boar came from a Ponongese hunter? Is there some obvious sign that a Ponongese killed the animal?"

"Death comes from slow suffocation as the paralysis takes the use of their lungs from them. They feel it, you know, the Ponongese. There's a psychic connection in their venom that makes them suffer along with their prey. The connection stops the moment the prey dies. That's why the snakes kill their prey as quickly and painlessly as possible."

"But the body, how could you tell Turyat – Governor Turyat – hadn't been dosed with venom to render him incapable of fighting back when he was struck?"

The mortician blinked. "My profuse apologizes if you thought I was not clear, Governor. No snake would allow a victim to die as slowly as the late Governor Turyat appeared to, as they would suffer through his death and maybe even slip into unconsciousness themselves along with him. They suffer when they kill prey, suffer the pain of death, so they are careful to do it in such a way that it does not kill them too. Can you imagine if every time you ate meat that you had to pay such a price? We Thampurians would all be vegetarians. Such is the curse of a more refined nature."

Kyam knew all of this, but had never connected the information like that. If the rumor were true, no wonder QuiTai had taken refuge in black lotus when the werewolves she'd paralyzed were torn to pieces by that mob. It was a wonder that she wasn't insane. Although, if he were honest, there were times when he thought she might be a little mad.

"Interesting," he said.

"In addition, Governor Turyat's fingernails and lips didn't show classic signs of suffocation. And his tongue wasn't swollen or discolored."

"Ah." That was much better. It sounded like real evidence rather than an opinion.

"Believe me, we look for such signs, under orders from Chief Justice Cuulon, even though, as I mentioned, I've rarely seen it. The Ponongese aren't especially violent people, unlike the Li Islanders, who are dirt." The mortician spat on the polished floor.

LiHoun was the only Li Islander Kyam knew. He wouldn't call LiHoun dirt. And he'd never seen the man act violently. Sneaky was a better description. But maybe LiHoun was as different from his people as QuiTai was from hers.

The mortician folded his hands. He had the look of a man taking out his memories and cherishing each one. "It's funny, odd, that Cuulon made it illegal for the snakes to show us their fangs. Way back, he used to beg their women to show their fangs to him. We all did. There were no Thampurian women for years. And we were curious about the rumors..."

Of course they had been curious. The first rumor Thampurian men heard about the Ponongese, even before anyone mentioned their reptilian eyes, concerned their venom. That time QuiTai had slid the tip of her tongue down her fangs, he'd almost grabbed her and pulled her into the jungle. In his most erotic dreams of her, he returned to that moment. Had she been threatening him or seducing him? Probably a bit of both. She liked layers of meaning in her words, why not her actions?

"We've all heard that rumor." Sometimes Kyam wondered if he were the only Thampurian in Levapur who hadn't tried a drop of venom with his sexual encounters. Maybe it was one of those rumors everyone believed but no one dared follow up on. Most of the Ponongese hanged for showing their fangs were men, after all, not women.

A flash of insight made him wince. Were his people really so intimidated by Ponongese men that they'd treat the mere flash of fangs as a sexual assault? They would. He knew they would, because he knew what Thampurians thought of the shiftless races. *Animals* was the kindest word they used.

Kyam missed the days when he had never thought about such things. Ignorance was a kind of bliss, which probably explained why QuiTai lived in a permanent state of rage. She knew too much.

The mortician leered. "You've heard about the psychic connection the snakes feel with their prey? It works with a lover, too. As long as you don't get a lethal dose, the woman, she knows exactly what pleases you. You don't have to say a word. And she feels pleasure by serving you."

Kyam's ingrained snobbery made him recoil from the lower caste man. He hated himself for the creeping sense of disgust inching up his spine.

The mortician's wife shuffled into the parlor, and the conversation slipped back into the expected propriety. Time ticked away with each practiced phrase. Tea was offered. To his surprise, they inquired after Nashruu. Gossip flew on strong wings in Levapur. He forced his attention back to the conversation. His knee bounced again. "Pardon me, but could you tell if Turyat was in dream when he died? If he had been, he might have fallen and hurt himself. It might not be a murder after all."

The wife gasped. She covered her mouth, but not before he saw her lips purse.

"I have no way of telling, but he had a pipe in his hand when he was brought in."

It was hard to tell if she were more aghast at Kyam or her husband. As a *thiree* and Governor, Kyam had more face to lose, but money could buy a lot of forgiveness. As low as their caste was, there was still a level or two to sink. She stared daggers at her husband.

"A pipe?" Kyam asked.

"Would you like to see it?" he asked.

Her hand shot out to smack his thigh almost faster than Kyam could see it, but he heard it.

Kyam nodded. He doubted it would tell him the most important part: someone had offered Turyat black lotus, and he was pretty sure it hadn't been QuiTai.

CHAPTER 8: AT THE DRAGON PEARL

Kyam rushed uphill from the mortuary and through the dodgy neighborhood. He slowed when he reached the peak of the hill near the Dragon Pearl to catch his breath. The Quarter of Delights spread out below him. The streets were busier than before, but the crowds wouldn't come until after it cooled down later in the evening. Then laughter and light would spill out of these buildings into the streets. The verandas would be crowded. No one would be mourning Turyat.

He stepped over a flowing sewer in the middle of the road. One of these days, he'd have to do something about the streets in Levapur. It seemed like the sort of thing a governor should do. The streets around the Red Happiness had real sewers, but that was the only place in Levapur that did. QuiTai had probably paid for the project herself. She wanted her customers to be able to enjoy the veranda without having to see or smell a river of excrement as it flowed past.

Kyam shoved his hands into his pockets and strolled to the Red Happiness. Maybe the scene of the crime wasn't as disrupted as he feared. He should at least give it a look. He wished some Ponongese were around to see him investigating the murder. It was important that they knew what he was doing. Dear Goddess of Mercy, he had no respect for himself anymore. He'd become a politician.

He reached for the typhoon shutter but pulled his hand away. He'd never been inside when the brothel was closed. He felt as if he were trespassing; but honestly, who would dare stop the colony's Governor from going wherever he pleased? He yanked open the shutter.

Inside, it looked as if there had been a brawl. Broken tables and chairs were stacked at the far end of the room. White stuffing had escaped from the cushions of several settees, and empty bottles covered the bar. Long splinters hung around the lock on QuiTai's office door.

Water pooled in the center of freshly mopped floorboards. The ceiling fans rotated slowly. Under the strong scent of whiskey and rum, he smelled blood and the resinous stink of black lotus. A large fly buzzed close to his face. As he swatted it away, it bit his hand.

"We're closed."

Even though the room was brightly lit, he had to search for the source of the voice. The brothel's Ingosolian Madam, Inattra, sat on the staircase. Only his curly strawberry-blond hair was visible over the banister.

Kyam walked up the stairs to the first landing and leaned against a post. "Turyat put up quite a fight."

Inattra sat with his knees spread and shoulders bowed. Despite the turmoil, he was dressed in a stylish brown suit that complemented his bluish skin. Lace flowed from his cuffs and down his shirt front.

"Your militia did that."

"All of that?"

With a great sigh, Inattra gripped the railing and pulled himself to his feet. He towered over Kyam until he stepped down to the same riser. "When have you ever known a vapor ghoul to struggle against a pipe?"

Inattra indicated the mess with a sweeping gesture as he walked down the stairs. "Your militia also broke the locks on the liquor cabinets and drank our stock. What they couldn't drink, they stuck in their pockets. What they couldn't put in their pockets, they broke open and poured onto the floor. I'd send the colonial government a bill, but from what I've heard, Turyat plundered the treasury so thoroughly that you can't even remit the rice tax to Thampur."

Bad news traveled fast; even faster when it moved through QuiTai's network. "Send the bill. We'll take it out of their pay," Kyam said.

Inattra picked up an empty bottle from the bar and put it into a large basket on the floor. "That would be a first, but I'll pretend you're serious."

"I am. So you gave Turyat some black lotus? I understood that QuiTai cut him off."

"Give that ghoul a pipe? Never. I'd lose my job, and I like working here." He set more bottles into the basket. He looked as if he hadn't slept in weeks.

"Then who did?"

"An idiot."

"Only if someone actually gave him some. Is it possible that someone took his coins and ran off with them?"

A short bark of laughter filled the bar. "Once a ghoul latches onto the idea of a pipe, it's all their decaying minds can focus on. Can you imagine the fuss Turyat would have raised if the black lotus never came? His friend Cuulon would execute anyone who tried to pull that trick."

"So you think he actually got his pipe?"

After thinking for a bit, Inattra slowly shook his head. "I'm not sure. There was a lit spirit lamp sitting on this bar. He was clutching a pipe, but I never saw a vial. Maybe it fell on the floor. Who knows? The militia made such a mess. It wasn't like this before they came, you know."

"Who found the body?" Kyam asked.

"Me. To be truthful, I'm not so sure he was dead yet when I came downstairs. The blood was still—" Inattra gulped. "Spreading. Slowly. As if it were leaking out of his head." Inattra drew a long breath in through his nose.

"What time was that?"

"It was horrible."

Kyam tried to look sympathetic while a hundred questions begged to be asked. "I'm sure it was."

"Yeah, well, thank you for making me relive it."

"Sorry. I'm…" He didn't know why, but he lowered his voice. "Trying to clear QuiTai's name."

"Sure you are. You arrested her."

Kyam leaned on the bar and hoped sincerity would be enough to convince him. "Not for Turyat's murder. And it was her idea, not mine. Don't ask me why. And I truly want to get her out of the fortress, so please help me figure out what happened here, so I can do that."

Inattra paused with a bottle in each hand. "You better hurry, because they'll hang her before the sun sets."

He didn't need anyone to remind him that he had to work fast. "That's why I need your help. Anything you can tell me about what you saw. Anything. Did you notice anything unusual?"

"Other than a body on the floor, no. And the lit spirit oil lamp. That's a fire hazard. QuiTai would fang me if she saw an open flame, especially right above the liquor. Half the Quarter of Delights burned down about six years ago when a dreamer knocked over a lamp in a black lotus den. QuiTai said the stink of cooked flesh hung over the quarter for days. Says the memory still makes her sick to her stomach. She's fired workers for leaving lamps lit in their rooms. Everyone knows that."

If QuiTai was that worried about fires, there was no way she would have left a lit lamp on her bar. He could see another killer panicking and forgetting to douse the flame, but not QuiTai.

Inattra suddenly gripped his wrist hard. Kyam saw his panic. "I was joking about her fanging me. She'd never do that.

Please don't tell anyone I said that."

"I wouldn't tell a soul. I'm trying to save her, remember? What time was it when you found the body?"

"Thank you. Thank you, Governor." Inattra pushed a red curl out of his eyes and tucked it behind his ear. "I, uh, came down a bit after ten, I think. Much earlier than usual. I'm... This doesn't seem real. I've only seen dead bodies at funerals, and then they're clean and pretty and there's no blood, you know? And you expect to see a corpse then. This morning, I wasn't prepared... It..." He pressed his hand to his mouth.

Around ten, QuiTai and Voorus were leading Mityam Muul across the wharf while the funicular began its ascent to Levapur. It would have been twenty minutes at least before she could have caught the next one. An hour later, she'd been in his office. That didn't give her much time. She could have murdered Turyat before she went to the harbor, though.

He pushed that thought aside while he tried to think of his next question. Large flies slammed into the typhoon shutters, a sound that made him flinch. A swarm of them had whirled through the air outside the mortuary. They always showed up in the marketplace within minutes of the butcher opening his stall. The vicious things bit hard.

"Where there flies yet? Were a bunch of them buzzing through this room when you found the body?" Kyam asked.

Inattra turned to look at the shutters. He moved in slow motion as if still in shock. Guilt pricked Kyam's conscience, but he tried to ignore it.

"Not that I noticed. There were a bunch flying around by the time they took away the body, though. Now they're almost all gone again."

"Did you see Lady QuiTai this morning? Cuulon? Anyone else, even if they belong here?"

Inattra shook his head to each.

"Did anyone else report hearing or seeing anything unusual?"

Inattra mouthed *No* as he shook his head again.

Kyam looked around the destroyed barroom. "Where are

the other workers?"

"Upstairs, with a priestess, singing Turyat's soul into the arms of the Goddess."

That surprised him. "That's kind of them."

Inattra looked at him as if he were stupid. "Would you want a vengeful ghost to materialize when you were with a customer? It's good business to make sure his spirit is ushered out of this building before it even realizes the body is gone."

Kyam tried hard not to show what he thought of that. Ingosolians were avid innovators of technology; yet they were also serious devotees of spiritualism. He saw those as diametrically opposed viewpoints. Ingosolians, apparently, did not.

He realized there was no need to be so superior about it. To be fair, most Thampurians also believed in all manner of demons and wrathful spirits.

Kyam was almost out of questions. "Did you hear anything unusual this morning?"

After a brief frown, followed by a moment of intense thought, Inattra finally spoke. "It's not unusual, but someone was moving out in the hallway. Or, at least, I think I heard someone. The outhouse is behind the building, so workers have to go downstairs to use it. But my room is almost at the end of the hallway. Why would anyone go past my door to get downstairs?"

Kyam jumped as Inattra slapped his palm on the bar. The transformation from bewildered to furious was instantaneous. Inattra shifted more male with each outraged flare of his nostrils. The spray of blue freckles across his cheeks darkened.

"That little bitch! PhaSun has the room across the hallway from mine. She knew the body was there. She had to!" Inattra jabbed a finger at Kyam. "She's been trying to get me fired ever since QuiTai named me Madam. And to think I sent her away to protect her from the militia!"

"PhaSun?" He vaguely remembered a pretty enough young woman who seemed to live in a perpetual party, laughing and talking with far more exuberance than anyone else in the bar.

She was one of the few Ponongese sex workers who lived in the Red Happiness. Most of the others lived with their families. He wondered why PhaSun didn't.

"She's probably hiding with her clan by now, in Old Levapur," Inattra said.

That was a problem Kyam didn't need right now. "The hillside slums. I'll never find her up there if she doesn't want to be found. And you know a Thampurian isn't safe there. Is there any way you could find her and bring her to me?"

Inattra raised his hands. "I'm staying out of this."

"I have only a few hours to come up with a better suspect in Turyat's murder. I can't waste that time poking my head into hovels and shouting PhaSun's name."

"And I can? I'm running a business here, Governor, one your militia almost destroyed this morning. Now I have to fix it and open our doors tonight, so I'm a little busy."

"Not even for QuiTai?"

"How long have you been on this island? Even I know the Pha hate the Devil for interfering in Old Levapur's clan business. By extension, they hate QuiTai, because for all intents and purposes, she is the Devil, isn't she?"

Kyam nodded.

"The Pha won't help me find PhaSun if they think I'm trying to help QuiTai." Inattra put his fist on his hip. "Not that PhaSun would be able to tell you much more than I can, and I guarantee you most of what she'll tell you is a lie. She's a troublemaker. Do you know that seconds after I found the body, she came running downstairs, went right into the street, and started screaming murder? Can you believe that? I had to drag her back inside and shove her into–" Inattra seemed to think better of finishing that comment. "Anyway, I made sure the militia didn't arrest her as 'the convenient Ponongese.' If I'd known they'd pick QuiTai instead, I would have let them have PhaSun. You have no idea the stupid little stunts she pulls to try to turn QuiTai against me."

Inattra was trying awfully hard to convince him PhaSun couldn't be trusted. He wondered what the woman knew. There were so many secrets here, and he didn't know which ones would help him solve the murder.

"You shoved PhaSun where? Are you holding her prisoner somewhere inside here? Tell the truth, Inattra."

His lips pursed as he folded his arms across his chest. He looked up at the ceiling for a while. "Okay, but this goes no further than us. There's a secret door in my room that leads down to the alleyway behind the café next door. I dragged her, screaming and flailing, upstairs and shoved her behind the hidden panel. She wanted to run into her room and pack some things. I could hear the militia downstairs and had to warn the rest of the workers that we were about to be invaded, so I slammed the door in her face. There's no way to open it from the inside. For all I know, she's standing there fuming still. But I didn't lock her in. There's an exit at the bottom of the stairs."

Kyam already knew about that passage, but he didn't want to tell Inattra that. "I believe you, about the secret passage. And about PhaSun."

Inattra relaxed a bit.

"I may have more questions later." Kyam nodded crisply and turned to leave.

"I'll be here. Cleaning up this mess." Inattra sighed as he set a chair back on its legs. "If you see LiHoun, tell him I want to see his wrinkled face right now more than I've ever wanted anything."

Kyam walked out of the Red Happiness more discouraged than he had been going in. He'd taken QuiTai to the fortress too soon. He should have asked her more questions.

He wished he could talk with her right now. What would she have seen in the Red Happiness that he didn't? The militia had destroyed any evidence he might have found there when they looted the crime scene. All he had was the victim's body.

Despite his wife's protests, the mortician had spoken about

the body in detail. He'd guessed that the weapon that had fractured Turyat's skull was probably a bottle. Given that the murder happened in a brothel bar, that wasn't much of a stretch of the imagination. But he'd also ventured a guess that the blow had come from someone shorter than Turyat. The former Governor wasn't tall for a Thampurian, but he was a head taller than most Ponongese men. QuiTai was short.

But why would QuiTai kill him? If Cuulon was telling the truth – and Inattra seemed to agree with his story – she'd enjoyed torturing the former Governor. Killing him would have ended her revenge.

As unsettling as it was, he'd always known she was cruel. It jarred him, but he had to admit she had every right to revenge after the way Turyat made her suffer. If he'd lost his entire family...

If he lost his family, it wouldn't change his life that much. The moment Nashruu disembarked from the *Golden Barracuda* this morning, he'd realized he had nothing to say to her. He didn't even know her. They'd gone through the public rites of courtship without ever really talking. The night of their wedding, he'd gone on a mission for Intelligence that required months of undercover work. They hadn't lived together or even seen each other since that day. He sent her boy Khyram gifts from time to time. That was the extent of their relationship. Losing family might not change his life, but leaving this island would.

He took the stairs down to the street as he mulled over the thought that bothered him. He kept assuming QuiTai was guilty. She had motive. But did she have opportunity? It seemed impossible, but he was used to her doing seemingly impossible things.

This wasn't helping. It would be far simpler to find out who was guilty than to prove her innocent. So who were the other suspects?

Grandfather, the Devil, the mysterious enemies who'd killed QuiTai's lieutenants... if he focused on who might want to frame QuiTai for Turyat's death, the list of suspects was endless. If he focused on the victim, there was Turyat's wife – now she had motive. She'd been dragged to Levapur with her exiled husband. For many years, they'd looted the treasury, but once Turyat lost his office, they'd been cut off. Then Turyat had become a vapor ghoul. Now that he was dead, his widow could return to Thampur. She probably had plenty of money and jewels stashed away to make a comfortable life for herself. That sounded like a good motive.

He stood in the middle of the crossroads and squinted against the sun. A man with a jungle fowl tucked under his arm walked past him. He turned to look the other direction. Heat thermals rose from the dirt road in waves. Everyone had gone indoors to nap through the hottest part of the day.

Where should he go next? Probably to question Turyat's widow. He didn't want to upset her, but it needed to be done. As he looked upslope, he saw the Dragon Pearl. Turyat had taken his pipes in the private rooms of the black lotus den on the second floor, as did many wealthy Thampurians in Levapur. Maybe the Ingosolian owner, Lizzriat, would tell him something.

"Forgive me for interrupting, Governor Zul, but you seem a man in search of something. Perhaps I can help?" LiHoun asked as he stepped out of the alleyway. He'd shrunk since Kyam had last seen him, and his whiskey-colored skin seemed coated in pallor.

"Madam Inattra asked me to send you along if we met."

The Ponongese woman beside LiHoun was trying to seem inconspicuous, but some people were too vivacious to hide in plain sight.

"I know you," Kyam said as he stared at her. From where? Her bright orange sarong was a common enough color, but the designs on it were unusual.

"We used to be neighbors," she said.

How could he have forgotten? Of course – those botanical designs on her sarong were made by someone from Cay Rhi. "You're RhiLan's cousin! That's where I know you. RhiHalla?"

"RhiHanya," she corrected.

She struck him as nervous, which seemed out of character

for her. He squinted at her as he tried to figure out what was off. "But I've seen you much more recently. In the marketplace. You bumped into me."

"It was a narrow aisle, Governor."

He realized she might be offended. "Forgive me, I'm sure it was I who bumped into you. And then I didn't apologize. How very rude of me."

A slow smile spread over her face as she relaxed. "Word has it that you're looking for Turyat's murderer. How are you coming with that, Governor Zul?"

"Too direct for Thampurian tastes," LiHoun muttered to her.

"You do it your way, uncle, I'll do it mine." She turned back to Kyam. "Well? Do you know who killed that Thampurian? Lady QuiTai is in danger every moment she sits in that fortress."

It was as if she suspected he didn't know how to investigate a murder. "I've just started looking into it." Should he admit he was already stumped? "I don't suppose either one of you was here this morning?"

"No."

Their answers came a bit too quickly.

"Did you see Lady QuiTai earlier today?"

They exchanged a glance that made him wary.

"Tell me," he said.

"We might have run into her upslope in the Quarter of Delights early this morning," RhiHanya said.

"Might have?"

"We chatted for a while. Then she headed down while we, uh, went on our way."

LiHoun nodded as she talked.

"Chatted about what?" Kyam asked.

"The murders of her lieutenants."

From the way RhiHanya said it, Kyam thought she was telling the truth about their conversation. She was hiding something else, though.

"When you say you went on your way, where did you go? Did you two stay together?"

LiHoun pointed beyond the Quarter of Delights to the steep mountainside rising above Levapur. "We went upslope, to my apartment, together."

"Can any witnesses verify that?"

"My wives."

Kyam sighed. He didn't speak Li and he doubted LiHoun's wives spoke Thampurian. With only LiHoun to translate, he'd only get the answers LiHoun wanted him to have.

"You seem troubled, Governor." LiHoun's expression was entirely sincere, although Kyam thought he detected a hint of dark humor glinting beneath it. "Is there any way we can help?"

"Only if you can tell me who murdered Governor Turyat."

LiHoun spread his hands. "Alas, my rice bowl has no meat today."

"Would you tell me if you knew?"

He looked hurt.

"QuiTai is in the fortress. Of course we'd tell you," RhiHanya said.

"I suspect there's plenty of meat hidden under your rice that you two don't want me to see. That's fair enough. I'm not after the Devil, and I'm not out to trick you into giving away QuiTai's secrets. All I'm asking for is a list of everyone who was in the Red Happiness this morning. In particular, I want to speak to PhaSun. Inattra has no idea where she went. You know everything that happens in this town, LiHoun, so I figure maybe you know where to find her."

RhiHanya and LiHoun whispered quickly in Li as their eyes flicked over to him and then away. RhiHanya lifted her palm. It was a Ponongese gesture very much like a shrug, but the subtle message behind it escaped him. LiHoun rolled a kur and lit it, as if that were his final say in the matter.

RhiHanya turned back to him. "PhaSun is in Old Levapur. I left a message with the Pha that it was safe for her to return to the Red Happiness, but who knows if she heard it?" Her sour frown made Kyam think that talking to the Pha clan leaders had been an unpleasant job, but she didn't want to complain about it.

"Inattra suspected as much." Kyam knew these two could gather information quicker than he could. He leaned toward them and lowered his voice. "Unfortunately, I can't go into Old Levapur. If I go alone, I'll never be seen again. If I take soldiers, I'll provoke a riot."

"They don't like us either," RhiHanya admitted. "If there's one thing the Pha hate, it's someone from another clan ordering them around. So of course they get stubborn at the worst possible times."

"I wonder if PhaSun would come out of hiding if she thought it would get Inattra into trouble. You know, pass on some sort of hint that I'm going to tell QuiTai rumors I heard when I go back to the fortress later this afternoon..."

LiHoun chuckled when RhiHanya said, "She'd come out of hiding in a heartbeat if she thought she could get convince QuiTai to fire Inattra. She's had it in for Inattra since the moment he became Madam."

Kyam tapped his bottom lip. "If only someone would go back to the Pha and tell them–"

"Hah! Don't for a moment think we work for you, Thampurian," RhiHanya said. "Go talk to them yourself."

A coughing fit shook LiHoun's thin body. "Too direct," he muttered from behind his hand.

"I'm not here to protect delicate Thampurian feelings. He takes what I have for him the way I see fit to give it, or he gets nothing," she said.

"She's in training, Mister Zul," LiHoun apologized to Kyam.

"Don't you go making excuses for me. I'm fine the way I am, brother." She turned back to Kyam. "Well? How many hours do you think you have to waste before your friends hang her? *Shu, shu, shu.* Get moving."

He felt like a jungle fowl caught pecking in the grain basket. Kyam checked his pocket watch. He'd lost too much time already with nothing to show for it.

"You have no idea what you're doing, do you?" RhiHanya asked.

Kyam glowered at her. "I know one thing – *you* can get the Pha to hear what you have to say, even if they pretend to ignore you. I can't. If I so much as set foot in the slums, there's going to be trouble, and I don't need that distraction right now. So you're going back there and you're going to convince them to tell PhaSun whatever she needs to hear to come talk to me. I don't care if it's hard or they're rude to you. Just do it."

As she drew in a sharp breath, LiHoun put his hand on her arm. "Time is wasting, sister. Teach the Thampurian manners on a day with too many hours, not one with too few." The old man gave Kyam an angry look and then tottered toward the Red Happiness on his bandy legs. RhiHanya followed him in a cloud of indignation.

CHAPTER 9: A SOCIAL CALL

The soldier stood in a gently rocking rowboat with one boot in an inch of filthy water and the other braced on one of the seats. He'd put his hand out for Nashruu's, but drew back. "Maybe we should ask..."

Nashruu's smile was her most ingratiating. She had hoped to get by on charm alone until she was forced to use the sterner stuff.

"What do you think?" he asked.

She knew the question was aimed at the man behind her. It was already clear he didn't care what she thought. It was so easy for Grandfather to say, 'Go to the fortress and offer Lady QuiTai our help in exchange for her promise to be my agent' and expect it to be done. But maybe she *could* get it done, after she convinced these two to do as she asked.

Perhaps if she stripped right here on the beach, calmly placed her clothing in her bag, shifted into her sea dragon form, and swam across the harbor to the fortress... No. She would be criticized for overreacting. If she wanted to force them to do what she wanted, she'd have to be ladylike about it. Subtle. Sneaky. She hated that.

"Oh!" With her most helpless squeal, she teetered into the soldier's arms, jammed her satchel into his knees, then squeaked again as he grabbed her around the waist. Her pretty blue sun spectacles dropped near his feet. There was much apologizing and stepping around each other as the soldier retrieved them for her. She plunked down on the tiny seat set into the bow and extended her hand for her glasses.

While she'd never gloat openly, she was rather pleased with herself. Lady QuiTai probably never had to resort to such silly scenes. She got to threaten them or have her thugs beat them. How Nashruu envied that!

The soldiers huddled together. They seemed to suspect her fall onto the little boat was an act. She held onto her parasol tightly as a gust of wind threatened to take it from her hand. She sat primly, set her jaw, and tried to appear as intimidating as her mother-in-law. The soldiers' conference ended in shrugs. Thankfully, one sat on the far bench and grabbed an oar while the other untied the boat's line from the cleat.

Nashruu had never seen such pale green water. In Thampur, it was either angry gray or cold sapphire. Here it was so clear. She could see reefs far below the rowboat surrounded by white sand, plants gently swaying in the current, and sharks endlessly circling.

The monolith stones that rose high overhead also fascinated her. She'd seen one standing as a lone sentinel in the midst of the Sea of Erykoli the day before, ferns and vines clinging to the white rock. Bird nests seemed to fill every crag and nook on the leeward side. At the water line, urchins and anemones hung on despite the constant waves. The monolith stones in the harbor were much the same, although the vegetation growing over them was more varied than on the one far out at sea.

This island was endlessly fascinating. She'd have to explore it more. Grandfather said no one except the plantation owners crossed the Jupoli Gorge Bridge. Levapur was such a small part of a big island. How could anyone resist exploring it?

There would be time for that later. Right now, she was on a mission. She twisted about to see where the rowboat headed.

The circular fortress at the end of the breakwater struck her as useless. The longer she looked at it, the less sense it made. From what she could see, the militia inside didn't seem to even take note of the ships sailing past its walls, except to occasionally wave at sailors in the rigging. They couldn't stop a Ravidian ship from sailing into the harbor. Perhaps, like the fortresses sitting on the seaward islands of Surrayya, it was equipped with ballistas to shoot flaming harpoons and oil at enemy ships, but she saw no evidence of such weapons on the ramparts.

It made no sense, though, to make it so difficult to reach the fortress by land. One could try to climb over the enormous, wet, barnacle-encrusted rocks of the breakwater, but it wouldn't be easy. They obviously wanted to make it as difficult as possible to walk to the front gates of the fortress.

Ah! She'd figured it out. The fortress had been built to protect Thampurians from the Ponongese, should the natives ever revolt. Thampurians could shift into their sea dragon forms and swim quickly to the protective walls. The Ponongese would have to row over.

She was quite pleased with herself.

Her theory also explained why twice as many arrow slots faced the harbor as the sea. And maybe that's why the executed prisoners were hung from the ramparts facing the harbor rather than the seaward side. She averted her eyes from the corpses.

They were nearly at the breakwater when she saw the short dock for the fortress. Up close, the stone walls were much more intimidating. She was going to walk in there, get Lady QuiTai to agree to work for Grandfather, and then tell Colonel Hurust to release her. That's what Grandfather expected her to do. Unfortunately, he hadn't told her how she was supposed to affect this miracle.

Nashruu had been lectured, quizzed, and tutored relentlessly for years. It had all been a waste. She was completely unprepared for this. Her shoulders slumped as a wave of doubt eroded her confidence. She was going to mess this up. Lady QuiTai would be hanged because of her, and Grandfather would make her come back to Thampur in disgrace.

Her mouth twitched. Wasn't that usually the other way around? One got sent to Levapur in disgrace, not recalled home. As she laughed at herself, her spirits rose.

Nashruu walked into Colonel Hurust's office in the fortress. It was a small room on the third floor with a view of the ramparts below. The battered furniture looked as if it had been bought as a temporary solution and never been replaced. His small desk was cluttered with files.

"Colonel Hurust–"

The colonel's secretary, Major Rheagus, spun around. His hair was curly, unusual for a Thampurian, and rose above the high dome of his bare forehead. Ill-advised academic's whiskers surrounded his wet little mouth that made smacking noises when he spoke. He gave Nashruu the most astonished look. "I told you to wait outside in the hallway."

"Did you? Oh, how dreadfully embarrassing. I didn't realize you meant me."

"There wasn't anyone else out there!"

Nashruu wiped away an offending bubble of spittle that had landed on her cheek. Colonel Hurust gripped the arms of his chair as if he might flee any moment. His neck overflowed his uniform collar as if he believed he was still the gawky youth he'd been when he'd entered the military academy.

Her eyes were drawn to his hair. There was an unreal quality to it, as if it had been waxed and then sculpted into shape by a doll maker. Something about his pursed lips and stubby fingers reeked of prissy habits.

When she managed to move her gaze from his astonishing hair to his eyes, she was startled to realize he was also judging her. She saw the sneer in the spread of his nostrils.

"Look at my manners. Colonel Hurust? How do you do?" She inclined her head just enough for it to count as a bow.

That should put him in his place, she thought.

After a long silence, in which the men stared at her, she quietly cleared her throat. "I suppose I must make the introductions then. I am Ma'am Zul, wife of Governor Zul."

"I humbly beg your pardon, Ma'am Zul. We don't receive many guests here," Colonel Hurust said. He didn't seem to regret that.

"How sad. You must feel so isolated." She sat down and placed her satchel at her feet.

If Major Rheagus' eyebrows rose any higher, he'd have a proper hairline for a man his age.

"We prefer to keep apart from the contamination," Colonel Hurust said. He suddenly leaned forward. "Does your husband know you're here?"

She didn't like to lie, but she knew what would happen if she told the truth. "Yes."

"He allowed you to come here without an escort or—"

"I'm surrounded by the gallant men of the colonial militia. How could I be any safer?"

Colonel Hurust apparently didn't like being interrupted. "This is a prison."

"Exactly."

Now he was ticked off. That didn't worry her. Maybe his wife shrank back when he scowled, but he wasn't nearly as scary as Grandfather.

"I came here to see a prisoner. Lady QuiTai."

Colonel Hurust chuckled. His secretary chortled. That was worse than any other insult. She hated the rising heat in her cheeks as they belittled her.

Then, for no reason she could understand, he rose from his desk and said, "Come on. I haven't got all day."

He strode from his office at a quick pace. She struggled to keep up as her narrow skirt forced her to take mincing steps. When she fell behind, he didn't slow down. At the stairs, she gritted her teeth and raised her hem almost to her knees so she could keep up. If a soldier saw her legs, she'd never be taken seriously.

She lost sight of him at the bottom landing as she quickly pushed her skirt back down. Hurrying as best she could, she turned a corner and found him waiting at a double-biolocked gate to the prison section of the fortress.

Hurust didn't have to say a word to make it clear he was doing this on a whim, and that he could easily change his mind. That was more unnerving than the laughter. Was she supposed to be grateful and obedient now? Or was he accommodating her because he liked her bravery? There was no telling with men.

Nashruu followed Colonel Hurust across the lush grass. The parade ground reminded her of the first time she'd seen Voorus at Thyrinmun, Thampur's elite military academy. He'd looked so dashing with his new stripes, and she'd felt so wicked. Men had affairs all the time, but outside of plays and operas, she'd never heard of a woman taking a lover and living to tell about it. Not that she'd ever told anyone. Grandfather made the price for letting out that secret graphically clear.

A delightful ocean breeze ruffled the longish grass, and gulls wheeled far overhead in the cloudless sky. As far as prisons went, she imagined this one was quite nice.

Colonel Hurust stopped at a thick door with a grill at eye level. He lifted the rusting iron ring to knock on the door.

"Why wasn't Lady QuiTai put in one of these cells?" Nashruu pointed to the empty cells built into the wall ringing the parade ground.

"Your husband demanded we put her in the dungeon." His tone made it clear that he'd had enough of her already, so she didn't press for details.

He knocked on the door again. They stood in silence. He seemed too surly to share information about his fortress or the militia, so she didn't attempt any polite chatter. She was a bit shocked he hadn't offered to carry her satchel. Even while annoyed, men of a certain social rank could usually be relied upon for such manners. Then again, if he were a good example of a gentleman, he most certainly wouldn't have been exiled to

Levapur, would he?

Although the Colonel's lips were a natural enough shade, she wondered if maybe he were a black lotus user. Not an addict; not yet. But she knew he'd been caught using his position to smuggle the addictive black tar into Thampur. She also understood she wasn't allowed to tell him she knew why he'd been exiled. Levapur's unwritten rules of society were odder than those in Surrayya.

Hurust shifted from foot to foot and pounded on the door. He cursed dreadfully but didn't apologize to her. Instead, he jangled a ring of keys irritably, found the one he wanted, and shoved it into the lock.

The door swung open under protest. Her nose wrinkled as a wave of air smelling of algae and mud oozed out of the dungeon.

Colonel Hurust stepped back and indicated she should go first. That struck her as bad manners, but if it were a dare, she would prove she had the nerve to step into the darkness.

She took off her blue sun spectacles. The room wasn't as dark as before, but the sunlight streaming through the door and the green light jellylanterns hanging from the stone walls didn't illuminate enough. She saw stairs leading down into pitch darkness ahead. To the side there was a space big enough for a roughly hewn table and a couple battered chairs. Tiles covered most of the table. Some were up, arranged in sets, but the rest were face down in the center. A game in progress, then. She rested her hand on the back to the chair closest to her and examined the tiles. The north seat was winning handily.

"My guards can escort you to the dungeon from here. Good day, Ma'am Zul."

Colonel Hurust's voice grew fainter. The little alcove darkened as the door swung closed. A half-forgotten nightmare of being buried alive sent her hand flying to protect her neck. She found her voice. "Colonel, there are no men here!"

"They're probably down in the dungeon with the prisoner. Simply call down—"

"I will not!"

Her hand ached where she'd been gripping the chair too tightly. She let go and went to the door. It was far heavier than she expected and didn't swing easily on its rusted hinges. Colonel Hurust hadn't walked away yet. He looked as if his lunch had turned viciously on him.

"Colonel, kindly wait with me for your men to return, or summon someone to escort me down."

He nodded as he turned to look at the parade ground. A sauntering guard appeared on the rampart across the way. Colonel Hurust yelled to get his attention, but the wind blew his voice away.

"Wait here." He walked stiffly to the flight of steps leading from the parade ground to the ramparts.

Nashruu pushed the door open wider to make sure it didn't close and lock her in.

Colonel Hurust was moving too slowly for her taste. Everyone on this island moved in slow motion. It was as if the heat sapped them of their will to get anything done. Impatient, she cast a glance behind her to the dark staircase leading down.

"Hello? Lady QuiTai? We met earlier. I'm Ma'am Zul, and I'm here to speak with you," Nashruu said. If the poor woman was locked down there in the dark, maybe another woman's voice would comfort her.

Nashruu tilted her head. The soft schussing she heard reminded her of pressing a seashell to her ear. Wait! Was that something moving? No. That must have been her imagination.

No matter how hard she squinted into the darkness or how hard she concentrated, she couldn't hear anything. The sounds from outside were muffled. Silence billowed over them and consumed everything.

A voice whispered from the pitch black staircase, "You shouldn't be here, Ma'am Zul."

It had to be a weird acoustical effect where the stone curved sound, or maybe like those entertainers who made voices come out of puppets. QuiTai couldn't be part of that darkness, could she? Was she close enough to reach out and touch Nashruu?

Nashruu refused to let her imagination spook her.

QuiTai wasn't a folktale demon. She should be feared, certainly, but she was mortal, like everyone else.

Two soldiers reluctantly edged into the room with her.

Colonel Hurust had found her escort, but he stood behind them and didn't cross the threshold.

"These men will take you down to see the Devil's whore, Ma'am. If you see my other men, tell them to report to me."

She didn't feel as if she should carry messages for him. Perhaps his men had taken a meal break, been relieved of duty, or... She glanced down the staircase again and gulped. Oh, this was silly. QuiTai could hardly be a threat to a fortress full of soldiers.

The soldiers didn't move. Apparently, she was supposed to go down the stairs first.

"I require a lamp," she said.

Jellylantern in hand, the three of them descended into the gloom. The stone stairs were slick and there was no handrail. The slow drip of water echoing through the dungeon could have been blood draining from a corpse.

The fading green light of a single jellylantern in the dungeon barely illuminated the first cell. It was impossible to know what lurked in the utter darkness outside the sickly halo of light. Nashruu's arms prickled as she peered into the gloom.

The soldier's shuffling boots on the stone floor sounded like the scrape of talons behind a wall. It made the hairs at the back of her neck stand.

QuiTai stood at the back of the first cell. It was hard to see where she ended and the shadows began. Even her face was difficult to see, but it was undoubtedly she.

Nashruu's relief to find her locked away was a bit embarrassing. She was glad no one knew how she felt.

The soldiers glanced around with wild eyes There was nothing to see, so their imaginations seemed to paint pictures for them. They edged toward the stairs as if they might abandon her.

"Wait!" Nashruu's voice ricocheted off the stone dungeon wall. She raised her hand as she peered through the cell bars. "Let me into the cell with her."

The soldiers drew themselves up as if a silent consensus had been reached. She knew the signs of men about to lie to justify something stupid.

The one with the luxuriant mustache spoke slowly, as if forming a lie took all his concentration. "Yes, well, that may be what you think you want, miss–"

"Ma'am."

He rolled his eyes as the other one smirked. "Ma'am. We can't let you put yourself in danger."

"Don't be ridiculous. Lady QuiTai won't kill me."

At least, she hoped not. Out of the corner of her eye, she watched the small figure waiting patiently for this scene to play out.

A quiet groan echoed through the chamber.

QuiTai stepped closer to the bars of her cell. Her unbound hair fell in matted, twisted locks down to her knees, as if she'd been floating face down in the sea for several days. In the sickly green light of the sole jellylantern, her eyes seemed to glow from the bottom of deep pits. It was silly to think this, but she looked exactly like the surkraim from that illustrated book of folktales that was probably in every nursery in Thampur. But QuiTai wasn't a vengeful marsh spirit. No adult believed in such things.

Somewhere else in the dark, something moved.

The soldiers bolted for the stairs, leaving Nashruu to face her alone.

"We haven't been introduced properly, Lady QuiTai. I'm Governor Zul's wife. Please call me Nashruu."

"Not for all the rice in Levapur." She sounded a bit annoyed, as if the interruption were barely tolerable.

"Are we enemies?" Nashruu was able to keep her voice light and pleasant. That was something, at least, although she suspected that QuiTai could hear her booming heartbeat.

"That has yet to be determined, Ma'am Zul, but you must appreciate my caution. In this place, I can't afford a single misstep."

It dawned on Nashruu that QuiTai's refusal to use her name hadn't been personal. If the soldiers overheard a Ponongese being familiar with a Thampurian, they'd probably use it as an excuse to beat her. Nashruu been warned that rules were different in Levapur: more formal, rigid, harsh. That was easy to forget in a place with no paved roads, where animals and plants seemed to wander where they willed, and most people walked around draped in little more than a bed sheet. At least QuiTai's reminder had been gentle. Grandfather would have roared at her.

She lifted her satchel. "Do you care for tea? I've brought cakes, too. One can't have proper tea without a little something to nibble on, don't you think?"

Her nerves were showing. She had to stop talking so much.

QuiTai's fingertips trailed across the cell bars as she sauntered the width of her cell. "Tea and cakes in the fortress dungeon? How delightfully absurd."

Her laughter didn't sound cruel or mocking. It was gentle. After all the warnings about QuiTai, Nashruu was surprised at her kindness. "I'd planned to have tea with you the moment I set foot in Levapur. Grandfather insisted I visit you here as soon as he heard you'd been arrested. I'm being efficient and doing both."

"You are either naive, Ma'am Zul, or you're the bravest

Thampurian I've ever met."

Brave? Since stepping into the dungeon, she'd imagined the weight of the fortress overhead crushing down on her. Every breath dragged the stench of the place across her tongue. She didn't trust the bars to protect her from this woman whom even Grandfather feared.

With some effort, she willed her hand from her jacket's frogs and down to her side. Her arm felt awkwardly posed, but there was nothing she could do about it. She had to prove she deserved Grandfather's faith in her.

Nashruu set the satchel on a stair and undid the heavy buckles. The compartments on one side held a box of little pink cakes, a tin of tea leaves, sugar, and a thermos of cream. The other held a teapot, spoons, saucers, and two cups. It wasn't practical; it was flash, the kind of toy most people liked to have but never used because it was more trouble than it was worth. "This is my favorite part." She unsnapped the base to reveal a rectangular metal canteen that was uncomfortably warm to the touch. "This end here has the fuel and enclosed flame. The rest is filled with water. It takes a while to boil."

"Ingenious. Made for train travel, I assume," QuiTai said.

Grandfather said QuiTai had a fascination for inventions of all sorts. She'd certainly smuggled enough of them into Levapur. He'd slipped a few items into those shipments to see what she might make of them, although Nashruu wasn't sure how he found out an answer. His spies watched QuiTai, but she had proven herself elusive many times.

"The protected flame was an innovation for ship passengers, since fire is the worst hazard on board. Cake?" Nashruu placed the thickly iced cakes on a plate with a gold edge and handed it through the bars to QuiTai.

"Perhaps it was in the past, before jellylanterns, which makes one wonder why the incidence of burns has risen sharply among the *Golden Barracuda*'s crew. Mm. Such a pretty cake. Suin's?"

"I was told it was the only pâtisserie in Levapur worth visiting." Nashruu took the plate from QuiTai and picked up a cake for herself. She bit into the corner. The filling wasn't the usual berry jam, but it was quite good. She popped the last bite into her mouth and flicked away the moist crumbs from her fingers. "Grandfather will be jealous that he didn't join us."

"You have no idea how much I also wish Grandfather were here."

There was menace in her tone. Nothing overt, of course, but her intent was clear.

"You call him Grandfather too?" Nashruu asked.

"It's a sign of greatest respect among the Ponongese. If he doesn't like it, I will use another name for him. I'd hate for him to think I underestimate him. Or his agent."

For a moment, she was taken aback, until she remembered that she'd told QuiTai herself that Grandfather had sent her here. Was QuiTai's seeming clairvoyance merely the result of listening to the things people forgot they'd said?

"That's quite flattering," Nashruu said.

"Not at all. Oh, I see. You're suspicious because I'm on my best behavior."

"Are you?"

QuiTai smiled to herself. "I'm not usually that generous. Such a warning, and for free!"

Nashruu thought back furiously over their conversation. What warning? "I'm sorry. I must have—"

QuiTai's very breath sounded impatient. "If I can spend an hour at the wharf and observe three crew members with obvious burn marks on their hands and arms disembarking from the *Golden Barracuda*, imagine what a spy who was looking for such things might learn. And it doesn't take much to extrapolate the rest of the story, does it? Three sailors, who from their jocular banter, work together. Their paler skin suggests they work below deck, but they are allowed shore leave, even though it's known that the *Golden Barracuda* sails tomorrow on the tide. So they don't work with the cargo or ship's stores, because those crewmen are working furiously to make sure everything is in order for tomorrow. Not to mention that their clothes reek of burned juam nut oil. And then there's the ship's doctor, openly negotiating the purchase of a large quantity of black lotus on the wharf where anyone might overhear. Black lotus has many uses, but in a ship's doctor's pharmacy, it's used for pain – intense pain. He also bought juikoo leaves, which are used to soothe burned skin. Need I go on?"

Nashruu's throat tightened. Did she know about the top secret engines on board Hadre's ship?

"Tell Grandfather that the crew of the *Golden Barracuda* needs to be much more discreet, or the Ravidians will figure out it's not a typical junk, if they don't already know," QuiTai said. "Remember, any farwriter can receive your transmissions if someone stumbles upon the frequency, even if you change it daily. That's why Grandfather delivers his most important messages in person. So chose your words carefully when you share my warning with him."

QuiTai had a way of clipping the end of her sentences to indicate she'd said all she meant to say. Nashruu certainly thought she'd said enough.

"Is the water hot?" QuiTai asked.

She changed subjects so abruptly.

"Yes."

"Go ahead and make your cup. I prefer you be settled before we start the next part of this conversation."

Nashruu rinsed out the pot with some of the heated water. "What is the next part?"

"We discuss why you're here. I gather Grandfather has instructed you to make some sort of deal with me."

"Do you take sugar?" Nashruu put leaves in the pot and poured the rest of the water over them.

"None for me, thank you."

"No sugar?"

"No tea. I don't mean to be rude. It's a little quirk of mine."

Nashruu laughed uncertainly. "But you ate the cake."

QuiTai held out her hand. It was almost too dark to tell, but the cake she held looked whole. Yet Nashruu was sure she'd seen her eat it.

"Never assume. What you believe you've seen may be an

illusion."

"Why would I poison you now? We haven't even begun to talk," Nashruu said.

"This is going to sound fanciful—"

"I've never heard you described that way."

QuiTai smiled down at her feet.

She's modest, or at least she pretends well. Grandfather never mentioned that!

"In the jellylantern serials, they always slip poison to the hero and then withhold the antidote until he does what they tell him to. Pure rubbish, I think, but one can never be too sure. The chemists in Thampur have been so busy in their laboratories lately. Busy, busy, making weapons of war, great and small. Who knows what they might be concocting?"

"And you're our hero, Lady QuiTai?"

"Oh no, my dear. Never. I'm the villain."

She knew the spike of fear that went through her was silly, because QuiTai couldn't possibly have magical powers. Nashruu had watched her every second since she'd entered the dungeon, hadn't she? It wasn't possible that QuiTai could have slipped between the bars and doctored her tea while she was watching, any more than it was possible that QuiTai had been standing inches away from her in the darkness at the top of the stairs earlier. The woman couldn't possibly glide through iron bars like a spirit, and she couldn't become invisible.

The dungeon walls echoed with a guttural moan. It had to be her imagination. This was a little play that QuiTai was staging for her benefit. That sound couldn't be real.

Nashruu set down her cup and pushed it away.

Two rings of gold glowed from the dark pits of QuiTai's eyes. With her chin lowered and the jellylantern casting dim light up on her face, she gave Nashruu the shivers.

"Now, let's talk about why Grandfather sent you here, Ma'am Zul."

CHAPTER 10: REPORTING TO GRANDFATHER ZUL

Nashruu knew she should tell Grandfather that QuiTai had turned down his deal, but she was putting it off. From the moment she'd returned to the compound, her servants had harassed her with a million stupid questions. Unpacked crates still sat in the foyer. The remains of their meal littered the dining table. Tempers were on edge.

Her maid, Simarn, followed her up the stairs and breathlessly delivered a list of complaints against the others. Nashruu made sympathetic noises and unbuttoned her jacket. Before it could fall to the floor, the maid snatched it away.

Nashruu drew in a deep breath as her maid unlaced her corset. Underneath, her shift was damp with sweat.

"No wonder those snakes wear nothing under their thin blouses," Simarn said.

"Maybe if I went without my corset I wouldn't get so hot. Oh, that look? You're the one who brought it up."

"It wasn't a suggestion, Ma'am."

Allowances had to be made for the heat, but that attitude had to change quickly. Simarn had received an outrageous bonus for agreeing to come to Ponong. She shouldn't blame Nashruu if the colony wasn't to her liking.

"Governor Zul says we are to refer to the natives as Ponongese, not snakes," Nashruu reminded her.

"Yes, Ma'am."

"Is my bath ready?"

"Yes, Ma'am, although you might wilt in that steam, so I also left you a pitcher of water by your basin. We drew it up from a well, so it's cool, but not enough to give you a chill."

The idea of getting a chill in Levapur was absurd.

"That was very thoughtful of you, Simarn. I'll need my blue dress when I go out this afternoon."

"You're leaving again?"

Being scolded by one's maid was simply too much. Nashruu gave her a stern look.

"Yes, Ma'am. Shall I close the doors?" Simarn indicated the typhoon shutters that were open to the veranda, although wood screens had been pulled across the opening for privacy.

"Leave them open. Perhaps the breeze will pick up."

Even if it hadn't been so hot, with her eyes closed, Nashruu would have known she was far from home. She'd never thought about Surrayya having a scent until now. It never smelled of dirt, verdant plants, decay like the jungle, the sharp spices of the marketplace, or the cloying sweetness of the flowers that grew on the trellis over the typhoon shutters. Surrayya smelled of the canals and damp velvet frocks, or like a storm coming over the ocean.

Simarn put Nashruu's afternoon frock into the wardrobe, bowed, and left the room.

Nashruu pulled her shift over her head and let it drop on the floor. It seemed so improper to stand naked inside her room with the doors wide open to the courtyard. No one could see through the wood screens unless they stood on the veranda, but still, it felt dangerous. She never would have done it in Surrayya. She wondered if Kyam would ever be tempted to creep across the veranda that linked their rooms to peek in at her.

How funny to think of her husband coming to her bedroom as scandalous, wicked even. The idea probably wouldn't have sent a shiver down her spine if it hadn't been forbidden. She'd never given much thought to Kyam as a husband. He'd always been more theoretical than a reality to her, but for the first time since their wedding, they would be living in the same house. Anything could happen on this island.

She dipped a sponge in a basin of water, squeezed it, and dragged it from her wrist to her shoulder. The warm breeze flowed over the drops of water on her heated skin. She lifted her hair to wipe the nape of her neck. It felt so lovely.

After the terrible things she'd heard about Ponong, she'd been prepared to hate it, but at her first glimpse of the agricultural terraces carved into the steep slopes of the mountains, the white streaks of waterfalls cascading hundreds of feet through the deep green of the jungle, and the turquoise lagoons, she'd felt free. Grandfather was miles away. The rules that had governed her every waking moment no longer seemed to apply. If one were smart, one could get away with almost anything here – she hoped. For eight years, she'd been forbidden a lover. Eight long years of listening to friends complain about their husband's physical demands, of fending off libertines, of praying for release.

Rivulets of water trickled down her thighs. If only she could have written to Voorus and told him she was coming to Levapur. Kyam couldn't have done anything to stop her from flinging herself into his arms at the dock.

Except that he might have beaten or killed her afterward. He would be expected to. Grandfather's protections were always such double-edged swords. Constrained and practically imprisoned in his house for years, she'd at least been safe from Kyam. She didn't think he was the type to do such a thing, but one never knew with men.

She assumed she was safe from him. Grandfather seemed to anticipate everything... with the exception of Lady QuiTai.

Nashruu smiled at the memory as she squeezed the sponge

and let water spill down her spine.

The evening before the rice riot in Levapur, back in Surrayya, Nashruu had gone to the ballroom with Grandfather. Grandfather had been genuinely shocked when QuiTai had used Kyam's farwriter to contact him. Then he'd chuckled. But the thing Nashruu remembered most about that night was how, for the first time, she'd seen fear on Grandfather's face, and she knew QuiTai was the person who'd made him feel that way.

She had to save QuiTai today, because QuiTai was the only one who could shatter Grandfather's shackles. QuiTai had done it for Kyam. Would she do the same thing for a woman she had just met? Maybe she would to thwart Grandfather...

Yes, QuiTai might help move her beyond Grandfather's reach. But first, she had to convince QuiTai to accept his deal. She had to hand him what he wanted to get free. A prisoner exchange. QuiTai for her. How could she trick QuiTai into it? There had to be something the woman wanted, something QuiTai valued above her own life.

Nashruu set down the sponge and looked about the room for her silk wrap. Simarn hadn't put it out. Perhaps it was still in the luggage.

It felt strange to move around the room absolutely naked. One stepped immediately from a bath into a warmed towel, from a night shift into an undershift. One was never naked for more than a few seconds at most. One never looked at one's own body, or touched it, or took pleasure in it. A Thampurian lady was above such animal behavior.

She tugged the top sheet from her bed and quickly wrapped it around herself.

Nashruu tucked the corner of the bed sheet between her breasts so she could type with both hands when she sat before the farwriter. How scandalized would Grandfather be if he knew her shoulders were bare and she was wearing a sarong of sorts?

Now *she* was one of those mysterious people sending messages to Grandfather. She pictured him hovering over the receiving farwriter. A card with her chop would be placed in front of the machine. A farwriter was dedicated solely to her.

After cranking the generator, she cleared her throat as if she were about to speak. Was someone reading what she wrote? Maybe QuiTai was right, but there was nothing she could do about it now. She had to report. Her short, slim fingers curved over the keys as she composed her message.

I went to the fortress as ordered. Made offer to Q. NaZ

And? TtZ

She could picture him tapping his fingernails on the table beside her farwriter. She'd never squirmed under the gaze of her parents or tutors, but she shifted uneasily now.

What would he want to know about first? She might as well get the worst out of the way.

Q refused deal. NaZ

Tell me the conversation, from beginning to end. TtZ

Nashruu realized she couldn't remember QuiTai's exact words. She wasn't sure what had been said, what was implied, and what she'd imagined anymore. Grandfather would be so angry.

The farwriter's bell rang again before she could type. He was impatient.

The conversation, in detail. TtZ

I'm typing as fast as I can, she told the farwriter.

We talked for a while. It's difficult to remember exactly what was said. NaZ

I warned you that with her, one must pay attention to every detail. TtZ

He always made her feel miserable and stupid.

She cleared her mind and let impressions of the conversation float through it. What was important to pass along? Except that QuiTai had turned her down, not much. She shared QuiTai's warning about the ship's doctor and the sailors giving away the secret engine on board the *Golden Barracuda* as cryptically as she could. The longer she typed, the more pieces of the conversation came back to her. Her confidence rose. She could do this.

She doesn't seem to care if she dies, or to want what you offered her. NaZ

Did she say what she wants? TtZ

Nashruu winced as she typed QuiTai's words as faithfully as she could remember them. She expected the secret police to crash through the door and arrest her for repeating them. It had to be treason to even think of the King kneeling to someone, much less apologizing for stealing their land.

A typical negotiating tactic. It would be more convincing if her situation wasn't so dire. Let her sit in the dark for a few hours and imagine the noose around her neck. Then go back and offer her less. She'll fold as the sun dips in the sky. TtZ

I don't think so. NaZ

You don't think so? You know nothing. TtZ

She shrank back. Nothing was ever good, no effort was ever enough.

It gave her grim satisfaction to type, *"She said she'd go to the noose smiling because she denied you what you wanted from her." NaZ*

Minutes passed. Nashruu picked at her fingernails and chewed on the cuticles. Simarn came in with her dress and parasol. She rose from the dressing table and let the sheet drop. Her maid averted her eyes as she helped Nashruu put on a sleeveless chemise with a pink silk flower at the neckline. Nashruu stepped into the skirt. It was always a tug-of-war to persuade her undergarments to stop bunching up under the silk. Once she'd donned the jacket, her maid smoothed her curls and placed a matching hat on her head.

Nashruu turned back and forth to examine the effect in the mirror. Would this outfit impress QuiTai? She felt it had an authoritative air. Satisfied, she dismissed Simarn.

The farwriter bell still hadn't rung.

How simple this all had seemed when she and Grandfather had discussed his agents in the past. 'Why don't they just...'

she'd often said about an agent who seemed to be taking too long to accomplish something. Now she knew. It wasn't so straightforward. Unexpected things happened. People didn't behave the way you predicted, and when your entire plan hinged on them doing something, you were stuck with a useless plan if they did something else. This game wasn't as fun as it looked from the outside.

The farwriter finally rang. She hovered over it and read the message as it typed out.

Go back to the fortress. Find out what she wants and give it to her. Then get her out of there before those idiots decide to hang her anyway. TtZ

She barely condescended to speak to me the first time. I don't see her as the type of person who would waste her time on a pointless conversation a second time. NaZ

Find a way. TtZ

Easy for you to say, Nashruu muttered.

Did you offer her Kyam? TtZ

How could she explain to him that an encounter with QuiTai wasn't like a dinner party? One couldn't steer the conversation. There was never an opportunity to drop in a well-practiced piece of information. The malevolent intent was there, the coded phrases, the use of wit as a weapon, but it was as different from playing salon hostess as swimming in your human form was from swimming as a sea dragon.

I mentioned Kyam once, but there wasn't so much as a flicker of recognition at his name. You told me she'd once been a prostitute, so maybe her kind thinks that way about men. NaZ

She was the mistress of the King of Houlton and other high ranking officials of nearly every country on the continent, so never make the mistake of thinking of her as a common whore. TtZ

"But you're the one–" Nashruu slumped in her chair. Arguing with a machine as useless. Of course she didn't think of QuiTai as a whore. Grandfather had made it perfectly clear that she was to be treated with the respect due any deadly, intelligent creature.

She looked at herself in the mirror above the dressing

table. A tendril of dark hair stuck to her neck. Frown lines marred her forehead. Leaning closer to the mirror, she stared into her eyes. How had she ever thought she would be able to play this game? Everything was so far above her abilities that she couldn't begin to compete against these people. Her gaze lowered.

Grandfather seemed to think his offer would work eventually, but she didn't agree. He hadn't seen QuiTai's indifference. He didn't understand what QuiTai wanted.

What could that woman want?

Nashruu made a face at her reflection. She had no idea. Grandfather thought he knew, but he was wrong. He'd framed a picture of QuiTai that was wrong from the beginning, and every decision he'd made about her since was still tainted by that error. It was as if he didn't see the obvious, or refused to learn from his mistakes. He thought he was so clever and could bend anyone to his will, but that only worked if you understood how a person thought. He didn't understand QuiTai. It was up to her to figure out how to deal with this woman. What did QuiTai want? Who knew her well enough?

Going to make inquiries. Signing off. NaZ

CHAPTER 11: LIZZRIAT EXPLAINS

*T*he Dragon Pearl wasn't the only casino in Levapur that banned Ponongese, but it was the only business owned by an Ingosolian that did. Kyam suspected the owner, Lizzriat, kept them out because his clients wanted him to, not out of any personal prejudice against the natives. Kyam wasn't sure how he felt about Lizzriat, because it was so hard to figure out where Lizzriat stood.

Like QuiTai, Lizzriat knew the value of information. It was coin of the realm in the Quarter of Delights. His alliances weren't clear, but his product was usually reliable.

Kyam had never heard the click of tiles in the Dragon Pearl before, but he'd never been in the casino this early. Bored dealers watched him climb the stairs without much curiosity. They were used to vapor addicts coming at all hours. He wondered how long it would take for rumors about him visiting the second story to spread through Levapur.

The door to the common den across the landing from the main staircase was open halfway. Dreamers shared a raised wooden pallet in heap of tangled limbs, uncaring for anything but the need for vapor. The strong, resinous scent of black lotus was stomach-churning.

Kyam crept down the hallway even though the thick carpet swallowed sound. Maybe it was the vapor fumes affecting his mind, but every time he walked past the opulent private dens where the rich took their pipes to the owner's office, the purple and brown striped walls appeared to converge and the hallway to elongate before him. It always seemed to take twice as long as it should to reach Lizzriat's door.

He knocked gently. While the ground floor of the Dragon Pearl was normally loud and boisterous, up here hush had settled like an overnight snowfall on a courtyard lantern. He thought he heard the rustle of silk and the quiet click of a lock, but it could have been a trick of his mind. He knocked again, this time sliding open the door as his knuckles rapped on the wood panel.

Lizzriat was reclining on a bed built into an alcove in the office's dark bookshelves. His curly red hair sprawled across the pillows that propped him into a sitting position. He extended a hand with weary grace.

Kyam pushed the fall of lace from Lizzriat's wrist and pressed his lips to the pale blue skin.

Lizzriat patted the mattress beside him, and Kyam sank into the soft bed. He wondered how Lizzriat could stand the layers of silken sheets and duvets swaddling him all night. The room was stuffy and too warm as it was, the air sour with sweat and another unpleasant scent he could not name.

"You're kind to see me," Kyam said. "I wouldn't have disturbed you this early, but I'm on a tight schedule."

Lizzriat's mouth hardened, but he tried to sound idly amused. "One does not rush in Levapur, *krith amaci*. One surrenders to lethargy." He reached for a small glass of garnet liquid on the nearby table and sipped it like a tonic.

"I don't have the luxury today."

Setting aside his glass, Lizzriat made a face. "I'm far too exhausted for cryptic messages. Let us borrow a tile from our

CHAPTER 11: LIZZRIAT EXPLAINS

native friends and be blunt."

That suited Kyam. "If you insist. Lady QuiTai has been arrested for murder and will be executed as the sun sets."

Lizzriat flinched at the mention of QuiTai and looked away. "It was bound to happen eventually. On suspicion, I assume. She'd never be stupid enough to leave evidence." A quick slide of his gaze to Kyam's face made that seem like a question. "Although I heard she was first arrested, and then she was accused of murder. Such a curious sequence of events, don't you think?"

Intrigue was part of daily life in the Quarter of Delights. Of course Lizzriat already knew what had happened. He wasn't asking. He was proving to Kyam the value of his network.

Smiling tightly, Kyam said, "I'm investigating former Governor Turyat's death, and wondered if you had any insights. He spent a lot of time here."

The ruffled edge of the blanket didn't need to be straightened, but Lizzriat passed the time aligning the fabric. "Not lately."

"I heard a rumor that he was off black lotus."

Lizzriat made a sound between bitter laughter and a harrumph. "Not by choice."

"So it's true QuiTai cut him off."

"She's as brilliant as the diamond dust that sharpens a drill's bit. You have to admire such a cruel imagination even if it repulses you. It's almost artistic."

"I think this is a folktale."

"We all suffer by her hand. We enjoy it. We hate ourselves for our addiction, but oh, do we ever relish the pain she doles out. And that, too, is her art. She tattoos our hearts with self-inflicted scars." Lizzriat grinned and winced.

That was far too close to the truth. Blunt was okay, but Kyam wasn't prepared to stare into the darkest part of his soul today. He cleared his throat. "The part I don't believe about–"

Where was it that Lizzriat was trying so hard not to look? He wouldn't turn around right now, but when he left, he'd find a reason to look at the room behind him. Something there drew

Lizzriat's eye.

Kyam struggled against the soft abyss of the blankets to find a more comfortable position before he continued. "I don't believe anyone could stop every single dreamer in Levapur from sharing their black lotus with Turyat. She can't possibly control every soul in this town. The population is small compared to cities on the continent, but it's no fishing village on the outer cays, either."

"Noted, although I respectfully disagree with one of your assertions."

"Back on the continent, possession of black lotus can send you to prison for life, but here, people use it like medicine."

"It is medicine," Lizzriat said.

"It's poison."

"All medicines are poisons. What do you think these concoctions our doctors give us do? They kill the sickness, and a little of the healthy part of us too." Lizzriat lifted his glass again, saluted Kyam, and took another sip.

"My point is – you can probably find black lotus in half the households in Levapur. So someone buys a little extra and slips it to Turyat for a tidy profit. How would QuiTai ever know? She can't control this many people. Simply not possible. It makes a nice story, but no. I don't believe it's true."

Lizzriat rolled on his side. His fingertip traced the cream on cream pattern on his sheets as he spoke. "Turyat stole a vial of black lotus from a dreamer here. She blamed me. Cut off my supply for weeks as punishment. Do you know how I got back into her good graces?"

"Seduced her?"

His hand covered Kyam's and squeezed lightly. "She and I, we flirt because it is in our nature to desire what is worst for us, but we're not meant to be."

"Because of the Devil?"

"The Devil? *Pffft.* Is he even fashionable anymore? No. QuiTai is terrifying enough on her own, which is part of her allure. I'm sure you agree."

Kyam couldn't deny it.

Lizzriat didn't seem to like what he saw when he gazed into his own soul. "I earned her partial forgiveness the old-fashioned way: I informed on someone else who dared to give Turyat a pipe."

"And they?"

"Know better now. We all do. She's the harsh headmistress of the school of life." His gaze flicked over Kyam's shoulder again.

Kyam wondered if maybe someone were sneaking up behind him. His back tensed.

"But maybe now my debt is fully paid..."

Lizzriat fussed with his nightshirt's sleeve. Kyam took advantage of the moment to look around the room. Clearly, it was more of an office than a bedroom. Where were Lizzriat's clothes, if this was where he lived? A suit hung over the back of the desk chair. Was that what he kept glancing at? Had he been out earlier this morning? Few denizens of the quarter rose before midday. The only person he knew who habitually rose with the sun was QuiTai. Had the two of them been up to something earlier today? Was that payment on Lizzriat's debt?

Kyam turned back to Lizzriat. "Who do you think would kill Turyat?"

Lizzriat's head jerked. He stared at Kyam for a moment. "No one. It's a nonsense murder."

"How do you mean?"

"Why risk a death sentence to kill a man like that?" Lizzriat didn't seem interested in the topic.

"Do you mean QuiTai?"

"I mean anyone. You'd have to be an idiot to murder a vapor ghoul."

"I agree. You agree. Everyone agrees with that. And yet, he's dead, and it was no accident."

Lizzriat gently tapped Kyam's thigh until Kyam got the message to rise from the bed, then shoved the covers down to his feet and then swung his legs over the side of the mattress. After wrapping a dusky red dressing gown over his nightshirt, he went to his desk.

"I think whoever killed Turyat made a huge mistake. QuiTai wanted him alive so he would suffer. Everyone knows that." He paused to smile at Kyam. "Everyone who matters. So whoever killed Turyat probably didn't mean to, and now they're scared to death. They'd probably welcome being arrested by you rather than face her wrath when she gets out of the fortress."

"If she gets out. And why don't you think someone framed her?"

"Do you see anyone trying to throw fuel on her funeral pyre? Is anyone offering the colonial government more information to make sure she's executed? Not that I've heard of. Think about that, Governor Zul." Lizzriat opened a ledger a placed it near the edge of the desk.

"So no one wants QuiTai to die?"

"As infuriating as this town can be, can you imagine what it would be like without her? But of course, you came after the Devil took control. You don't remember the bad old days of assassinations in the streets, or the time the werewolves burned my Dragon Pearl to the ground for refusing to pay protection money. That's not the official story, of course, but everyone knows that's why sixteen dreamers roasted alive that night. Even QuiTai's enemies fear chaos more than they hate her. Except, of course, those lately arrived opportunists who are foolish enough to believe they are the embodiment of order."

Pointed words meant Lizzriat had someone in mind. "Now who might that be?" Kyam asked.

"Is that the time? Goodness. My books need updating before tonight."

Kyam knew it was useless to press for more right now, so he bowed.

"Tell Ma'am Zul that if she cares to gamble, we can open a line of credit for her. We can assume that you vouch for her?" Lizzriat's eyebrow arched as he reached for his pen.

Kyam hadn't given much thought to the subject of his wife. Nashruu had always been his Grandfather's problem. She'd never asked him for as much as a coin. He had no idea where the money came from that kept her in designer clothes, or how her servants were paid. She'd need accounts with merchants in Levapur, and someone would have to keep the household budget, but did that come from his pocket now, or did she have her own money? He should have asked before she arrived. He should have known. But all he knew was that if Nashruu couldn't handle money, they were in trouble. He'd done a terrible job of managing his remittance before he'd become Governor.

"If she plays deep, it's at her own peril," he said.

Lizzriat clicked his tongue. "Is that private information, or should I warn the other merchants?"

"I wouldn't want you to go to any trouble."

"I assure you it would be no trouble, Governor. None at all."

Lizzriat now had a coin of rare value to spend. Kyam wasn't sure if he'd gotten anything in return for it.

CHAPTER 12: THE WIDOW TURYAT

The gate to Turyat's compound swung open half a foot and then abruptly stopped, as if a foot had blocked it. A servant peered at Kyam and swept an appraising eye over him. The gate closed a few inches. A hand jabbed through the narrow opening and turned palm up. When Kyam was slow to react, the thumb and two fingers came together and rubbed in the universal gesture for currency.

After he slapped a few coins into the greedy palm, the gate opened a few inches. Kyam impatiently shoved it the rest of the way. The servant's soft grunt made him smile.

Like most entry courtyards in Thampur and Levapur, the one behind the gate was the size of a modest ship's cabin. A thick layer of gravel covered the ground. Earlier in the day it had been meticulously raked into patterns that were visible only at the edges now.

A privacy wall embellished with a family chop blocked the view of the festoon gate and the inner courtyard. Several gemstones had fallen away, leaving gaping pits of white mortar among the glass tiles. Kyam went to the stone urn in the corner and peered around the wall into the inner courtyard while he waited for the servant to dip the ladle into the water and pour it over his hands.

"The widow says you're not to be allowed in, Governor Zul." The servant rubbed his bruised nose and glared at Kyam.

Undeterred, Kyam washed his own hands. He flicked drops off his fingertips. The servant watched like a skulking dog as Kyam snatched up the drying cloth and wiped his palms.

Kyam tossed the cloth at the servant. "Tell them I beat you."

He went around the privacy wall. Carved dragons coiled up the festoon gate's pillars. Blisters marred the deep blue and green enamel, and the gold leaf had been scraped from the dragon's talons.

The gate perfectly framed the view of a raised pavilion that appeared to float in the center of a pond. Unlike the gate, the pavilion's teak posts were simply carved and varnished, an oddly Ponongese touch in an otherwise Thampurian setting. Through the pavilion's mosquito netting curtains, he saw dreamer's couches. On hot nights it would be much cooler to sleep there than inside the main house, although no Thampurian would ever admit to sleeping outdoors.

Sunlight glinted off the scales of slowly swimming fish in the courtyard pond. The water lily leaves were enormous, like something from a fairy tale. He wondered how big the flowers were. The plant had to be native; no Thampurian water lily was that exotic. Perhaps Turyat had developed a fondness for his adopted home over the years.

Fruit trees grew in blue and green glazed pots set in neat lines across the tiled patio. Their branches were unkempt, and it appeared they hadn't been pruned for some time. Moss covered the tile roof of the kitchen house, ferns sprouted from the stucco on the main house, and a vine with purple trumpet flowers had taken over most of the third story veranda. The kitchen building's roof bowed under the weight of thick vines.

Through the glass doors on the first floor he saw clusters

of people standing in several rooms. The facial expressions of the crowd in the dining room were only as grave as propriety demanded, and the din of their conversations could be heard even out where Kyam stood. In the salon, a line of people moved slowly, and if they spoke at all, their mouths barely moved. He figured he'd find the widow with them.

Knocking on wood was bad luck after a death. The stately doors of the main house had been left open so that no guest would accidently summon a minor demon. He walked through the foyer and into the salon. No one seemed to notice he'd joined the line of visitors waiting to express condolences to Turyat's wife.

Captain Voorus was hovering at Mityam Muul's elbow near the front of the line. Kyam doubted either one of them had met the woman before, but in Levapur, people often went to strangers' funerals. It was the way Thampurians showed a sense of community, even though they probably would have cut the deceased in public, while that person were living, if they were of a lower caste.

Kyam wasn't sure how he felt about Turyat's widow. She'd lived well beyond her means for years on the money Turyat plundered from the colony's treasury, but she'd also been forced to leave Thampur over forty years ago because of him. It couldn't have been easy for her to forgive her husband, but if she'd left him, she would have been sent right back to Levapur by her family. Being unfairly punished for a marriage that she'd probably been forced into would have tested the disposition of the sweetest woman in existence – which according to rumor, she wasn't.

He chided himself. A person didn't have to be nice to deserve pity, and there was plenty of reason to pity her. She was expected to stand through the entire funeral ordeal. No matter how long it took to greet all the visitors, attend to prayers, and go through the proper rites with Turyat's ashes, she would not take a break, drink even water, sit, or eat. He remembered his mother, aunts, uncles, cousins, and Grandfather spending twenty hours on their feet when his father had died. He'd been so numb that he'd spent most of that time in a miserable daze somewhere between daydreams and hallucinations. Luckily, he'd been young enough that no one had expected him to say much. Turyat's widow didn't have that luxury. Her children had escaped banishment and lived in Thampur; they wouldn't arrive for weeks. Until then, she had to endure this alone. No wonder she looked so angry.

Kyam felt even worse for her when he focused on her yellow mourning frock. She had to be melting in this blistering heat. If she'd only taken up the new style of dress, as Nashruu and QuiTai had, she would have been spared several layers of undergarments and possibly her corset. Nashruu and QuiTai also favored silk over velvet, a sensible nod to the island's climate. He had no idea how the widow withstood the torment of her clothing, unless she'd somehow managed to hide a block of ice under her layers of petticoats.

Kyam shrank behind the curtain at the doorway to cover his inappropriate amusement at the idea of the widow clutching a block of ice between her knees.

When he dared to peer into the room, he caught the eye of the mortician. Before he could hide again, the man leaned close to Turyat's widow and whispered. Her head snapped in his direction and her eyes narrowed. He braced for her anger, but she only glared at him over the heads of her visitors.

The line hardly seemed to be moving. Ten minutes later, he was barely inside the salon. His feet were uncomfortably hot. The widow caught his gaze again as he tried to run his finger under his collar. Despite the itch under his shoulder blade growing more intense as the moments slowly ticked by, he didn't try to scratch it.

This was a waste of time. He wouldn't learn anything here. It wasn't as if he could question her. Taking a widow away from the people paying their respects was unthinkable, and he obviously couldn't ask if she'd killed her husband when he reached the front of the line.

If he ever reached the front of the line.

QuiTai would be hanged before he paid his respects. He shifted from foot to foot, hoping the unbearable heat building up in his boots would somehow disappear.

Voorus and Mityam finally shuffled away from the widow. As they headed out of the room, Voorus came over to Kyam and leaned close to his ear. "The widow asked that I escort you out of here. She thinks it's disrespectful that you came. Do me a favor and walk out with us."

"I arrested someone for his murder."

"You took his post as Governor. Guess which one she thinks is more important?" Voorus asked.

Kyam caught her eye across the room and bowed. She lifted her chin and looked away. Relieved to be excused, Kyam followed Mityam and Voorus out of the salon.

Several of the guests had spilled out of the dining room into the foyer, clutching small plates piled high with food. Kyam gestured for Voorus to come out to the courtyard with him where they could speak privately. Mityam shuffled toward the dining room with an anticipatory gleam in his eye.

More guests had taken over the pavilion by the pond. Finding a place for a quick, private chat was proving more difficult than he'd anticipated.

"I take it the widow blames me for her husband's death," Kyam whispered.

Voorus nodded.

"She didn't look too upset."

Voorus spread his hands. "Up close, it's easier to see. She might not have loved him, or even liked him, but she seems stunned."

"Is it real or faked?"

"I have no idea. Not everyone is as skilled of an actor as QuiTai, but everyone lies to some extent."

"Do me a favor and try to find out," Kyam said.

Voorus nodded. "I'll listen and keep an eye out for anything strange. We'll probably stay for at least another hour. Meet us at my place after that." He glanced around the courtyard. "How is your investigation coming?"

Kyam didn't want to admit he hadn't learned much. "I have QuiTai's people out looking for PhaSun. She may know something."

"PhaSun?" Voorus winced.

"You know her?"

Voorus tugged on his earlobe until it was nearly as pink as his cheeks. "Took me a while to figure out that everything she said was ear poison, because she seemed like a fun person, but I got tired of hearing that the whole world was out to get her. Everyone is jealous. Life isn't fair. You know the type. Hirun, a captain in the militia, is like that too. You start out sympathetic, but soon you'd gladly chew off your arm to get away from them. PhaSun hits, too. Hard. Throws a temper tantrum faster than a tidal wave sweeps on shore." He pulled back his hair to show a faint scar above his brow. "I didn't dodge fast enough."

Kyam slipped his hands into his trouser pockets as the gate of the Turyat family compound slammed shut behind him, and strolled down the shaded lane. This line of inquiry might lead to a solution in the jellylantern serials, but it didn't feel right. He didn't think Turyat's widow was a murderer. The problem, he decided as he tapped a pebble with the toe of his boot, was that there were too many possibilities. Levapur seemed like such a dull place on the surface, but underneath, it was rotten with strange hidden alliances. Why had the widow picked Voorus to evict him from the funeral? Were they friends? And when had Voorus and QuiTai become such good pals? For that matter, how had she been able to entice Mityam Muul to a place like this? What about Lizzriat? Were he and QuiTai only flirting, or was there more to it than that?

No. He had to stop thinking about it. He did not care. QuiTai was going to become one of those memories old men dragged out of keepsake boxes on winter nights. He was going to figure out who murdered Turyat and release her from the fortress; then she would keep her end of the bargain, and he'd be on a junk bound for Thampur by the end of the week and she'd be out of his life.

Nashruu wasn't going to like it. She'd just arrived in Levapur. He hadn't sent for her, of course – Grandfather had ordered her to come. She probably had several assignments. If he left the island, would she feel as if she had to follow him back home? Probably not. It wasn't as if he mattered to her, especially considering how he'd treated her this morning.

Kyam made a face. He shouldn't have abandoned her at the house. That was behavior unworthy of him. The poor woman had walked off a junk into a new life, and he'd left her to face it alone. Ashamed of himself, he turned toward home.

As he walked through the foyer, he glimpsed Nashruu's son in through the parlor door. The boy's tongue stuck out as he concentrated on the instrument balanced on his lap. A tutor hovered and pounced on each wrong note with a tut of disapproval. Kyam flexed his hand as he remembered his piano teacher hitting him at every mistake. All he'd learned from those lessons was to hate music. The boy was Nashruu's concern, of course, but he'd speak with the tutor sometime soon about acceptable discipline. No one was going to have their hands smacked under his roof.

Nashruu appeared on the top landing of the main staircase. She paused to adjust her hat and turned to speak to someone he couldn't see in the upstairs hallway. Kyam darted toward his office and hoped she hadn't seen him. As he closed the sliding door to his office, he shook his head. She was a perfectly nice person, from what little he knew of her. Running from her was cowardly. Doing it twice in one day was downright rude.

Before he could work up the courage to open the door, Nashruu did it for him. "Oh, there you are," she said.

Kyam retreated behind his desk. "Yes. Here I am." He cleared his throat. "I know that we haven't spoken since you arrived, and we should talk, soon, but I'm quite busy at the moment."

Uninvited, she sat in a chair. "You just returned, husband.

How could you be too absorbed to set it aside for a moment?"

Despite the pleasant expression on her face, he could have sworn there was some malice in the way she said 'husband.' Maybe she'd decided to blame him for her life. It had been explained to her, and they'd both agreed to the arrangement; but that was years ago, and maybe the deal didn't look so good now. That wasn't his fault, though, and he was miserable too —although it didn't take a genius to see that she was trapped in ways no man ever could be.

He had to start treating her better. Wasn't that why he'd come here rather than to his office in the government building? "Are your rooms to your liking?"

"You did a lovely job furnishing them. Thank you. That was kind of you, Kyam. I feel quite at home."

At least one of them did.

That was the sum of what he had to say to her. They were complete strangers. He wondered if she found this as awkward as he did. "And how was your voyage?"

"I believe we had this conversation already."

Now he swore he saw a glimmer of humor in her expression. It irritated him that she could mock him and still be so perfectly polite. It was almost like talking to QuiTai, only it could never be the same. Never.

"How dark it is in here. One wonders how you read. Shall I have the servants bring more jellylanterns?" she asked.

The dark wood bookshelves built into the walls, the ponderous desk, and even the carpet seemed to absorb light. Except for the ceiling fans, his office looked like a miniature version of their Grandfather's study. He'd only used it twice since the house had been refurbished, and both times to hide from people.

"No. The lighting is fine."

"Good, because I have yet to find a servant of yours in this place. Except the Ponongese kitchen staff. They're quite nice, although they don't speak much Thampurian. They don't seem to know where the house servants are either."

"The staff I imported went back home after only a month

here, or they abandoned their posts for other work."

"Are you that horrible to work for?"

"You'll soon learn that the trials of keeping Thampurian servants is a favorite topic at dinner parties here. Back home, many of the lower castes work as servants, but here, it's seen as Ponongese work. The general consensus is that you have to hire someone sent here in disgrace, and you have to have enough to blackmail them into…"

"Into what?"

A glimmer of an idea shone brightly in Kyam's mind. If Turyat had been blackmailing one of his servants into staying-- like that scoundrel at his gate-- that was a good motive to kill him. The only problem was that Turyat was too much of an addict to be a real threat to anyone's reputation. His wife, on the other hand, probably knew all sorts of wicked things about her staff and could wield that knowledge like a spiked war club.

He sighed. "Into staying in servitude. Never mind. I had a thought, but it was wrong."

She seemed perfectly willing to let him keep his thoughts to himself. "But the house is so tidy. Don't tell me you dusted and made the beds yourself."

"I hired relatives of the cooks to come through here yesterday and put everything in order."

"They did an excellent job. Maybe I should simply hire them, if Thampurian servants are too scarce."

He sucked in his breath through his teeth. "There would be talk," he said slowly. "You'd be considered an original or naive by most people here. It would be a brave move on your part."

"Funny. She said much the same thing to me earlier today."

A bad feeling settled in Kyam's stomach. "Who?"

"Lady QuiTai."

His stomach dropped the rest of the way. Nashruu seemed oblivious to the social disaster she'd set in motion. How could she be so pleased with herself? He struggled to suppress his temper and dread. A real Thampurian husband would have scolded her as if she were a stupid child, but Grandfather had selected her as his agent in Levapur, and Grandfather would never place his trust in an idiot.

Her glance was almost coquettish as her fingers traced the arm of her chair. "Aren't you curious? Do you want to know if we gossiped about you?"

"Surely two women of your caliber could find something more interesting to talk about than me."

If she were surprised by his reply, she hid it well. "When Lady QuiTai turned to you for help before the rice riot, Grandfather became convinced you two were lovers. He primed me for an ugly little squabble over you. The injured wife versus the evil mistress. That sort of thing." She clasped her hands together and leaned forward with shining eyes. "I think he looked forward to it, and now I shall have to disappoint him. Honestly, I mentioned you only once and she didn't so much as bat an eyelash. Poor Kyam. A discarded conquest."

"If you're that worried about Grandfather, make something up. If you're worried about my pride, don't be."

Her lips formed a little moue of pity for him, but he doubted she cared about the state of his heart. "In Thampur, QuiTai would hire away my cook and whisper that I use cosmetics if she wanted to destroy me socially. I'm not acquainted with Ponongese-style revenge. What should I tell Grandfather she did to me?"

He owed her for having abandoned her earlier. This one time, he'd help her; but after this, she was on her own. "It's a mistake to assume Lady QuiTai behaves in any way like a normal Ponongese."

"Well, then, what would she do if she hated me?"

"Kill you."

Shocked into silence, Nashruu snapped her mouth shut. It pleased him in a grim way. Hadn't Grandfather warned her about how ruthless QuiTai could be?

"She arranged the deaths of those werewolves, but–" She was still flustered.

"Oh, she wouldn't kill you over me. As you said, I'm only a discarded conquest. It would have to be something important, something she cared about deeply, before she'd bother to make you bleed. That's when you know you've arrived. But trust me when I say that she's dangerous. You have no idea who you're tangling with."

Nashruu seemed to be collecting herself quickly, but not nearly as fast as she'd need to when she dealt with QuiTai.

She cleared her throat. "But she's in no position to negotiate anything, now that she's been accused of the former governor's murder."

The bad feelings piled on top of each other. Why was Nashruu talking about negotiations? Was she trying to cut in on his deal with QuiTai?

"So you know about the murder," he said.

"It was all the talk when I went to that pastry shop near the bank."

"You're been busy."

"Grandfather likes results."

It was like being back in Thampur. Sometimes, he hated that place. The humidity in Ponong during monsoon season made the air seem to weigh heavily on his lungs, but it was nowhere near as stifling as the atmosphere in the salons of Surrayya.

"Why did you go to the fortress?"

"About an hour after you deserted me in our courtyard, Grandfather ordered me to visit her. We had tea and cakes, and talked about the murder, among other things."

He would have laughed at the image conjured in his imagination if matters hadn't been so dire. "Thus the visit to the pastry shop."

She nodded.

"How'd your meeting with Lady QuiTai go?"

She glanced away.

"Don't feel bad. I know you're used to living in a world where Grandfather controls all, knows all, and wins all, but this isn't Thampur. She will eventually beat you and, you will never even see it coming. Ask Grandfather about that."

A thought dawned on Nashruu. He could read that much from her face. She'd have to learn to control her expressions better.

"You respect her," she said.

He wasn't sure how he felt about QuiTai anymore, but every time her name was mentioned, his emotions roiled.

"Grandfather respects her too," she said.

"That alone should warn you what sort of person you're dealing with."

Nashruu leaned forward. "What does she want? I can't even figure out how she thinks."

Damn it. Grandfather was up to something. He wasn't sure if he should ask Nashruu about it.

Nashruu slapped her glove in her lap as if she'd lost patience already. She'd never last if she thought things happened quickly, especially in Levapur. Every action had a reaction, but it was delayed, or muffled, or oblique. In Levapur, you pushed, and then ran for cover and waited for the pendulum to swing back at your head, no matter how long it took.

"She must want something," Nashruu said.

"For herself? I have no idea."

"Would you tell me if you did?"

He had to be careful here. "I wasn't aware that you and I were enemies."

"You and Grandfather have suffered a rift. I'm his agent in Levapur now, although you probably don't need to be told that. You might feel that puts us at odds, but I'm more than willing to work with you when our interests are similar."

She'd been tutored by Grandfather for years. The training showed. He shouldn't underestimate her, ever. Yet rather than being more guarded, he relaxed. Marriage was beyond him, but professional relationships he understood. "I don't know what QuiTai needs or wants. I don't think anyone knows her well enough to answer that question. She's not the chatty type."

"You'd think her life would be enough leverage, but she turned down my offer to save her from the noose."

Save QuiTai? That was his job.

He couldn't say that out loud, though. He couldn't even hint at it, because she'd report it back to Grandfather, and the old man would try to use it to get him back under his control.

He leaned back in his chair and crossed his legs. "It seems her life would be the ultimate bargaining tile, but it wasn't, was it? Sometimes, I think she doesn't particularly care if she lives or dies. After Jezereet, and her daughter and her parents..."

He realized the truth of what he said as the words came out of his mouth. It gave him pause to think that QuiTai might be willing to die. Might want to. How hard had this last year been for her?

Nashruu huffed as she slouched. "So she doesn't want anything? How can I negotiate with that?"

"I didn't say she doesn't want anything. I said there's nothing I can think of that she wants for herself. What she wants, I think, is justice."

Nashruu slowly rose to her feet. The expression on her face looked a lot like QuiTai during one of her *aha* moments. The similarity unnerved him. What if he was married to the Thampurian version of QuiTai?

Once Nashruu had a thought, she evidently ran with it. She ignored him as she mused aloud. "Of course! She's Qui. Grandfather told me the Qui clan's goddess is the Oracle of Justice, or Vengeance. I'm not sure of the exact translation. Grandfather used the words interchangeably. QuiTai was raised to think of herself as the vessel of justice. So all I have to do..."

Kyam dreaded the words that weren't spoken. Nashruu's building excitement worried him. Who was this woman he was married to? What was she thinking? If he stared at her long enough, would he figure it out?

"By the way, Kyam, I know you're at odds with Grandfather, but don't even think of meddling in this to get even with him."

"Revenge would never be my motivation."

That was a lie so big he was embarrassed by it. Of course he'd get revenge on his Grandfather if he could. He waited for her to call him out on it, but she was completely wrapped up in thoughts of QuiTai. He could almost commiserate with her.

He wondered what deal she was trying to make with QuiTai. What would Grandfather want with QuiTai this time?

And why would he send Nashruu to get it? What special powers of persuasion did Nashruu have?

As he watched Nashruu's agitated pacing, something nagged at the back of his mind. There was something different about her. It wasn't only her manner. His breath caught as he watched his wife cross the room. "You changed clothes."

She gave him a look as if he were an idiot. "And here I thought men never noticed such things."

He pointed at her. "You were in a different outfit this morning."

The idea dawning on him was terrible. He slowly rose from his chair. Had QuiTai tricked him? He felt a little queasy. A bit embarrassed. And heartsick.

No. He wasn't heartsick. He was over her, and she'd never draw his soul's blood again.

He had to turn off his emotions and be logical. That was the way to get through this day.

There was no way QuiTai could have been at the harbor and at the Red Happiness at the same time. She couldn't have killed Turyat. But why had she changed clothes? Not just once, but twice.

Nashruu stared at him. "You're onto something."

He knew where his investigation had to go now. His fingers fumbled with the top button of his jacket.

"Whatever you're doing, don't you dare interfere with my mission, Kyam. Grandfather will crush you."

"Pardon me. Have to go." He slipped past her, through the door, and was running at full stride by the time he reached the courtyard.

CHAPTER 13: IN QUITAI'S OFFICE

*K*yam stepped around Ponongese women caning the seats and backs of damaged chairs on the veranda of the Red Happiness. Inside, several people on their hands and knees were sanding the old finish from the floor. The smell of fresh paint was strong. Another group was pasting the wallpaper's curling corners to the plaster. Even the brothel's workers had been put to work on the banister and stairs.

Inattra watched Kyam pick his way around the newly stained patches on the floor from behind the bar. He plunged a glass into a bucket of steaming, soapy water and wiped it with a rag before rinsing it in another pail. "How can I help you, Governor Zul?"

"I have a few more questions."

Inattra sighed heavily.

"I know you're busy, so I'll be quick. Early this morning, Lady QuiTai was seen on the veranda in a yellow dress in the newest continental style: a military style jacket and a narrow skirt."

"I'm aware of the latest fashions in Rantuum."

Kyam ignored the sour tone. "An hour later, she was at the harbor in her traditional green sarong. Now, I know that she doesn't tell anyone where she sleeps, and she has many safe houses around Levapur, but she didn't have much time to change clothes, so she may have done it here. Does she keep a room in the brothel?"

"No."

Kyam scratched his brow. "You do realize that I'm trying to help her, don't you?"

"Yes."

When had Ingosolians become so tight-lipped? An ugly idea sprouted in his mind. What would happen to the brothel if QuiTai were to die? She didn't own it; Jezereet's sibling did. But that sibling, Evoreet, had never been to Levapur, as far as Kyam knew, so he'd probably let Inattra continue to run the place.

"How much more do you make as the Madam here than you did as a worker?" Kyam asked.

Inattra's freckles flushed a deeper shade of blue.

"I know money is a sensitive topic," Kyam said.

Inattra's short bark of laughter made him wince. As the scion of one of the richest families on the continent and colonial Governor, those words took on a completely different meaning when they came from him.

"QuiTai said I can still take customers even though I'm the Madam, and sometimes I do, but not often. I don't need to."

QuiTai had a reputation for paying her people well, so that didn't surprise him. Still, for some people, no stack of coins would ever be high enough. He tried to remember how many tables and chairs had been in the bar before, and used that number to calculate what the bar might bring in. How many rooms were upstairs, and how often were they used per night? Plus the take from the liquor and drug sales… and maybe he was wrong, but that added up to a tidy sum. Take away the average rent for a building this size and the worker's cut, and there was still quite a bit left over.

"This place mills coin faster than a mint, doesn't it?" he said.

Inattra seemed even more wary. "We do all right."

"Have you ever thought of opening your own place?"

Inattra picked up another glass and dunked it into the suds. "It's a big, bad world out there, Governor. PhaJut's brothel was robbed last month. His workers and customers were roughed up by a gang of men. Thampurian men, but ones not often seen in town."

"From the plantations?"

"Two months ago, the Madam of the Pink Orchid was murdered by a customer. Here, I enjoy QuiTai's protection. No one in this town would be stupid enough to bring that kind of violence under this roof. Other than the damage the militia did here this morning, of course. I'm paid twice what the Madams of the other brothels make, QuiTai doesn't charge rent for my room, and I don't have an owner's headaches. Ask anyone in the Quarter of Delights and they'll tell you my job is the best one in Levapur." He rested his hands on the edge of the bar. "But only a fool would want it."

"Why is that?"

Inattra sighed again. "I'm exaggerating. It's been a difficult day."

Kyam made a sympathetic noise.

Inattra licked his lips as he squinted at Kyam. After a long moment, he seemed to have reached a decision. "QuiTai has standards that no one else would demand from their workers. They aren't impossible to meet, and she rewards people who uphold them, but sometimes it's a huge pain in my ass. Most people don't have any idea how meticulous she is. Some of the workers here grumble about how I don't do anything but flit around the room and chat with our guests every night as if I'm at a party. They crawl into bed when the last customer leaves; I'm still awake two hours later doing the books. They rise after noon and have a leisurely breakfast while their rooms miraculously clean themselves. The bar is always stocked, problem customers magically go away, the jellylanterns never fade, and the floor is never sticky. Sometimes, I think QuiTai is the only person who appreciates what I do." His expression hardened. "Some lazy little liar may think she can take my place, but I'm not going anywhere, and if she does get me fired, she's going to learn real fast that it isn't as easy as she thinks."

Every business had internal squabbles, Kyam supposed. The bickering in the government building was deafening at times, so why should the Red Happiness be any different? He didn't have time for workplace gossip, though. There was a murder to solve.

"About QuiTai – if she doesn't have a room here, where might she change clothes?"

Inattra jerked his thumb toward the splintered door to QuiTai's office. "She has a wardrobe in there."

"I need to have a look."

"And I suppose I need to accompany you, because QuiTai would never forgive me if I ever let someone in there without watching them. Make it quick, Governor. I have a lot of work to do before we open tonight."

QuiTai's office door swung open part way and then rebounded toward Kyam. It wouldn't open further no matter how hard he pushed against it. Splinters snagged his trousers as he sucked in his breath to slip inside.

The small room was well lit by jellylanterns. It had no windows and only the one door, although he assumed at least one hidden passage had been built into the walls, because QuiTai would never leave herself only one escape route.

A tall iron safe stood behind the door. From the deep drag marks in the flooring, someone had tried to move it but had given up. Scrapes on the metal dial and around the edges of the safe door showed futile efforts to pry it open.

"The militia did that too," Inattra told him. "The plan was to carry it down to the fortress so they'd have time to figure out the combination."

"Too heavy?"

"That, and one of them was smart enough to measure the doorway before they tried to push it through." He knocked on the door frame. "She had this made of metal too, so they couldn't saw away the wood. This room was built around the safe. They could push it back and forth over the floor all day, but they'd never get it out of the room, and it would take months to try all the combinations."

"But you know it?"

Inattra showed him bruises ringing his wrist. "That's what the militia thought. I use the smaller safe inside the wardrobe. The soldiers didn't even look for it. Once they saw the behemoth, they focused on that. I'm lucky they didn't try to beat the combination out of me."

"Why didn't they?"

"They got in a few blows before I lost my temper and shifted masculine. They recognized testosterone-fueled rage when they saw it. My muscles ripped my best jacket into rags." He squeezed his biceps. "We Madams have to deal with belligerent drunks all the time. We make sure we have the strength to beat them. The militia is no different from a drunk – except drunks rarely rob you."

Kyam knew he should do something about the militia's thuggery, but soon they would be another Governor's problem.

"It's not that I don't care what the militia did, but I have to concentrate on the murder. Can you come in here and tell me if anything strikes you as odd?" Kyam asked.

Inattra's slim frame easily slipped around the door. They stood shoulder to shoulder and looked at QuiTai's office.

It was difficult to know where to look first. The far wall was covered in clocks, most of their workings exposed. The pendulums were swinging out of synch, and he had to resist the urge to force them into unison.

Books filled every shelf of the bookcases. Many were stacked on top of other books. He knew QuiTai spoke several languages, so it didn't surprise him that the math, science, and technological manuals seemed to come from every country on the continent. That didn't interest him as much as the fantasies on the opposite shelves. People might call them toys, but the beautiful mechanical gadgets were so much more. Inventors in Ingosol built scale models of their machines to show potential investors. Some were crafted by professors to demonstrate concepts to their students, but others, such as the motion picture viewer on the middle shelf, were sold in stores.

He could have spent all day exploring her private collection. It was a rare insight into the most private person he'd ever met. If only Inattra would go away and let him absorb this peek inside QuiTai's brain! But the mismatched ticking from the wall of clocks reminded him that he didn't have time for that.

The scale model of a rigid balloon sat in pieces on a side table. Kyam thought at first that the militia had broken it, but then he saw the journal with sketches of the parts underneath the model. Beside the drawings were formulas and notes that went to the bottom of the page and then turned up the side and continued. He moved a set of tiny gears off the page and lifted the journal to show Inattra.

"I don't recognize this alphabet. Do you?" he asked.

Inattra shrugged. "Maybe it's Ponongese."

He set the journal down. "They don't have a written language."

Inattra gingerly reached out to touch the motion picture viewer. "These were Jezereet's. QuiTai was always bringing them to her. Sweets, too, imported all the way from Rantuum. Jezereet wouldn't eat them, so she always gave them to us. Jez didn't like the fantasies and follies either." He sounded wistful. "I can't imagine being loved like that. I can't imagine being loved like that and not caring."

Inattra turned around and leaned against the cabinet. "I knew Jez back in Rantuum. Not friends, you understand, but our social circles overlapped. He– She– Your genders are too clumsy for my people, too limited. *She* was amazing. So talented. Black lotus stole that from her. Toward the end, all she cared about was her next pipe, and I had to watch QuiTai desperately try to distract Jez from it, even though she had to know it was useless. Vapor is evil. I won't touch it. I don't stop the workers here from offering it to their customers, but it makes my skin crawl to have it under the roof."

More gossip. They were determined to distract him.

Kyam pointed to the empty desktop. "Anything odd here?"

"The desk is always bare like that. She demands that everything be put away in the safe, even if I leave the office for only a minute."

"But not her journal?"

"I can't read that. Can you? She doesn't need to hide it. Business records and coins are another matter. Things like that you don't leave out."

"Are the records in the big safe only for the Red Happiness?"

Inattra snorted. "Do you actually think I'd tell you if QuiTai kept details of her network in there too? Do you think I'd dare look at anything I wasn't supposed to? She's not stupid enough to leave that sort of information around where anyone could see it. She's careful, always. Never slips."

"She doesn't trust you?"

"Don't try to sow discord, Governor. I know my place. She trusts me within the scope of my job, and that's all I care about. She doesn't give people a chance to betray her. If I messed up the things she entrusts to me here, she'd shove me out in the street so fast I wouldn't have time to blink. I have no illusions about that. But at least this job is all I have to worry about."

"You expect me to believe she's never once let anything accidentally slip in front of you? Not once?"

Inattra glanced away and fiddled with the side propellers on the rigid balloon. "I occasionally hear about her business outside the Red Happiness, but I don't want to disappear like some other people I could name, so don't even bother asking what it was that I heard." He walked to the wardrobe beside the settee and yanked open the door. "Now find what you came for and go. We're both trying to beat the sun, so let's get out of each other's way."

Kyam was tempted to turn around and leave. So what if QuiTai had changed clothes? She'd obviously been down at the wharf for a reason, and if that reason was to meet Mityam Muul, she most certainly would have worn her finest continental fashion. So why had she changed?

It probably didn't matter.

No matter how hard he tried to convince himself of that, he couldn't believe it. QuiTai always played to her audience. She was always aware of costume and script. He'd watched her try to climb the veranda stairs in that ridiculously tight skirt that bound her legs. But she hadn't frowned until that subtle double-take at her sleeve.

Did he really want to know why? Would it tell him who murdered Turyat?

He clenched his jaw and strode to the wardrobe. Inattra folded his arms across his chest.

She'd hung the jacket and skirt in the wardrobe. Her scent wafted to him as he touched the jacket. He lifted the sleeve so the light fell on the raw silk. His eyes closed. It wouldn't change the truth, but he could pretend for a moment it was mud, or tamtuk grease – anything except what he knew it was.

How could he have been so stupid as to believe in her? It was what he'd most feared he'd find. He tore the jacket from the hanger. His temper was on the boil, and a storm was gathering in his mind. With a grunt of dismissal, he stomped past Inattra, who flattened against the wall to get out of his way.

CHAPTER 14: A DUNGEON MEETING

There weren't any soldiers guarding the dungeon. Kyam feared they'd already executed QuiTai – although the way he felt, he could do it himself. She'd fooled him for the last time.

He grabbed a jellylantern from the hook on the wall and stomped down the stairs. Oh, the things he would say to her! Terrible words welled up on his tongue.

Maybe it was his imagination, but it seemed far darker in the dungeon than it had been earlier. There was only one jellylantern down there now.

"I assumed that when they locked you in a dungeon cell, you spent your time either being tortured or in isolation. That only goes to show how wrong I was. There's a constant stream of visitors down here. Hello, Governor. Have you eaten today?" QuiTai asked.

He squinted until he saw her shadowy form. She was sitting against the far wall with her head tipped back. She rose and walked toward him. Her hair fell to her knees in twisting, fuzzy locks as if she were a child. Kyam knew how much she hated being seen like that. He was angry enough with her that it made him happy, although he wondered which soldier had been brave enough to force her to let it down.

"Oh, dear. A storm seems to have settled on your brow and you're swelling with outrage. Could it be you have come here to scold me, Kyam?"

He flung the jacket at her face.

"That would have been much more effective if the cell bars weren't in the way. Would you like to open my cell so you can try again?"

He hated it when she mocked him like that. He ground his fist into his palm. "I might lose control and leave fingerprints on your lovely throat like the Devil does."

Her smirk faded. This must be what she looked like when she killed: absolutely calm, in control, and without a trace of humanity in her eyes. "I'd like to see you try, Governor Zul."

"That's a neat trick. Have you been practicing with the acoustics in here?"

"What trick?"

"The way you make it sound as if there's something in the dark corners down here, and the way your voice slithers behind me and makes the hair at the back of my neck stand up."

It wasn't her voice that was giving him chills despite the heat. She looked like a vengeful surkraim spirit, half drowned and full of malignant fury. But he was the one with the right to be angry here, not her.

She pulled the jacket through the bars and examined the ripped seam at the shoulder as she walked to the back of her cell.

"Don't you turn your back on me, QuiTai! Don't you dare." His chest rose and fell quickly as he glowered at her. He knew most of his anger was about humiliation, even though he'd duped himself. The shame was almost unbearable, so he lashed out at her as if it were her fault.

Her head turned, but not enough that she could look at

him. It reminded him of the day they'd first met. If he'd known how treacherous she was, would he have spent so much time trying to figure her out? Yes, a thousand times yes, because even though he knew she was poison, he couldn't resist her.

"There's blood on that sleeve," he said.

She turned to face him. "Yes."

What could he do with that? He realized he'd hoped she would lie. "It makes you look damn guilty."

"Do you want me to explain it away to ease your mind?"

How did she say what he was feeling when even he couldn't put it into words? "It's not like that."

"Yes, it is, Kyam."

He took a deep breath. "Why can't you ever answer a question? Why is there blood spatter on your sleeve? You always dress in continental fashions when you're dealing with Thampurians, but today, you changed from this outfit into a sarong before you went down to the harbor."

"I did?"

"You were seen."

What was that flicker that crossed her face? Fear? Concern? It went away too quickly for him to figure it out.

He gritted his teeth. "Why did you change clothes?"

"There, now. Was it so hard to ask me in a reasonable tone?"

Did she have any idea how irritating she was? He couldn't let her get the better of him. He had to calm down. "The blood. Explain it."

She lifted a finger. "Before I do, I feel a preliminary discussion is called for."

"One of your word games?"

"A word game? Yes and no. I prefer to think of it as clarification," she said.

"You would."

"Do you want to know about the blood, or do you want to know specifically if it's Turyat's? Keeping in mind that you only have a few hours left to find his killer. If you fail, you lose your only chance at freedom."

No one could be that infuriating by accident. He ran his hand over his hair as he counted to ten a few times.

A low growl, or maybe it was a groan, echoed through the dungeon. Was she mocking him? He felt like growling back at her. But how did she do that? It had to be a stage trick.

"It's—"

"No, it isn't the same thing, Kyam, if that's what you were about to say. Far be it from me to tell you what to think, but if I were trying to figure out what happened in the Red Happiness this morning, I'd limit the scope of my questions to Turyat's death."

His mouth snapped shut. Lizzriat had told him to narrow his focus too. Did he want to know more? He was never sure. "I know you're up to something. It's always a game with you."

Her gaze traveled slowly down his face to his chest. By the time it reached his thighs, he had to take a deep breath and close his eyes for a moment.

"Of course it's a game for me. That's a given. You want to find Turyat's real killer, so you can get me out of here and use me to buy your freedom. I'm not quite ready to leave the fortress, though, so I'm not going to give you the answer."

"And what do you want? Why are you here?"

She was like the surface of a calm lake, reflecting sky rather than let anyone peer into its depths. "I wanted you to investigate the murders of my lieutenants and bring their killers to trial. I asked you to stop Cuulon from arresting my people for simply gathering in the marketplace and during our festivals. But I had to settle for this."

That stung. "There is no such thing as justice, QuiTai. No one gets it."

She grabbed the cell bars and looked up at him. "We should still try."

For once, she wasn't cold or distant. She looked now like an actress playing a surkraim spirit, as if the mask was floating above her true face and only he could see beyond it. What he saw was worry and sorrow. She'd started down a grim path and was determined to see it to the end, no matter the cost.

Maybe he could bend a little and do this her way.

"Is the blood on that sleeve Turyat's?" he asked.

"Ah! You've decided to focus on the right questions. No, the blood isn't Turyat's. And to anticipate your next question, it has nothing to do with his death."

His relief was telling. He cared much more than he'd admitted to himself. "If you say so."

"I'm here to help, Governor."

A slow smile spread across his face. This was like before, when they'd worked together. He shouldn't have been so happy. "Of course you are. Your lovely neck never entered into it, sweetheart."

She batted her eyelashes at him.

"So... Do you have any idea what happened at the Red Happiness this morning?" Kyam asked QuiTai.

He wasn't sure if she was acting again or if she was truly reluctant to answer him. She rubbed one hand over another. Emotions cast shadows over her face in a constant kaleidoscope unlike her usual serene mask. The deliberations clearly made her unhappy. "I've been giving it serious thought since I heard he'd been killed. I have a theory," she finally admitted.

"I'd like to hear it."

QuiTai shook her head. "As you often say to me, 'It's an interesting story, but where's the proof?'"

"And as I told you once, I'd take your theories over most people's 'facts' any day."

She stepped back from the bars and hugged her arms. "We shouldn't work together. You have to know that you have the true answer."

"But I'm too damn slow, and you're running out of time! At least give me a hint."

"Don't tempt me."

"You pick the oddest things to be stubborn about."

Was that the real reason he'd come to her? Maybe he'd wanted her to convince him that he could believe in her innocence, despite what he'd found.

He had no idea how to investigate a murder. He didn't

know what to do next. Time was slipping away, and if he ran off in the wrong direction, he'd waste what little he had. How did the police solve crimes? They asked questions. They verified answers. He could do that; but how did anyone know what questions to ask?

For a moment, he thought she might speak, but she frowned and slightly shook her head. Why wouldn't she give him a hint?

"Listen, these are your options, as far as I know. You probably have something else up your sleeve," he told her.

Did she react a little? He couldn't be sure.

"Either you help me, or you take Grandfather's deal. I don't know what he's offering you, but it can't be good."

"He wants me to work for him."

A horrible suspicion dropped on him. Was he racing against Nashruu to recruit QuiTai? What would happen if he lost? "Grandfather wants you to work for him? Not for Thampurian Intelligence?"

She shook her head.

"Doesn't that strike you as a bit treasonous?"

"Maybe to you, since you're now bidding against him for my help. Oh, calm down. You and I have a deal, and I'm not about to ruin my hard-earned reputation by breaking it. However, if you fail to hold up your end, I'd be free to accept a better offer."

"I'm working on it. If you'd help me..." He realized that wasn't going to work. She wanted him to find the real murderer, but not because it would get her out of the fortress. He had to know with steadfast certainty that she was innocent. Unless he found the answer himself, he'd always have a bit of doubt. What a risk she was taking!

Kyam wanted to be flattered that she wanted him to have faith in her, but he couldn't help being angry that she was gambling with his freedom.

"Your arrest couldn't have come at a better time for Grandfather. He has much more power than I do to get you out of here."

"But does he have the power to figure out who murdered

Turyat? I think you have the edge there."

He acknowledged her compliment with a sour smile. Too many things were happening too fast, and he'd been asleep while everyone else set their plots in motion.

"It's probably pure coincidence that Nashruu arrived the day Turyat was murdered. Remember, the old man plays a long, long game. He's patient. Nashruu all but admitted that she was sent here to woo me for him. She's an interesting person, by the way. I liked her," QuiTai said.

"Apart from your obvious charms — and by that, I mean your network of informants and smugglers — why would Grandfather try to recruit you?" Kyam asked.

"There is that pesky war looming on the horizon."

"War on the continent. You're a thousand miles from the battlefields of the last war."

"Different war, different battles. Don't discount the strategic importance of the Ponong Fangs. Thampur chased the Ravidians out of the Sea of Erykoli during the last war, making trade with the rest of the continent almost impossible. They want back in. Their economy relies on it."

"Their caravans still come over the desert."

"Caravans are inefficient and are pirated more often than ships. And before you mention trains, their rail lines are constantly devoured by sand storms or warped by heat in the great salt pans. Ships are the only way to trade with the rest of the continent."

"Thank you for the big picture, but let's focus on the local story. You may be many things, but you can't be the key to stopping the war," he said.

"If anyone would listen to me, they'd avoid it by giving the Ravidians, and anyone else who asks, the charts to the Ponong Fangs. Let them back into the Sea of Erykoli. Don't block the other routes around the Ponong Archipelago. Their excuse for war? Poof. Gone. We all move on."

She was insane. "We're not giving up our charts," he said.

"Then you deserve everything that's coming your way."

He rubbed his forehead. "We were talking about why

everyone in Thampur wants to get their hands on you. Wait! I put that the wrong way."

"I know what you meant."

"I suppose they want you to help with interrogations of spies and enemy soldiers. That psychic bond through your venom – if you injected some of it into a prisoner, you'd feel their physical reactions. At least, that's the rumor. So if you were good enough at reading them, you'd know when they lied, or when they reacted to something. I can see where that would be useful."

"And this, Mister Zul, is why I consider you the most dangerous man I've ever met. In all my life, I've never known any other Thampurian to figure that out. They get as far as the sexual possibilities, and then their minds wander off into the vast jungle of lust never to return again. But you, you have vision. You always make that leap beyond."

He was quite pleased with himself.

"But you're wrong. I mean, that *should* be why they want me; but as I said, they're lust-addled idiots. Your Grandfather has another of my rumored talents in mind for exploitation, and I'm going to assume someone in Intelligence is after me for the same reason. The funny thing is that it's the fake talent."

"You're going to have to remind me what this fake talent is."

"They think I can see the future."

"You can't?"

She shook her head and quietly said, "No."

"I've seen you predict many things that came true."

"I'm a good guesser, but so are carnival hustlers and con artists."

"You know I'm going to deliver you to them even if you are a fake," he said.

"As well you should. Deliver what they asked for. If it doesn't work out, it's not your problem."

"I could swear you almost want to work with them."

She made a face that made him uneasy. Maybe she did. Who knew what sabotage she had planned?

The muscles along his spine flexed when he heard something big move in the far, dark corner. He lifted the jellylantern and took a few steps toward the sound.

QuiTai spoke so quietly he had to turn back and lean close to hear her. "Pay attention, because this may be my only chance to share this information with you."

"You changed your mind?"

She still seemed reluctant to speak. "I won't tell you who murdered Turyat, but I'll tell you what happened leading up to his death. Late morning, I found Turyat and Cuulon passed out on the veranda at the Red Happiness. Turyat woke as I opened the shutters and followed me inside."

That was what he'd seen.

"Turyat begged me for black lotus and even threatened me, but I turned him down."

"Is it true that you forbade anyone to sell black lotus to him, practically torturing him with his addiction?"

"Yes."

She didn't hesitate a moment about admitting that. She looked him right in the eyes. Killing Turyat would have been an act of mercy on her part, and she wasn't the merciful type. Torture was more her style. He couldn't blame her, though. And Cuulon should be careful. QuiTai might be biding her time, but eventually, she'd find a way to torment him too.

"While Turyat was bothering me, PhaSun came creeping down the staircase. She about jumped out of her skin when she saw me there."

"PhaSun again? Inattra mentioned he had to practically pull PhaSun out of the street and hide her from the militia."

"Inattra is an excellent employee." Her voice sounded oddly flat.

"He's had a rough day. The militia destroyed the bar and drank all your liquor. He's trying to get the place ready to open by tonight, but he's stopped to help me several times."

"The militia reminds me of Petrof's werewolves. Thugs, all of them. Criminals, really, trying their hand at intimidation. One wonders who their shadowy overlord might be."

"Yes, yes. The militia are bad. I get it. I thought you wanted me to focus on Turyat's murder." Kyam wiped away the bead of sweat trickling down his temple. "Inattra said PhaSun was actually trying to summon the militia. Does that sound right to you?"

QuiTai paced the cell as she pulled at her bottom lip. "It fits my theory. Yes, I can see it. It was a stupid thing to do, but she isn't the smartest person, obviously. I strongly urge you to find her, and soon."

"We're trying. I have RhiHanya and LiHoun working to lure her out of Old Levapur."

"They will," she promised.

His relief at her renewed sense of urgency must have shown.

"You were talking about the Red Happiness. Go on."

"I told PhaSun that I had to go meet a passenger on the *Golden Barracuda* this morning and didn't have time to listen to her try to get Inattra in trouble. I went into my office to change out of my soiled dress – something that I'm surprised you knew about, or did you simply guess from what you know about me?"

If he admitted he'd watched her from behind a tree, it would sound like he'd been spying on her. "I believe I mentioned that you were seen by a witness."

"Oh, yes. I forgot."

The hell she did. She never forgot anything.

"Alas, I didn't have another continental style dress in my wardrobe, so I was forced to change into a sarong. When I came out of my office, Turyat was still there. I'm fairly certain he and Cuulon were waiting on the veranda for PhaSun. My workers don't rise before noon unless there are many coins involved."

He pushed his bangs out of his eyes. It was like standing in an oven down here. He had no idea how QuiTai could look so composed after several hours in the dungeon, especially since she'd been wearing two layers of clothing when he'd brought her here. If it had been acceptable, he would have taken off his jacket.

She was speaking so quickly he was afraid he'd miss something important. He had to solve this mystery and bring the real murderer to the fortress as soon as possible, or the military would execute her for the crime. If only he knew what questions were the right ones to ask. If only she'd answer. If only he'd be able to figure out the truth in spite of her answers.

"Do you think PhaSun was planning to sell Turyat black lotus despite knowing you'd cut him off?"

"I had my suspicions that's what was happening, but since I had to leave and no one else was awake, I didn't feel it was a good time to fire her. She destroyed drapes and a chair when I announced that Inattra would take Jezereet's position as Madam. Quite the temper, that one, and no attempt at self-control. So I didn't tell her that I knew what she was up to. I thought I'd have time to take care of the matter this afternoon."

Every word counted, he reminded himself. He hoped he could remember all this, because she wouldn't be able to resist the temptation to hide clues for him in her story. All he had to do was pick them out.

"I told her that when I returned from the harbor, Turyat had better still be itching for vapor, or someone–" She caught Kyam's gaze and held it. "Someone would lose their job. My exact words: someone."

"Then?"

"I left. Turyat was still alive."

"PhaSun can verify that?"

She spread her hands. "I'm in a difficult spot here. If I want you to believe her when she swears Turyat was alive after I left, I shouldn't mention that she's a troublemaker and a liar. If I want you to ignore aspersions she might cast on Inattra, then I'd want you to know her true character."

"I see. And she won't cast aspersions on you?"

That clearly troubled her. "I can't imagine why she would. If she does, let me know. I may have to reassess."

"If I can't find her soon, you may have to rethink this noble but stupid stance of yours and tell me the solution to this mystery."

"What good does my version do you if you don't have proof? I'm telling you to find the clues – find the proof. Then, if you still have trouble figuring out the story they tell, I will give you my interpretation. But you know as well as I do that you'll never believe I'm innocent unless you prove it to yourself."

"Why does that matter to you?"

"I'm taking the long view here, Kyam. It's a risk. I know that. But it's one I'm willing to take because things are going to get very complicated from here on out. The arrival your wife in Levapur proves that. So does this race to recruit me."

"I don't get it. You want me to start trusting you again because Grandfather sent my wife here?"

"Find PhaSun. Hurry, Kyam. Time is ticking away."

He wanted to ask her so many more things, but she made him feel as if he were falling behind, so he reluctantly left.

By the time he was on the beach, doubt was nagging at him. It seemed as if she'd wanted him to leave her. He couldn't put his finger on any exact thing, but he was sure she'd tricked him somehow. Again.

CHAPTER 15: VOORUS LEARNS THE LAW

Voorus had never given much thought to his living quarters before. He didn't have visitors. But now that Mityam sat in his sagging best chair, the apartment embarrassed him. A dusty spider web hung from the ceiling. His plates were gaudy. The prints that hung on his walls hadn't been popular in a decade. He should have paid extra for a white light jellylantern rather than his usual green, but once he opened the doors to the veranda, natural light overpowered the sickly glow.

Mityam clutched a teacup in his curled fist and stirred in sugar. Voorus thought about offering help, but hesitated. That might be an insult. Not offering to help might be an insult. The entire day had been full of moments like this. He was so on edge that he almost wished QuiTai hadn't hired Mityam to tutor him.

They'd only met several hours before, so the subject of how much help was wanted seemed embarrassingly personal. Maybe in the thirteen families they taught you how to gracefully work through this situation, but the only thing he'd been taught was repulsion for anyone who seemed ill.

He sank into the wingback chair opposite Mityam and kept sinking until his knees were higher than his backside. Maybe he should have picked up some cakes to serve.

"You have something on your mind, Captain," Mityam said.

Voorus immediately blushed. Was he supposed to acknowledge that it took forever for Mityam to climb the stairs? Did a proper Thampurian ignore his guest's struggles? "I'm going to say something that might offend you, but I'm not sure how else it might be said. Unfortunately for us both, it is a matter I feel must be addressed." He rubbed his thighs as he tried to figure out how to say it. "It appeared to me that three flights of stairs were a difficult climb for you, although you know yourself better than I, so please correct me if I'm being presumptuous."

Mityam shrugged, but Voorus thought it was agreement.

"If this is too much for you to do every day, I should probably come to your apartment to study. Unfortunately, I wasn't told that a ground floor apartment would be more convenient for you, so I arranged for a place up one flight."

"I was quite a bit spryer when QuiTai last saw me, and I wasn't exactly forthcoming in our letters." Mischief lit Mityam's eyes as he leaned forward. He confessed with a conspiratorial wink, "I didn't want her to think of me as an old man. Pretty young girls don't talk to you when you look thirty years older than you are in your mind." He tapped his temple.

Did elderly men still think about things like that? He realized with some surprise that Mityam did. The idea that he considered QuiTai a young girl, and someone to flirt with, was too odd for Voorus. He decided to ignore it, as one would any embarrassing social gaffe, and prayed that there wouldn't be any more comments like that.

"I'll find another place for you soon. If only Lady QuiTai were free, I'm sure she'd find something suitable by tomorrow," Voorus stammered.

If only she were free. But she wasn't, and the day was slipping away. What was he doing having tea with a *thiree* instead of helping Kyam find a way to free her?

Voorus hated to be petty, but if QuiTai were executed, who would pay Mityam's fees?

"I noticed that you and Governor Zul call her Lady QuiTai. I wasn't aware that our mutual friend was titled. Is she a native princess? She never mentioned a family name, so many of us suspected she had a secret past. She always had a regal aloofness to her," Mityam said.

Newcomers to Levapur always had strange ideas about the island and the Ponongese. Voorus remembered with some embarrassment things he'd believed even after living in Levapur a few years. "It's not like that. They don't believe in a central authority. How it works, I don't know. It seems like chaos to me. Did you know that if a child knows more about something than everyone else, they will listen to her opinion?"

Mityam seemed as aghast as he'd been.

"Qui is QuiTai's clan name, or her tribe, or something like that. It's confusing at first because Old Levapur is in the ancestral lands of the Pha clan, so it will seem as if half the Ponongese you meet in Levapur have the same name. Pay attention to the second half, so you can tell them apart." Voorus winced. A year or so ago he wouldn't have thought twice about saying something like that, but now that he heard it in his own voice, it sounded so insulting. The Ponongese didn't all look alike.

"Are there many Qui around? Do you called her Lady QuiTai so everyone knows who you're talking about?"

Voorus snorted. "There's no question people will know who you mean if you say QuiTai. And no, there aren't many Qui. Aren't any Qui, I guess. Not since..." He winced at the memories. "I'm not sure why we call her Lady QuiTai. If we were Ponongese, I suppose we'd call her auntie, or grandmother–"

Mityam chuckled. It took Voorus a moment to figure out why, and then he laughed with the old man, because he could imagine the horror on a Thampurian woman's face if anyone hinted she was old enough to have grandchildren. His own grandmother had demanded he call her Aunt Iolya. He wondered now if that was vanity or embarrassment that he was a bastard. He stopped laughing.

"Anyway, I'm not sure who started it, but someone recognized that she's in a class by herself, so they gave her a title befitting her stature."

Mityam couldn't seem to find the words, until he could. "You can't go around handing out titles. Someone might mistake her for real nobility."

It struck Voorus that only a *thiree* would be upset by the idea of someone being treated as their equal. He was shocked when the next realization came to him – that all Thampurians would react the same way if they suspected someone might be treated as if they belonged to a higher caste. Thankfully, the Ponongese could never pass as Thampurian because of their eyes, but when QuiTai wore continental fashions and arranged her hair in upswept curls rather than her braid, she appeared uncomfortably similar to a Thampurian lady of means. He'd been fooled by her once, until she'd raised the heavy mourning veil on her hat. If she ever conquered the curse of her eyes, no one would ever suspect the fanged menace among them. The idea made him shiver.

"It's too bad she isn't a secret princess, though," Mityam grumbled. "I saw her play a bare-breasted native queen once on the stage. Very exotic."

As Mityam's eyebrows wriggled, Voorus tried to picture QuiTai on a stage without a blouse. The mental picture didn't strike him as exotic. In his vision, she looked fearsome, and the audience cowed by her power.

Mityam's eyebrows stopped their lascivious dance to arch. "It bothers you when I speak of this."

"I can't imagine my instructors back in Thampur ever discussing something so racy."

"Instructors? You do mean tutors, don't you?"

There was no use pretending to be someone he wasn't. "No, sir. Only regular school."

"Yes, yes. I've lectured many times to rooms full of young men, so I know that system. It's an efficient way to teach many students at once, but what I dislike about it is that I must make speeches and you must take notes, and then I must test to see what you've memorized. Memorization isn't the same as knowing something, really knowing it and understanding it. You have to take it off the shelf and turn it over and poke inside it to learn what it means. Memorization is only the ability to tell me what it looks like on that shelf."

To Voorus, school was rows of small desks in a bleak school room, with boys in matching uniforms writing the same lesson while the teacher loomed over them. It was chanting the lesson in unison for the headmaster. It was misery.

"Have you heard of the Ingosolian Ikoreet Orsuna?" Mityam asked.

"I saw his bust in the library at the military academy. Someone had put a festival hat on his head and flower leis around his neck."

"I have a copy of his writings in my trunk if you'd like to borrow them. Back in his day, lessons were more like a conversation. He'd say something, his student would ask what it meant, and they'd explore the answers together. If that method was good enough for the greatest philosopher in antiquity, who am I to say he was wrong?" Mityam shrugged with false modesty.

Voorus rose and went to his desk. His entire library stretched across the back of it. He had never learned to enjoy reading. "I have here a copy of the Thampurian legal code. All thirty-two books. Plus this little one for the colony. Is that where we start?"

A professorial air came over Mityam as he settled back in his chair. His voice rang through the room as if he were addressing someone in the hallway. "Normally, I'd spend a week explaining the fascinating history and structure of our legal system, but I'm interested myself to read these colonial laws that allow people to be executed without a trial, so let's start there."

Voorus tried to hand Mityam the book, but he waved it away.

"Find the judicial code relating to murder and read it to me. You should ask questions when something confuses you. And if something confuses me, well, we have a problem, don't we?"

It would take them weeks to get through a single page if they stopped every time Voorus got confused. He felt as if they should be doing something for QuiTai, something quick and active, something he was good at. All morning he'd felt as if his dreams were stupid, and now he felt useless too.

But QuiTai wouldn't have wasted her money if she'd thought he was hopeless. She wouldn't have gone to such lengths to help him. Sure, she seemed to think he was an idiot; but she thought everyone was an idiot, and some of those idiots did quite well despite her opinion of them.

"There's nothing about trials or murder in the colonial laws. I've read this cover to cover three times. It's all about taxes and land. There must be another book, because there are laws the militia enforces that I can't find anywhere in here, and I've looked, believe me. When I asked the clerks for the book with those laws, they said it doesn't exist."

"That's rather interesting." Mityam scowled at the book in Voorus' hand. "Do you know why Chief Justice Cuulon was exiled to Ponong?"

Voorus was mortified. "No, and we don't—"

"I can see from your face that it's a taboo subject. I wonder who conned people into believing that the past is best left buried. Although I guess everyone here is guilty of something they're ashamed of." Mityam winked, although it was hard to see under the weight on his wild white brows. "Cuulon was a policeman of some repute for his tough stance on crime. He kept the lower castes in line. Brutally. And everyone looked the other way when he punished or executed people he said were criminals. Of course their families complained, but when someone dies, we're used to the family cutting a fine burial shroud for them. We assume they lie about the virtues of their dead. The lower castes, after all, are inherently criminal classes."

From the way Mityam said it, Voorus didn't think he actually believed what he said. Not too far in his own past, though, Voorus knew he would have agreed with that statement. To his embarrassment, he still tended to assume that the lower castes were guilty when they were arrested. It was hard work to constantly climb out of that mindset.

"What finally brought Cuulon down wasn't the disappearances or pile of bodies at his feet. It wasn't the brutal beatings or the lack of trials. No. What got him exiled was the time he roughed up two scions of one of the thirteen families when he caught them burglarizing their aunt's house. You see, they were upstanding lads from a good family, even though they'd apparently been breaking into homes of family and friends for almost a year. Boys of our caste have high spirits and play pranks; they aren't criminals. But Cuulon treated them like the thieves they were, and that's when he suddenly became an object lesson to the rest of the police in Thampur: make sure the person you've arrested has no powerful friends before you bang his head against the rocks and throw him into a cell with the rapists."

"I shouldn't be listening to this," Voorus said uncertainly. It was fascinating, though.

"I'm a newcomer here. I can be forgiven for a little social blunder." Mityam sipped of his cooled tea. "It sounds as if he took up exactly where he left off in Thampur. He's judge, jury, and executioner. Which means, of course, that he's a common murderer with the power of the state behind him." He leaned back in his chair. "He'll probably do very well when this war starts. His sort always do."

CHAPTER 16: NASHRUU RETURNS

*V*oorus gladly set aside the thick book when there was a knock on his apartment door. His brain was numb and his mouth dry from reading aloud and discussing the text. It had been an hour, and they were only on the second page. He'd take any break he could get. Maybe it was Kyam, bearing good news. Or even better, maybe it was QuiTai herself, come to let them know she'd been freed and to see if Mityam was settled comfortably. That was the kind of thing she'd do.

Expectations buoyed his mood as he rose. "Excuse me a moment, sir."

Mityam motioned for Voorus to go ahead.

Voorus opened his apartment door, and the smile slid off his face. It was her, but the wrong her.

How had she found him? Why was she walking around Levapur without an escort?

He tugged the door tight against his body so Mityam wouldn't be able to see around him. He couldn't breathe. It was worse than the way he'd felt at the wharf earlier, because this time she saw him. He wanted to grab her by the arms and demand she explain everything. He wanted to kiss her and tell her he didn't care that she'd disappeared without a word. He wanted to hug her and close his eyes and dream that they'd gone back in time eight years. But all he could do was save her reputation.

"You can't be seen here. It isn't proper," he whispered.

"Is that any way to greet me after all these years?" Nashruu asked.

Her genteel voice sent him reeling back a step. Years ago, he'd hidden smiles when she'd imitated cultured tones. Only now he realized that was her real accent. No one ever expected a *thiree* to try to slum below caste. Was anything he knew about her real?

Nashruu lowered her voice but not her gaze. "We need to talk."

"Not now," he said between clenched teeth.

He turned back to see if Mityam were eavesdropping. All he could see was the old man's arm and the back of his chair. However, Mityam's hairy ears might be as sharp as his wit, so he shuffled closer to her and tried to close the door behind him. She might be seen in the hallway, though. He couldn't decide if it were safer to let her into his apartment or risk a gossipy neighbor.

She pushed on the door. "I have to talk to you about Lady QuiTai. Right now."

He didn't understand. This woman looked like his Nashruu, but didn't act like her. Her gaze was too direct and her bearing almost unfeminine. She didn't look as if she cared what a man or her family thought of her, which was unthinkable. Ladies didn't behave that way. Where was the obedient lover who had joyfully sacrificed herself in every way for his happiness? This *thiree* woman wouldn't have lived in an apartment where cold air seeped around the windows and the hallways smelled of poverty dinners, as his Nashruu had. And how could she possibly know about QuiTai? How could QuiTai concern her?

She'd only been in Levapur a couple hours.

"Is that Ma'am Nashruu Zul I hear?" Mityam asked.

Nashruu drew back. Now she had to understand why she shouldn't be here. Voorus put his finger to his lips as he silently implored her to go away, even though they knew it was too late. She leaned against the wall and drew in quick breaths. Then the color came back into her face and she pushed the door open enough to walk inside.

"Yes, it is. Is that you, Mister Muul? What a pleasure to see you again." She extended her hands to the old man as she walked around his chair. That darling dimple in her cheek showed as she smiled down at him.

Completely confused, Voorus watched his dream lover turn into a real person before his eyes. He wasn't sure how he felt about that.

Nashruu settled into the chair Voorus offered. With downcast eyes and her hands folded into her lap, she looked like a proper Thampurian lady. Had it only been this morning that he'd found out she was alive? It seemed he'd always known, although the news that she was married to his half-brother had been a shock. QuiTai had explained things to him, things he hadn't wanted to hear.

"This whole thing has the stench of Grandfather Zul to it," QuiTai had whispered to him.

As Voorus looked at Nashruu, he began to hate her as passionately as he'd once loved her. Heat rushed over his face. He wanted to yell at her. He wanted to send her away. He would die of embarrassment if he cried, but his emotions were so muddled that he didn't think he could control himself much longer. He was glad he was standing behind Mityam's chair, so only she could see his shameful trembling.

"I'm so pleased to see you again, Mister Muul," Nashruu said. Her gaze flitted up to Mityam's face as she gave him a warm smile, and then fluttered back down to her hands. She pressed them together as if any moment she'd wring them in distress. It reminded Voorus of QuiTai's deceptions.

"And I you. We were fellow passengers on the *Golden Barracuda* and spent many delightful hours playing tiles with Captain Hadre," Mityam told Voorus. "What brings you here, dear lady? Shouldn't you be resting?"

For a second, Voorus thought her expression hardened, but he blinked and she looked soft and biddable again. He was a bit annoyed at Mityam himself. This was his apartment; he was the host. If anyone should be chastising Ma'am Zul, it should be he, but the things he wanted to say couldn't be repeated in front of a witness.

"I'm afraid that I have urgent business with Captain Voorus that can't wait. I hate to impose, but it's a personal matter." She shyly glanced at Mityam as she left it to him to act on the implied request.

Curious to see what Mityam made of that, Voorus crept around the chair. Mityam seemed shocked, as well he should be. Married ladies didn't have business with unmarried men, personal or otherwise, and certainly not in private. Voorus noticed she had yet to look at him again. Not even a coy glance. Why would she come to him and then ignore him?

Seething, he asked, "What interest could you possibly have with QuiTai?"

Now Mityam was truly alarmed. He turned to Nashruu. "Oh, my dear! A woman like that? No, no. This won't do."

Nashruu's fleeting look of disgust changed quickly back to a properly docile mien. "I realize that it's a bit unusual, but I have my orders."

"I think your husband would agree with me that it's best that you ignore these 'orders' you think you have. This isn't befitting a woman of your station," Mityam said.

Mityam struggled to rise from his chair, and Voorus put a hand on his shoulder. "I'll escort Ma'am Zul back to her home. You can wait here for my return."

Groaning, Mityam sank back into the chair. "Only sensible

thing to do. I'd escort her myself, but…"

"Oh, absolutely. Ma'am Zul?" He bowed and indicated she should precede him to the door. To his relief, she didn't make a scene, but they'd lived together long enough that he knew she was fuming underneath her polite expression. That made two of them.

"Have a talk with her husband," Mityam called out.

Voorus nodded as he opened the door for Nashruu. He realized that they'd be alone. She might talk to him. He didn't think he could bear it. He wanted explanations even though he already knew that none would satisfy him. There wasn't an apology sincere enough to make him forgive her, but he wanted her to try so he could coldly, cruelly, let her know exactly what he thought of her. Some matters of honor could only be satisfied by drawing the soul's blood. He wanted hers to pour onto the ground where he could spit on it.

"You wanted to speak to me?" Voorus winced at the pinched sound in his voice.

Now that they were out of his apartment, Nashruu seemed less bold. She stared forward grimly as she walked, as if the strangeness of Levapur already bored her. At the next road, she suddenly stopped and faced him.

"I'm sorry. Sorry for everything. Sorry for leaving you without a word. Sorry for returning in this manner. I'm not supposed to apologize to you, but I feel it's in order. We've treated you poorly. If it's any consolation, he uses all of us horribly."

"He? Who? What?" he asked, although he knew already. Not all of it, of course. Even QuiTai admitted she hadn't known all of it, but she'd known – guessed – enough the moment Nashruu had walked down the *Golden Barracuda*'s gang plank. He'd frozen in terror, anger… he couldn't even name all the emotions that had washed over him in that moment.

Thank goodness QuiTai had had the sense to drag him behind the crates as Nashruu, Khyram, and Kyam strolled past.

"I think I know why I was exiled," he'd told QuiTai when he was able to speak.

"Me too," she'd said.

His throat had hurt. "I didn't know she was married."

QuiTai had put her finger to his lips. "Spies, everywhere, Captain. You don't want them to know your business."

A burst of hysteria had overwhelmed the confusion and grief. He'd laughed, bitterly. QuiTai was right, though: he didn't want anyone to know his business – except her, because right now she was looking at him with such sympathy that he realized it had been a very long time since anyone had been kind to him. He'd bowed his head so their foreheads nearly touched. This woman, whom he'd tried to have hanged more times than he could count, shed a tear for the injustices he'd suffered.

Voorus didn't touch Nashruu as they walked through the Quarter of Delights toward the Dragon Bridge. He didn't need to. A spark flowed between them as if they held onto one of those new electrical fantasies.

"My Grandfather," she said.

It took him a moment to realize she was answering him. He corrected her carefully. "Our Grandfather."

Nashruu's hand went to her mouth.

"I slept with my cousin. I guess I really am a Zul," he'd told QuiTai.

"So you figured that out," Nashruu said. She started walking again.

"I'm not stupid. I have a mirror." He was angry with her, with their Grandfather, with the entire Zul clan.

They crossed over the Dragon Bridge, a small stone arch that spanned a gully, into the neighborhood where only members of the thirteen families lived. It was the flattest land in Levapur. Each compound was huge, with massive main houses and several outer buildings around the large inner courtyard.

The compound walls sat behind a row of trees that shaded the dirt road. Despite the wealth behind them, the walls were plain stucco and the gates that broke the long expanses were small and often unpainted. By each gate there was a bell pull that would summon a servant. It was very much like Thampur, and yet no one would ever mistake Levapur for Surrayya. The colors were too vivid. The sun was unrelenting. Everything simmered here.

"Even though we're the only two people on this road, take my arm and I'll whisper. Oh come on, I won't contaminate you. That's much better. We look like friends now. I hope we are," Nashruu said.

"You were talking about our Grandfather."

"He's your true Grandfather. He's more of a second cousin to me, I think. The charts are complicated. And like you, I'm only half Zul. You'd be surprised how many of us are. Half Zuls pretending to be full Zuls, that is. Bastards, all of us, which explains a lot."

Voorus wondered if others behind the compound walls they passed were suffering through their own turmoil too, if the entire world were constantly unhappy and hurting, but none of them would dare show it.

What would it be like if people were permitted to be fragile when they were going through hell? Would everyone speak in gentle voices and try to make their way easier, or would they attack? You never knew. People surprised you. QuiTai had surprised him.

And what about Nashruu? Should he try to make her feel how much hurt she'd put him through, or should he treat her soul like delicate glass? Was this awkward and hard for her? Had she also been used?

"Why does he do this to us? What's the point of sending you to seduce me, then making you leave me? He did make you leave me, didn't he?" Voorus hated that his heart so plainly rode his voice.

She nodded, but not with any conviction. "I left because I had what I was sent for."

"What could I possibly have given to you?"

"A son."

He couldn't breathe. So it was true. That boy on the wharf

looked too much like Kyam. But Voorus looked like Kyam too. QuiTai had whispered all of this to him as they'd hidden behind the crates, but the meaning of her words hadn't sunk in until now.

Voorus repeated QuiTai's prophetic words. "Fresh blood."

How did QuiTai see such a vast conspiracy from the way he looked at Nashruu? All he'd done was look. QuiTai had let go of the boy she'd saved from falling off the wharf and turned to him. Then she'd looked back at Nashruu. When she'd turned back to him, he'd seen the truth dawn on her as if a god sat on her shoulder and whispered the secret to her. One glance from him to Nashruu, and QuiTai had known they'd been lovers. All from a single glance.

Nashruu's hand wrapped tighter around his forearm. "Yes. Exactly. Our King likes the idea of a pure line and doesn't think of the consequences of inbreeding. Thankfully, Grandfather does. He learned from his father. Kyam's son and the King's eldest daughter would have been first cousins through all four parents. Our son and the princess are first cousins only through two. It isn't perfect, but it's better than a prince with no chin and the wit of a flounder."

They spoke of treasonous deception and unforgivable manipulation as casually as the weather. If the people living in these expensive estates had any idea… They wouldn't believe it. Who would? It was a monstrous fantasy. He felt as if the real him walked like a ghost beside his shell and someone else were inside his body. His life couldn't be this complicated, could it? Intrigue was for QuiTai and Kyam and the rest of the dammed Zul clan, not bastards from the wrong part of town. He didn't belong in the historical annuals, not even as a footnote.

"The King should be grateful to be saved from his own folly, but I can't be thankful for being forced into this scheme," Voorus said.

His son was betrothed to the King's eldest daughter. His *son*.

Maybe if he thought about the next generation instead of himself, he could be at peace with Grandfather's schemes.

They walked over interlaced tree roots spreading over the road's surface. In Thampur, a road through the richest part of town would be paved with bricks. Here, it was dirt.

"It was the best year of my life," Nashruu said. "I didn't leave because of you. I wrote a note that said that, but lost my nerve and took it with me. I still have it, if you want to read it. It was just that I didn't dare give you hope. You were the type who would look for me forever if you thought there was hope, so I thought it was kinder to make sure you had none. But it was never because of you. Please believe me. The best part of coming here was that I could say that to you."

And just that quickly, he forgave it all and loved her again.

Voorus and Nashruu stood at the Zul family compound's gate, but didn't go inside. Up close, Voorus could see the fine etching of time on Nashruu's face. After so many years in Levapur, the sun had done worse to him. But now that the shock was over, he saw the Nashruu he'd known.

"Grandfather argued against it, but I thought you deserved the truth finally. Besides, it's clear that Lady QuiTai would gladly spill our secrets to you. She doesn't like Grandfather," Nashruu confided, as if he didn't know that.

"I need time to think about all this."

She smiled kindly at him, even took his hand. "Take all the time you need."

He could have stood there until the sun set.

"But," she said.

He held his breath. What was it with the Zuls that they never let anyone enjoy a moment?

"I've been ordered to save Lady QuiTai from the fortress. I have the power of a writ, signed by the King, to let her out, but I was told only to use it as a last resort. So I went to the fortress—"

"You went…" Horrified, Voorus braced a hand against the

compound wall for support. He was glad the only other person on the road was a Ponongese servant far off in the distance. A Thampurian would have hurried over to see if there was gossip to gather.

"Lady QuiTai is stubborn. She seems to prefer to die than to pledge her support to Grandfather," Nashruu said.

Under the toe of his boot, he crushed a thin layer of brittle mud left from a rain puddle that had dried months ago. He wondered if he should blurt out that he'd been faithful to her all these years. That he'd only ever loved her. But she was worldly now. Such an outburst would make him sound like a schoolboy, and it would only embarrass her, but he wanted her to know.

He squinted at the dappled shade down the lane and tried to figure out if the far-off person was walking toward them or away. "I can see her point."

Nashruu leaned away from him. "Yes, well, don't we all wish we were free of him? But since that's not going to happen, I have to be practical. She won't budge to save her own life. There must be something she wants, though. Kyam wouldn't tell me. But you're friends with her. I saw you two huddled together in the shadows at the wharf."

"That wasn't–" Why did he have to keep explaining that? Why was it anyone's business?

"Please, tell me what I can offer Lady QuiTai. I have to get her to agree to serve Grandfather. You have no idea how I'll suffer if I fail. How your son will suffer."

He winced at the crude attempt at manipulation. He'd only just learned he had a son. Wasn't it too early to try to use the boy as a lever? Did they think that fatherly concern took only a minute to develop?

"I don't know QuiTai well enough to give you any insight," he said stiffly.

"You looked awfully close on the wharf."

"We aren't lovers. We've never been lovers," he blurted. Nashruu looked a bit alarmed. He spread his hands. "She's not the type to have close relationships with anyone. Have you asked her what she wants?"

Nashruu tugged on her gloves, a gesture he recognized: she was frustrated. Her gaze shifted to the long, shady lane. "She had ridiculous demands."

"Let me guess. She wanted Ponong to be independent again."

She scowled. "And for the King to bow down to her people and apologize. What sort of insane person asks for something like that?"

He was as offended as Nashruu was.

"Can't you think of anything? Please, this is important. It's not just for Grandfather. I'm asking for Thampur. We need Lady QuiTai on our side when the war starts. I can't fail. Please."

Thampur had never done a damn thing for him, but his son was to become part of the royal family. Thampur was going to belong to his son. Giddy joy swept over him and he couldn't hide his smile. He had a son!

He had a son whom he could never acknowledge because it would ruin the boy's rise to the top of Thampurian society. Could he risk a relationship, though? Something more than silence and distance? Could he pretend to be an uncle, a family friend?

He had a son.

She couldn't drop something like that at his feet and expect him not to stagger. Yet here she was, talking about the nation and duty and making him want to give everything to their Grandfather in return for this miracle.

He had a son. His heart was buoyant.

"I know you must be angry with me, but please, this is important. Is there anything you can think of?" Nashruu asked. She reached for his arm. He barely felt the weight of her fingers through the thick material of his jacket.

"Let me think about it."

"No time to think. I need something now."

Voorus tried to concentrate on what he knew of QuiTai. She wouldn't ever need something from another person. She could do everything for herself. He didn't even know that much about her except the things that everyone knew, like how she'd paralyzed those werewolves and left them in the marketplace for her people to dismember, and why she'd done that. He shivered as he imagined his son being eaten by wolves right in front of him.

"If I were her, before I died, I'd want to make Cuulon pay for my daughter's death. I'd want to destroy anyone who stole that from me," he said.

QuiTai wouldn't let a wound like that go unavenged any more than he would. She understood honor.

"Cuulon, again. His name seems to come up a lot when anyone speaks of QuiTai."

"Do you know the story?"

Nashruu gave him a pitying look. "More than even QuiTai knows."

"Don't bet on that. She knows a lot. It's eerie how much she can figure out from a glance." He wasn't a superstitious man, and wasn't given to believing in folktales like so many of his caste, so he was a bit embarrassed to say, "It's as if she has a god in her pocket."

"She may well have." Nashruu's head jerked slightly, as if she suddenly realized she'd said something indiscreet. "About QuiTai…"

"I'd want Cuulon dead, but QuiTai doesn't think like most people. If Cuulon is alive now, it's because she wants him to be."

"We are of one mind on that. She is formidable. So, whom should I send to arrest Chief Justice Cuulon?"

She had to be joking. Could she do that? An ungentlemanly thrill jolted through him. There was something bad, forbidden, and sexy about this new side of her. He reached to grasp her hand but then thought better of it. They were in public. She was a *thiree*; He was a bastard. She was married.

"Your husband, I suppose," he said.

Nashruu snorted. "When Kyam gets mixed up with Lady QuiTai, unexpected things happen to our plans. He's to stay out of it. I told him."

Voorus laughed. "He obeys you?" His mother wasn't the type to obey a man either. He'd always thought that was why she hadn't remarried. Now he wasn't so sure.

"It's not a question of obedience to me. Or even his filial duty to our grandfather. I have a writ from our royal cousin. I'd like to see him ignore that."

CHAPTER 17: EDUCATING NASHRUU

"You're angry, Ma'am Zul," QuiTai said as Nashruu entered the dungeon.

Nashruu was cross at Colonel Hurust, who had first refused to let her visit QuiTai again and then abruptly abandoned her at the top of the dungeon stairs. If it wasn't such a ridiculous idea, she'd swear he was afraid of the dark. And of course no guards were on duty. She felt as if she could walk in and out of their dungeon with far too much ease.

"There are only a couple of reasons you'd be angry with me, so let me posit a scenario, and you can tell me if I'm right," QuiTai said.

Nashruu raised her chin. There was no way QuiTai could know why she was out of sorts. All she could do was guess. Perhaps she was like one of those charlatans who persuaded weak-minded women that they were in touch with the spirit world. That wouldn't fool Nashruu. She already knew that QuiTai had the best network of informants in existence to gather gossip for her. Down here, she was cut off from her sources, but she could still read people with uncanny accuracy. This time, she wouldn't be able to guess. "Go on."

QuiTai smiled down at her hands. "The Thampurian men you've been dealing with today are using a tone of voice with you that's usually reserved for small children with sticky hands. Because you are a clever woman, you know that if you raise your voice the slightest bit, you'll be seen as a shrew, and if you don't, they'll talk right over you. If you stand firm, you're troublesome and should be put in your place. They may even threaten to turn you over to Kyam in the hopes that he'll control you. And by that, they mean beat you into submission. Or they grip your elbow and steer you toward the door. Yes, it must have been a frustrating day for you, even though you've had to negotiate this delicate balance your entire life."

Anyone could have guessed that. Nashruu clamped her mouth shut and tried not to react.

QuiTai seemed to take that as an answer. "You feel you should be shown some courtesy, due to the seriousness of your mission, but at every step you're forced to resort to threats and waving the King's writ under noses. You might even have to drag out the farwriter and get your Grandfather to tell the men to do as you say, something that undermines your personal authority and worse, wastes time."

How could QuiTai possibly know she had a writ from the King? Maybe she'd overheard the militia talking. She wished she could remember exactly what she'd told QuiTai during her last visit. Maybe she'd let the information slip herself.

For a moment, she wondered if it could it be true that QuiTai spoke directly to the gods. No, that was nonsense. QuiTai had to be getting the information from a terrestrial source. Grandfather could believe what he wanted, and she was more than happy to indulge him if it meant her freedom.

"But what saddens me, Ma'am Zul, is how you've turned that frustration toward me. I have done you no wrong. I did not decide that today should be this hot and you this weary. It's not my fault that Thampurian men are patronizing fools. Be angry with them, not me," QuiTai said.

She thought she'd been prepared for QuiTai, but Nashruu was shocked by her disregard for convention. The truth should never be shoved unceremoniously into the light to be exposed raw and naked in front of people. It deserved to be clothed in grace and dignity.

"I wouldn't have to put up with them if you'd agree to serve Thampur," she remarked acidly. In the next second, she regretted the display of temper. Her orders were to be charming and sympathetic. If necessary, she was to try to seduce QuiTai. Sniping at her was not in the plan.

"Why does Thampur want my help? It's a big, strong nation. I'm simply the owner of a small brothel who dabbles in smuggling and extortion."

Grandfather said that QuiTai seemed to value honesty above everything else, so Nashruu was to be truthful if nothing else was working. Should she be truthful now? Back home, it seemed that orders were orders and all you had to do was follow them; but out here, there were so many decisions to be made, and orders provided far too little guidance.

"You have on your liar's face, Ma'am Zul."

She had been preparing to lie.

"This is the part of the game where you put your tiles on the table face up, not the time when you bluff," QuiTai said.

Nashruu drew in a breath.

"All your tiles."

QuiTai frightened her, but Nashruu was a Thampurian lady, and she would not let it show. "You said earlier that you were willing to die rather than let Grandfather have what he wants."

"That sentiment hasn't changed."

"Then why–"

"You came to speak to me. I did not send for you."

She sensed that QuiTai was smirking, although her face remained impassive. "Oh! I give up," she snapped, exasperated, abandoning her intended self-discipline. "Hang if you want to."

QuiTai pressed her hands together and bowed.

Nashruu had nearly reached the top of the stairs before she turned around and descended back into the dungeon. QuiTai hadn't moved. If she'd seen even a hint of triumph on QuiTai's face, she would have struck it off with the back of her hand.

"Grandfather knows about the Qui. He always assumed your lot were con artists. Like all priests are, he said. But now he thinks you're the real thing. He thinks you can talk directly to your goddess. That explains how you always know so much and can see the future."

QuiTai obviously didn't think much of Grandfather's idea. "I suppose divine assistance is the only other possible solution, although it's the least probable one."

"More improbable than what?"

"That I'm smart enough to do it myself, without any help, divine or otherwise."

"It's vulgar to brag," Nashruu said with disgust.

Instead of being abashed, QuiTai seemed to find this outburst funny. "If I were a man, that would simply be a candid observation about my abilities. You know you're smarter than almost every man you've had to deal with today. Is it wrong to say it?"

QuiTai was getting inside her head. She'd been warned about this.

Nashruu's shoulders squirmed as she tried to think of a way to gain the upper hand. "No well-bred Thampurian woman would ever think such things."

"You mean no well-trained Thampurian woman would dare say such things out loud. Well-trained, well-trampled."

"Women who act like you are unfeminine."

"It's impossible for a woman to be unfeminine. Would you like me better if I pretended to be clumsy, or stupid?"

Nashruu bit her lip. How many times had she pretended to be clumsy and weak-minded to get along better with the women in her circle? Too many. And if someone complimented you and you didn't deny every good thing they said, you'd be attacked.

"I would never force you to hide your talents or invite your friends to say vicious things behind your back," QuiTai said. "Never make you live in misery. Isn't that what the famed salons of Surrayya are really about? Cruelty as entertainment?"

"How dare you!"

QuiTai clicked her tongue like a scolding teacher. "Don't lecture me on my behavior, because I don't give a damn what you think of me."

Nashruu reeled. She secretly thought the same thing about the salons, so why did she want to shout that it was a lie? She didn't like feeling uncomfortable in this way. Was QuiTai deliberately provoking her? When had she lost control of this conversation?

"Go be offended elsewhere, Ma'am Zul. It's been a difficult day for me, and it's only going to get worse." QuiTai massaged her temples.

It was hard to tell in the dim lighting, but Nashruu thought QuiTai didn't look as robust as before. From the furrow in her brow, it appeared she truly had a headache.

"Are you in need of medication?"

QuiTai's laughter bounced off the stone walls. "I will be hanged in a few hours. Do you have a cure for that in your purse also?"

Nashruu clasped her hands primly at her waist. "As a matter of fact, I do, but you insist on refusing it."

That made QuiTai laugh even more. Despite Nashruu's sour mood, the sound was contagious. She put her hand over her mouth in a last attempt to rein in her laughter. The tension shattered as she and QuiTai laughed together until their eyes ran with tears.

After wiping the corners of her eyes, QuiTai sobered, but she seemed more lighthearted than before. "It's a shame that we won't have much more time to talk. Even though you're Grandfather Zul's agent, I've decided that I like you – so I'm going to help you."

Charlatans only told you what you wanted to hear, but did that make the message wrong? Nashruu knew she *was* smarter than most of the men she'd had to deal with today. She hated the way they treated her, but it hadn't much abraded her sensibilities until QuiTai pointed it out.

She knew she was being manipulated, but she was also being offered a glimpse of what it would be like if she stopped hiding her intelligence and behaving in the expected ways. It was Grandfather's fault that it appealed to her. He'd given her a taste for scandalous behavior when he'd sent her to seduce Voorus. QuiTai seemed to be offering an honest friendship of a kind she'd never known before. The opportunity might be short-lived, so she should make good use of it both personally and professionally.

"I think you're the one in need of help, Lady QuiTai."

QuiTai made a little sound of dismissal. "Tell me, Ma'am Zul, if I were to agree to your Grandfather's terms, do you really think you could stop my execution? Cuulon is determined to see me die. Could you convince the militia to follow your orders instead of his?"

"Yes."

QuiTai shook her head. "No."

Nashruu tugged at her purse strings, "But, as you know, I have a writ from the King."

"A piece of paper versus the man who has ruled this island for forty years. A king far across the sea, or the king they know? Who are they going to obey?"

"Chief Justice Cuulon isn't a king. He isn't even Governor."

"And yet everyone here knows he's the real power. Your paper will be ignored."

Nashruu had seen it already. The men who allowed her into the dungeon made sure she knew they were indulging her. At any time they could change their minds and ignore her. "Tell me how I make them listen to me."

"Kill one as a warning to the others."

Nashruu sighed. The last thing she needed now was dry wit. "Real advice, please."

"I'm serious. Do it calmly as you can, in front of witnesses, then step over the body and continue the conversation. I'm assuming, of course, that you know how to kill. I hope Grandfather didn't neglect that area of training as well."

QuiTai couldn't be serious. Simply kill a man, let his body drop, and keep talking? Who could be that callous?

"But doesn't that get you into trouble, killing people as an example to others?" Nashruu asked.

"Loads of trouble. Then you find a way out of that trouble. And then no one can stop you." QuiTai's head tilted. "But that might not work for you. I can see it isn't in your nature. Pardon me while I think out loud on this."

Feeling that she'd somehow stepped into one of those dreadful experimental Ingosolian plays where the distorted sets made you feel as if you'd smoked a black lotus pipe and the dialog consisted of people shouting about fish, she gestured for QuiTai to continue. None of Grandfather's lessons had prepared her for this. He'd never talked about killing. He'd never questioned that people would obey her if she mentioned his name.

QuiTai rubbed her temples as she paced. "You've lost everything the moment a man uses a patronizing tone of voice on you. Anything you say after that will seem petulant. You could try talking down to them from the beginning, since the first one to treat the other like an idiot usually wins these things, but ideally you want your conversations to remain as professional as possible."

"Yes. I suppose." She wasn't sure.

"Respect is key. The problem there is that Thampurian men demand that you respect them while they treat you like an idiot child."

That summed up Nashruu's entire life.

"I still say killing the first one who questions your authority sends the quickest message, but failing that, remind them once that you are an agent of the King. That's fair warning. Then if they ignore you, stop the conversation immediately. It will only weaken your position to say more."

"But what if that doesn't make them listen?"

QuiTai gestured for her to calm down even though she didn't feel as if she were agitated.

"Do you have a portable farwriter? Good. You may want to keep it with you from now on."

"It's heavy."

"Hire someone to carry it for you. That's the Thampurian way." QuiTai waved that aside and continued pacing. "Immediately after you've reminded someone that you have a writ from the King and they refuse to recognize your authority, get out that farwriter – remember, your conversation with that person is absolutely over, not another word – and send a message to Grandfather Zul. Tell him what you're trying to do and that this person isn't complying, so you need them removed from their position immediately. No delays. No discussion. Instant dismissal. It isn't death, but it will have to do."

Just like that? Nashruu's heart pounded. "What if Grandfather won't do that for me?"

"Pack your bags and go home. But if that happens, don't imagine that you've failed. He will have failed when he didn't back you up."

Failure was scary, but not as overwhelming as the idea of following QuiTai's instructions. "What do I do after Grandfather acts?"

"Turn to the next man and make the exact same request. If he balks for even a second, tell him that he, too, is dismissed from duty. If you have to force half the garrison to resign, so be it. Eventually one of them will get the message that you have the power, and he will obey you. Be ruthless. Be quick. Don't give them time to think it over. And don't reach out to Grandfather too many times. You have to make it clear you wield authority."

It was a tempting idea, but Nashruu wasn't sure she could do it. What if the men ignored her? What if they laughed? "It sounds so simple when you say it."

"I understand that every inch of your soul rebels against the idea of behaving that way. You've been taught it's unnatural. Remember, you don't have to enjoy it to do it well. You can quake in your shoes through the whole thing. But it's the only way."

A forbidden thought crossed Nashruu's mind. She covered her mouth as she laughed. "Short of murder."

QuiTai seemed to find it funny too, and then her smile faded away. "That's always an option."

Nashruu wondered how to lead their conversation back to Grandfather's offer. If QuiTai's life wasn't enough of an incentive to come work for Grandfather, what could tempt her? She hoped Grandfather knew QuiTai better than he seemed to.

The sound of the dungeon door opening echoed down the staircase.

"I'm afraid it's time for you to leave, Ma'am Zul. Matters are about to get quite intense," QuiTai said.

"I'm not done yet."

QuiTai's gaze hadn't left the stairs. She tensed. "This might be a very good time to run home and gather your farwriter. Bringing Grandfather up to date might not change anything, but it's worth a try."

It sounded as if more than one person was coming. Nashruu gripped the cell bars. Who would it be? QuiTai seemed to already know. Maybe she did speak to the gods.

"I can save you. Just give me your word," Nashruu said.

"I'm not leaving this cell yet. And you need to go. Right now."

Nashruu felt like a child sent off to bed just when things got interesting. So much for QuiTai being her mentor.

Chief Justice Cuulon sauntered down the steps with a jellylantern held high. Colonel Hurust hung back from the pale orb of light surrounding Cuulon, as if he were afraid to be seen.

"Enough tea and cakes, Ma'am Zul. It's time for the professionals," Cuulon said. He reached for her arm.

"My work here isn't complete yet. I suggest you wait." Nashruu heart thudded as she stepped back.

Colonel Hurust slunk around Cuulon. She yelped when he

gripped her waist with far too much familiarity. He dragged her toward the steps. "Why don't you come with me, Ma'am Zul? You don't want to be here when Chief Justice Cuulon questions the Devil's whore. You might faint."

"Return to me after you've shown her out, Colonel," Cuulon said.

It was all very well for QuiTai to say one should demand respect, but they acted as if Nashruu didn't matter.

QuiTai moved her fingers as if typing on a farwriter. Her glance shifted to the Colonel.

There was such focus in QuiTai's stare that Nashruu feared for the Colonel, although she didn't understand why. Why wasn't she afraid for Cuulon? Or for QuiTai, for that matter? Yet she couldn't shake the feeling that she should warn the Colonel. Maybe his affiliation was different from hers at this moment, but he was a Thampurian, someone she understood at a gut level, while QuiTai was something alien and deadly.

She was sure of it now. QuiTai was coiling to strike. She should warn Colonel Hurust. And yet, she held her tongue.

Lady QuiTai and I are fighting together against the colonial government. How did she twist me into this?

Colonel Hurust's eyes looked like a spooked horse's, too wide and showing too much white. He moved behind Nashruu. Was he using her as a shield?

"Chief Justice Cuulon, Colonel Hurust, I warn you that the King himself wants this woman alive. If she dies, so do you." Nashruu wanted to say so much more, but QuiTai signaled her to stop talking, and she obeyed.

Chapter 18: Cuulon

"*I* wondered when you'd show up, Cuulon," QuiTai said. She mocked him even though she was the one behind bars. He couldn't wait to see the look in her eyes the moment she realized she was about to die. She'd regret everything. She'd beg for mercy. She'd break. And he'd simply smile down at her.

"And Colonel Hurust. How very nice to finally meet you. I've been waiting all day for this honor," QuiTai said.

Offended pride pricked Cuulon's complacency. Why was she taking notice of the Colonel? *He* was the most important man in the room. He held her life in his hands. Hurust was no one.

He hated the way her dark magic still made him want to drop to his knees before her even in this filthy place. He'd make her regret every night she'd sent dreams to torment him. Once she was dead, he'd finally be free.

A smile played across her mouth as if she read his mind. He remembered those long silences when she'd weighed his soul and found it wanting.

"Unlock her cell, Colonel," Cuulon snapped, turning to Hurust. He'd show her he wasn't afraid.

"I don't – Governor Zul took the key."

Cuulon looked back at QuiTai and recoiled in shock – somehow, in the second he'd glanced away, she had transformed into the image of a wrathful water demon. Her unbound hair twisted in long locks as if tangled by the shifting tide while she'd floated face down in a lagoon. The thin yellow rings around her oval pupils glowed like candles in her skull. Even though he knew she couldn't be a demon spirit, fear dropped into his gut and sat there, hard and unyielding.

"Oh come now, Colonel Hurust. We all know there's another key. There's always another key," QuiTai said.

The odd way her voice reverberated against the stone walls, as if it came from anywhere but her mouth, made his skin crawl.

"I left the key in my office," Hurust said.

"Then what's the ring on your belt for?" QuiTai snapped.

Colonel Hurust flinched.

Cuulon clasped his hands behind his back and lowered his gaze to the stone floor. It embarrassed him how that tone of voice could make him revert to that stance. He peeked at her. Had she noticed? Why wasn't she looking at him?

He stood straight again. He was in charge here. "Get one of your soldiers to fetch the key if it's not on that ring," he told Hurust.

Time was slipping away. That damned fool Kyam Zul might come dashing in here any moment to stop him. Everyone knew Theram Zul had brought a private army to Levapur before the rice riot. No one knew where they'd gone. They might have gone back to Thampur, but what if they were lurking in Levapur still? The Zul clan was making a move. He was sure of it. Why else would Mityam Muul have come to Ponong?

Words seemed stuck in Colonel Hurust's throat. His gaze flicked to QuiTai again. "My men have vanished."

QuiTai clicked her tongue. She shook her head as if

confronted by a great sorrow. "Surely not all of them. It would be so careless of you to lose track of them."

Hurust rushed to the cell and shook the bars. "Shut up! I know why you're here."

Cuulon looked around the dungeon. Why was it so infernally dark down here? "Where's the torture chamber? Near your office?"

"No. Down here." Colonel Hurust gestured away from the stairs as if the motion exhausted him. He seemed to deflate. He lifted a ring of keys from his belt and put one in the lock. Cuulon shot him a look, but the Colonel's back was to him as he pulled open the cell door.

"Was that so difficult?" QuiTai crooned. She slunk across the opening like a cat deciding if it wanted to go outside, and was in no rush to.

Cuulon took the jellylantern and waded into the darkness even though it gave him the chills to turn his back on her. Was that a door ahead? Hurust must have grabbed QuiTai's arm and dragged her with him, because the scuff of their shoes seemed to come close on his heels.

"So it's torture and a chat? Or just torture? Because you know I didn't murder Governor Turyat, so I can't imagine we have much to talk about, Chief Justice," QuiTai said.

"You killed him."

"You know I didn't. I enjoyed playing with him too much."

He opened the door to the torture chamber. "Bitch snake."

"Snake? Oh, I am crushed, Cuulon. You used to call me Ma'am."

He prayed Hurust thought she was lying. There were many interesting devices in the chamber to make her stop talking. The spiked iron ball, for instance, would pin her tongue to her chin, and every sound she uttered would drive it deeper into her flesh.

"Bring her inside, Colonel, and shut the door. We don't want to be interrupted."

The snake woman walked around the torture chamber as if she were thinking of leasing the place. Colonel Hurust had seen plenty of her people come into this room with their heads held high, but even they'd balked at the board, with its iron cap and the shackles for wrists, ankles, thighs, and shoulders. If they turned away from it, they saw the cruel implements hanging from the iron grid on the wall, and they showed fear. But this one coolly extended a fingertip to a slim metal spike and tested the point.

So this was the Devil's whore. Hurust didn't leave the fortress often, so he hadn't known her by sight. Everyone talked about her peculiar beauty, but she looked like a half-remembered childhood nightmare to him. The last time she'd been in his prison she'd escaped before he'd even seen her. This time he'd avoided her as best he could, but Cuulon had forced him to come down here. What made the Chief Justice think he had authority over the militia? For too long they'd served the powers in Levapur rather than running the place. He was changing that, but first he had to help Cuulon get rid of her, because she was the symbol of everything wrong and decadent in Levapur.

She was so calm. Nearly cheerful. Maybe she was drugged, although nothing in her movements or voice seemed as if her senses had been dulled. Could it be that she truly had no fear?

He drew back from her as her snake's eyes turned on him. Her lips formed into a cruel vee, the most malevolent smile he'd ever seen. It was ghastly.

"So many instruments of torture, Colonel. They overwhelm a girl. Kindly point me to the ones with hooks," she said.

Wordlessly, he pointed to the far left of the metal grid bolted to the wall. This creature was loose in his fortress. Far more dangerous than werewolves, more crafty than an octopus, as soulless as a drowned corpse. She probably ate livers, or souls.

"So kind. Thank you. That's exactly what I was looking for."

Hurust jumped when Cuulon slammed shut the heavy door and threw the bolts.

He was locked inside with her.

Nashruu was glad she'd forgone her corset despite Simarn's scandalized tutting. Even without it, her clothes felt as if they clung too tightly. Her skin felt slick and unclean.

Colonel Hurust's secretary made her wait outside his office again, a game she had no time for. She leaned forward in the hard wooden chair until she saw him at his desk. He tried to pretend he couldn't see her waiting. Another soldier, perched on the edge of his desk, chatted about his lucky evening at a place called the Dragon Pearl. Major Rheagus grew more distracted as she continued to stare at him.

If only QuiTai had warned her this morning to keep her farwriter with her. Now it was too late. Why did everything in this strange place move as if struggling through knee-high snow? Everything except the clock. It relentlessly moved forward while the militia made her wait in a hard wooden chair in a bare hallway.

What was Cuulon doing to QuiTai? She shivered as her imagination went to a dark, bloody place. Cuulon obviously hated QuiTai, but why? He'd started it when he'd paid Petrof to kill the Qui. QuiTai hadn't even known he was behind it until last year. Although, when one thought about it, the reason wasn't important. All that mattered was the palpable loathing. QuiTai might loom large in the imagination, and her personality certainly filled a room, but her body was a fragile vessel for that power. In his rush to make her suffer, Cuulon could easily go too far.

Nashruu jumped to her feet and walked into Major Rheagus office. "Chief Justice Cuulon is about to torture Lady QuiTai against my direct orders. Our King wants her alive. I insist you stop him immediately."

Major Rheagus clearly wasn't used to women storming into his office. She could almost read the progression of his thoughts as his face reflected them. He was outraged, but she was the Governor's wife. Respect for *thirees* – how that word irritated her – had been drummed into him since birth, so he hated them while probably also believing deep down that she was superior to him. And while she was only a woman, she claimed to speak for the King. Those warring facts put him in a difficult spot.

He looked at the other soldier. A silent agreement seemed to pass between them. He placed his palms on his desk. "Ma'am Zul..." he said with false reluctance.

Could she simply kill him?

Alas, no, but she understood why QuiTai recommended it. Instead, she raised a hand to stop him from saying something that might incite her to pick up the pen beside his inkwell and jab it into his eye.

"Is your plan is to move as slowly as possible without actually refusing to obey?" she asked.

He jerked back. The other soldier chuckled warily.

"I'll take that as a yes. Make your farwriter available at once."

Major Rheagus leaned back in his chair. He smirked as he put his boots up on his desk. "No."

She rose as she felt heat flood her cheeks. She couldn't fail, not matter how humiliated she felt.

The other soldier laughed openly at her now.

There was nothing wrong with her glove, but she tugged at the wrist while she steadied her nerves. She didn't like this. If only people would be reasonable – but they wouldn't, because they always had to show you they were powerful and you were not. They were cruel simply because they could be. She used to cry from the frustration and humiliation, but years of living with Grandfather had wrung every teardrop from her, every foot stomp and outcry. "Your children, your wife, and your parents. Your sisters and brothers, cousins, aunts, and uncles," she said wearily. She pointed to the other soldier. "Yours too."

Of course Major Rheagus was confused. He probably thought she'd gone strange, so he chuckled the way you did when your employer said something a ten-year-old boy would find unsophisticated. "What is that, Ma'am Zul?"

"The list of people who will die tomorrow at the hands of assassins if you allow Cuulon to murder Lady QuiTai."

One. Two. Three. Four.

That was long enough to hold his gaze so he knew she was serious.

She spun around and walked out of his office. Once you'd made a threat like that, there was nothing left to say. She forced herself to walk slowly even though she wanted to run. As QuiTai had predicted, she was shaking in her boots.

Her pulse drummed as she strained to hear what might be happening behind her. Would Major Rheagus call out for her to stop? Would he yield? She didn't think so, but she hoped, right until the moment the fortress gates slammed shut behind her, that they would take her seriously. Then she was out in the sunshine. The mist from a wave was light on her skin, and only the gulls heard her cry out her frustration into the wind. The families would have to die. Once you made a threat like that, you had to go through with it, or you were forever lost.

Chapter 19: PhaSun

"Governor Zul, why are you in my office again?" Lizzriat asked.

"Because, honestly, I don't know where to go anymore."

"I told you. The Red Happiness."

Kyam sat down in a wood chair. "I didn't learn anything there."

Lizzriat rolled a kur and lit it. He didn't offer it to Kyam. "QuiTai swears you're smarter than this, but I don't see it."

"You talk about me?"

A puff of exhaled smoke rose toward the draped fabric on the ceiling. "Don't be flattered. It wasn't that kind of conversation. We were talking about your mistakes in governing this town and which one of us should be the unlucky one to pull you aside for a chat."

They had no idea how hard it was to push the clerks and department heads in the government building to do anything. It wasn't fair to judge his efforts by his results. That was yet another reason why he'd never miss this stupid town.

"You haven't visited me. She hasn't either."

Lizzriat stubbed out his partially smoked kur and picked up a pen that he fiddled with. "It's an ongoing negotiation. It requires many drinks late at night. Long silences. Rueful laughter. Lightly stroking the inside of her arm. I'm sure you understand."

There was no reason to be jealous of Lizzriat. QuiTai could do what she liked.

"I came back because I think you have more to tell me about Turyat."

Lizzriat put his feet up on his desk and leaned back. "No wonder you aren't getting anywhere. All you do is walk in circles. Are you sure you're investigating the right murder? His death is so trivial."

"Who killed him?"

"Cuulon is the only one who loved him enough to put him out of his misery."

"Not Turyat's wife?"

"She donned her widow's veil the day you were named Governor. One might suspect that she – well, it would be unkind to suggest she smiled behind it, because I don't know her heart, but I never got the impression she was devastated. Thampurians don't show their emotions in public, though, so maybe she was truly upset but hid it skillfully." Lizzriat rolled his pen across his knuckles. "Very skillfully."

That confirmed Kyam's observations. "Can you think of anyone else who might have killed him?"

"Maybe it was the militia. The ones who live in the fortress. They used to keep to themselves, but lately they've spent a lot of time in the quarter, making trouble."

"Why would the militia murder Turyat?"

Lizzriat jabbed the tip of his pen against his desk blotter, making dots across the paper. "Have you spoken to QuiTai, or are you still sulking? She probably knows who killed him."

"I was not –" Kyam lowered his voice. "Yes, I asked her if she knew. She told me I had to figure it out for myself."

Chuckling, Lizzriat set down the pen. "Did she really?" A

smile not only lit up his eyes and face but seemed to invigorate his body as well. "She still surprises, doesn't she?"

"Always. Do you know why she wanted to be arrested earlier today, before Turyat's body was found?"

What gave liars away was how long it took them to respond. Too quickly – or as in Lizzriat's case – far too slowly. It was as if a difference engine had churned into action inside his head. Kyam half expected Lizzriat's mouth to open and a ribbon of paper to roll off his tongue like a farwriter message.

He shook his head to clear away the image. How did Lizzriat stay so sharp while breathing in vapor-tainted air day and night?

"Do you know something you'd like to tell me?" Kyam asked. Sometimes a question like that had surprising answers.

Lizzriat leaned across the desk to pat his hand. "I know lots of somethings, none of which I'd like to give away to you. Information has value."

"Do you want QuiTai to hang?"

"What a very interesting question, Governor. I can see the benefits and drawbacks of her death, as well as her continued existence. So call me neutral."

This was going nowhere. Kyam knew he was wasting his remaining time. He could feel freedom slipping from his fingers. "If you hold anything back, you're making sure she's executed. That doesn't sound neutral to me."

"I'm no expert at investigating murders, Governor, but if I were you, I'd concentrate on the scene of the crime and who was there."

"So you do know–"

"That's common sense. You pretty much have to be present at a murder to commit it. Unless, of course, one has a newfangled contraption– Oh, damn it. Now you're going to waste time thinking QuiTai set up one of the toys in her office to kill him. Use the brains QuiTai swears you have and realize how very lucky you'd be to get someone to stand at the exact spot and wait patiently to be killed by a little contraption."

"Point taken." If only Lizzriat would be helpful instead of

making him feel defeated already. "I tried to interrogate the workers over at the Red Happiness, but their petty squabbling and stupid little personal vendettas drive me crazy. I can't stand listening to them bicker. It's as if they expect me to solve it for them."

"They expect QuiTai to step in, not you. They're giving you the message to carry to her since they can't visit her and you can."

"Even if I tell her everything they say, she can't step in as long as she's in the fortress."

"Exactly. That probably has someone very worried."

Kyam perked up. "Who? Tell me."

"I can't. I don't dare. You're Governor. You should know what's happening in this colony."

Kyam's last drop of patience had been wrung from him. He opened his purse and tossed a handful of coins at Lizzriat. "Is that enough to buy the information from you?"

"It isn't even close to enough. If I'm seen siding with QuiTai, she had better win, or I'm finished. It's safer for me to stay neutral."

"Sides? Winning? What's going on?"

"Don't come see me again. You've put me in a bad enough position already. Go solve your case on your own, and let everyone see that you did it without my help."

Desperation was a swift tide engulfing him. "Please, Lizzriat. Give me a hint."

"Everything you need to know you'll find at the Red Happiness. And that's all I'll say. Now get out."

Lizzriat opened his office door. Two huge Ingosolians lurked in the hallway. When an Ingosolian shifted gender, they rarely went for subtlety. These two were caricatures of men: brutish, overly muscled, and bristling with red facial hair.

"I take it I'm to be dragged out to the curb," Kyam said.

"If you don't mind. I have a reputation to maintain, after all." Lizzriat turned to his thugs. "Make it look good."

They gripped Kyam roughly by the arms. His boot heels dug tracks in the thick carpeting the length of the hall and raised the nap on every stair. They didn't push hard when they shoved him out on the veranda, but he reeled back a few steps to make it look good. They turned and walked back inside, trusting him to complete the performance. Lizzriat would never make an enemy carelessly.

It had seemed like a good idea when Kyam headed for Voorus' apartment, but now that he was there with a cup of tea in one hand and plate of sweets balanced on his knee, he wasn't so sure. Something was odd about the way Voorus was blushing and wouldn't look him in the eye. Mityam Muul, however, seemed quite content to talk.

"It's been a busy first day here for you. Things aren't usually this exciting in Levapur," Kyam told Mityam.

"Good. I wanted slow. The heat is wonderful. I can feel it down in my bones." Mityam grasped his tea cup between two cruelly twisted fists and brought it to his lips.

With time slipping out of his grasp, Kyam didn't feel he could waste it on pleasantries. "You said you were with QuiTai from the moment you left the harbor–"

"Even earlier. We rode the funicular down together," Voorus said.

Kyam nodded. "Her sarong looked normal at the harbor, but when she got to my office, it was lumpy and odd."

"That would be because she put another one on under it. Don't ask me why. On our way to your office, after we brought Mityam here and left him to rest, she stopped in the marketplace and bought a men's sarong from one of those women who walk around with a basket on her head. She bought a man's blouse too. Then she put them on under her clothes, right there in a tamtuk stall."

"And you never left her side?"

"I didn't watch her put on the extra clothes, but she wasn't more than five feet away, right until she walked into your office."

She was innocent of Turyat's murder, or she had pulled off an impossible trick.

Kyam turned to Mityam. "I know your reputation was made interpreting our constitution, but do you have any insights into murder, Mister Muul?"

Mityam grinned at his tea as if he shared a secret with it. "Not professionally, but it is a little hobby of mine. Cases, I mean. I haven't left a trail of bodies behind me in Surrayya." He smiled at his tea again. "That you know of."

"Your wit in court is legendary."

"Your grandfather, Theram, doesn't always find me so amusing."

"He wouldn't."

Rather than pull his desk chair over, Voorus settled behind Kyam and extended his long legs under the coffee table. Kyam's neck twinged every time he turned back to include him in the conversation, so he concentrated on Mityam. He had a feeling Voorus might prefer that. They'd never been close friends, but they'd never been awkward together. QuiTai had only told Voorus this morning that he was Kyam's half-brother. Maybe he was still in shock.

"I'm looking into the murder of ex-Governor Turyat," Kyam said. "I've never had to make a case that could bear legal scrutiny. It's different in Intelligence. Motives are presumed to center around espionage, and you proceed under the assumption that it's your right and duty to be judge, jury, and executioner."

Mityam directed a knowing nod at Voorus. "How is that different from how Chief Justice Cuulon runs Levapur?"

"We have a lot of work to do here to reform the justice system, I'll admit." Kyam waved off the refill of tea offered by Voorus. "But I don't have time for that now. I want to talk to you about murder. What kind of person is a typical killer?"

"A husband. Or a father."

"Are you being funny?"

Mityam sighed. "Sadly, no. If your victim was a woman, forty percent of the time her husband or lover killed her. Higher than that if she was pregnant. That's not just Thampur. Across the continent, it's a sadly consistent number. Except, of course, in Ingosol, but let's ignore them since most people on this island have a fixed gender. Men tend to be killed more often by strangers than women are, but still overwhelmingly they are killed by someone they know. No wonder some people chose to be hermits."

"That doesn't help me. Turyat knew QuiTai."

"Are you trying to prove her innocent, or find the killer?"

"That's the same thing, isn't it?" Voorus asked.

"Innocence is almost impossible to prove. Find a better suspect instead." Mityam suggested.

"I'm trying! Either I can look at who might want to kill Turyat – I haven't had much luck there – or I can look into who might want to frame QuiTai for murder. That list is longer and much more complicated."

"Frame QuiTai?" Mityam laughed. In the uneasy silence that followed, he glanced from Voorus to Kyam. "She's a retired actress who runs a brothel. Who would want to frame her for murder? Another brothel owner? Did she have a rival in love? Is she up to her old tricks seducing the power brokers?"

Kyam wondered if Voorus wanted to handle this, but the captain raised his hands and shrugged elaborately.

"You knew QuiTai back in Surrayya?" Kyam asked.

Mityam settled back as if ready to take a long sail through his sea of memories. Kyam's teeth ground together.

"The first time I met her, I brought flowers for Jezereet and handed my cloak to QuiTai. I never made that mistake again. Fascinating girl – once you got past the eyes and her nature, of course."

Voorus choked out, "Her nature?"

Kyam bristled too, but he didn't have time to lecture Mityam. The more interesting thing was Voorus' seeming change of heart about QuiTai. Something clearly had been going on between the two, even if they weren't lovers.

Even though he felt it was a waste of time, Kyam decided to give Mityam a truer picture of QuiTai in the hopes that it would trigger the man's insight. "Maybe you're not aware of

QuiTai's career since she returned to Levapur. She opened the Red Happiness with her spouse, Jezereet Karula—"

Mityam made sympathetic noises. "I understand our beloved Jez passed away last year. A great loss to the stage. QuiTai was devoted to her."

"Before that, QuiTai and Jezereet's daughter was killed by werewolves," Kyam said.

"The whole family was slaughtered, right in front of her," Voorus said.

Polite sorrow sat like a mask on Mityam's face. "I hadn't heard. How terrible."

Kyam hoped Voorus would stop interrupting. "At which point QuiTai took up with a local criminal known as the Devil."

"Isn't that always the case with women of her caste? They're sexually attracted to the brutes."

Even though he sometimes thought the same thing about QuiTai, Kyam was deeply angered by Mityam's words. Voorus grunted and shifted in his chair. They didn't have time to behave like frosty, overly polite, wounded Thampurians, though, so he plunged ahead with her history. "The Devil was, by all accounts, merely a local thug among many small gangs. He didn't stand out enough to make a lasting impression on anyone. But after she took up with him, he consolidated power. Anyone who didn't join him disappeared, or so I've heard. This was before I arrived in Levapur."

Voorus nodded. "Although there are always fools who test the Devil's power."

And sometimes, they win. Kyam thought about the two bodies found in the alley last week. Someone was after the Devil. He could probably protect QuiTai from the militia, but not from the Devil's enemies. He wouldn't even know where to look for them.

"So you see, if you look at who might want to frame QuiTai for murder, you have all the thugs forced to surrender power to the Devil, and anyone wanting to take over the Devil's networks," Voorus told Mityam.

Kyam wondered when Voorus had become such an expert on the Devil.

Mityam seemed to think they were telling sailors' tales. "But why would they go after the Devil's woman?"

How could he explain it to Mityam? "It's... she's... No one knows who the Devil is. You can't attack him. It's like trying to grasp a smoke wraith. He's nowhere. He's everywhere. Only QuiTai seems to know who he is. But his anonymity is his weakness too. Kill her, and you've hit the Devil where it hurts. Her lieutenants wouldn't know who to report to. A dozen people could claim to be the real Devil. It would be anarchy." It left a bad taste in his mouth to admit it, but it was true. Lizzriat was right. Without QuiTai's iron fist, Levapur's underworld would be far more dangerous and deadly than it was now.

The Devil, though – Kyam could execute him and no one would miss the bastard. He could free QuiTai from the Devil's clutches.

No! He couldn't think that way. He wouldn't choose the Devil's name over his freedom.

Did QuiTai know those thoughts would creep into his mind? She probably put them there.

"This is a fantasy." Mityam laughed uneasily.

Kyam forced himself to stop obsessing about the Devil. "That's just the local angle on who might want to frame her. My Grandfather is another good suspect," Kyam said. "Although he'd be acting through an agent, and who knows who his agents are?" Except that he knew one. Nashruu.

Voorus sprang out of his chair. He smoothed back his hair as he paced the room.

Mityam leaned back and watched Kyam over the rim of his teacup. "This is interesting. Why would Theram Zul be interested in a former actress? Although did you know she was once a magician's assistant? And before that, she was a lady pugilist. She had to flee Thampur after she knocked out a Thampurian woman in the ring. It seems no one explained to her that the barbarian girl is supposed to lose. She thought it was a real fight, not a staged one." Mityam clapped his fist against his thigh as he laughed heartily. "Knowing our QuiTai, she knew she was supposed to lose but won anyway. She told me that she escaped the country in a dirigible, minutes ahead of the police."

When this was over and QuiTai was safe, Kyam vowed to sit down with Mityam and listen to every QuiTai story the old man had – but this was not the time.

He tried to keep the impatience out of his voice. "Mister Muul, you have to stop thinking of QuiTai as a performer. See her for what she's become. She wields major influence on Levapur's political landscape. From the fashions Thampurian women wear to the price of whiskey, her fingers are in every rice bowl. She's started riots–"

"And stopped them," Voorus said.

Kyam shot him a look and turned back to Mityam. "She's a shadow government."

"And she's a thorn in Theram Zul's side." Voorus smiled.

Mityam seemed pleased about that. No doubt he'd pass that gossip back to his family in Surrayya as soon as he could get to a farwriter. There were many members of the thirteen families who would love to see the Zul family's grip on power broken. Kyam didn't care. By its nature, power was fleeting. To think the Zul family could remain on top forever was foolish.

"Well, my boy, you had better hope that the murderer meant to kill Turyat and only framed QuiTai by accident, because if she's as nefarious as you say, there's no telling who might want her out of the way," Mityam said.

"If she were Thampurian, she wouldn't have been accused. I mean, her alibi would have been enough. Instead, it's ignored," Voorus grumbled.

Kyam agreed with that but didn't want to prompt Mityam into another lecture. He got quite enough of that from QuiTai. "That's because Cuulon is seizing the opportunity to get rid of a witness to his crimes instead of looking for Turyat's real killer."

Voorus grumbled, "Unless he is the real killer." From his expression, it was clear that that had slipped out before he thought it over.

"Oh, hell." Kyam covered his face as he realized Voorus might be right. "And I warned him that I'm looking for the truth. I think I moved her execution up by several hours."

His ticket out was slipping away. He had to fix this. He had to save her.

As if he read Kyam's thoughts, Voorus jumped to his feet. "I'm coming with you."

As Kyam and Voorus rushed toward the town square, Kyam pulled his watch from his pocket and consulted it. He also glanced at the sun, and saw it was already below the top fronds of the palm trees. There wasn't much time left. Executions were typically held at sundown, although if Cuulon wanted to, he could kill QuiTai before then.

It seemed as if the entire town had risen from the midday rest and gone to the marketplace so they could be in his way. Kyam and Voorus pushed through the throngs to the funicular station. Fishmongers swarmed the funicular cars to haul the daily catch to stalls in the marketplace. The engine behind the shack puffed the stench of overcooked juam nut oil into the air. Kyam wasn't sure which stink was worse. At least the fish smelled of ocean.

His hand passed over his eyes. He missed the sea. Although he lived on an island, the water taunted him, rushing over the sand to greet him on the beach and then dancing away from his outstretched fingers. He wanted to stand on a deck again and feel the ship heave under his boots as if it were a great beast. He missed skies of churning gray clouds and foam-topped waves breaking over the railing, uncertain winds changing direction like a school of silvery fish on the reef. He wanted off Ponong. He hated his Grandfather for marooning him here, but he hated QuiTai even more for offering to help him escape and then betraying him. She'd broken his heart for this damned island. But now she could give him his ticket home.

"Governor Zul!"

Kyam lowered his hand. He saw RhiHanya first, because

she was the sort of woman who drew your attention, but LiHoun had been the one to call out his name. He saw the old cat-man through a narrow break in the crowd. He also saw a young Ponongese woman with them.

"Is that PhaSun with them?" he asked Voorus.

"Yes. The little viper."

Kyam shot him a warning look. He glanced around at the crowd to see if any of them had heard the slur. They seemed too intent on the hard work of offloading the heavy baskets of fish to notice a couple of Thampurians.

"We're surrounded by them, Voorus, try to be a bit more polite," he whispered.

Voorus looked confused for a moment and then grimaced. "I didn't mean like a snake. I meant she's... Oh, never mind."

The crowd moved for RhiHanya, and LiHoun was able somehow to contort around baskets and people with odd grace despite his age, but PhaSun shoved and cursed to get through.

"Governor Zul, we have brought PhaSun, as you requested." LiHoun gestured to the petite, curvaceous young woman wearing a bright pink sarong.

"Can it wait? We have a bit of an emergency down at the fortress," Kyam said.

RhiHanya and LiHoun exchanged a worried look, but PhaSun stepped forward. "Are you going to see QuiTai? Are you going to tell her what Inattra did?"

Kyam looked at the funicular. It would be empty soon. He couldn't risk missing it when it left the station, but when would he have another chance to talk to her? Too much was happening at once. "Captain Voorus, could you tell the funicular operator I need him to hold the train for us?"

Voorus bowed and slipped away.

Kyam turned back to PhaSun. She smiled up at him, but her eyes were full of malice. She probably thought she was cunning.

"Have you eaten, little sister?" he asked.

She regarded him with her hand on her hip. "Yes I have, uncle. And you?"

Voorus caught his eye. He shook his head and shrugged.

Kyam glanced at the funicular.

Seemingly impatient to be past the courtesies, as if he were the one wasting her time, PhaSun drew closer to him. "Tell QuiTai that Inattra let Turyat into the Red Happiness early this morning. I think he was selling Turyat black lotus."

"Inattra was?"

Voorus tapped on Kyam's forearm.

"Yes, I saw. He won't hold the funicular for us."

"No. Look. Inattra is coming this way. He must have heard that they found PhaSun. And it looks like he's angry." Voorus pointed into the crowd.

If Inattra shifted any further masculine, his burgundy suit would rip at the biceps. His jaw jutted forward as if it were leading him through the crowds. The blue tones of his skin deepened as he cast a poisonous look at PhaSun. The feeling was mutual. She stared fangs at him.

"Whatever she says, it's a lie, Governor," Inattra said when he came closer.

"Inattra, I'm on a tight schedule. I have to be on this funicular when it leaves. So please, let me ask PhaSun a few questions," Kyam said.

"You're always spreading lies about me, but QuiTai is too smart to believe you," Inattra told PhaSun.

Spitting angry, PhaSun circled Inattra. Kyam backed away and slid his baton out of its holster under his jacket. He hoped they wouldn't attract a crowd, because this was good gossip in the making.

"She lets you get away with all kinds of things because you remind her of Jezereet, but she won't forgive you this time," PhaSun said.

"Forgive me for what?" Inattra asked. "What did I do?"

PhaSun's expression got sly. "As if you don't know."

Outraged, Inattra shoved her. "Oh, no! You're not going to pin that black lotus thing on me! See, I told everyone you'd be nosing around for some to slip to Turyat. And I told them that if anyone gave you some, I'd let QuiTai know that you defied her ban. I heard about you going from room to room late last night begging for a vial. The workers will testify to it."

PhaSun's fists slammed Inattra's chest. "Liar! You horrible, evil liar!"

Inattra easily grabbed her wrists. Screaming obscenities in Thampurian, Ponongese, and Ingosolian, PhaSun writhed but couldn't escape his grasp. She kicked Inattra. Voorus stepped in to stop Inattra from striking back.

"Okay, I think that's enough." Kyam grabbed PhaSun by her waist and pulled her toward the funicular. If he could get her inside, he could talk to her on the ride down. PhaSun's arms and legs sought every target they could hit. Her elbow caught Kyam in the cheek, and he dropped his baton.

"Let go of me!" she screamed.

"You're fired!" Inattra said. "Don't ever let me catch you in the Red Happiness again."

PhaSun nearly wriggled out of Kyam's arms. "My clothes! You're trying to steal them. Let me take my things!"

"As if I'd want some cheap sarongs in ugly colors. I could buy better in this market."

Fingers curled, PhaSun lunged for Inattra's eyes.

Kyam dragged her toward a car. She gripped the sides of the doorway as he tried to push her inside. "A little help would be nice," he called out.

LiHoun smiled and shrugged.

PhaSun's kebaya blouse bunched under her arms. Her torso was slick with sweat, and he could barely hold on as she squirmed.

"I'd help you, but you won't let me thrash her," Inattra said. He folded his arms over his chest. As he shifted androgynous, his bulky muscles disappeared.

Kyam grunted as he took another blow to the cheek.

RhiHanya rolled her eyes and sauntered over. "You tell anyone about this, Thampurian, and you and I are going to have words." She bowed over the smaller woman as if she were going to whisper something in PhaSun's ear.

PhaSun went into frantic motion again. "I'll tell the militia you showed fang in front of a Thampurian! They'll hang you!

No!" She knocked RhiHanya to her knees.

To Kyam, it looked as if RhiHanya fell forward, but her arms wrapped around PhaSun's thighs as if she'd planned it. PhaSun sagged. She still screamed and lashed out with her arms, but her legs gave out under her.

"Can you do her arms so I can get her safely into the car?" Kyam asked between gasps. His cheek throbbed where she'd hit it.

"Not without risking paralyzing her lungs. Dosing someone with venom isn't an exact science." RhiHanya pushed her fangs back with the tip of her tongue. "You did not see that."

Kyam touched his brow. It felt wet. "See what? Thank you, auntie." He looked for his baton. It wasn't much of a weapon, but he needed something for protection when they went into the fortress.

RhiHanya spat. "The flavor of her personality is nothing but bitter. I may not be able to control my anger while I'm connected to her."

LiHoun and Inattra stared down at PhaSun. She looked like a toddler throwing a temper tantrum, except that she couldn't move her legs. Her hair stuck to her sweaty face, and she rolled on the ground. She switched between vile insults and pleading with Kyam to save her from Inattra.

"We can't let her go after the venom wears off. She'll get RhiHanya in trouble," Inattra said.

"What about the things she said about you?" Kyam asked.

Inattra shrugged. "Only QuiTai cares about the black lotus, and she can easily check my story with the others, if she escapes the noose. RhiHanya is the one who risked her life for you. You better make it count, Governor."

Kyam looked up. The funicular operator was methodically going up the line and locking the car doors.

Voorus stepped over PhaSun to get into the car. "Is she coming with us? This is going to be a fun ride."

Kyam was exhausted. It was amazing how much effort it took to hold down a crazed person. "We can't let her go, but we can't take her with us. Can you take her to the Red Happiness and detain her somewhere private until I can deal with her?"

"We can carry her there," LiHoun said.

RhiHanya nodded. Inattra seemed to look forward to it. Perhaps he planned to drop PhaSun a few times or pinch her mercilessly as he carried her across town.

Kyam nodded wearily. He grimaced as he bent over to pick up his baton, but not because of the pangs shooting down his back. He'd ruined his only chance to talk to PhaSun. From the hatred in her eyes, she'd never give him any information. What was he going to do now?

He squatted close to her head but beyond her reach. "Was Governor Turyat alive when QuiTai left the Red Happiness this morning, little sister?"

He didn't usually throw down a luck sign, but he did it quickly now and hoped his sleeve hid his fingers.

"Are you riding or not?" the funicular operator asked.

"Riding, but give me a moment."

"I've got to keep on schedule, Governor."

"A schedule? On this island? Don't make me laugh. Give me a moment. Go lock the rest of the cars." Kyam gestured to the rest of the funicular.

The operator glared at him then stomped off.

"Now, PhaSun, an answer, please," Kyam said.

"Of course Turyat was still alive after QuiTai left the brothel this morning. He was waiting for someone, you know." PhaSun's gaze shifted to Inattra. "He was alive until I came downstairs and caught Inattra standing over his bloody corpse."

"Liar!" In his male form, Inattra's voice was surprisingly high.

Kyam held out a hand to warn Inattra to stay quiet. "Was he still alive when you went to use the outhouse?"

"I don't remember."

"You don't remember." He didn't need to tell her he didn't believe it.

Her gaze darted everywhere, but she had no friends here. Her mouth snapped shut with such finality that he knew he wouldn't get another word out of her.

The operator came back to them. He cast suspicious glances at LiHoun and PhaSun, but his dirtiest look was saved for Kyam. "Governor, I can't wait for you any longer."

He had to choose between trying to get more from PhaSun and saving QuiTai. Kyam jumped into the car. He barely had time to move his hands before the door slammed shut.

Chapter 20: At the End of Their Ropes

The funicular jolted as it began its slow descent down to the harbor. Thankfully, few people were headed downslope this time of day, and Kyam and Voorus had a car to themselves. There were no seats, so they gripped the railing at the bottom of the windows and leaned against the walls.

Kyam rubbed his jaw. PhaSun hit surprisingly hard.

"Do you think Cuulon has gone to the fortress already?" Voorus asked.

"We should have asked the operator before he locked the car door. Cuulon wouldn't have walked, would he?"

"In this heat? It's faster to ride anyway."

"So Cuulon murdered Turyat." Now Kyam understood why QuiTai refused to name the murderer when she clearly knew. He wouldn't have believed her if she'd named Cuulon. The first time they'd worked together, she'd suggested blaming Cuulon for Jezereet's death. Although she hadn't been far from wrong, now that he thought about it. Jezereet's death had been... not an accident, but not part of the plan either. Cuulon had hired the killer, so that made him responsible for her death.

"I'm glad I don't have to work with those two." Voorus nodded upslope. "It must be torture to get between Inattra and PhaSun when they're fighting."

"I'm surprised QuiTai puts up with it."

"That's why I don't live in the barracks in the fortress anymore. There's a strange mentality down there, like its own little world. Some of those soldiers don't leave the fortress for months at a time. They get odd ideas, and there's something about the isolation and heat that seems to cook the crazy into their brains. They have real contempt for Levapur. Say it needs cleansing."

"Wonderful. As if I need another faction with a fanatical agenda to deal with."

Voorus drew up. "I wonder if they murdered Turyat."

"That idea has been floated today. I wish I could remember who said it. But I thought we'd decided Cuulon murdered Turyat in order to frame QuiTai." He looked at Voorus and lifted an eyebrow.

"Is that a question or a statement?" Voorus asked.

"Truthfully, I'm not sure. Ideas?"

Voorus exhaled slowly. "Even if he didn't, I think we made the right decision going to the fortress. You're not only protecting QuiTai from Cuulon, after all. Most of the militia have been waiting for this day ever since the werewolves killed four of our men in the fortress when she escaped unharmed."

"That wasn't her fault."

"Maybe not, but she's the only one left to blame. She... and you."

Kyam realized Voorus knew the situation there better than he did. "Damn it. Are there any men down there you can count on?"

Voorus shook his head. "Maybe one or two. After a while on this island, you stop accepting Thampur's rule and start following the colonial government. I think that really means we're ruled by Chief Justice Cuulon. No offense, Governor, but do you actually *do* anything? Turyat sure didn't. Cuulon makes up laws, and the militia blindly enforces them."

He didn't look happy as he admitted, "And you have to include me with the militia. *We* overlooked crimes we knew he and Turyat were committing because they let us do what we wanted. I didn't realize how far out of hand it had gotten until I saw it through Mityam's eyes. Now I'm ashamed."

"QuiTai said that all the time." Kyam knew she would never forgive him for believing it only because Voorus said it too. He could tell her he'd always believed her, but she'd know he'd lied.

He'd never seen Voorus so enthusiastic before. He'd talked about studying the law. Now that he was, he seemed happy.

"She's right. And she's going to be angry when she finds out what Mityam and I uncovered. Do you know that it's not illegal for a Ponongese to show their fangs to a Thampurian?"

Kyam snorted. "Oh, come on. Everyone knows that's against the law."

Voorus shook his head. "It isn't in the legal code, and according to Mityam, that means it isn't against the law. So RhiHanya didn't actually risk her life when she fanged PhaSun in front of us – although she thought she did, so we still owe her gratitude. She's a brave woman. Not that you'd expect less from one of QuiTai's people."

Realization opened Kyam's eyes to a horrible truth. "But... All those people, Voorus. All those Ponongese the militia executed."

"Murdered, Kyam. We murdered them. I murdered innocent people in the name of the state, which destroys not only my honor, but also our King's honor, and that of every soldier and citizen of Thampur. We are unclean."

The funicular broke out of the jungle canopy. Ponongese women with huge baskets of fish balanced on their heads waited for it to pass so they could continue their climb upslope. Their teenage sons helped carry younger brothers and sisters. Kyam felt a pang of guilt. Those same youths, who looked so harmless now, worried him when they gathered on the steps of the government building. But what was the difference? Not who they were, but how he chose to look at them.

The waiting Ponongese looked back at him with uninterested gazes. He had no idea what their opinion of him was, but they didn't seem to fear him. Why had that worried him earlier but comforted him now? Nothing changed in Levapur, ever; only the way he saw it changed.

As soon as their car crossed the intersection with the road, the jungle canopy arched over the rails again and he couldn't see the harbor road.

"It's a huge problem," Voorus said.

It took a moment for Kyam to remember what they'd been talking about. "I wish you hadn't told me," he admitted. Playing politics made him sick. The truth should always come out. People of honor didn't cover up evil, especially when the government was the source of it. Expediency was moral corruption. He liked the Ponongese. But…

"What will we do about it? Keep it to ourselves and mull it over until we think of the most advantageous way to use the information? Do we keep letting people die, or do we risk giving the Ponongese reason to murder us in our beds?" Voorus asked.

"Not now! We'll discuss this later."

Voorus looked queasy. "Are we bad people?" he asked plaintively.

Kyam wished he had the answer to that too.

Kyam and Voorus rushed out of the funicular the moment their car was unlocked. They ran across the white sand on the narrow beach to the militia's dock. The afternoon wind was rising, and with it white caps formed on the waves beyond the breakwater.

"Is that–" Kyam frowned at the rowboat crossing the harbor.

Voorus shielded his eyes from the sun and peered across the turquoise water. "Ma'am Zul was at the fortress again?"

Kyam was more surprised that she'd already met with Voorus than he was to see her in the rowboat coming from the fortress. He was a bit jealous to see her accomplishing so much while he foundered. "I'm sure she had her reasons."

"I escorted her home. She was safe."

"What danger do you imagine she was in at the fortress?"

"I– Well– It's no place for a woman," Voorus said.

"No, indeed, especially if she's Ponongese." Kyam paced the dock. "Could they row any slower?"

"I think she's trying to tell us something."

Nashruu was waving her hands frantically over her head. She cupped her hands around her mouth, but her voice was swept away in the breeze. She gestured emphatically to the fortress and pointed somewhere upslope, but they couldn't guess the message. She tried to grab an oar from one of the soldiers. They easily shoved her away, but they moved a bit faster.

"She's something, isn't she?" Voorus grinned.

Kyam turned to him slowly. It only took a little slip to reveal the truth. Voorus and Nashruu. His half-brother and his wife. His gaze lifted to the sky as his mouth set in a grim line. The only swear word strong enough was a guttural, "Grandfather."

He wasn't even sure why his temper snapped. He knew when he'd married Nashruu that any child she bore wouldn't be his. But the way Thampurian men saved face when their woman cheated was to kill her. He hated that way of thinking, but years of being told that real men wouldn't allow her to live if she shamed him were hard to ignore.

"It wasn't her fault. I seduced her. Please, don't hurt her," Voorus begged.

Kyam clapped his hand on Voorus' arm. "I won't. You're a good man to try to protect her."

Voorus still looked worried. "She's entirely innocent."

"Oh, ho! I doubt that. Now look here, don't panic. It's okay. She's not in danger. Not from me. You have my oath on it."

"You're not just saying that? Don't hurt her."

"I'm not going to hurt her." Kyam realized his raised voice wasn't making his case. He motioned for calm. "We need to have a long talk about Grandfather and this clan, and why you have to believe me when I say that I will not harm Nashruu."

"You looked angry."

Kyam would not lose his temper. He would not. He set his jaw and patiently explained. "I'm sorry if you misread my facial expression. It had nothing to do with her."

"You're sure?"

"I'm—" He had to bite his tongue and soften his voice again. "I'm sure."

"Then what were you thinking about?"

Why wouldn't Voorus let it go? Now he had to lie. "I was thinking about Lady QuiTai."

Voorus chuckled. "She will do that to you. Make you a bit crazy." He rubbed his chin. "Are you and Lady QuiTai…?" He made hand gestures that might have implied sex, although Kyam found them incomprehensible.

"No."

"It's just, sometimes it seems you two are…" Voorus shrank back from Kyam's grim look. "Oh, look. The rowboat is almost here."

Kyam stood back as Voorus leaned over to reach for the rowboat's sturdy bow. It rocked violently as Nashruu rose. He helped her up onto the dock as one of the soldiers tossed the bowline to Kyam.

Nashruu gestured frantically toward the fortress. "We don't have a moment to spare. Cuulon's there, and he's taken Lady QuiTai into the torture chamber. I ordered Colonel Hurust to stop him, but he simply ignored me." She gasped as if this outburst had used the last of her breath. "You wouldn't happen to know where I can find a farwriter, do you?"

Kyam put a foot on the bench in the rowboat but kept

the other on the dock. "Try the Harbor Master's office at the end of the wharf. Contact Grandfather and see if he has any soldiers hidden in Levapur. If he does, gather as many as you can and bring them to the fortress, quickly. If he doesn't, warn Intelligence that we have a situation here and the colonial militia may have gone rogue."

"Oh no! You're not going to drag Intelligence into this! Grandfather won't stand for it," Nashruu said.

Voorus stepped between them. "We need help right now. Don't be picky about who sends it. You two can work out credit for her rescue after she's been saved."

Nashruu made a face, but she nodded.

"Go now. I'll do what I can at the fortress." Kyam finished boarding the rowboat. "Go with Nashruu, Voorus. Persuade people to be helpful to her."

"You may need my help."

Kyam reached over to remove the rope from the cleat holding the boat to the dock. "That's why I need you to join me at the fortress as soon as you can."

"Oh!" Nashruu clasped her hands over her mouth. Her eyes were wide. She pointed at the fortress with a trembling hand.

The boat rocked wildly under Kyam as he turned to see what had frightened her.

A prisoner convulsed at the end of a rope beneath the fortress rampart. The legs kicked frantically as the prisoner tried to get her hands free. The body swung and twisted, bouncing against the stone walls with each kick.

Kyam staggered back a step. Horror silenced him as a tsunami of hopelessness engulfed him. He sank to the bow bench as his knees weakened.

QuiTai didn't have one last scheme up her sleeve. She was gone.

Despair punched his gut. Nothing felt real. He wanted to claw back time and do it over again. He wanted to go to the fortress instead of going to see Lizzriat again. Why hadn't Nashruu stayed by QuiTai's side and protected her? Hadn't she understood the danger QuiTai had been in?

A wave of disbelief hit him. It couldn't be her. But hope died in his heart. Who else would they have killed? Cuulon had gotten to her.

You could drown in despair, he thought. It was heavy water that seeped into your clothes and pulled you under the surface. Even if you managed somehow to stay afloat, the misty misery clogged your lungs and made you breathe in great sobs.

Hopeless, he tried to find something to grasp onto. All he had was anger. This was all QuiTai's fault. She'd made him arrest her. She'd tricked him into it, and now it had backfired on her. She wasn't as smart as she thought she was. She shouldn't have risked this much. And for what? He'd never know.

How could she do this to him? She'd promised freedom and then snatched it away. She was a cruel devil, a demon. For years, he'd made it clear that all he wanted was his old life back. She knew that. She knew it and she took it away from him again.

Kyam pursed his lips and drew in a deep breath.

He hated her.

"Are we going or not?" one of the soldiers asked.

He turned away to hide the tears brimming in his eyes. Why had she insisted on going to the fortress? She should have let him know what she was up to. Maybe he could have helped her.

But why would she have confided in him? He'd done nothing but sulk since the rice riot. It was his fault they'd grown apart.

Damn her. Damn her to hell. She shouldn't have let him treat her like that.

Kyam forced himself to look at the fortress, but couldn't make his gaze go to the body dangling, lifeless now, from the rope. Soldiers were leaning over the ramparts to watch the hanging. He was too far away to see their faces, but he imagined them smirking.

The soldiers in the rowboat with him laughed as they imitated the prisoner's frantic kicking. Kyam came to his feet and grabbed the nearest one by the collar. He knocked the soldier down and pummeled his face.

Voorus jumped into the boat and grabbed his arm. "We don't have time for this."

He had all the time in the world to wipe the smile off the soldier's face forever. The other one huddled against the stern as he tried to pull the oar out of the oarlock.

QuiTai was dead. The universe had come to an end.

Nashruu shouted from the dock. He ignored her.

Voorus grabbed his arm and held on tight. "It's a man, Kyam. Look. A man. It isn't her."

Panting, Kyam looked up.

He couldn't see the purpling face, but he saw now that the prisoner was a man. So why did his heart still feel as if it were going to crack his ribs? He knew the hanged man's tongue was swelling now, his last breath burning in his lungs. Terrified and desperate, he'd spend his last seconds in horrible pain.

"From his sarong, he's Ponongese, but he's a man," Voorus said.

He heard what Voorus said. Part of him understood, but he was so blinded by grief that he didn't see immediately. Slowly, the truth dawned on him. QuiTai was still alive; he wasn't too late.

Kyam slowly groped his way back to the bench. He licked his lip, tasted blood, and knew it wasn't his.

He looked at the corpse. How had he ever thought that tall man was his QuiTai? Even the sarong was the wrong color. His relief was short-lived, though, as he realized Voorus was right. He'd let another innocent person die because it felt like wasted effort to make things right. His stomach clenched with a new kind of sickness.

"What did he do?" Voorus grabbed the beaten soldier by the collar and glowered down at him. "Why is he being executed?"

"Don't ask me. We didn't have any prisoners except the Devil's whore. Not that I knew about. He's just a damn snake. Why do you care?" the soldier whined. He shot a fearful glance at his companion. The other man shook his head hard and gripped the oar to his chest.

"Why did that happen?" Voorus shouted as he pointed at the fortress.

The soldier's face scrunched up, as if bracing for a blow. "I don't know! Maybe he fanged someone."

Enraged, Voorus shoved the soldier back down. His nostrils flared as his chest rose and fell rapidly. Completely disgusted, he shook his head. "That!" he said to Kyam. "That's what happens when good men hold their tongues. Take a good look, Governor, because you know who it will be next time."

Voorus climbed onto the dock and stomped to the beach. Hands on hips, he looked up at the cliffs and shook his head several times as if struggling to keep his temper. He turned suddenly and waded back through the deep sand. "Okay. We have to stop Cuulon from killing her. But this matter does not go away. Do you hear me?"

Should he make a promise when he knew he wouldn't be around to see it through? Kyam wished he had QuiTai's talent for bending words into artful paper cranes. He wasn't proud of himself for doing it, but he was politician enough to nod as he pushed away from the dock with one of the oars and began rowing. One thought of QuiTai at Cuulon's mercy made him put his back into it.

CHAPTER 21: A DUNGEON DECEPTION

*H*urust couldn't move his head. He was at the far end of the torture chamber, yet only a second ago he'd been ten feet away, at the door. He felt as if he were falling backward, and he tried to use his arms to brace or balance, but they wouldn't move. Struggling didn't help. He'd shackled enough prisoners to the torture board to know there was no escape. He tried to shout, but only gurgled. His eyes darted back and forth.

He didn't know how this had happened. Cuulon had shut the door to the torture chamber a mere second ago. He remembered a sharp pain on the back of his hand and looking down to see a thorn in it. Then, suddenly, being transported across the room and secured to the board. There was nothing between.

Cuulon was slouched in a chair with a foolish grin on his face. He had dreamer's eyes. Hurust didn't smell black lotus in the stale air of the torture chamber, so how had Cuulon taken vapor?

He saw two thorns sticking into Cuulon's cheek and understood. They weren't thorns; they were darts. Somehow, that snake had smuggled a hunting pipe into the fortress.

Hurust flinched as a familiar voice whispered in his ear.

"Normally, I wouldn't waste my time chatting with you. That's for stage villains. But I want you to suffer as much as possible, so that means letting you know what's coming."

A young, small soldier walked into his line of vision. Why didn't the lad do something to help him?

"When you sent your dogs to attack PhaJut's brothel and the Pink Orchid, I wasn't unduly worried. Militia dirt have been swaggering through the Quarter of Delights since long before you came here. Cleaning up after your sort is the cost of doing business. But then you had had my lieutenants murdered. That got my attention."

Hurust recoiled as he heard her voice coming from the soldier. Where had she found a uniform? How had she turned Thampurian?

Her Thampurian eyes rose, as if rolling back into her head, but underneath were snake's eyes. His fingernails scrapped the board as he tried to dig through them.

"Killing my people was a foolish mistake, Colonel. They're valuable. You aren't."

The iron band around his forehead stopped him from shaking his head. He struggled against the shackles. His heart beat fast and hard against his ribs. Her kind didn't have a soul. She'd do terrible things to him no civilized man would think of.

She watched him writhe with a wry smile. There was no pity in her. He'd heard so many stories, but none of them had prepared him for the pure evil before him.

"I understand business. I built my organization by eliminating my competition. Did you think for a moment that I'd let you get away with killing my people so you could take over the black lotus trade? When you hanged all the werewolves, you thought you were free to resume your trade – yes, I know that's why you were exiled from Thampur – but you only removed the lowest level of distribution. The werewolves were unimportant and easily replaced. When you move into someone's territory, you take out the brains of the operation, not the brawn. Do you know what galls me? I mean, other than the waste caused by your excessive stupidity? All this sanctimonious talk of racial purity to get these moronic soldiers to do your dirty work. It's ear poison. It seeps into the rest of the filth you Thampurians brought to this island, like a disease. It ruins lives in small ways and big ways you're far too stupid to realize."

Her eyebrow arched. "But you're going to get a glimpse of it very soon."

Enraged, he shook.

"Well, this has been a lovely chat, Colonel, but as I told you, it bores me. You bore me. To death."

She dragged the small table Cuulon sat behind to the torture board and climbed up on it. She knelt gracefully and leaned close to his face. He tried to shrink away, but couldn't.

QuiTai pulled a long gold necklace from inside her blouse and unscrewed the top of the vial hanging from it. Her little finger pressed into it and came out with a daub of black lotus tar. He tightly closed his eyes as she reached for his face.

She daubed the black lotus into the corners of his eyes. Against his will, his eyelids relaxed. She forced his upper and lower lids wide apart.

He tried to blink as her finger came close to his eye again, but she had complete control over him. A small lens balanced on the tip of her finger. He screamed as her finger neared, and then touched, his eyeball. His legs tried to kick, but the unyielding shackles allowed him only to twitch.

The uncomfortable lens made him blink rapidly as she released his eyelid.

"Have you never worn a costume lens before? They're a bit scratchy, but I assure you that you can't blink them away." She put one in his other eye.

QuiTai hopped off the table. Hands clasped behind her back, she perused the grid of torture devices as she had before, only this time her tiny feet moved at a purposeful pace. "Aha! That's what I was looking for."

She stood on the tips of her toes and reached for one of the metal gags. Testing the weight of it in her hand, she came back to him and climbed back onto the table. She paid no attention to him as she arranged items around her within easy reach.

"Open wide." She gave him a stern look. "Now really, do you think you're going to be able to stop me?"

He'd be damned if he'd help her torture him. He clamped his mouth shut.

"I was hoping you'd do that." Her hand shot out and gripped his nose.

His throat clenched. He tried to twist away but couldn't.

"How heavy do your lungs feel? What would you pay for one deep breath?" She leaned over to pick up the metal gag and examine it.

One little gasp of air. Just one. He didn't need to open his mouth that much. She wasn't looking; he could do it before she realized—

Her gaze locked on his. Slowly, the corner of her mouth curved.

His face flooded with heat as his lungs burned. So this was what it was like to drown. His body fought him. His lungs demanded fresh air. If only he could push her away!

He couldn't hold out any longer. If only he could take a quick breath when she didn't expect it. He tried to breathe through his nose, but she had it pinched so tight that his ears popped from the pressure.

She watched him closely as she held the bar against his lips. Her eyes glowed as she watched him struggle.

Desperate for air, Hurust gasped in a breath.

She shoved the bar into his mouth. It was like a horse's bit. Sharp pains jolted through his teeth as it banged against them. His lips felt like they would rip. She pushed it so far back he began to retch. He'd used it on prisoners before; the idea that Ponongese tongues had touched the bar made him nauseous.

"Why?" he tried to ask as his tongue pressed against the

bar. The taste of rusty metal filled his mouth. Drool spilled from his lips.

"I went to so much trouble, and considerable risk, to arrange our meeting today. Imagine how crushed I was that you refused to visit me. Everyone else trooped in to pay their respects, but you? No." She pressed the back of her hand against her forehead. "Absolutely crushed."

His strained his eyes trying to see if Cuulon were coming around. If they'd both been dosed at the same time, why wasn't Cuulon coming out of dream?

Her gaze followed his. "Don't worry about him. I gave him a double dose."

He reluctantly looked into her eyes as her fingertips lifted his chin.

"I put a lot of thought into this," she cooed. "Originally, I expected to mutilate and torture you in the exact same way your men killed my lieutenants."

She wouldn't. He was a Thampurian, a sentient being, not an animal! She was a monster.

"But then I decided to give myself a little gift. Your death would be an amusement, something to make me chuckle fondly when I look back on this afternoon. Would you like to know what makes me laugh, Colonel?"

She was so cold. He'd never seen anything as terrifying. It wasn't even as if she were angry. Tears streamed down his face. He tried to shake his head. He'd rather die than know what made such an alien creature laugh. She was the devil himself. A demon.

"I'm going to feed you a delicious dish of pure irony. I don't think it will agree with you. You could say you'll be forced to choke it down."

QuiTai pushed something into his mouth. Thinking it was poison, he tried to spit it out. His front teeth felt weird, as if something were compressing them. It was uncomfortable enough, but the pressure made him squirm.

"A low tolerance for pain, I see." She clicked her tongue and slowly shook her head as if scolding him. "That's unfortunate.

For you. Oh, stop blubbering. It's a set of costume fangs. We have to give the cement time to set."

She kept the pressure on the ill-fitting caps for a while longer. Her gaze traveled over the torture chamber as if she were bored, or possibly searching for something to use on him. He winced as he envisioned the tools in her hands.

She gave the teeth a slight tug. "There. The cement is set."

QuiTai hopped off the table and pulled it back into place near Cuulon. She stepped back, eyed it, and then moved it a few more inches. Satisfied, she turned back to Hurust.

"So that your death won't be a complete waste, I decided to give you a unique honor of historical importance. You, Colonel Hurust, will be the last Ponongese to be executed on this island without the benefit of a trial."

She was mad. Evil, and insane. He was so terrified he could hardly breathe.

"I know what you're thinking. You're thinking you aren't Ponongese. Duly noted, but costume lenses and fangs are good enough to pass quick inspection. Change your clothes for a sarong and blouse, and ta-da! Instant Ponongese."

He strained to look down. He was dressed in native clothes. How long had he been insensate? Had she seen him naked?

Hurust quaked. There was no escaping her. He prayed to the Goddess of Mercy as he turned his eyes to the ceiling. He didn't believe in miracles, but he hoped for one from the depths of his soul.

"Well, this has been amusing, but Governor Zul has probably solved Turyat's murder by now and is no doubt racing here to save me from your clutches, so I don't dare waste a moment. I'd hate for him to ruin my fun." She put her hands on her hips. "I do wish you weren't so tall. Dragging you up those stairs is going to be a pain."

QuiTai's fangs sprang forward. She advanced on him. Snot and tears streamed down his face. He begged for his life, but his tongue couldn't get around the metal bar.

She milked a drop of her venom from her fang and smeared it on his tongue. He screamed and writhed until his mouth went numb.

Hurust clutched the cell bars to hold himself up. He'd made QuiTai fight every inch to get him out of the torture chamber. He'd flopped on the ground and refused to move. She'd dragged him this far, but her hair was sticking to her face and she gasped deep breaths.

"Keep going. At this rate, it will take all day to get outside, and I don't have that kind of time, so move," she said.

He shook his head.

She showed him her palm. An ugly welt crossed it. "Sea wasp sting. It nearly killed me. Since then, I've wanted to experiment with their stingers to see how much a person could tolerate, but there aren't that many people I hate enough to torture that way."

The vial that hung from her second necklace was a bit larger than the one for black lotus.

"Must be very careful. I spilled a drop of this on my foot a couple weeks ago." She gingerly unscrewed the top. "As you can imagine, I have no desire to go through that again. Now, Colonel, the stairs, or shall we find out how high you can scream?" She cast a meaningful glance at his trousers.

She wouldn't dare.

She would. She had no sense of decency.

He'd show her how a Thampurian went to his death. He fumbled toward the stairs. She threatened him again to make him climb.

Half way up the winding stone staircase, he staggered. He pretended to try to keep going so she wouldn't use the sea wasp on him.

Her eyes narrowed. She took out the vial. "I know what you're thinking. So here's incentive to stop pretending."

A drop fell on the back of his hand. He'd never felt such pain before. His heart raced as sweat poured down his face. Her face twisted in agony too. Of course. She'd put her venom on his tongue. Hurust grinned sloppily and extended his hand. He motioned for her to go ahead and pour more on him.

"Calling my bluff! Nicely played. Alas, we're on a tight schedule. Can I assume that you're not going to take my threats seriously now? Fine." She stooped down and put his arm across her shoulder. Between pressing him against the wall and lifting, she got him to his feet. With each step, he sagged a bit more.

At the guard's table, she propped him up in a chair while she caught her breath. "I really, really wish I could have caught you in Levapur instead of having to come here. This is a ridiculous amount of work to kill a sniveling dirt Thampurian."

If only he could find a way to signal his men. Maybe if he tapped out a message in code? He couldn't move his arms well, and his hands felt clumsy, but he thought if he could touch a wall, he might be able to do it. His spirits caught this slim chance and soared with it.

"You obviously know how know how my venom works. I can feel your fear and your pain. So after I convince the soldiers that you showed me your fangs–" QuiTai flicked the tip of his prosthetic fangs with her finger. "They're going to drag you up to the ramparts, put a noose around your neck, and shove you off. No trial. No second thoughts. They won't even look closely at your face, because you're just a snake as far as they're concerned. But the worst part is going to be the end of the fall, because I will be right there with you through the whole thing. I'll feel your neck snap, unless these idiots mess up and you slowly suffocate at the end of the rope. It will be awful for me, worse than the time the werewolves were torn limb from limb in the marketplace. Back then I had the luxury of escaping into dream. This time I won't. But you know what? I look forward to suffering with you. I hope it lasts and lasts."

She knelt before him and lifted his hand to her mouth. He couldn't watch as her head bowed like a penitent wife begging his forgiveness. She kissed each of his fingertips before piercing them with her fangs. As the numbness spread, his hope ebbed.

The dungeon door opened. A soldier stuck his head inside. He looked from Hurust to QuiTai. "What's going on here?"

QuiTai grinned up at Hurust. Her inner eyelids snapped

down, turning her eyes Thampurian. She staggered to her feet and clutched the table. "Fucking snake attacked me." Her proper Thampurian slipped into the guttural tones of a marshlander.

"He did, did he?"

"Thought he got the slip on me. Look! His fangs are still out!"

"We know how to cure that, don't we?" The soldier gripped Hurust by the collar and brought him to his feet. He called across the parade ground for help.

"Yeah, let's teach this snake a lesson!" QuiTai said.

Her bravado seemed infectious. The guards puffed out their chests. Their grip on him got rougher.

"Show them they can't get away with showing their fangs, the perverts!"

She smirked as three soldiers dragged him out into the sunlight. One was calling for a rope. He was going to die. Goddess of Mercy, he was going to die.

Cuulon turned his hands over and stared at them. They looked normal. Why had he been thinking that they were odd? He remembered them seeming so very odd and giggling at the way his thumbs bent. That puzzled him because that instant of thought felt as if it had stretched over a long period of time.

The hushed clink of metal drew his focus away from his palms.

Oh, yes. He was at the fortress. Why was that something he had to recall?

QuiTai was shackled to the torture board. She looked ill, as if her head ached. Being on the board did that to you. At that slightly reclined angle, you couldn't quite stand, but you couldn't lie back either. It felt as if you were perpetually falling backwards. Your shoulders bore most of your weight while your toes strained to push against the ground.

She gasped so frantically he almost rose to free her, but his leg muscles felt weak. She was probably acting. Her face went purple and foam gathered at the corners of her lips.

She was an amazing actor. He'd always thought so. But she looked so ill that it worried him.

He gripped his head to stop a wave of dizziness that made him reel. His skin was clammy. There was something he'd forgotten. He knew there was, but his thought was a shy thing that would not come back to him.

He was in the torture chamber. QuiTai was here.

Torture implements hung on an iron grid against the stone wall. If he used the spiked iron ball gag, he could pin her tongue down and silence her.

He remembered thinking that only a moment ago.

As quickly as the dizziness engulfed him, it passed. His mind was clearer. He was thinking of using the spiked ball gag on QuiTai. He remembered now. Putting that in her mouth would make it clear he wasn't there to ask questions, though he rarely pretended to anyway. This room was about suffering. It was about being cruel because he could be.

He began to rise, but his eyes couldn't focus, so he slid back into the seat. Doubt oozed into his mind.

She would always have the upper hand, no matter what he did. She'd find a way to disgrace him. Colonel Hurust would tell everyone about it. The gossip would spread beyond the fortress to the government building and into the family compounds, and those damn *thirees* would laugh behind their hands and say they had always known he was nothing but dirt.

She could probably smell his fear. He wiped his upper lip as he forced himself to his feet. He looked around the chamber.

Where was the Colonel? He'd been here only a moment ago. Cuulon felt as if he were shrugging off dream, but the flavor of vapor wasn't in his mouth. He closed his eyes. When he opened them again, he stared directly into her gaze.

Cuulon stumbled back a step.

He'd dreamed of revenge for so many years, but revenge against what? She'd told him many times she didn't care for him. Back then, he'd believed it to be a lie she told to hurt him, but now it struck him as the truth. He'd loved, worshiped, adored her, and she'd never cared for him. Nothing he did would change that. He couldn't beat love into her heart.

Cuulon wanted this day to be over.

"Where is the Colonel?" he asked.

She glanced to the door and shrugged, a movement that must have sent jolts of pain through her shoulders. She winced but hid it well. Only the tightness of her mouth and deepening lines around her eyes betrayed her exhaustion.

Cuulon perched on the edge of the working table and let his leg swing. How any times had he dreamed of torturing her to death? How many times had he savored a look of surprise in her eyes as she realized he'd finally overcome her? Many times a night he'd resurrect her only to kill her again. He was only getting one chance this time.

He didn't think he'd be able to surprise her. That had been childish fantasy. She looked as if she thoroughly expected him to kill her, and she seemed not to care. Dreams were so much more fulfilling than reality.

She was watching him. The corners of her mouth curved.

"Shall we begin, sea dragon?" she said.

Cuulon wanted to strike QuiTai, but he imagined her laughing at him in triumph. Why did she have to be so difficult? Why did she have to be so cruel?

"We have nothing to talk about, bitch."

He reached for the device that crushed fingers. She'd once told him that she had no doubt she'd break under torture, that believing you could withstand it was the first mistake. He'd show her she'd been right.

She must have been frightened, but she didn't show it. The metal tool in his hand seemed to provoke only a mild interest, not the terror he'd hoped to inspire. Tired – she looked tired, as if it had been a very long day for her too and only stubborn pride kept her going. She didn't even try to clasp her hands into tight fists so he'd have to pry her fingers apart before he crushed them. Was all the fight already drained from her?

"How much punishment will be enough, Cuulon? How much must I suffer for not loving you? My family. My daughter. My Jezereet. And now my life too."

"You made me do those things."

She clearly didn't believe him. "A year from now, will you feel you had complete revenge? Or will you wake in the middle of the night with a thirst that can't be quenched?"

"As you said, it is time to begin. And it is time to end this."

"Absolutely. And now that we're alone, we can be honest, yes?"

"About what? Where is Colonel Hurust?" He didn't want to share her with anyone, but he didn't trust himself alone with her. She had a way of getting into his brain and making him do things he'd never intended to.

"He had to go."

Cuulon didn't remember the Colonel saying goodbye. Had he been that preoccupied with his hands? What sort of man drifted off into daydreams when he was about to get revenge? It worried him that time seemed to have slipped away from him. The harder he looked for it, the most disturbed he was. The immediate past was blank, like a blink that stretched an hour.

"Are you afraid of me still, little boy? I'm shackled. At your mercy." It sounded as if she were trying to recite serious lines but couldn't quite suppress her laughter.

"Don't mock me!" His pride ached. "I will not get on my knees for you, ever."

"You were always far too invested in the idea of sex. Think, Cuulon. I'm obviously not here to seduce you."

What did she expect him to think of her? She'd worked in a brothel, yet she made him feel as if he were the one in the wrong. He'd forgotten what it was like to talk to her, how she could read the merest shift of his feet or hear confessions in a sigh.

He had her complete attention again. That's what he'd craved all those nights when he'd missed her. She was the only person who could reveal his truth to him. His eyelids were the ones peeled back now. He was the one staring into the starkness of his soul. That was her art.

"You could have softened my edges, my lady. Instead, you hardened them. You were the anvil and the fire, and the hammer." His voice caught as anguish rent his chest. She'd pay for making old wounds fresh again.

"It's always about you, isn't it? Your friend Turyat is dead, and you're whining about your broken heart." Her anger was chilling.

"Do you know who killed him?"

The slightest hint of approval played over her face. He hated himself for being elated by it, but it was a drop of rain on a sere desert.

"I have my suspicions," she said.

"Tell me!"

Thank goodness Colonel Hurust had left. What if she said it was his Ravidian masters? What if it were his fault they'd made an example of Turyat? Fear of getting into trouble washed away with his rising anger. Turyat had died because she'd refused to.

He pushed his face close to hers. "Tell me."

"Ooh, you're so commanding and forceful when your spittle flies into my face. I may swoon."

"Whore! Bitch!"

Her eyes gleamed with unshed tears, or was that mirth?

"By the way, your Ravidian masters say hello, and they also say that if you kill me, there is no death painful enough for you."

He gasped. "How do you—"

"If you don't believe me, verify it with them. But until you can, you should be very careful about harming me. You might find out how they turned Petrof. Imagine a werewolf so frightened of the jungle that he couldn't bear to run with his pack. Your thugs made it worse when they tortured him with the ants, but he was already broken. I wonder what the Ravidians might do to make a sea dragon too afraid to ever touch the ocean again?"

Cuulon stumbled back to the table and gripped it for support. No matter where he turned, she was there, waiting to attack.

"Did you know that after I moved to the continent, I worked as a magician's assistant? I survived being impaled by seven swords every night. Twice for matinees. The job sounds more fascinating than it was. Once you know how a trick is done, well, life's one disillusionment after another, isn't it?"

What was she talking about? He didn't care what she'd done after she ran away from him. "What are you getting at?"

"That sometimes we lose people we love in senseless violence, and when we find out why, all it does is add to the frustration and anger. Trust my words of experience."

"I want to know anyway."

QuiTai donned her cruelest smile for him. "I know you do, pet."

She had him twisted around her finger again. It was like before. Because she was telling him that he didn't want something, he wanted it with all his heart. She was usually right, though. Once he got it, it was nothing like he'd dreamed. Still, he had to have the answer.

QuiTai grinned. "I'll gladly tell you what I think happened at the Red Happiness this morning. You don't even need to torture me."

Chapter 22: The Murderer Revealed

Three militia soldiers slouched at the Dragon Bridge's railing, watching the road like sulky delinquents waiting for someone to bother.

Voorus got a bad feeling. He pulled Nashruu off the road. "Cuulon must have sent them to make sure you couldn't contact Grandfather," he said. It was odd calling a man he'd never met Grandfather, and even odder that he and his lover should share that relation. The Zuls were a strange clan. For years, he'd dreamed of finding his real father. Now he wasn't so sure he wanted anything to do with that side of his family.

"You can't possibly know they're going to stop us. What if they were simply patrolling the town, met on this bridge, and decided to pause for a bit of gossip?"

He wasn't sure how he knew, so explaining it to her wouldn't be easy. "I just—"

"Let me at least try to walk past them. I've only been in Levapur half a day. Surely they have no idea who I am yet."

What was he going to do with her? She didn't seem to understand that she should be afraid, or at least concerned.

"Wait–"

It was too late. He paced a quick circle as he tried to figure out if he should follow her. Women were turning out to be far different from what he'd been told they'd be.

Hating himself for being a coward, he ducked behind a glossy leaf and peered through a gap on the frilled edge. Nashruu sauntered toward the bridge. The soldiers slowly stood up straight. Her parasol hid her face, but he could read the conversation well enough from her movements.

She pointed down the lane on the other side of the bridge. The soldiers shook their heads. She tried to walk past them anyway.

He pushed through the plants as one grabbed her arm.

She lowered her parasol, snapped it shut, and swung it at the soldier's legs. After a tight little shake of her shoulders, she walked back toward Voorus, passed him, and then ducked into the thicket beside him.

"I stand corrected, darling. You were right. They're very sorry, but they can't let me pass. Some nonsense about a dangerous snake being seen in the neighborhood. I'm not sure if they meant a Ponongese or an actual snake. There must be another way to the compound other than crossing the bridge." She picked flowers out of the folds of her parasol and flicked them to the ground.

"There is, but it's a long walk around the hills, and that entrance is probably guarded too. Maybe we should simply find another farwriter. I have no idea where, since we've been blocked from almost every place I can think of."

She placed her hand on his forearm and leaned closer to him with a look of earnest feminine distress. She'd had that same look on her face the first time they'd met, when he'd rescued her little nephew from a tree in the park. She'd seemed so sweet and innocent back then. He gulped when he realized he'd been her prey that whole time. Had she shoved the poor little boy up onto the high limb?

"If you think that's the sensible thing to do, then by all means, I bow to your superior understanding of the situation – this time. So where do we find one?" she asked.

"There are a few places in town with machines, but this is hardly a message you want to send through a clerk."

"Would Lady QuiTai have one in the Red Happiness?"

"It's illegal for Ponongese to have farwriters."

She made a face. "I know that. But that wouldn't stop her, would it? Her main lieutenant, LiHoun, used to have one, and the Li Islanders aren't allowed to have them either. Unfortunately, he hasn't responded to Grandfather's messages since the rice riot, so we're not sure if he still has it."

Voorus sucked in a breath. "LiHoun was Grandfather Zul's agent?" Was it possible that QuiTai didn't know her most trusted lieutenant gave Grandfather Zul information? If she did, why was LiHoun still alive? Then again, Cuulon was still alive, and Turyat still would be too if QuiTai had had any say in the matter.

Nashruu pursed her lips and shook her head as if angry with herself. "Forget I said that."

"You can't say something like that and then expect me to forget it simply because you want me to."

"Sh! Those soldiers are looking this way."

The leaf sprang up to slap his face when she let go of it. They skulked through the trees until they were far enough from the bridge that they could risk walking on the road.

Voorus had to ask the question burbling in his brain. "Were you always this way? You seem so different now."

She opened her parasol and took his arm. "I'm not sure I can answer that. I've never felt as if I wasn't me. Then, now, I'm essentially the same. You too. You always look as if you'd rather be anywhere else."

He stopped and looked into her eyes. "No."

"Come now, you can be honest. I know you hated being a soldier."

"That? Yes. But being with you made it tolerable." He cleared his throat. "I only ever wanted to study the law and live quietly."

Her laughter traipsed down a musical scale. "You're a Zul. You'll never be allowed to live quietly." She crushed enticing parts of her body against his arm. "At least we're on this adventure together. There's no one else I'd rather crawl through a jungle with."

It didn't matter if she were saying that only to get him to help. He wanted to believe it, so it had to be true. "We should find LiHoun, then. He might still have that farwriter, and if he doesn't, he might know where to find one."

"If he doesn't, we should try Lizzriat." She noticed his surprise. "The Ingosolian owner of the Dragon Pearl."

"I know who Lizzriat is. I'm surprised you do."

"Grandfather keeps me well informed."

She strode briskly toward the Red Happiness. With his long legs, Voorus had no problem catching up to her.

"I've always been curious about the Red Happiness. Who would have imagined I'd get to see inside?"

He gripped her elbow hard enough to bring her to a stop. "I can't let you go in there. I'm sorry, but as family, I have to protect your name."

Her gloved hand covered her mouth as she giggled. "Voorus, my love, I understand what you're trying to do, but you have exactly two seconds to forget all that nonsense and stop getting in my way, or I will destroy you." She smiled angelically at him as her eyelashes fluttered. "But if you insist that the Red Happiness is off limits for me, find a way to sneak me past those soldiers and get me to the compound. I *desperately* need to fetch something from my luggage."

Colonel Hurust's secretary, Major Rheagus, sighed when he saw Kyam. "I was warned you'd probably come back. You have no authority here, so why don't you go back to your office and paint some pretty flowers?"

Kyam wanted to punch him.

"The King himself has interest in this matter, Major. We have to stop Cuulon before he tortures Lady QuiTai to death."

Major Rheagus scratched his ear. "You're not in charge here."

Kyam wanted to grab him by the throat. "Where's Colonel Hurust?" He might have imagined the look of worry in the major's eyes, but he decided to press the young man anyway. "I'm not only the Governor; I'm a Colonel in the Intelligence division. Do I need to point out that I outrank you? And before you make any smart remarks about the military not being under the command of Intelligence, you may want to consider my fists." The blood had washed off as waves had splashed over him while rowing across the harbor, but bruises and an old scar gave his knuckles an aura of lurking violence.

Major Rheagus' wide eyes stayed focused on Kyam's hands as he sank back into his desk chair. "This is our chance to be rid of the Devil's whore. You should be thanking us for cleaning up the filth up there for you instead of trying to stop us."

Kyam took a deep breath. Then another. He leaned close to Major Rheagus and glowered. "It's possible Cuulon, not Lady QuiTai, murdered Turyat, and I know you wouldn't dare execute someone for a crime they didn't commit. But even if you want her to die because she's Ponongese, let me explain that our king wants her alive. Do you know what the punishment is for defying him? They take you out into the salt plains of the Great Malisium Desert and bury you up to your neck in sand."

No one had ever done such a thing to a Thampurian. Kyam hoped Major Rheagus didn't know that.

The major reached into his sleeves to scratch his arms like a vapor addict craving dream. "Do you have proof that Cuulon is guilty?"

"The sand in the salt plains is so alkaline that when your sweat mixes with it, you suffer chemical burns. It's also so dry that it sucks the moisture out of your skin and mummifies you alive. You'll be delirious in hours, but we'll make sure you survive for weeks."

Major Rheagus grabbed his keys. "I'm taking you to my commander. That's all you can order me to do." He rushed out of the office and hurried for the stairs.

The four guards at the table appeared confused when Kyam opened the dungeon door. They shrank back from the sunlight.

The major's lips pursed. He grabbed a jellylantern hanging from the wall and headed down the stairs.

Kyam inhaled deeply. He didn't smell vapor, even though the guards had dreamer's eyes. The tiles on the table hadn't changed since his first visit to the dungeon this morning. Frowning, he followed Major Rheagus down the stairs.

Someone had replaced the jellylanterns in the dungeon since his earlier visit. They didn't illuminate much, but at least he could see into each of the cells. This was what it had been like when he'd first brought QuiTai to the dungeon this morning. He had a good idea who'd done it, but he couldn't guess why.

Major Rheagus led him to a squat wooden door at the far end of the cavernous room. His mouth set into its prissiest clench. "I better not get in trouble for interrupting them."

"You can always tell them you were just following orders."

"The door is probably locked."

Kyam shoved open the door and rushed inside.

He didn't dare show his relief. She was alive. He staggered back a step as the rush of emotion overwhelmed him.

She was alive.

QuiTai was bound to the torture board by her wrists and ankles. Iron bars crossed her chest and hips. She looked weary, but he didn't see any blood. He hoped the wicked hooked instrument at her feet had only been used to menace her.

He'd never forgive her for putting him through this. He shot her a look of pure venom; her most devilish grin spread across her face in triumph.

Cuulon's chair fell to the floor when he leapt to his feet.

He seemed flustered and a bit embarrassed to be caught not torturing her. "What is the meaning of this, Zul?"

"Chief Justice Cuulon, you're under arrest for the murder of Governor Turyat," Kyam said.

"What?" The finger crusher clanged loudly when he dropped it on the table. "I didn't murder anyone. What sort of nonsense is this?"

QuiTai clicked her tongue in disapproval. "Wrong. Not even close, Governor."

"This wasn't my idea," Major Rheagus told Cuulon. "I only came down here to find Colonel Hurust."

"What in the name of infernal darkness is going on here?" Cuulon roared. "She was about to tell me who murdered my friend."

"Was I?" She sounded bored.

Cuulon glared at her. Kyam wasn't sure who was torturing whom in this room. Cuulon only had things that maimed and tore flesh; she was armed with a far more vicious weapon.

"I don't understand what's going on," Major Rheagus grumbled. "How does she know who killed Turyat?"

Her eyes worried Kyam; he'd seen her this exhausted before. She'd been busy since he'd left her. He found the keys to the shackles on the table and grabbed them. "Why do I have a feeling this is all for show?" he whispered to her as he unlocked one at her wrist.

"Test them. You'll see they're all real." Despite how tired she was, mischief danced through her eyes.

"Where is Colonel Hurust?" Major Rheagus asked. "He's supposed to be here."

"He was, earlier, but had to go," QuiTai said. "Thank you, Governor." She rubbed her wrist and smiled down at Kyam as he squatted to unlock her ankles.

"What do you mean, 'Had to go'?" Cuulon asked.

Kyam stepped in front of QuiTai. "Let's not lose focus here. Lady QuiTai was accused of murdering Governor Turyat. New information has come to light that will exonerate her."

"Such as?" Major Rheagus asked.

Kyam cast a glance over his shoulder at QuiTai. She seemed amused, and not inclined to help him. He rubbed his hands together. "Well, there's her alibi."

"That's hardly new information, Zul," Cuulon snapped.

"There's also the fact that she didn't want Turyat to die. She enjoyed torturing him too much. Which isn't proper behavior for a lady, but I guess we all know she's..." Kyam wished she'd rescue him from this humiliating exercise. Her lips trembled as if she'd laugh any second.

"Zul, why don't you shut up? She was about to tell me who killed Turyat when you barged in here," Cuulon said. His neck grew pink above his collar and he twitched like man who chain-smoked kur. "And it wasn't me!"

QuiTai pushed away the last metal bar securing her to the board and walked around the room. From the way she moved, her muscles were sore. Kyam was relieved that was the worst of her injuries.

As if she'd just remembered the men who were waiting anxiously to hear what she might say, she turned around, smiling apologetically. "I'd rather tell you somewhere else, such as in the marketplace."

"You don't leave here unless I'm convinced you're innocent," Major Rheagus said. He set the chair upright and plopped into it.

"It's quite simple," QuiTai said. "And deathly dull."

Cuulon grabbed her arm. "Stop toying with me!"

"I thought you liked that."

Cuulon's hand rose. He didn't hit her, but the threat was obvious. "Tell us who killed Turyat, or so help me, I'll have the soldiers push you off the ramparts with a rope around your neck, then haul you up before your neck breaks, and do it over and over again until your neck is bruised and you've forgotten what it's like to have air in your lungs."

Instead of being scared, as any sane person would be, QuiTai seemed mildly annoyed. "You don't understand the premise of dramatic tension, do you? Oh, very well. I'll tell you."

"Who?"

"But first—"

"Oh, for the love of deep water, just start removing her fingers." Major Rheagus grabbed the iron tool from the table and lunged across the table.

She stared him down. "If I'm harmed, I will take the name to my grave."

To Kyam's amazement, Cuulon stepped between Major Rheagus and QuiTai. "Don't you dare touch her."

The major's mouth dropped open.

"Tell me. Give me peace from this torment," Cuulon begged QuiTai. A tear dropped down his cheek.

QuiTai caressed his face. "There will be no peace with the answer. You'll be up nights howling at the moon for the unfairness of it. Tears will flow until your eyes are dry as the salt plains of Ravidia. You'll call down the gods themselves to demand an apology for the stupidity of it all. No rest, no satisfaction, no peace, ever. The absolute waste of Turyat's death will torment you to your last breath. And I'm more than happy to be the person who unleashes that torment in your heart. But first—"

Kyam groaned. "Can you have two firsts?"

She motioned for silence. "I want your promise – Chief Justice Cuulon and Governor Zul – that the murderer will be brought to trial. It won't be fair, of course, but there must be a trial, with evidence and a legal defense and all the other actors necessary for a farce."

Kyam bowed his head as revelations swarmed his brain. He didn't understand her plan, but the glimpses were astonishing enough. She never played for petty stakes.

"I don't understand. If it's a farce, then why do you want a trial?" Major Rheagus asked.

"Precedence. She's setting a precedent," Kyam said.

The men stared at him. He smiled sheepishly, because it was embarrassing to show how slow he was compared to her. Then he realized the other men had no idea what he knew. They hadn't seen and heard everything he had today. They didn't know what he did. And yet, how superior could he feel when the answer had been screaming in his ear all day and only now he was hearing it?

"I agree. Do you, Cuulon? Come on," Kyam said.

Cuulon made a face then tersely nodded. "Then who murdered Turyat?"

Kyam couldn't resist interrupting QuiTai. She had to know that he had, finally, figured it out. "PhaSun did it."

QuiTai inclined her head to him. "Very good, Governor," she murmured.

"PhaSun? Who is PhaSun?" Major Rheagus asked.

"A worker at the Red Happiness. A stupid, useless, meaningless sex worker." Cuulon sagged against the table. "But why? He never hurt her."

Kyam paced. "She wanted to frame Inattra for selling black lotus to Turyat, so that QuiTai would make her the Madam. But Inattra had already warned everyone in the Red Happiness not to sell any to her." It was all coming together. His conviction grew as he talked through it. "So early in the morning – early by Quarter of Delights standards – she crept downstairs to meet Turyat. Having been promised a pipe, he was still lingering on the veranda with that tenacity we've all seen in vapor ghouls. After QuiTai left the brothel to go meet the *Golden Barracuda* at the harbor, PhaSun told Turyat to wait while she went to buy a vial. It was possible that word hadn't gone beyond the brothel and she'd find a seller. That's when something went wrong. Maybe he got violent. She struck him and posed a pipe beside his body, and left a lit spirit lamp on the bar for good measure, knowing that QuiTai would return from the harbor shortly. Then the blood began to flow, and she realized she'd hit him too hard. She ran upstairs to hide in her room. She probably changed quickly out of her sarong and blouse, which may have had blood spatter on them–"

His eyes narrowed. Blood spatter. Earlier this morning, QuiTai had to change clothes because of blood spatter too. Where was Colonel Hurust? Where had all the jellylanterns gone earlier? For that matter, where had the dungeon guards disappeared to, for all those hours when QuiTai was locked in the cell? She'd wanted to be brought to the fortress. She'd wanted to be in the dungeon, where no one would watch her.

Their gazes locked.

He didn't know exactly how she'd done it, but he knew she'd made Hurust disappear. That was why she'd come to the fortress. And he knew that she saw he'd figured it out.

"What? Is that it?" Major Rheagus asked. "Are you finished?"

He turned to the major and Cuulon, expecting to see a sign that they suspected something was terribly amiss in the fortress. They didn't. They were so many steps behind her that they might never catch up.

He had to get her out of here before they did.

After drawing in a deep breath, Kyam rushed through the rest. "After PhaSun struck the lethal blow, she went upstairs to hide. Inattra heard her door slam, woke, dressed, and went downstairs to find the body. Thinking she could turn it to her advantage, PhaSun raced downstairs, pretended to see his body for the first time, and then ran out in the street to summon the militia."

QuiTai nodded.

"That's it?" Cuulon roared. "My friend died because of a fight between whores?"

"Yes. Absolutely." Kyam placed his hand at the small of QuiTai's back and ushered her toward the door. They had to leave.

"To show there are no hard feelings, I'll see to it that PhaSun is delivered to you," QuiTai said.

Kyam moved her firmly to the door. "She has to live long enough for a trial, so don't let Cuulon at her." He opened the door.

"He died by accident?" Cuulon shouted even louder. "I'll kill her. I'll dig her bowels out of her belly and burn her eyeballs!"

"For once, exit the stage without delivering your line," he growled at her. He'd felt her draw in a breath. He shoved her out of the chamber before she could say anything.

"But what about... She's the Devil's whore! We should

keep her here," Major Rheagus said.

"Find your Colonel and see what he says." Before they could object, Kyam bowed to them then rushed after her.

"Wouldn't want to leave this behind." QuiTai picked up a small case and her jacket from the floor of her cell. "I've only worn it once, after all."

He could tell from her voice that she wasn't as calm as she was pretending. She might have defeated the odds again, but she was terrified of the fortress and didn't have the energy to hide it much longer.

Kyam strode to her and grabbed her elbow. He spun her around, yanked her against him, and hugged her hard. "I thought you were dead. I thought–" His pent-up sob of relief, the one he hadn't dared release in front of Cuulon and Major Rheagus when he saw she was alive, welled out of him as he pressed his lips to her forehead. "I went a little mad."

She buried her face against his chest. "I am sorry, tamtuk."

He almost kissed her, but paused. "Did you call me 'little fried dumpling'?"

She made a face. "I guess I did. Can we pretend I didn't?"

"Are you kidding? I'm going to bring it up every chance I get."

Kyam felt her smile when he kissed her. She dropped her jacket and slid her hands up his back. He cupped her head in his hand. How could he have let so much time slip away? Why had he denied himself this?

He chased her lips as she leaned back. Her hungry kisses grew more intense until they were forced to part and pant for air.

With a flirtatious smile, she stepped out of his arms. "It sounds as if the guards are awake. I thought I heard them talking. And we should save any..." – she pointed from him to herself – "for when we're..."

"Alone?"

She nodded. "Meet LiHoun at the Jupoli Gorge Bridge in three hours. He'll bring you to me."

He grabbed her hand and pulled her into his arms again. "Not sure if I can wait." He kissed her neck below her ear.

"Eight months, Kyam. What's a few more hours?" Her fingers trailed down his lips. "You're right. Meet LiHoun in two hours." Her hand stopped at the top button of his jacket.

"I've been an idiot," he confessed.

"Yes, you have, but I forgive you."

Kyam grabbed her hand. "I think your line was, 'No, my love. You're brilliant.'"

"You accused Cuulon of murdering Turyat."

He knew she was teasing him, but he was a little upset. "Hey, I figured it out. And if I hadn't come when I had, Cuulon might have changed his mind and decided to torture you anyway."

"I had him where I wanted him."

"You were shackled to that board."

"A mere technicality—"

Footsteps clattered on the staircase, and they sprang apart. QuiTai checked her sarong as Kyam fussed with his cuffs.

Nashruu clambered down the steps, followed by Voorus. She held a strange contraption in her hand, with a fat glass cylinder similar to a jellylantern set in a metal framework.

"Oh!" Nashruu said. Voorus bumped into her when she stopped suddenly. "So, we're not too late?"

"You're a little too early," Kyam grumbled.

Nashruu pouted. "And I'd so hoped I'd get to use this."

QuiTai's breath caught. "Is that...?" Mesmerized, she crept closer to Nashruu.

Nashruu proudly held it up. "A sea wasp gun? Yes, it is. Like it?"

Kyam hadn't suspected the Thampurians were developing something like that. They'd taken the bulky tanks from the Ravidian weapons they'd found on Cay Rhi and made them small enough to fit into a handheld device. He had no idea how many shots one could get from that small tank, or how accurate it was, but the potential for such a weapon was horrifying.

"May I hold it?" QuiTai extended both hands.

"Absolutely not." Nashruu yanked it out of reach. "Unless..."

Kyam saw how tempting it was for QuiTai. After seeing the fantasies strewn around her office, he knew she itched to tear the sea wasp gun apart to see how it worked.

"I will not sell my freedom to your Grandfather for that." QuiTai dismissed the gun as if it already bored her. "I don't wish to be an alarmist, but there's a major in the torture chamber who would gladly use any excuse to keep me imprisoned here. Before he thinks one up, I intend to leave. Excuse me, Captain Voorus." She went around him to climb the steps.

Nashruu followed her up the stairs. "The sea wasp gun is part of a bigger offer, Lady QuiTai."

Kyam didn't have anything like that to offer her. They had a deal, though. He had to get her out right now, before Nashruu offered her something she couldn't resist.

"I'll take you back to the Red Happiness," he said. He rushed to her side and firmly ushered her up a step.

"Wait, Kyam! Don't you dare interfere." Nashruu leveled the sea wasp gun on him. "This is between Lady QuiTai and me. And she doesn't leave this fortress until we have an understanding." She grinned at QuiTai. "What do you want? Coins? Land? Power? This gun? I can give you many things."

"But not what I want," QuiTai said.

Nashruu gestured toward Kyam. "You can have him."

Kyam had always known he was disposable, but it stung to hear his wife say it. She was the new generation of family agents. His time was over.

"Or, if you prefer, you can have Cuulon. You can torture him any way you please, with impunity. You can make him suffer, QuiTai. Make him hurt for everything he's ever taken from you. Think of it. Revenge without limits. Our torture specialists in the secret police will advise you on methods to keep him alive while making him experience more pain." Eyes gleaming, Nashruu stepped closer to her. "Think of him suffering like your daughter did while Petrof ripped apart her flesh. Imagine making him feel that every day and begging for death that never comes."

QuiTai blinked. Kyam wanted to plead with her, but how could he appeal to her better nature when he planned to use her the same way Nashruu would?

"Your father, mother, and aunts, avenged. Scream for scream, horror for horror." Nashruu's voice seemed to creep into the back of his mind. It wove a repellent dream of ugly desires. It made old wounds bleed again.

The tip of QuiTai's tongue darted across her bottom lip.

Could she betray him again? He wouldn't blame her if she did. From her point of view, working for his Grandfather and for Thampurian Intelligence was practically the same thing. He'd only offered her a way out of the fortress, but it was clear Nashruu could give her the same thing... and more. Oh, so much more. QuiTai probably wanted this as much as he wanted to leave Levapur.

"I want you to know that my decision isn't personal. It's business," QuiTai said.

Kyam wasn't sure whom that was meant for. He had a terrible feeling he was about to pay for ignoring her all those months. QuiTai was patient when it came to revenge. She waited until it had the biggest impact.

Sensing she'd swayed QuiTai, Nashruu went in for the kill. "Your Jezereet would still be alive if Cuulon hadn't sent Petrof after her. Because of Cuulon, Petrof turned her into a vapor ghoul. Don't you want to make him pay for all the pain he put you through?"

Kyam's heart sank. He was trapped here, and he'd never get to leave. It was over.

QuiTai drew in a breath. Her lips parted.

Nashruu was radiant in her triumph.

QuiTai's expression hardened. "No one gives me revenge. I take it."

Nashruu pushed onto the stair beside Kyam. She gripped QuiTai's arm. "Grandfather is prepared to be generous. You only need ask. Do you want books for your school? Immunity from prosecution for your crimes?"

That was a better offer. She'd be a fool not to take it. If only he had more to bargain with... but it was too late now.

QuiTai looked over Nashruu's head to meet his gaze. He pleaded with his eyes. If only he could beg on his knees.

"I'm tired. Let's speak at another time, Ma'am Zul."

Kyam sagged against the stone wall. He closed his eyes, gulped in a breath, and opened them again. Was that yes or no?

"You won't like Grandfather when he's angry, Lady QuiTai. His private soldiers could return to Levapur. The assembly law is only the beginning. Your people could be pushed to the brink. Children might get hurt," Nashruu said.

QuiTai smoothed her sarong. Her palms pressed together at her waist.

Kyam took a step back. So did Voorus.

Her face was a mask, but Kyam saw rage in QuiTai's eyes. Her voice had never been this quiet before. "You know as well as I that the problem with a threat like that is that you'd better be willing to see it through. One of the guards upstairs told me that you've sent the secret police in Thampur after his family, and that of Colonel Hurust's secretary, for failing to obey you. While I commend you for taking the necessary steps, are you prepared to live with the slaughter?"

Nashruu lifted her chin.

"I see. So go ahead. Pass your vile laws and make my people miserable just to show you can. Incite them to rebel. Let the blood run in the streets." QuiTai's upper lip curled as she drew inches from Nashruu's face. "I dare you."

Chapter 23: And for Her Final Trick, a Disappearing Act

*T*he scented smoke of grilled evening meals faded as Kyam climbed the twisting road through Levapur. The onshore breeze brought welcome coolness to the sunset hour. It was a peaceful end to the day, a time best spent on a veranda gossiping with neighbors; but he was on his way to meet LiHoun at the Jupoli Gorge Bridge. He couldn't remember ever coming this far upslope. The road narrowed at the edge of a cliff beyond the last dilapidated apartment building and then dissolved into jungle. This, then, was where Levapur ended.

With his hands on his hips, he gulped deep breaths. Up here, it was clear how hilly the town was. Even the flat land sloped from the mountainsides down to the sea cliffs.

When he walked around Levapur it seemed like a bustling, sprawling town. Now he saw the truth: it was only a tiny cluster of buildings backed against a cliff. The jungle laid siege to its borders. Swaths of green through the buildings showed that the jungle had already breached the ring of civilization and infiltrated deep into the heart of the town. Holding it back was a constant battle, probably futile.

Beyond the island, the ocean was deep turquoise. The past few years, he'd tried not to torture himself with longing glimpses of the open water. Today the pull had been more urgent than usual. He'd relished the taste of salt on his lips left by the sea spray as he'd rowed to the fortress. His pulse had beat with the surge of waves against the breakwater. He was a sea dragon. He wasn't meant to live chained to land.

Past the monolith stones jutting out of the Sea of Erykoli, junks navigated the shipping channels. One of them might be the *Golden Barracuda*. Next time it was in port, he would swallow his pride, board it, and shake cousin Hadre's hand. Or maybe it wouldn't be here, but he'd find a way to repair that friendship, he vowed to himself. It was time to stop sulking.

He felt burdens lifting from his soul as he drank in the view of the vast blue sea. Somewhere beyond where the horizon curved was home.

Unlike the green water of Ponong, the harbor water in Surrayya was dark gray. Junks flying the chops of the thirteen families gathered there after returning from months at sea. Their rich cargos had built the capital city from marshland into a sophisticated metropolis of small islands connected by canals.

The Zul family compound encompassed almost an entire island in that network. Only the road connecting the bridges was outside the walls. That wasn't the home he was going to. He'd never liked living under his Grandfather's unrelenting rule. After several years out of the world of espionage, he probably wouldn't be allowed to return to that work anyway. All male Zuls worked on their fleet of junks for several years, so he might return to the sea, but he couldn't call himself a master at any task on board. He couldn't think of anywhere he'd be useful.

He wasn't sure where home was anymore.

"Governor Zul?" LiHoun called out.

Kyam turned around and walked to the bridge where the old cat-man was waiting for him. The Pha River thundered below them, although it was almost impossible to see the rapids through the mist.

LiHoun handed him a sack to put over his head. The rough fabric stank faintly of wet dogs. Kyam made a sour face, but he put it on because it was the only way to get to QuiTai.

LiHoun took his hand and led him across the bridge. They climbed up a small rise and turned toward the setting sun. For a while, he heard the engine of one of the funicular lines that ran to the upslope plantations, but it grew fainter. Only the sound of rushing water and the jungle remained.

His boots slid in patches of mud. The path rose and fell and sometimes turned. He'd tried to count his steps but lost his place.

LiHoun stopped him. "One little step up."

Kyam lifted his foot too far and lurched as he stepped down on what felt like timber grass.

"This is narrow. Careful please."

LiHoun put his hand on a timber grass railing as thick as his wrist.

"Now three steps to your right, Governor Zul."

He knew now he was on a walkway leading to a house. Zigzagging paths thwarted demons that could only travel in straight lines. When vines trailed over his shoulders, he guessed they'd passed through a moon gate. Between that and the stink of the cloth over his face, he suspected he was at Petrof's hidden den.

Had Petrof been alive all this time?

"Wait here," LiHoun said.

He heard something heavy moving.

"She does not like to be disturbed. We draw back the bridge so that no one can cross it," LiHoun explained.

The old man took his hands again and led him into darkness. His boots shuffled across a smooth wood floor. The sounds of the Pha River suddenly muted.

LiHoun dropped his hands. His footsteps faded.

Kyam was sure she was there, and that they were alone now, even though he hadn't heard a door close.

"Can I take this off?" He pulled off the sack before she answered. He stood in the center of a bare room in a house that wasn't Thampurian, but wasn't Ponongese either.

She sat in a large, ornately carved chair too big for her petite frame, and yet she looked quite at home in it. A low table sat to the side of her chair. The large sliding door behind her was closed.

He smelled kur smoke. He turned around and saw a narrow front doorway. LiHoun squatted outside, under a moon gate covered in flowering vines. The smoke from a kur curled from his fingers.

Kyam turned back to QuiTai. She wore a kebaya blouse richly embroidered with Ponongese designs. He'd never seen one that elegant. The wide hem was gold. Like her blouse, the design was Ponongese, but not like any other one he'd seen before. The Pha tended to use small repeating geometric shapes while the Rhi took inspiration from nature, but this wasn't either of those. He wondered if hers were a Qui pattern.

He gestured to her sarong. "I already know you're the most poisonous thing in this jungle. No need to warn me."

"You always say such sweet things."

Kyam drew close to her throne – there was no other word for it – and put his boot up on the little table. He leaned on his thigh. "I got you out of the fortress. Time to uphold your end of the bargain."

"Of course."

"No games."

"No games." Her restless hands traced the chair's carved lines.

"But first–" he said.

The corner of her mouth curved.

"I have to know. How did you do it?"

"I'm in no mood to be arrested again today, so I'm going to pretend I have no idea what you're talking about," QuiTai said.

He took her hand and turned the palm up. His fingertips traced the welt left by the sea wasp sting so many months ago. He pressed his lips to the scar. "I spent all day running around trying to solve a mystery that didn't matter. Meanwhile, you were committing an almost perfect murder. Only you would be clever enough to ask to be arrested before committing the crime."

"Flirt."

"Unless there's a secret passage in that dungeon, I swear what you did was impossible. Oh, I know you flitted in and out of that cell at will, but the shackles on your wrists and ankles in the torture chamber were real, as you were careful to point out."

"They're always real in the best tricks."

"I can see how you could have locked yourself in them, except..." He held up his hands as if he were on the torture board and looked from one wrist to the other. "The last one. How did you reach from here" – he nodded to the left – "all the way over there?" He wriggled the fingers on his right hand.

She pretended to be as mystified as he was.

There was no way she could have hidden something in that small room. The answer had to have been right in front of him. Of course! The hooked metal bar that had been at her feet. He'd thought they'd used it on her, but she'd used it to close the last shackle. Sweet Goddess of Mercy, she was brilliant.

As if she knew he'd figured it out, she clapped politely.

He bowed. "For a moment there, I was afraid you'd lose faith in me."

"Never."

It was such a simple word. If spoken in jest, it meant nothing, but there was something so honest about the way she said it. Stripped bare of tone and insinuation, it struck him as a promise. They didn't talk like that to each other.

This was too new and awkward. She turned away.

He couldn't bear even the briefest silence. "How did you dose the guards with black lotus? I didn't smell it down there. The air was musty, but not enough to cover the stink of it. Yet they all had dreamer's eyes."

She seemed glad to return to the subject. "Blow pipe and darts. Sometimes, the old ways are best."

"Was it worth it? So much trouble—"

"And expense!" Comfortable with this subject, she leaned forward. "You wouldn't believe how much black lotus I went through today. Some of those guards must be heavy users, because I had to dose them four and five times to keep them quiet. They kept groaning."

He didn't trust this face of hers. She was playing a role, pretending to be carefree, when she had to still feel that moment between them. If only they could loop back a few seconds in time and she'd look at him the way she had when she'd said 'never.' He should have made it last somehow.

"And all of it for what? To make Colonel Hurust disappear?" he asked.

"Colonel Hurust was behind the murders of my lieutenants. I'm sure you've figured that out by now."

"Lizzriat danced around it."

"Why would you – never mind. I won't question your methods. How is Liz?" she asked.

"Neutral."

"You mean selectively helpful, I'm sure. He's a crafty one."

Kyam sauntered away from her. "High praise coming from you." He ran his hand along the sliding door behind her throne. "Tell me about Hurust. Why was he targeting your people?"

He tried to see what was behind the door, but the crack was too slim, so he gave up and explored the rest of the room. From the faded wood, it looked as if there had been a lot of furniture in there at one time. It felt deserted, the way empty places did when people visited them, as if the shadows in the corners absorbed light and sound, hoarding it to feed upon when the people left again. No one lived here now, he was sure of it. It was simply another stage on which for her to perform.

"The racial cleansing of the Quarter of Delights was a nasty excuse to hide his targeted murders. His real aim was to take control of the black lotus market. According to my sources, he was a smuggler back in Thampur. He saw a chance to get back in the business when the militia executed the werewolves," she said. "All of which is irrelevant. He ordered his men to kill my people. For that, he had to die."

"But, the Devil..."

"During my inquiries, I learned his plan was to approach the Devil. He planned to push me out." That brought a wry smile to her lips.

"Inquiries?"

"One of Colonel Hurust's men was at the Dragon Pearl. Upstairs, you understand. He'd gone there to discuss the possibility of supplying Lizzriat, and then decided to take a pipe. Liz has been very careful lately not to anger me, so he sent a messenger offering the soldier for questioning. Ponongese aren't allowed in the Dragon Pearl, as you know, so in order to interrogate him thoroughly, we had to spirit him out of the place without being seen. Unfortunately, he slipped out of our hold as we carried him to a hidden staircase. He fell face down onto Lizzriat's desk and broke his nose. Blood went everywhere."

"The spatter on your jacket." He didn't know why he was so relieved that blood had an innocent-enough explanation, when he knew she'd murdered so many other people. Could it be Hurust disappeared because she couldn't stand for anyone to think she was stupid enough to leave a body behind as evidence? Even now, he and she were the only two people who knew that Hurust was dead. Back in the fortress, they merely thought he was missing, and no one seemed too alarmed about it. Even Nashruu didn't seem to suspect anything was amiss.

"If you see a soldier with a broken nose and a bruise across his chin, tell him he owes me a new jacket if those stains don't come out. But don't bother asking him to confirm our conversation. He won't remember it."

She could have been telling him about the weather for all the interest she showed. That meant she was glossing over something she didn't care to talk about.

"How can you interrogate someone in dream?"

A chill ran down his back. QuiTai was cold and hard again. She might have been a statue except for the growing tension running through her body.

"I've always said you're a dangerous man," she finally said.

"You're one to talk. Will we ever find Hurust?"

"He's in plain sight."

"I have no idea what that means."

"He will not be seen by Thampurian eyes, even when they look directly at him."

"Another damn political lecture."

"Oh no, Governor Zul. A harsh truth."

"Let's assume I'll never figure out what you did, much less how you did it. But I have questions."

"I may have answers."

"Explain the second sarong. You had on your usual one at the harbor. By the time you were in my office, you had one on under your usual green one, and you wore two blouses. Voorus claims he never left your side, but you weren't wearing the second one down at the harbor. So when did you add the second layer?"

"I bought them in the marketplace and donned them before we entered the government building. You can ask him."

"I did. I wanted to hear it from you."

"You don't trust me?" She feigned innocence and batted her eyelashes. "I am hurt, Governor Zul. Absolutely crushed."

"Take me through it. What happened to Colonel Hurust?"

"Did you find PhaSun's bloody clothes in her room at the Red Happiness?" QuiTai asked.

Kyam gave her a stern look. "Yes. And she confessed when we arrested her. But that's not what we were talking about. The subject is Colonel Hurust, QuiTai."

"He must have suspected I was there for him, because he wouldn't come down to the dungeon despite all the trouble I went to arrange our meeting."

He shook his head ruefully. "Such poor manners."

Despite his obvious sarcasm, she said, "That's what I thought too. Strangely enough, while he knew enough to stay away from me, no one seemed to care that the guards kept disappearing from the dungeon. And to think that was the part of the plan that worried me most, the thought that the watch would bring a bunch of men and jellylanterns down there to search for the men who had gone missing."

"That's what worried you? Not the threat of execution, or torture?"

She gave it barely a moment of thought. "Not really."

He felt a headache coming on.

"Then, finally, Cuulon, of all people, managed to drag Colonel Hurust down into the dungeon. Once I had them where I wanted them, in the torture chamber—"

"Where you wanted them?"

"Kyam, if you insist on interrupting... Yes, where I wanted them." She was enjoying this too much. It didn't bother him that she did things no normal person would dream of; it was the cheerful, matter-of-fact way she talked about them.

He definitely had a headache. Any moment now, he was going to lose his temper with her. He ground his teeth. "Do you have any idea how many things could have gone wrong?" She'd put him through hell when he'd thought she was the prisoner executed before his eyes.

"Don't take that tone with me. I pleaded with you to investigate. You turned me down. I had no choice."

"I... You..." He hated it when she was right, which was always.

"You're sexy when you glower over me. Did you know that? You're breathing hard. Do you want to grab me? Shake me? Drag me to bed and enjoy violent passion?" she asked.

"You are a very, very bad woman."

That clearly pleased her. "I'll take that as a yes. Anyway, the rest is simply details. I dosed Cuulon and Hurust as soon as we were in the torture chamber."

Was Hurust still in the torture chamber? It was a small room, low ceiling, stone walls and floor. There wasn't even a chest to fold a body into. Kyam shoved that mental image out of his mind, but not quickly enough.

"As soon as they were in dream, I stripped the Colonel and

put him into a men's sarong," she said.

Kyam sensed where this was going, but his imagination wouldn't let him finish the tale. "That couldn't have been enough to fool the militia." He rubbed his forehead. "RhiHanya. In the marketplace. We were next to a stall that sells festival costumes. You signaled her to bump into me so I wouldn't see you swipe... what, fake fangs and those lenses that make your eyes look Ponongese?"

"Very good, Governor Zul."

"I'm amazed that you didn't already have them with you. You were wearing the second sarong. No doubt you also had a makeup kit and burglar tools on you too."

"A woman likes to be prepared, but sometimes she has a last-second inspiration. I'm not, despite rumors to the contrary, a perfect machine. Sometimes details do escape me in the rush to put a plan together, especially when I only have an hour. I saw the festival stalls from the stairs of the government building and was inspired."

"So you gave Hurust Ponongese eyes and fangs and put him in a sarong so the other soldiers would believe he was Ponongese. But what about you? They know who you are. Why would they have trusted anything you said to them?"

"I borrowed a uniform from the smallest guard in my little collection."

"You passed as a Thampurian soldier?" He wouldn't believe it if he hadn't seen her dressed as a Thampurian boy before the rice riot. She had a miraculous ability to transform herself. It wasn't simply a costume and makeup, it was the way she moved, the gestures and the way she mimicked others.

"I've passed as a soldier before. People see what they want to. The other soldiers saw one of theirs struggling with a Ponongese inside the dungeon door. It was dark. I was on the ground as if he'd struck me down, so the height difference wasn't as noticeable as it might have been." She winced as she rubbed her biceps. "Hurust made me work for it. I'll give him that."

He was sure he knew the rest.

Hurust was in plain sight, where everyone could see him but no Thampurian would notice. Hurust must have been the prisoner he, Voorus, and Nashruu had seen hanged from the ramparts. If there had been any justice in Levapur, the soldiers would have looked beyond the festival costume she'd wrapped around him. The Colonel would have ended up in one of his own cells awaiting trial, woken from dream, and yelled until his men came running to let him out. But there was never justice for a Ponongese, so the soldiers put a rope around his neck and shoved him off the ramparts.

Ruthless. Dangerous. Lethal. He should never forget what she was.

QuiTai rose from her throne and slid open the door behind it. He rushed over to help her.

The revealed room was nearly as large as the front room. A darker square in the center showed there had once been a large rug covering the wood. A bed draped in plum silk sat against a wall decorated with the chop in a werewolf's symbol.

"Is this Petrof's bed?" he asked.

"I couldn't get the smell of dog out of the mattress. I gave it away. This bed was delivered only an hour ago from one of my safe houses."

"Good."

Petrof had to be long dead. The werewolf wouldn't have stopped trying to kill her. He wondered if Petrof's body were nearby or if he'd been dumped unceremoniously into the gorge. He was sure she'd killed him. Maybe one day he could ask her, and many years after that, she might give him an honest answer.

"Good that it isn't his bed, or good that I planned ahead?" she asked.

"Both."

"So I'm forgiven for taking matters into my own hands."

She sauntered across the room to open the typhoon

shutters.

"I should care that you murdered Hurust, but you're right. I forgive you. I guess I'm as morally selective as you are," Kyam said.

"You're getting interesting. Don't ruin it with gloomy musings over a whiskey glass."

Something caught her attention. His hand moved to his baton. She tilted her head as she listened intently.

"It's raining," she said.

He released his baton.

She pushed opened the typhoon shutters and walked out on a veranda. It took a moment to separate the steady rush of the Pha River through the Jupoli Gorge from the quiet drumming on the roof. He felt it in the air too. His spirits soared.

"Monsoon. Finally." The long hot spell wasn't over yet, but relief was coming.

He followed her out onto the veranda. It thrust into the middle of the jungle canopy. Across the gorge, an unhappy troop of monkeys huddled in a tree. Ferns covered the stone wall of the gorge's north rim below them. Mist from the churning river rose to meet the rain, creating a scrim of gray that muted the vibrant flowers.

He leaned on the railing. He could see why she liked it here. It was a private place. If only it had a view of the ocean, it would have been perfect.

"Can you see the future?" he asked.

"I already told you I can't."

"You once warned me that I would wish I'd listened to your lectures on politics. It was as if you knew somehow that I'd be Governor."

She leaned on the rail beside him. Raindrops fine as mist sparkled in her hair. "I used to believe my goddess, The Oracle, revealed things to me. Now I know it's only me, gathering facts and guessing what will happen next." Contemplative, she wiped the rain from her arm. "One disillusionment after another."

He knew she'd been talking to herself.

"You're a very good guesser, though."

She seemed to agree.

"So everyone wants to recruit you because they think you can do something you can't – talk to a goddess – but you can predict the future with some degree of accuracy despite that."

"That sums it up rather well."

"Does it matter, if the end result is the same?"

"I honestly don't have an answer to that." She patted his hand and then headed back inside. "But don't tell your former commander I'm a fraud. At least, not until you've received your signed articles of transport."

He leaned against the shutter. "I wouldn't call you a fraud."

"What would you call me?"

"Maddening."

She chuckled.

He wondered if she'd practiced that slow walk toward the bed. When she moved liked that, it had to be an invitation to follow.

"Fascinating," he added.

"Oh, ho!" She seemed to think he was teasing.

"And I may never forgive you for scaring me like that. I thought it was you when they hanged Hurust. I thought the sun had been swallowed by the sea."

Her gasp was too quiet to be heard, but he knew this was the second time today he'd surprised her.

"I thought you knew how I felt about you. You know everything."

"A long time ago, you were, shall we say, infatuated with me. We'd shared an adventure, survived moments of peril together, and had one memorable romp in a ship's cabin, so that was to be expected. I assumed you'd moved on since then."

He couldn't love her more. Nothing she'd done, no matter how terrible, would change the way he felt. "Never."

She looked at him like she wanted to believe but couldn't. He'd give her no reason to.

"I won't tell my commander you're a fraud, because I'm not turning you over to them."

Anger darkened her face. Kyam stopped, baffled. He didn't

understand. She was supposed to be relieved.

"Don't be an idiot, Kyam. Of course you're handing me over to them."

She was infuriating. He glowered down at her. She tried to walk away, but he blocked her way. "Give me the Devil's name."

QuiTai rolled her eyes and stepped around him. "One year working for Intelligence isn't much. It's not as if you're selling me into slavery."

"*You* said one year. They didn't. And maybe you keep your word, but they don't. If they promise you a year, they'll find a way to keep you longer."

"I'd like to see them try."

Her defiance was so typical. She believed she could think her way out of anything. She was lucky, and of course she was brilliant, but this reckless disregard for her life was going to get her killed.

Clearly annoyed, she stalked away from him. "What do you think you'll learn by chasing the Devil? He doesn't matter. He's nothing, a smoke wraith."

"Of course he matters. You matter, I should say."

She recovered from her shock quickly. A slow smile spread across her mouth. "Very good, Governor Zul. How long have you known?"

He shrugged and went to her. He slipped his arm around her waist. "Sometimes it's what you don't hear that matters, and what I didn't hear much today was anyone talking about the Devil. It was all about you. Even you didn't seem that interested in the Devil, when you used to fear him." He lightly stroked her neck. "Then I thought about how much the Devil has changed over this past year. How much smarter he seemed to be. No more kidnappings or murders for hire, while the scale of the smuggling operations increased dramatically, which was always your contribution to the organization. Your network focused more on information and less on intimidation. Our militia, as ill-equipped as it is for police work, was able to catch the rougher element of the Devil's gang in the commission of crimes. One might even wonder if there was a concerted effort to weed them out."

She spread her hands as if she had no idea what he was talking about.

"Oh, you're good. I'd almost believe you, but I know you too well."

"Your Grandfather also knows I'm the Devil, so we have to assume soon everyone will."

"Is that a bad thing?"

"It makes me a target, which is why I'm going to have to keep out of sight for a while."

"You mentioned when you came to my office that you delayed your plans because of this mess. So you aren't going into hiding inland. You're going somewhere."

She was impressed. "Dangerous man."

"Every time I think we'll catch a break, you abandon me. Us."

"You didn't think we'd get to have this, did you?" She gestured to the room. "Not people like us. Never. You and I are the best at what we do. We can't stop, not with the war coming. So we will take our hours together when and where we can, but don't ever fool yourself into thinking we're going to settle down into a dull marital triangle of husband, wife, mistress. We both have too much to do."

He knew she was right. He didn't want the easy life. If only he could run off with her and join her adventures!

"You know my plans. What are yours? The only thing keeping you here is the Governor's office. And your wife. She's very nice."

She yelped and then laughed when he pinched her.

"Yes. I hope she and Voorus are extremely happy." He nuzzled her neck. Her hair smelled so good.

"My offer still stands. I will spy for Thampur, if that's what it takes to get your articles of transport. It's my fault you're Governor."

"Oh, no, you don't."

"You said I owe you."

"I was sulking. Nothing I said while sulking matters. And

I'm not going to let you be my ticket out. I can damn well do that on my own."

He loved the admiration in her eyes.

"I never doubted it, Kyam. What do you have in mind?"

"I was thinking about something you said earlier in my office. This trial for PhaSun is going to anger a lot of people. Imagine how they'll react when I pave the streets and put in sewers. Or stop corruption. And if I fire everyone in the government building who tries to stop me, they'll be begging the King to put me out of office."

She threw her arms around his neck and kissed him hard. His back pushed against the wall as she tugged at his buttons.

"You like my idea, I take it."

He didn't want to let her go when she backed out of his arms until he saw the glint in her eye. She unbuttoned her blouse and dropped it on the floor. Her sarong left an undulating trail across the floor as she unwound it. He followed the green and gold silk path to her.

He covered her mouth with his. She pushed his jacket from his shoulders as he pulled off his boots.

"It will take a while for my plan to work. As soon as it does, I'm coming after you. Leave a trail of crumbs for me to follow."

"We'll make it a game."

"Don't you always?"

"You like that. How about if I–" she purred as she caressed him.

He wrapped his arms around her and rolled them over. His hands slid to her thighs. "But first…"

QuiTai's contented sigh was all the encouragement he needed.

Chapter 24: The Beginning

Kyam knew before he opened his eyes that she was gone. Still, he slowed his breath and listened carefully. He could have jumped out of the bed, thrown on his clothes, and dashed about calling her name, but he knew it wouldn't do any good.

His arm stretched across the sheets. There was no lingering warmth. She'd been gone a while.

Was she the type to leave a note? Probably not. But she'd promised to leave behind a trail. It might take him months to figure out what it was, but he had time. He had to make his escape. There was a lot of work ahead of him, and he had to be smart about it.

He dressed slowly as he moved around the house. Nothing looked like a clue left by her. He'd have to stay alert so he'd recognize a trail when he saw it.

LiHoun was squatting by the moon gate when he stepped outside. Kyam helped the old cat-man slide the timber grass bridge across the chasm to the road.

He wasn't given a blindfold for the hike back to town. That made it official. She'd never return to that house again.

Kyam and LiHoun crossed the Jupoli Gorge Bridge together, but LiHoun stopped at the crumbling apartments at the outer edge of Levapur.

"She says, 'You have a trial to plan, Governor.'" LiHoun laughed, showing teeth like the monolith stones in the harbor – singular and crooked. "You're going to be a pariah in this town if you give a Ponongese a fair trial."

Kyam nodded. "That's the plan, uncle. May your rice bowl always be full." He bowed then headed downslope, hands in his pockets, shoulders square. Grandfather was going to howl. So were a lot of people. The corner of his mouth curved into a sardonic smile. This was going to be fun.

THE END

Glossary

Foreign Words, Terms, and Cultural Notes

ahmni: Ponongese word for Mama.

ambrosia fruit: Thampurian. Honey scented with a pink interior. They are bitter and woody unless eaten at the peak of ripeness.

ambush spiders: Spiders that weave a web between their longer legs. When prey come by their hiding place, they leap out and 'throw' the web over the victim and then drag it in.

anmau: Thampurian. A liver-eating demon that punishes the wicked.

anoin (seeds): Ponongese. Fragrant seeds used to flavor dishes.

articles of transport: Permission to leave/enter a country.

auntie / uncle: Ponongese. A term of respect, showing deference to their experience or skill. May be used to address someone younger. Not necessarily a relative.

biolock: A lock theoretically keyed to only one person. When the fingertips come in contact with the copper plate, a slight electrical charge unique to that person unlocks the device.

black lotus: Black tar made from fermented, roasted roots. It is usually smoked (**taking the vapors**), but it can be ingested in other ways. Medicinally, its primary use is to relieve pain, although its use is punishable by death in most countries on the continent to because of its highly addictive qualities. Recreational users seek the dream state it induces.

compound: A walled area around a family home. Wealthier families often have several houses around an inner courtyard, which are used by different generations or branches of the family. In Levapur, the kitchen is never in the same building as the living quarters; but in Thampur, it is.

conduit: A person who shares his or her visions with the Qui while under the influence of red tar or black lotus.

cutting a fine burial cloth: Thampurian. Praising the dead in such a way that the truth is completely ignored.

Day of the Spirits: The most holy day for the Ponongese, when the clans gather to remember and honor their dead.

dirt Thampurian: The lowest castes, including butchers, tanners, and morticians, as well as addicts or anyone who has been shunned by their family.

downslope: Toward the ocean/downhill.

dreamers: Users of black lotus.

ear poison: Words that seep into your brain and eat at your soul.

fantasies: Scale working models of mechanical devices, used for education or to entice investors to a project. The term can also be used for a full-sized piece of technology that is small enough for a person to pick up and use. As most of these are created by Ingosolians, they are usually works of art in and of themselves.

farwriter: Thampurian. A radio that conveys typed messages to a receiver tuned to the same frequency.

feeling your rum: A Thampurian saying. Disgracefully drunk, as a Thampurian would never stoop to drinking rum.

festoon gates: The highly decorated columns and archway separating the outer courtyard of a Thampurian family compound from the inner courtyard.

Flying Dragon: The oldest junk in the Zul fleet.

Full Moon Massacre, the: The night Petrof and his werewolves killed and ate the members of the Qui clan living in Levapur, all except QuiTai who survived by a quirk of fate. In retaliation, she paralyzed the werewolves she was told were responsible for the deaths of her daughter, mother, aunt, and father (among others) and left them in the town square for the mob to rip into pieces while they were still alive. Petrof was paid to slaughter the Qui by Cuulon and Turyat, on the orders of their Ravidian masters.

funiculars: There are four funiculars on Ponong. The main one runs from the harbor to Levapur. The other three are on the other side of the Jupoli Gorge, where the mountainside aqua plantations took over the Ponongese agricultural terraces carved into the mountains.

Golden Barracuda: Under command of Hadre Zul, this prototype junk can sail by wind or engine power. It also had a rudimentary navigational computer.

grandmother/grandfather: Elderly person or someone you greatly admire.

green jellyfish (medusazoa): Ponong. Freshwater jellyfish that feed off the algae that grow in their bodies in a symbiotic relationship. The algae, not the jellyfish, are bioluminescent, and emit a greenish light much fainter than the white light jellies. However, because their food source is incorporated into their bodies, they survive much longer in jellylanterns than do the white light jellies that must have an outside food source.

gregru: Ponong. Jungle birds known for their lavish nests that the males decorate with shells, rocks, and anything they can steal from another male's nest. They will fight to the death over a shiny bit of decoration.

hitouh root: Ponongese. Used to bring down fevers.

huwewe: Ponongese. Fruit with spikes. Only the gelatinous pulp surrounding the seeds is edible.

in dream: Under the influence of black lotus.

jellylantern: A sealed glass tube filled with live bioluminescent jellyfish. Used for lighting. The ones that glow green only thrive on the island of Ponong in fresh water pools and live off the algae in their bodies as a symbiotic relationship. White light jellyfish must have salt water and eat fish, so they don't live nearly as long, but the light they give off is stronger.

jikal root: Ponongese. A starchy, purple root roasted and then pounded to the consistency of mashed potatoes. The dried buds are used in medicinal teas and are said to strengthen the blood.

juam nut (oil): Li. Juam nuts are a source of oil used in spirit lamps and engines as well as for cooking. The trees only grow on the Li Islands.

juikoo: Ponongese. A succulent plant. The interior of the leaves is used in medicines and as a topical ointment for burns or abraded skin.

jungle fowl: Ponong. Gold, blue, and red pheasants.

Kinertate (the Saga of): a traditional Ingosolian pantomime. It was made into one of their first motion pictures.

krith amaci: Ingosolian. Lover, but literally, 'tasty snack.'

kur: Ponongese. A widely used drug that temporarily invigorates the user. Most often smoked.

kuriwei: Ponong. Colorful fish about the length of an adult's hand. Reef dwellers.

little sister: Ponongese. Someone younger or less of an expert. Can be an insult, but can also be used to tease someone.

maishun: Ponongese. Shy jungle spirits that take the form of people. They usually flee when seen. They're said to be the gardeners of the jungle.

moon mad: The state of a Rujick feeling the effects of the moon. Figuratively, anyone who is uncontrollably violent.

night spirit moths: Ponong. Small white moths that live around banana trees. Thought to be another form the maishun spirits take.

Oin Affair, the: Under orders from his grandfather, Theram Zul, Kyam Zul leaked information about a top secret mission he was on for His Majesty's Intelligence Service while he was an officer. Theram Zul profited from the inside information. There was an investigation and Kyam was found guilty, but his superiors were willing to overlook it since the secret never went beyond his grandfather. Theram Zul, however, demanded that his grandson be exiled to Ponong in disgrace.

pillow sister/brother: A lover who is also your best friend.

pui: Ponongese. Money, coins.

queltumonz: Ingosolian. A passionate affair that burns out quickly due to its intensity.

red tar: The poisonous psychoactive drug used by the Qui clan to evoke the Oracle.

rice-and-eggs: Thampurian, but common across the continent and in Ponong. Comfort food made from leftover rice and any meat or vegetables on hand. Scrambled with eggs and fried in juam nut oil quickly over high heat.

ring-tailed lizards: Ponong. Large lizards with banded black and green tails several feet long.

sea wasps: Te'Am Ocean. Jellyfish with extremely painful, often lethal, stings.

smoke wraith: Several countries. City spirits related to maishun spirits, but not as shy, and not as kind.

surkraim: Thampurian. A vengeful spirit that appears as a drowned woman. If she catches you in the water in your human form, she will drag you under the surface and drown you too.

sweet seed oil: Ponongese. Oil derived from **anoin seeds**.

tamtuk: Ponongese. A fried dumpling made from **jikal root** mash, usually filled with highly seasoned meat.

The Book of Carnal Bliss: Traditional Ingosolian erotic literature. This is actually a collection of works that include poetry, drawings, hygiene, and reproductive health information.

thiree: Thampurian slang. Member of the Thirteen Families of Thampur. This is the ruling class, although the royal family is not included in the thirteen. These families are (in no particular order): Zul, Muul, Kortun, Orul, Quonn, Karour, Turul, Himuun, Zournn, Mirtyat, Rheun, Tooruun, Vartat.

tikkut: A mild spice. "A grain of tikkut" is something unnoticeable or without meaning.

tiuhon (tea): Ponongese. Bitter tea made from the bark of the tiuhon tree. Reduces fever and swelling.

tumejra powder: Ponongese. Deep yellow spice from ground root, prized for its color more than the flavor it adds to dishes.

upslope: Away from the ocean/uphill.

vapor ghoul: A black lotus addict in the final stages of the addiction. Signs are unnaturally red lips, pale skin, and skeletal thinness.

vapor nightmare: A frightening or disturbing dream while taking vapor.

water pipe: An afternoon pastime for gentlemen with nothing better to do than gossip.

white (or **blue**) **jellyfish** (**medusazoa**): Sea of Erykoli. Bioluminescent jellyfish that glow white light.

Wolf Slayer: Ponongese nickname for QuiTai, used mostly by Ponongese who live outside Levapur.

NAMES OF RACES AND BEINGS

GODS

Erykoli: Thampurian. Goddess of the Sea.

Goddess of Mercy, the: Thampurian. The daughter of Erykoli (the sea) and Kiruse (the sun).

Hunt: Ponongese. Goddess of the Hunt. The Sung clan are her priestesses.

Kiruse: Thampurian. God of the Sun.

Monsoon God: Ponongese. The Su clan are his priestesses.

Moon Goddess: Ponongese. The Chi clan are her priestesses.

Oracle, the: Ponongese. Goddess of Justice and Vengeance. The Qui clan are her priestesses.

PONONGESE

The **Ponongese** are natives of the Ponong Archipelago. They are one of the "shiftless" races, in that they do not fully shift between a "human" form and an animal form, but rather combine elements of both. They have fangs and are venomous. Their venom is a combination of a neurotoxin and a paralytic that can be fatal in sufficient doses. It provides a psychic link between them and their prey. Their eyes are perhaps their most striking feature, with a narrow, bright yellow iris surrounding an oval pupil, and an inner eyelid. Many races from the continent use the racial slur of "snake" to describe them, but they are mammals.

PONONGESE CLANS

QUI: The Qui are said to be from QuiYalin province, but no such place exists except in folk tales, where it is the court of the gods, where souls are weighed. They are from the island of Quinong, which lies across the Ponong Fangs from the big island of Ponong. The Qui are the priestesses of the Oracle.

QuiTai: Former actress. Former prostitute. Former mistress of the King of Houltan and at least one ambassador. Scourge of Levapur. Formerly the Devil's Concubine, and now the Devil. She rules the criminal underworld of Levapur.

QuiZhun: QuiTai and Jezereet's daughter, killed by Petrof for Cuulon and Turyat, who were following Ravidian orders.

RHI: The Rhi are from Cay Rhi, a small island off the west coast of Ponong. Their sarongs are prized for the vivid colors and botanical prints. The Rhi mostly make their living from the sea, although some worked at the small aqua plantation on the far side of the island. Before the time of peace, the Rhi's warriors regularly raided the coastal villages of Ponong and were feared for their brutality.

RhiFa: A man who escaped from Cay Rhi with QuiTai and RhiHanya.

RhiHanya: Helped QuiTai and others escape from slavery on Cay Rhi in the bioweapons aqua plantation taken over by the Ravidians. Later became one of QuiTai's lieutenants.

RhiLan: RhiHanya's cousin. Kyam Zul's neighbor. She hid QuiTai in her apartment from the colonial militia following the escape from Cay Rhi and helped nurse her back to health.

RhiLiet: RhiLan's eldest son.

RhiNyam: Died on Cay Rhi at the bioweapons aqua plantation

RhiTeek: RhiLan's daughter.

PHA: Levapur sits on the ancestral lands of the Pha clan, which are bordered on the north by the Sea of Erykoli and the south by the Pha River. They agreed to allow the Thampurians to settle on their lands, which led to the entire archipelago being claimed as a colony by Theram Zul for the King of Thampur. The rest of the Ponongese will never forgive them for this.

PhaJut: Brothel owner in the Quarter of Delights. Former employer of QuiTai and LiHoun.

PhaSun: Sex worker at the Red Happiness.

PhaNyan: QuiTai's lieutenant. Killed on Cay Rhi by Ravidians.

PhaChiu: Her stall in the marketplace is known for the best tamtuk dipping sauce in Levapur. Don't even ask what's in it; her burly sons will escort you out of the town square.

MEMBERS OF OTHER CLANS FROM THE INTERIOR OR COASTS OF PONONG

SunYan: A professional dominatrix and worker at PhaJut's brothel.

SungHi: QuiTai's lieutenant, tortured and mutilated by a radical faction of the colonial militia under orders of Colonel Hurust.

ChiHui: QuiTai's lieutenant, tortured and mutilated by a radical colonial militia under orders of Colonel Hurust.

FalLoun: While PhaChiu may make the best dipping sauce for tamtuks, FalLoun's fillings could make the gods weep with joy. If she catches you buying a tamtuk from PhaChiu's stall, she will never let you eat another of hers.

THAMPURIANS

THAMPURIANS are one of the fully shifting races, from a human form to a sea dragon form. Like most fully shifting races, they consider their human form to be superior to the shiftless races. Despite being strong swimmers in sea dragon form, they built an impressive fleet of merchant ships (junks), which brought wealth and power to the small country.

HOUSE OF ZUL

Kyam Zul: Grandson of Theram Zul, Governor of the Crown Colony.

Hadre Zul: Grandson of Theram Zul, cousin to Kyam, commander of the *Golden Barracuda*, pride of the Zul family fleet.

Grandfather Zul (Theram): The richest and most powerful head of the Thirteen Families of Thampur, cousin of the king.

Liragme Zul: Kyam's mother.

Nashruu Zul: Kyam's wife and cousin.

Khyram Zul: Nashruu's son.

Malk Zul: Captain of the *Winged Dragon*, and for seven glorious months, the *Golden Barracuda*.

Virham Voorus: Captain in the colonial militia. Exiled to Ponong eight years ago. Kyam's secret half-brother.

OTHER THAMPURIANS

Cuulon: Chief Justice of the Colonial Government. Turyat's best friend. Former police captain in Thampur, exiled to Ponong for arresting and brutally beating two sons of the House of Turul.

Turyat: Governor of the Crown Colony after Theram Zul returned to Thampur. Ruled for forty years. Forced out of office after the rice riots.

Mityam Muul: The finest legal mind in Thampur, often called the nation's sage uncle.

Simarn: Nashruu Zul's personal maid.

Colonel Hurust: Commander of the colonial militia. Family connections barely saved him from execution after he was caught dealing black lotus in Thampur. After he executed all the Rujicks in Levapur (except Petrof) he decided to take over their black lotus business.

Major Rheagus: Colonel Hurust's secretary.

Ma'am Thun: A school teacher exiled to Ponong after her husband's senseless death by drowning.

Hirun: A captain noted for his persecution complex and lack of friends.

Korours: A plantation owner on Cay Rhi who married a Ponongese woman. He, his wife, and children were tortured and then killed by the Ravidians, who took over their remote aqua plantation to convert it into a bioweapons facility.

INGOSOLIANS

INGOSOLIANS are often called the ultimate shifters. They can shift anywhere along a continuum between male and female genders, but are always "human." The Ingosolians are also known for their love of inventions and the arts.

Jezereet Karula: QuiTai's spouse and business partner, retired actress, and sire of QuiZhun.

Lizzriat: Owner of the Dagon Pearl, a casino.

Inattra: Madam of the Red Happiness after Jezereet's death.

Evoreet Karula: Jezereet's sibling.

Ikoreet Orsuna: A great philosopher from antiquity, renowned across the continent. Founded the first university on the continent. Set forth the first rules of scientific methodology and logic that are still taught as the basis of critical thinking.

Gernert: An actor in Jezereet and QuiTai's former troupe.

Inaza: An actor Jezereet and QuiTai worked with.

LISUDTAN ISLANDERS (also known as Li Islanders):

LI ISLANDERS are a shiftless race with the hearing and sight of a jungle cat; thus referred to as cat-men. They are stealthy, secretive, and excellent climbers.

LiHoun: On his native island, he is simply known as Houn. As a member of a religious minority, he was unable to find steady work at home. His fate wasn't any better in Ponong, but he never had enough money to return home. His lung worm infection is incurable.

LiHoun's wives and children: These sisters are a racial minority in their homeland because they have spots down their spines while the majority race have rosette dots. They fled to Ponong at the same time as LiHoun, but not with him. Similarly marooned, they formed a clan with him. They work for the funicular company as rail inspectors.

RAVIDIANS

A "shiftless" race with pale skin and white-blond hair. They have a prominent bony neck ruff that protects their necks from attack. They also have a sharp dewclaw on both feet that can gut prey. Much is said about their savagery, but how much of it is true is unknown. They are second only to the Ingosolians in their scientific advances.

RUJICKS

From the northernmost lands of the continent, where the males and females live apart. Commonly known as werewolves, they are tall and muscular. While they are often referred to as hairy barbarians, they have a tradition of poetry and music unrivaled on the continent.

Petrof: Forcibly evicted from his home keep in the stark fjords of northern Rujick, he wandered the continent for several years. Despite being small for a Rujick, he worked as muscle for several criminal enterprises in Houltan, Ingosol, and Chimit before finding his way to Ponong on a smuggler's ship. There, he worked on plantations sporadically but made most of his money in the criminal underworld, mostly in contract killings and black lotus. He was hired by Cuulon and Turyat to kill all the Qui on the island. He only missed one, a mistake that came back to haunt him. The rest of his pack found his fascination with QuiTai puzzling, but he admired her fearlessness. After she made him the mysterious Devil, he secretly understood she was the key to his power. As such, she could take it away as easily as she gave it to him. He feared her for that. He also desired her more because of that danger she posed to him.

Casmir: The model for heroic statues in Rujick, this tall, muscular, gravel-voiced werewolf was most often chosen by Petrof to keep watch on QuiTai, as well as sometimes serving as her maid. He was one of the few werewolves to witness the mob in the marketplace tearing his fellow countrymen apart limb by limb after QuiTai paralyzed them and handed them to the mob in retaliation for the

Full Moon Massacre, so his hatred and fear of her are greater than the rest of the pack.

Ivitch: The bloom of youth was still on his cheeks when he came to Ponong. He grew older on the island but never grew up. Stupid and evil is a bad combination, and he was plenty of both.

HOULTANS

Houltan is one of the biggest countries on the continent, but much of the land is artic desert. It shares a long border with Rujick that is mostly unpopulated. Many Houltans are still nomadic herdsmen with the great migrating ruminant herds of the northern tundra. The only known race with three shifting forms: person, dog, and fire. One of the ethnic minorities in their easternmost province take the form of firebirds rather than as open flame. Houltans are known for their ribald sense of humor, love of theater, and vast repertoire of drinking songs. If a Houltan ever pours a tiny glass of Furskvaszer for you, sit down and grab hold of the table before you drink it. Also, don't have any plans for the next two days.

Names of Places

Ponong

Dragon Bridge: A small stone bridge over a ravine that separates the toniest Thampurian neighborhood where exiled *thirees* live from the Quarter of Delights.

Dragon Pearl: A casino and black lotus den owned by the Ingosolian information broker Lizzriat.

fortress, the: A round building on the end of a breakwater at the sea edge of the harbor. It is a prison, but also a place of refuge for Thampurians, should the Ponongese ever revolt against their occupation.

government building, the: Sits on the southern side of the town square. The entire colonial government, except the militia, is run from this massive three-story building with a center atrium.

Jupoli Gorge: A deep gorge cut by the Pha River. It separates the north shore from the majority of the island of Ponong.

Jupoli Gorge Bridge: A stone bridge over the Jupoli Gorge built by the Thampurians to help bring jellyfish from the upslope aqua plantations down to the harbor. One hundred seven Ponongese died during construction.

Levapur: Capital of the colonial government on Ponong. Home to about 1800 Thampurians and 8000 or more Ponongese, as well as a several thousand people from the continent. It sits on cliffs high above the harbor, which can be reached by a winding road or funicular. While it is the largest town on Ponong, it occupies only a small fraction of the island. Other than the coastal and mountain plantations, few Thampurians dare wander far from this outpost.

marketplace, the: The most democratic place on the island, where all races and castes mix together to buy and sell goods. As most Ponongese are not allowed in Thampurian shops, it is the only place they can buy many goods, and the only place they are allowed to gather to sell theirs.

Old Levapur: The hillside slums where the Pha clan live after letting the Thampurians take their lands.

Petrof's Lair: A remote house cantilevered over the edge of the southern rim of the Jupoli Gorge. It served as the den for the werewolves, who preferred to live in the jungle where they could run rather than in Levapur.

Pha River: A river that begins in a wide inland valley. By the time it reaches the Jupoli Gorge, it is a fast moving torrent.

PhaJut's: A brothel. Known for its Ponongese workers.

Pink Orchid: A brothel in the Quarter of Delights owned by a Houltan emigre. It also has a small casino for low-stakes tile games.

Ponong: The largest island in the Ponong Archipelago. The north side has a large protected natural harbor.

Ponongese Quarter: Far upslope on the outskirts of Levapur, bordering on the Jupoli Gorge. This area is extremely steep. At its highest point, it sits five hundred feet above the town square.

Quarter of Delights: Casinos, bars, brothels, cafés, and black lotus dens are concentrated in this section of Levapur, although others exist outside it

Quarter of the Guests: A mixed neighborhood with a high concentration of exiles from the continent.

Quarter of the Unclean: A neighborhood of lowest caste Thampurians on the backside of the hill the Quarter of Delights is on.

Quinong: The true home of the Qui. An island thought to be uninhabited. QuiTai's estate is hidden on this island.

QuiYalin Province: A place that exists only in folktales, said to be the homeland of the Qui clan.

Red Happiness: The brothel Jezereet and QuiTai built when they retired from the stage and moved to Levapur with their daughter. This pink building is ringed by verandas on both stories. It is popular with people from the continent.

Suin's Pâtisserie: The best Thampurian-style bakery in Levapur.

Thampurian Quarter: The posh neighborhoods built on the only flat land in Levapur.

The Home Port: A Thampurian bar in Levapur that tries very hard to pretend it's in Thampur.

town square, the: The center of life in Levapur. The marketplace is held here every day. The northern edge is a cliff that drops several hundred feet to the Sea of Erykoli. The southern edge is the government building. The bank and shops line the eastern edge. Site of the Rice Riot, and the mob dismemberment of the werewolves thought to be guilty of the Full Moon Massacre.

West Levapur: A cluster of apartment buildings past Old Levapur where middle class Thampurians live if they can't afford to get into the posher neighborhoods.

THE CONTINENT

Great Malisium Desert: Separates Ravidia from most of the other countries on the continent. It is brutally hot and arid, with alkaline sands that can burn human skin.

Ingosol: A country on the continent. Ingosol is known for its culture, arts, and love of technology.

Lirhumet Canal: A high-end shopping area in Surrayya.

Rantuum: The capital of Ingosol.

Salt Plains of Ravidia: The driest, most desolate section of the Great Malisium Desert.

Surrayya: The capital of Thampur. This city is built on thousands of tiny islands connected by canals and bridges. Some islands are as small as a family compound. Others are much larger. It is a cold, windy port on the northern shore of the Sea of Erykoli.

Suvat Park: A park between the palace and the Lirhumet Canal, popular with wealthy Thampurians as a place to stroll.

Thyrinmun: Thampur's elite military academy.

OCEANS AND ISLANDS

Cay Rhi: An island off the eastern coast of Ponong.

Li Islands (formally known as the **Lisudtan Islands**): This cluster of volcanic islands sit several thousand miles south east of Ponong in the middle of the Te'Am Ocean. This island group was also claimed by Thampur. It is home to the Li people, and the only source of juam nut oil.

Ponong Archipelago: A long chain of tropical islands that separates the Sea of Erykoli from the Te'Am Ocean.

Ponong Fangs: The only deep water passage between islands (Ponong and Quinong) in the Ponong Archipelago. This treacherous passage features rapidly shifting currents where the Sea of Erykoli and Te'Am Oceans meet, as well as many submerged monolith stones.

Te'Am Ocean: This ocean separates "the continent" from the southern continent. It lies south of the Ponong Archipelago.

Sea of Erykoli: This sea is separated from the Te'Am Ocean by the Ponong Archipelago. The northern and eastern borders are "The Continent," which is more correctly called the northern continent. Thampur, Ingosol, and Ravidia, as well as several smaller nations, border this sea on the north and west. It is named after the Goddess Erykoli.